PRAISE FOR
THE BEAUTIFUL CREATURES NOVELS

"A hauntingly delicious dark fantasy."
— **CASSANDRA CLARE,** *New York Times* bestselling
author of **CITY OF BONES**

"In the Gothic tradition of Anne Rice.... Give this to fans of
Stephenie Meyer's *Twilight* or HBO's *True Blood* series."
— **SLJ**

"Gorgeously crafted, atmospheric, and original."
— **MELISSA MARR,** *New York Times* bestselling
author of **WICKED LOVELY**

★ "The authors ground their Caster world in the concrete,
skillfully juxtaposing the arcane, magical world with Gatlin's
normal southern lifestyle.... [Fans will] plead for more."
— **VOYA** (starred review)

"A lush Southern gothic."
— **HOLLY BLACK,** *New York Times* bestselling
author of **TITHE: A MODERN FAERIE TALE**

"[Readers] will be swept up by the haunting and detailed
atmosphere, the conventions and strictures of Southern life,
and a compelling and dimensional mythology."
— **PUBLISHERS WEEKLY**

"Smart, textured and romantic.... Ethan's wry narrative voice will
resonate with readers of John Green as well as the hordes of supernatural-
romance fans looking for the next book to sink their teeth into."
— **KIRKUS REVIEWS**

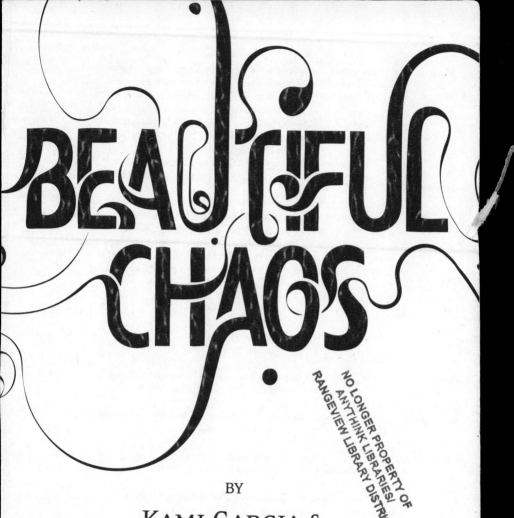

BEAUTIFUL CHAOS

BY

KAMI GARCIA &
MARGARET STOHL

LITTLE, BROWN AND COMPANY
New York • Boston

Copyright © 2011 by Kami Garcia, LLC, and Margaret Stohl, Inc.
Excerpt from *Dangerous Creatures* copyright © 2014 by Kami Garcia, LLC, and Margaret Stohl, Inc.
Excerpt from *Icons* copyright © 2013 by Margaret Stohl, Inc.
Excerpt from *Unbreakable* copyright © 2013 by Kami Garcia, LLC

Little, Brown and Company

Hachette Book Group
1290 Avenue of the Americas, New York, NY 10104
Visit us at lb-teens.com

Little, Brown and Company is a division of Hachette Book Group, Inc.
The Little, Brown name and logo are trademarks of Hachette Book Group, Inc.

The publisher is not responsible for websites (or their content) that are not owned by the publisher.

First Paperback Edition: June 2012
First published in hardcover in October 2011 by Little, Brown and Company

Library of Congress Cataloging-in-Publication Data

Garcia, Kami.
Beautiful chaos / by Kami Garcia & Margaret Stohl.—1st ed.
    p. cm.
Sequel to: Beautiful darkness.
Summary: Swarms of locusts, record-breaking heat, and devastating storms ravage Gatlin as Ethan and Lena struggle to understand and control the impact of Lena's claiming, which is even causing her family members' abilities to dangerously misfire.
ISBN 978-0-316-12352-5 (hc) / ISBN 978-0-316-12351-8 (pb)
[1. Supernatural—Fiction. 2. Psychic ability—Fiction. 3. Love—Fiction. 4. Weather—Fiction. 5. South Carolina—Fiction.] I. Stohl, Margaret. II. Title.
PZ7.G155627Bec 2011   [Fic]—dc23   2011012957

20 19 18 17 16 15 14
LSC-C
Printed in the United States of America

For our mothers

Susan Racca,
who raises baby squirrels and
feeds them with an eyedropper,
&

Marilyn Ross Stohl,
who could drive a tractor before
she could drive a car.

They are true Gatlin Peaches.

Tumult and peace, the darkness and the light—
Were all like workings of one mind, the features
Of the same face, blossoms upon one tree;
Characters of the great Apocalypse,
The types and symbols of Eternity,
Of first, and last, and midst, and without end.

—WILLIAM WORDSWORTH, *The Prelude: Book Sixth*

⚔ BEFORE ⚔

Sugar and Salt

In Gatlin, it's funny how the good things are all tied up with the bad. Sometimes it's hard to tell which is which. But either way, you end up taking your sugar with your salt and your kicks with your kisses, as Amma would say.

I don't know if it's like that everywhere. I only know Gatlin, and this is what I know: By the time I got back to my usual seat at church with the Sisters, the only news being passed along with the collection plate was that the Bluebird Café had stopped serving up hamburger soup, peach pie season was winding down, and *some hooligans* had stolen the tire swing from the old oak near the General's Green. Half the congregation was still shuffling down the carpeted aisles in what my mom used to call Red Cross shoes. With all the purple knees puffing up where the knee-highs ended, it felt like a whole sea of legs was holding its breath. At least I was.

But the Sisters still propped their hymnals open to the wrong pages with their curled knuckles, wadded up handkerchiefs buried in the spotted roses of their hands. Nothing kept them from singing the melody, loud and shrill, as they tried to drown one another out. Except Aunt Prue. She accidentally hit on a real harmony about three notes out of three hundred, but nobody minded. Some things didn't have to change, and maybe they shouldn't. Some things, like Aunt Prue, were meant to be off-key.

It was as if this summer had never happened, and we were safe within these walls. Like nothing but the thick, colored sunlight streaming through the stained-glass windows could force its way in here. Not Abraham Ravenwood or Hunting and his Blood Pack. Not Lena's mother Sarafine or the Devil himself. Nobody else could get past the fierce hospitality of the ushers handing out programs. And even if they did, the preacher would keep on preaching and the choir would keep on singing, because nothing short of the apocalypse could keep folks in Gatlin out of church or each other's business.

But outside these walls, this summer had changed everything, in both the Caster and Mortal worlds, even if the folks in Gatlin didn't know it. Lena had Claimed herself both Light and Dark and split the Seventeenth Moon. A battle between Demons and Casters had ended in death on both sides and opened a crack in the Order of Things the size of the Grand Canyon. What Lena had done was the Caster equivalent of smashing the Ten Commandments. I wondered what the folks in Gatlin would think about that, if they'd ever know. I hoped they wouldn't.

This town used to make me feel claustrophobic, and I hated it. Now it felt more like something expected, something I would miss someday. And that day was coming. No one knew that better than I did.

Sugar and salt and kicks and kisses. The girl I loved had come back to me and broken the world. That's what actually happened this summer.

We'd seen the last of hamburger soup and peach pie and tire swings. But we'd seen the start of something, too.

The beginning of the End of Days.

Linkubus

I was standing on the top of the white water tower, with my back to the sun. My headless shadow fell across the warm painted metal, disappearing off the edge and into the sky. I could see Summerville stretching out before me, all the way to the lake, from Route 9 to Gatlin. This had been our happy place, mine and Lena's. One of them, at least. But I wasn't feeling happy. I felt like I was going to throw up.

My eyes were watering, but I didn't know why. Maybe it was the light.

Come on, already. It's time.

I clenched and unclenched my fists — staring out at the tiny houses, the tiny cars, and the tiny people — waiting for it to happen. The dread churned in my stomach, heavy and wrong. Then the familiar arms slammed into my waist, knocking the air out of me and dragging me down to the metal ladder. My jaw hit the side of the railing, and I stumbled. I lurched forward, trying to throw him off.

Who are you?

But the harder I swung, the harder he hit me. The next punch landed in my stomach, and I doubled over. That's when I saw them.

His black Chucks. They were so old and beat-up, they could have been mine.

What do you want?

I didn't wait for an answer. I lunged for his throat, and he went for mine. That's when I caught a look at his face, and I saw the truth.

He was me.

As we stared into each other's eyes and clawed at each other's throats, we rolled over the edge of the water tower and fell.

The whole way down, I could only think one thing.

Finally.

My head hit the floor with a crack, and my body followed a second later, the sheets tangled around me. I tried to open my eyes, but they were still blurred with sleep. I waited for the panic to subside.

In my old dreams, I had tried to keep Lena from falling. Now I was the one falling. What did that mean? Why did I wake up feeling like I'd already fallen?

"Ethan Lawson Wate! What in our Sweet Redeemer's name are you doin' up there?" Amma had a particular way of shouting that could haul you right back up out of Hades, as my dad would say.

I opened my eyes, but all I could see was a lonely sock, a

spider working its way aimlessly through the dust, and a few beat-up, spine-busted books. *Catch-22. Ender's Game. The Outsiders.* A few others. The thrilling view under my bed.

"Nothing. Just shutting the window." I stared at my window, but I didn't close it. I always slept with it open. I'd started leaving it open when Macon died—at least, when we thought he'd died—and now it was a reassuring habit. Most people felt safer with their windows closed, but I knew a closed window couldn't protect me from the things I was afraid of. It couldn't keep out a Dark Caster or a Blood Incubus.

I wasn't sure anything could.

But if there was a way, Macon seemed determined to find it. I hadn't seen much of him since we came back from the Great Barrier. He was always in the Tunnels anyway, or working on some kind of protective Cast to Bind Ravenwood. Lena's house had become the Fortress of Solitude since the Seventeenth Moon, when the Order of Things—the delicate balance that regulated the Caster world—was broken. Amma was creating her own Fortress of Solitude here at Wate's Landing—or Fortress of Superstition, as Link called it. Amma would've called it "taking preventative measures." She had lined every windowsill with salt and used my dad's rickety stepladder to hang cracked glass bottles upside down on every branch of our crepe myrtle tree. In Wader's Creek, bottle trees were as common as cypresses. Now whenever I saw Link's mom at the Stop & Steal, Mrs. Lincoln said the same thing—"Caught any evil spirits in those old bottles yet?"

I wish we could catch yours. That's what I wanted to say. Mrs. Lincoln stuffed in a dusty brown Coke bottle. I wasn't sure any bottle tree could handle that.

Right now, I just wanted to catch a breeze. The heat rolled over me as I leaned against my old wooden bed frame. It was thick and suffocating, a blanket you couldn't kick off. The relentless South Carolina sun usually let up a little by September, but not this year.

I rubbed the lump on my forehead and stumbled to the shower. I turned on the cold water. I let it run for a minute, but it still came out warm.

Five in a row. I had fallen out of bed five straight mornings, and I was afraid to tell Amma about the nightmares. Who knew what she would hang on our old crepe myrtle next? After everything that happened this summer, Amma had closed in on me like a mother hawk protecting her nest. Every time I stepped out of the house, I could almost feel her shadowing me like my own personal Sheer, a ghost I couldn't escape.

And I couldn't stand it. I needed to believe that sometimes a nightmare was just a nightmare.

I smelled the bacon frying, and turned up the water. It finally went cold. It wasn't until I was drying off that I noticed the window had closed without me.

—☙

"Hurry up, Sleepin' Beauty. I'm ready to hit the books." I heard Link before I saw him, but I almost wouldn't have recognized his voice. It was deeper, and he sounded more like a man and less like a guy who specialized in banging on the drums and writing bad songs.

"Yeah, you're ready to hit something, but I'm pretty sure it's not the books." I slid into the chair next to his spot at our chipped kitchen table. Link had bulked up so much that it looked like he was sitting in one of those tiny plastic chairs from elementary school. "Since when do you show up on time for school?"

At the stove, Amma sniffed, one hand on her hip, the other pushing at scrambled eggs with the One-Eyed Menace, her wooden spoon of justice.

"Morning, Amma." I could tell I was about to get an earful, from the way she had one hip cocked up higher than the other. Kind of like a loaded pistol.

"Feels more like afternoon to me. 'Bout time you decided to join us." Standing at a hot stove on an even hotter day, she didn't break a sweat. It would take more than the weather to force Amma to budge an inch out of her way of doing things. The look in her eye reminded me of that as she sent a whole henhouse's worth of eggs tumbling across my blue and white Dragonware plate. The bigger the breakfast, the bigger the day, in Amma's mind. At this rate, by the time I graduated I'd be one giant biscuit floating in a bathtub full of pancake batter. A dozen scrambled eggs on my plate meant there was no denying it. It really was the first day of school.

You wouldn't expect me to be itching to get back to Jackson High. Last year, with the exception of Link, my so-called friends had treated me like crap. But the truth was, I couldn't wait for a reason to get out of my house.

"You eat up, Ethan Wate." Toast flew onto the plate, chased by bacon and sealed with a healthy glop of butter and grits. Amma had put out a placemat for Link, but there was no plate on it. Not even a glass. She knew Link wouldn't be eating her eggs, or anything else she whipped up in our kitchen.

8

But not even Amma could tell us what he was capable of now. No one knew, least of all Link. If John Breed was some kind of Caster-Incubus hybrid, Link was one generation removed. As far as Macon could tell, Link was the Incubus equivalent of some distant Southern cousin you ran into every couple of years at a wedding or a funeral and called the wrong name.

Link stretched his arms behind his head, relaxed. The wooden chair creaked under his weight. "It's been a long summer, Wate. I'm ready to get back in the game."

I swallowed a spoonful of grits and had to fight the urge to spit them out. They tasted weird, dry. Amma had never made a bad batch of grits in her life. Maybe it was the heat. "Why don't you ask Ridley how she feels about that, and get back to me?"

He winced, and I could tell the subject had already come up. "It's our junior year, and I'm the only Linkubus at Jackson. I got all the charm and none a the harm. All the muscle and none a the—"

"What? You have a rhyme for muscle? Hustle? Bustle?" I would've laughed, but I was having a hard time getting my grits down.

"You know what I mean." I did. It was a little more than ironic. His on-again, off-again girlfriend, Lena's cousin Ridley, had been a Siren—able to get any guy, anywhere, to do whatever she wanted, whenever she wanted it. Until Sarafine took Ridley's powers, and she became a Mortal just days before Link became part Incubus. Not long after that bite, we could all see the transformation beginning, right in front of our eyes.

Link's ridiculously greasy spiked hair became ridiculously cool greasy spiked hair. He packed on the muscle, popping out biceps like the inflatable water wings his mother used to make him wear long after he knew how to swim. He looked more like a guy in an actual rock band than a guy who dreamed about being in one.

"I wouldn't mess with Ridley. She may not be a Siren anymore, but she's still trouble." I scooped grits and eggs onto my toast, slapped bacon in the middle, and rolled it all up together.

Link looked at me like he wanted to puke. Food didn't have the same appeal now that he was part Incubus. "Dude, I'm not messin' with Ridley. I'm stupid, but I'm not that stupid."

I was starting to have my doubts. I shrugged and stuffed half my breakfast sandwich into my mouth. It tasted wrong, too. Guess I undershot on the bacon.

Before I could say another word, a hand clamped down on my shoulder, and I jumped. For a second, I was back at the top of the water tower in my dream, bracing for an attack. But it was only Amma, ready for her usual first day of school lecture. At least, that's what I thought. I should've noticed the red string tied around her wrist. A new charm always meant the clouds were rolling in.

"Don't know what you boys are thinkin', sitting here like today's just another day. It's not over—not the moon or this heat or that business with Abraham Ravenwood. You two are actin' like done is done, the lights are on and it's time to leave the picture show." She lowered her voice. "Well, you're as wrong as walkin' barefoot in church. Things have consequences, and we haven't seen the half a them."

I knew about consequences. They were everywhere I looked, no matter how hard I tried not to see them.

"Ma'am?" Link should have known to keep his mouth shut when Amma was going dark.

She clenched Link's shirt tighter, creating fresh cracks in the Black Sabbath iron-on decal. "Stick close to my boy. There's trouble runnin' through you now, and I'm ten kinds a sorry 'bout that. But it's the kind a trouble that may keep you fools from gettin' into any more. You hear me, Wesley Jefferson Lincoln?"

Link nodded, scared. "Yes, ma'am."

I looked up at Amma from my side of the table. She hadn't relaxed her grip on Link, and she wasn't about to let go of me anytime soon. "Amma, don't get yourself all worked up. It's just the first day of school. Compared to what we've been through, this is nothing. It's not like there are any Vexes or Incubuses or Demons at Jackson High."

Link cleared his throat. "Well, that isn't exactly true." He tried to smile, but Amma twisted his shirt even harder, until he rose up from the seat of his chair. "Ow!"

"You think this is funny?" Link was smart enough to keep his mouth shut this time. Amma turned to me. "I was there when you lost your first tooth in that apple, and your wheels in the Pinewood Derby. I've cut up shoe boxes for dioramas and iced hundreds a birthday cupcakes. Never said a word when your water collection up and evaporated like I said it would."

"No, ma'am." It was true. Amma was the constant in my life. She was there when my mom died, almost a year and a half ago, and when my dad lost himself because of it.

She let go of my shirt as suddenly as she had taken it, smoothed her apron, and lowered her voice. Whatever had brought on this particular storm had passed. Maybe it was the heat. It was getting to all of us.

Amma looked out the window, past Link and me. "I've been

here, Ethan Wate. And I will be, long as you are. Long as you need me. Not a minute less. Not a minute more."

What was that supposed to mean? Amma had never talked to me that way before—like there would ever be a time when I wasn't here or I wouldn't need her.

"I know, Amma."

"You look me in the eye and tell me you're not as scared as I am, five miles down." Her voice was low, nearly a whisper.

"We made it back in one piece. That's what matters. We can figure everything else out."

"It's not that simple." Amma was still talking as quietly as if we were in the front pew at church. "Pay attention. Has anything, even one thing, felt the same since we got back to Gatlin?"

Link spoke up, scratching his head. "Ma'am, if it's Ethan and Lena you're worried about, I promise you as long as I'm around, with my superstrength and all, nothin's gonna happen to them." He flexed his arm proudly.

Amma snorted. "Wesley Lincoln. Don't you know? The kind a things I'm talkin' about, you could no more keep from happenin' than you could keep the sky from fallin'."

I took a swig of my chocolate milk and almost spit it out all over the table. It tasted too sweet, sugar coating my throat like cough syrup. It was like my eggs, which had tasted more like cotton, and the grits more like sand.

Everything was off today, everything and everyone. "What's wrong with the milk, Amma?"

She shook her head. "I don't know, Ethan Wate. What's wrong with your mouth?"

I wish I knew.

By the time we were out the door and in the Beater, I turned back for one last look at Wate's Landing. I don't know why. She was standing in the window, between the curtains, watching me drive away. And if I didn't know better, and I didn't know Amma, I would have sworn she was crying.

Mortal Girls

As we drove down Dove Street, it was hard to believe our town had ever been anything but brown. The grass looked like burnt toast before you scraped off the black parts. The Beater was about the only thing that hadn't changed. Link was actually driving the speed limit for once, even if it was only because he wanted to check out what was left of our neighbors' front yards.

"Man, look at Mrs. Asher's azaleas. Sun's so hot, they turned black." Link was right about the heat. According to the *Farmers' Almanac*, and the Sisters, who were Gatlin's walking almanac, it hadn't been this hot in Gatlin County since 1942. But the sun wasn't what had killed Mrs. Asher's azaleas.

"They aren't burnt. They're covered in lubbers."

Link hung out the window to get a better look. "No way."

The grasshoppers had shown up in droves three weeks after

14

Lena Claimed herself, and two weeks after the worst heat wave in seventy years hit. Lubber grasshoppers weren't your run-of-the-mill green grasshoppers, like the ones Amma found in the kitchen every now and then. Lubbers were black, with an angry slash of yellow running down their backs, and they traveled in swarms. They were like locusts, devouring every inch of green in town, including the General's Green. General Jubal A. Early's statue was standing on a brown circle of dead grass, his sword drawn and covered with a black army of its own.

Link sped up a little. "That's nasty. My mom thinks they're one a the plagues a the apocalypse. She's waitin' for the frogs to show up and the water to run red."

For once I couldn't blame Mrs. Lincoln. In a town built on equal parts religion and superstition, it was hard to ignore an unprecedented infestation of grasshoppers that had descended on Gatlin like a black cloud. Every day seemed like an End of Days kind of a day. And I wasn't about to knock on Mrs. Lincoln's door and tell her it was most likely the result of my Caster girlfriend splitting the moon and disrupting the Order of Things. We were having a hard enough time convincing Link's mom that his new physique wasn't the result of steroids. He had already been to Doc Asher's office twice this month.

When we pulled into the parking lot, Lena was already there, and something else had changed. She wasn't driving her cousin Larkin's Fastback anymore. She was standing next to Macon's hearse, in a vintage U2 T-shirt with the word WAR written across the top, a gray skirt, and her old black Chucks. There was fresh Sharpie inked across the toes. It was crazy how a hearse and a pair of sneakers could cheer a guy up.

15

A million thoughts ran through my head. That when she looked at me, it was like there was no one else in the world. That when I looked at her, I noticed every detail about her while everything else faded away. That I was only myself when we were together.

It was impossible to put into words, and even if I could I wasn't sure the words would be right. But I didn't have to try, because Lena and I never had to say the things we felt. We could think them, and Kelting took care of the rest.

Hi.

What took you so long?

I climbed out of the passenger seat, the back of my shirt already soaked with sweat. Link seemed immune to the heat, another perk of being part Incubus. I slipped into Lena's arms and breathed her in.

Lemons and rosemary. The scent I had followed through the halls of Jackson before I saw her for the first time. The one that had never faded, even when she walked into the darkness and away from me.

I leaned down carefully to kiss her without brushing against any other part of her body. These days, the more we touched, the less I could breathe. The physical effects of touching her had intensified, and even though I tried to hide it, she knew.

I felt the jolt as soon as our lips met. The sweetness of her kiss was so perfect and the shock of her skin so powerful that my head was always left spinning. But now there was something else—the feeling she was inhaling my breath every time our lips met, pulling an invisible string I couldn't control. Lena arched her neck and pulled away before I could move.

Later.

16

I sighed, and she blew me a kiss.

But, L, it's been...

A whole nine hours?

Yeah.

I smiled at her, and she shook her head.

I don't want you to spend the first day of school in the nurse's office.

Lena was more worried about me than I was. If something happened to me—which was a pretty big possibility, since it was becoming harder to kiss her, and even harder to stay away—I didn't care. I couldn't stand to think about not touching her. Things were changing. That feeling—the pain that wasn't pain—was still there even when we were apart. There should be a name for it, the perfect ache I felt in the empty places she usually filled.

Is there a word to describe that? Heartache, maybe? Is that how they came up with the word? Except I felt it in my gut, my head, my entire body. I saw Lena when I was looking out windows and staring at walls.

I tried to focus on something that didn't hurt. "I like your new wheels."

"You mean my old ones? Ridley threw a fit about riding in a hearse."

"Where's Rid?" Link was already scanning the parking lot.

Lena gestured at the hearse behind her. "She's in there changing her clothes."

"She can't change at home like a normal person?" I asked.

"I heard that, Short Straw," Ridley called out from inside the car. "I am not"—a ball of crumpled fabric flew through the driver's side window, landing in a heap on the steaming asphalt—"a *normal person*." She said it like normal was an affliction. "And I am not wearing this mass-produced piece of mall crap." Ridley was squirming around, the leather seat squeaking as flashes of blond and pink hair whipped in and out of view. A pair of silver shoes flew out the window. "I look like I belong on the Disney Channel."

I bent down and picked up the offensive piece of clothing. It was a short, printed dress from a chain store at the mall in Summerville. It was a variation of the same dress Savannah Snow, Emily Asher, Eden Westerly, and Charlotte Chase—the queens of the cheerleading squad—and therefore half the girls at Jackson High, wore.

Lena rolled her eyes. "Gramma decided Ridley needed to dress more appropriately now that she would be going to a Mortal high school." Lena dropped her voice. "You know, as a Mortal."

"I heard that!" A white tank top flew out the window. "Just because I'm a disgusting Mortal doesn't mean I have to dress like one." Lena glanced over her shoulder and moved away from the car. Ridley stepped out of the hearse and adjusted her new outfit—a bright pink T-shirt and a black sliver of material that she was passing off as a skirt. The shirt was slashed all over and safety-pinned in a few places, hanging down on one side to show off Ridley's shoulder.

"I don't know if you'll ever look like a Mortal, Babe." Link tugged uncomfortably on his own T-shirt, which looked like his mom had shrunk it in the wash.

"Thank God for small favors. And don't call me Babe." Ridley grabbed the dress, holding it between two fingers. "We

18

should give this thing to Goodwill. Maybe they can sell it as a Halloween costume."

Lena stared at a belt buckle slung low around Ridley's waist. "Speaking of Goodwill, what's that?"

"What? This old thing?" It was an oversize buckle on a battered black leather belt, with some kind of insect caught in a rock or plastic or something. I think it was a scorpion. It was creepy and weird, and very Ridley. "Just trying to fit in." Ridley smiled, smacking her gum. "You know. All the cool kids are wearing them." Without her signature lollipops, she was about as cranky as my dad when Amma switched him to decaf.

Lena let it go. "You're gonna have to change back before we go home, or Gramma will figure out what you're up to." Ridley ignored her and dropped the crumpled dress onto the hot asphalt, stepping on it with her superhigh sandals.

Lena sighed and held out her hand. The dress flew up toward her fingers, but before it reached them the fabric burst into flames. Lena yanked her hand back, and the dress hit the ground, the edges already charred.

"Holy crap!" Link stomped on the material until there was nothing left but a smoldering black mess. Lena turned red.

Ridley was unfazed. "Way to go, Cuz. Couldn't have done it better myself."

Lena watched the last curl of black smoke disappear. "I didn't mean—"

"I know." Ridley looked bored.

Lena's powers had been out of whack ever since she Claimed herself, which was dangerous, considering she was both Light and Dark. Her powers had always been unpredictable, but now she could cause anything from downpours and hurricane-force winds to forest fires.

Lena sighed, frustrated. "I'll get you another one before the end of the day, Rid."

Ridley rolled her eyes, digging through her purse. "Don't do me any favors." She pulled out her sunglasses.

"Good idea." Link slid on his scratched black wraparound shades, which had been cool for about ten minutes when we were in sixth grade. "Let's groove, Sugar Cube."

They turned toward the steps, and I saw my chance. I reached for Lena's arm and pulled her close. She pushed my brown hair, which was always a little too long, out of my eyes and looked up at me from under her thick black lashes. One perfectly gold eye and one dark green one stared back at me. Her eyes had never changed back after the night Sarafine called the Seventeenth Moon out of time. She looked up at me with the gold eye of a Dark Caster and the green eye of a Light one—a constant reminder of the moment Lena realized she possessed both types of power. But her eyes were also a reminder that her choice had changed things for both the Caster and the Mortal worlds. And for us.

Ethan, don't—

Shh. You worry too much.

I wrapped my arms around her, and the feel of her burned through my veins. I could feel the intensity of it as I struggled to keep my shallow breaths even. She tugged gently on my lower lip as we kissed, and I was light-headed and disoriented in seconds. To me, we weren't standing in the middle of the parking lot. Images flashed through my mind, and I had to be hallucinating, because now we were kissing in the water, in Lake

Moultrie—on my desk in English—at the lunch tables—behind the bleachers—in the garden at Greenbrier.

Then a shadow passed over me, and I felt something that wasn't the result of her kiss. I'd had the same feeling before, on top of the water tower, in my dream. A suffocating dizziness wrapped itself around me, and Lena and I weren't in the garden anymore. We were surrounded by dirt, kissing in an open grave.

I was going to pass out.

As my knees buckled, a voice cut through the air and our kiss, and Lena tore herself away from me.

"Hey there. How y'all doin'?" Savannah Snow.

I collapsed against the side of the hearse, sliding to the ground. Then I felt someone pulling me up, my feet barely touching the asphalt.

"What's wrong with Ethan?" Savannah drawled. I opened my eyes.

"The heat, I guess." Link grinned and put me down. Lena looked shocked, but Ridley looked worse. Because Link was smiling like someone had just offered him a record deal. That someone being Savannah Snow—cheer captain, Third Degree Burns–level hot—and the Holy Grail of unattainable girls at Stonewall Jackson High.

Savannah stood there, squeezing her books against her chest so hard her knuckles turned white. She was wearing almost the same dress Ridley had tossed onto the asphalt seconds earlier. Emily Asher was trailing behind her, wearing her own version of Savannah's outfit, looking confused. Savannah stepped closer to Link, with only her books between them. "What I really meant was, how are you?"

21

Link ran his hand through his hair nervously and took a step back. "I'm good. What's up?"

Savannah flipped her blond ponytail and bit her lower lip suggestively, sticky pink lip gloss melting in the sun. "Not much. Just wonderin' if you're goin' to the Dar-ee Keen after school. Maybe you can give me a ride."

Emily looked as surprised as I was. Savannah was more likely to give up her position on the cheer squad than agree to ride in Link's rusted shell of a car. Since riding around with Savannah was one of the requirements of being her sidekick, Emily spoke up. "Savannah, we have a ride. Earl is takin' us, remember?"

"You ride with Earl. I think I'd rather ride with Link." Savannah was still staring at Link like he was a rock star.

Lena shook her head at me.

I told you. It's the John Breed effect. Not too shabby for a quarter Incubus. You can't expect a Mortal girl not to feel it.

That was an understatement.

Just Mortal girls, L?

She pretended not to know what I was talking about.

Not all Mortal girls. Look —

She was right. Link didn't seem to be having the same effect on Emily. The more Savannah licked her lips, the more nauseated Emily appeared.

Ridley grabbed Link's arm, jerking him away from Savannah. "He's busy this afternoon, sweetheart. You should listen to your friend." Her eyes weren't yellow anymore, but Ridley looked as intimidating as her former Dark Caster self.

Savannah didn't think so, or she didn't care. "Oh, sorry. Are you two together?" She paused for a second, pretending to appear thoughtful. "No. That's right, you aren't."

Anyone who spent any time at the Dar-ee Keen knew that Link and Ridley's on-again, off-again relationship was off at the moment. Savannah hooked her arm through Link's other arm. A challenge. "I guess that means Link can make his own decisions."

Link untangled himself from both of them and draped his arms over their shoulders. "Ladies, ladies. There's no need to fight. There's plenty a this to go around." He puffed out his chest, even though it was big enough already. Normally, I would've laughed at the idea of two girls fighting over Link, except they weren't just any two girls. We were talking about Savannah Snow and Ridley Duchannes. Supernatural or not, they were the two most powerful Sirens mankind had ever been lucky—or unlucky—enough to encounter, depending on how they used their powers of persuasion.

"Savannah, let's go. We're gonna be late for class." Emily sounded disgusted. I wondered why Link's Incubus magnetism didn't work on her.

Savannah wedged herself tighter under his arm. "You should find yourself a guy who's more"—she looked at Ridley and her safety-pinned shirt—"like you."

Ridley shrugged Link's arm off her shoulder. "And you should be careful who you talk to like that, Barbie." Savannah was lucky Ridley didn't have her powers anymore.

This is about to get ugly, L.

Don't worry. I'm not going to let Rid get kicked out on her first day. I won't give Principal Harper the satisfaction.

"Ridley, let's go." Lena walked over and stood next to her cousin. "She's not worth it. Trust me."

Savannah was about to fire back, when something distracted

her. She crinkled her nose. "Your eyes—they're two different colors. What's wrong with you?"

Emily wandered over to get a better look. It was only a matter of time before someone noticed Lena's eyes. They were impossible to miss. But I had hoped we would make it past the parking lot before the first wave of gossip hit. "Savannah, why don't you—"

Lena interrupted before I could finish. "I would ask you the same question, but we all know the answer."

Ridley crossed her arms. "Let me give you a hint. It begins with B and rhymes with bitch."

Lena turned her back on Savannah and Emily, heading for Jackson's broken concrete steps. I grabbed her hand, the energy pulsating up my arm. I expected Lena to be shaky after facing off against Savannah, but she was calm. Something had changed, and it was more than just her eyes. I guess when you've faced a Dark Caster who also happens to be your mother, and a hundred-and-fifty-year-old Blood Incubus who is trying to kill you, a few cheerleaders aren't that intimidating.

You okay?

Lena squeezed my hand.

I'm okay.

I could hear Ridley's shoes smacking against the concrete behind us. Link jogged up alongside me. "Man, if this is what I have to look forward to, this year is gonna rock."

I tried to convince myself he was right as we cut across the brown grass, dead lubbers crunching under our feet.

Stonewalling

There's something about walking into school holding hands with a person you actually love. It's strange—not bad strange. The best strange. I remembered what made couples hang around attached to each other like cold spaghetti. There were so many ways to be knotted up together. Arms draped around necks, hands crossed in pockets. We couldn't even walk next to each other without our shoulders finding a way to bump, as if our bodies gravitated toward each other on their own. I guess when electric voltage marked each of those tiny connections, you noticed them more than the average guy.

Even though I should've been used to it by now, it still felt weird to walk down the halls while everyone stared at Lena. She would always be the most beautiful girl in school, no matter what color her eyes were, and everyone here knew it, too. She was that girl—the one who had her own kind of power, supernatural or not. And there was a look a guy couldn't help but give that girl, no matter what she'd done or how much of a freak she would always be.

It was the same look the guys were giving her now.

Calm down, Lover Boy.

Lena bumped her shoulder against mine.

I forgot what this walk was like. After Lena's sixteenth birthday, I lost more and more of her every day. By the end of the school year, she was so distant I could barely find her in the halls. It was only a few months ago. But now that we were here again, I remembered.

I don't like the way they're looking at you.

What way?

I stopped walking and touched the side of Lena's face, below the crescent-shaped birthmark on her cheekbone. A shiver shot through both of us, and I leaned down to find her mouth.

This way.

She pulled back, smiling, and dragged me down the hall.

I get the picture. But I think you're way off. Look.

Emory Watkins and the other guys from the basketball team were staring past us as we walked by his locker. He nodded at me.

I hate to break it to you, Ethan, but they're not looking at me.

I heard Link's voice. "Hey, girls. We shootin' hoops this afternoon or what?" He bumped fists with Emory and kept walking. But they weren't looking at him either.

Ridley was a step behind the rest of us, letting her long pink nails trail along the locker doors. When she got to Emory's, she let the door close beneath her fingers.

"Hey, *girls.*" The way Ridley rolled out the words, she still sounded like a Siren.

Emory stammered, and Ridley let her finger trail across his chest as she walked past. In that skirt, she was showing more leg than should have been legal. The entire team turned to watch her go.

"Who's your friend?" Emory was talking to Link, but he didn't take his eyes off Ridley. He'd seen her before—at the Stop & Steal when I first met her, and at the winter formal, when she trashed the gym—but he was looking for an introduction, up close and personal.

"Who wants to know?" Rid blew a bubble, letting it pop.

Link looked at her sideways and grabbed Ridley's hand. "Nobody."

The hallway divided in front of them as an ex-Siren and a quarter Incubus conquered Jackson High. I wondered what Amma would have to say about that.

Sweet baby in a manger. Heaven help us all.

———❧

"Are you kidding? I'm supposed to keep my things in this filthy tin *coffin*?" Ridley stared into her locker like she thought something was going to pop out of it.

"Rid, you've been to school before, and you had a locker," Lena said patiently.

Ridley flipped her pink and blond hair. "I must've blocked all that out. Post-traumatic stress."

Lena handed Ridley the combination lock. "You don't have to use it. But you can put your books inside so you don't have to carry them around all day."

"Books?" Ridley looked disgusted. "Carry?"

27

Lena sighed. "You'll get them today, in your classes. And, yes, you have to carry them. You should know how this works."

Ridley adjusted her shirt to expose a little more shoulder. "I was a Siren the last time I was in school. I didn't actually go to any of my classes, and I certainly didn't carry anything."

Link clapped his hand down on her shoulder. "Come on. We have homeroom together. I'll show you how it's done, Link-style."

"Yeah?" Ridley sounded skeptical. "How is that any better?"

"Well, for starters, it doesn't involve any books...." Link seemed more than happy to walk her to class. He wanted to keep an eye on her.

"Ridley, wait! You need this." Lena waved a binder in the air.

Ridley slipped her arm through Link's and ignored her. "Relax, Cuz. I'll use Hot Rod's."

I slammed the locker shut. "Your gramma is an optimist."

"You think?"

Like everyone else, I watched Link and Rid disappear down the hall. "I give this whole little experiment three days, max."

"Three days? You're the optimist." Lena sighed, and we started up the stairs to English.

The air conditioning was running full blast, a pathetic mechanical hum echoing through the halls. But the outdated system didn't stand a chance against this heat wave. It was even hotter upstairs in the administration building than it was outside in the parking lot.

As we walked into English class, I stopped for a minute under the fluorescent light, the one that had burned out when Lena and I had collided on the way into this room the first day I saw her. I stared up at the cardboard squares in the ceiling.

28

You know, if you look really close, you can still see the burn mark around the new light.

How romantic. The scene of our first disaster. Lena followed my eyes up to the ceiling. *I think I see it.*

I let my eyes linger on the squares speckled with perforated dots. How many times had I sat in class staring up at those dots, trying to stay awake or counting them to pass time? Counting minutes left in a class period, periods left in the day—days into weeks, weeks into months, until I got out of Gatlin?

Lena walked by Mrs. English, who was buried in first day of school papers at her desk, and slid into her old seat on the infamous Good-Eye Side.

I started to follow her, but I sensed someone behind me. It was that feeling you get when you're in line and the person after you is standing way too close. I turned around, but no one was there.

Lena was already writing in her notebook when I sat down at the desk next to hers. I wondered if she was writing one of her poems. I was about to sneak a look when I heard it. The voice was faint, and it wasn't Lena's. It was a low whisper, coming from over my shoulder.

I turned around. The seat behind me was empty.

Did you say something, L?

Lena looked up from the notebook, surprised.

What?

Were you Kelting? I thought I heard something.

She shook her head.

No. Are you okay?

I nodded, opening my binder. I heard the voice again. This time I recognized the words. The letters appeared on the page, in my handwriting.

29

I slammed it shut, clenching my hands to stop them from shaking.

Lena looked up at me.

Are you sure you're okay?

I'm fine.

I didn't look up once for the rest of the period. I didn't look up while I failed the quiz on *The Crucible*. Not when Lena participated, straight-faced, in a class discussion about the Salem witch trials. Or when Emily Asher made a less than clever comparison between dear, departed Macon Ravenwood and the possessed townsfolk in the play, and a ceiling tile suddenly came loose and smacked her on the head.

I didn't look up again until the bell rang.

Mrs. English was staring at me, her expression so unnerving and blank that for a second I thought both her eyes could have been glass.

I tried to tell myself that it was the first day of school, which could make anyone crazy. That she'd probably just had a bad cup of coffee.

But this was Gatlin, so there was a pretty good chance I was wrong.

Once English was over, Lena and I didn't have any other classes together until after lunch. I was in Trig and Lena was in Calculus. Link—and now Ridley—had been bumped down to Con-

30

sumer Math, the class the teachers enrolled you in when they finally admitted you weren't going to make it past Algebra II. Everyone called it Burger Math because all you learned was how to make change. Link's whole schedule read like the teachers had decided he was going to be working at the BP station with Ed after graduation. His schedule was basically one big study hall. I had Bio; he had Rocks for Jocks. I had World History; he had CSS—Cultures of Southern States, or "Checking Out Savannah Snow," as he called it. Compared to Link, I looked like a rocket scientist. He didn't seem to care—or if he did, there were too many girls following him around for him to notice.

To be honest, it didn't matter, because all I wanted to do was get lost in the familiar blur of the first day of school so I could forget about the crazy message in my binder.

I guess there's nothing like a crappy summer filled with near-death experiences to make the first day of school seem great in comparison. Until I got to the cafeteria, where it was sloppy joe day. Of course it was. Nothing said first day of school like sloppy joes.

I found Lena and Ridley easily enough. They were sitting alone at one of the orange lunch tables, with a steady stream of guys circling like vultures. Everyone had heard about Ridley by now, and all the guys wanted to check her out.

"Where's Link?"

Ridley tilted her head toward the back of the lunchroom, where Link was moving from table to table like he was the MVP at the state championship or something. I noticed her tray, full of chocolate pudding, red Jell-O cubes, and slices of dry-looking angel food cake. "Hungry, Rid?"

"What can I say, Boyfriend? Girl's got a sweet tooth." She picked up a bowl of pudding and dug in.

"Don't tease her. She's having a bad day," Lena said.

"Really? That's a shocker." I bit into my first deflated sloppy joe. "What happened?"

Lena glanced back at one of the tables. "That happened."

Link had one foot up on the plastic bench, and he was leaning over the table, talking to the cheer squad. His attention focused on one cheer captain in particular.

"Aw, that's nothing. Just Link being Link. You don't have anything to worry about, Rid."

"Like I'm worried," she snapped. "I could care less what he does." But I looked down at her tray, and four of the pudding bowls were already empty. "I'm not coming back tomorrow, anyway. This whole school thing is moronic. You move around from room to room like herds or flocks or—"

"Schools?" I couldn't resist.

"That's what I'm talking about." Ridley rolled her eyes, annoyed that I couldn't keep up.

"I was talking about fish. A group of fish is called a school. If you went to school you'd know that." I ducked to avoid her spoon.

"That isn't the point." Lena shot me a warning look.

"The point is, you're sort of a solo act," I said, trying to sound sympathetic. Ridley went back to her pudding with a serious level of sugar dedication I respected. She didn't take her eyes off Link.

"Actually *trying* to make someone like you is totally demeaning. It's pathetic. It's…"

"Mortal?"

"Exactly." She shuddered, moving on to the Jell-O.

A few minutes later, Link worked his way over to our table. He dropped down next to Ridley, and the side of the table where Lena and I were sitting lifted right off the ground. At 6'2", I was one of the tallest guys at Jackson, but I only had an inch or so on Link now.

"Hey, man. Take it easy."

Link eased up a little, and our side of the table smacked down against the linoleum. People were staring. "Sorry. I keep forgettin'. I'm Transitioning. Mr. Ravenwood said this would be a rough time, when you're the new kid on the block."

Lena kicked me under the table, trying not to laugh.

Ridley was less subtle. "I think all this sugar is making me sick. Oh wait, did I say sugar? I meant sap." She looked at Link. "And when I said sap, I meant you."

Link smiled. This was the Ridley he liked best. "Your uncle said no one would understand."

"Yeah, I bet it's really tough being the Hulk." I was kidding, but I wasn't far off.

"Dude, it's no joke. I can't sit down for more than five minutes or people start throwing their food at me, like they expect me to eat it."

"Well, you did have a reputation for being a human garbage disposal."

"I could still eat if I wanted to." He looked disgusted. "But food doesn't taste like anything. It's like chewin' on cardboard. I'm on the Macon Ravenwood diet. You know, snackin' on a few dreams here and there."

"Whose dreams?" If Link was feeding off my dreams, I was going to kick his ass. They were confusing enough without him.

"No way. Your head's too full a crazy for me. But you wouldn't believe what Savannah dreams about. Let's just say she's not thinking about the state finals."

No one wanted to hear the details—especially not Ridley, who was stabbing at her Jell-O. I tried to spare her. "That's a visual I can live without, thanks."

"It's cool. But you'll never guess what I saw." If he said Savannah in her underwear, he was a dead man.

Lena was thinking the same thing. "Link, I don't think—"

"Dolls."

"What?" It wasn't the answer Lena was expecting.

"Barbies, but not the ones girls had in elementary school. These puppies are all dressed up. She's got a bride, Miss America, Snow White. And they're in this big glass case."

"I knew she reminded me of a Barbie." Ridley stabbed another cube.

Link slid closer to her. "You still ignorin' me?"

"You're not worth the time it takes to ignore." Ridley stared through the jiggling red cube. "I don't think Kitchen makes this. What's it called again?"

"Jell-O Surprise." Link grinned.

"What's the surprise?" Ridley examined the red gelatin more closely.

"What they put in it." He flicked the cube with his finger, and she pulled it away.

"Which is?"

"Ground-up hooves, hides, and bones. Surprise."

Ridley looked at him, shrugged, and put the spoon in her mouth. She wasn't going to give him an inch. Not as long as he

34

was creeping around Savannah Snow's bedroom at night and flirting with her all day.

Link looked over at me. "So, you wanna shoot some hoops after school?"

"No." I shoved the rest of the sloppy joe into my mouth.

"I can't believe you're eating that. You hate those things."

"I know. But they're pretty good today." A Jackson first. When Amma's cooking was off and the cafeteria's was on, maybe it really was the End of Days.

You know, you can play basketball if you want to.

Lena was offering me something, the same thing Link was. A chance to make peace with my former friends, to be less of an outcast, if that was possible. But it was too late. Your friends were supposed to stand by you, and now I knew who my friends really were. And who they weren't.

I don't want to.

"Come on. It's cool. All that crazy stuff with the guys is history." Link believed what he was saying. But history was hard to forget when it included tormenting your girlfriend all year.

"Yeah. People around here aren't into history."

Even Link caught my sarcasm. "Well, I'm gonna hit the court." He didn't look at me. "I might even go back on the team. I mean, it's not like I was really off."

Not like you. That's the part he didn't say.

"It's really hot in here." Sweat was dripping down my back. So many people, crammed into one room.

You okay?

No. Yeah. I just need to get some air.

I stood up to go, but the door looked like it was a mile away.

This school had a way of making you feel small. As small as it was, maybe even smaller. I guess some things never change.

———⁊

Turns out, Ridley wasn't interested in studying the cultures of the Southern states any more than she was interested in Link studying Savannah Snow, and five minutes into the period she convinced him they should switch to World History. Which wouldn't have surprised me except switching classes usually involved taking your schedule to Miss Hester—then lying and begging and, if you were really stuck, crying. So when Link and Ridley showed up in World History and he told me that his schedule had miraculously changed, I was more than suspicious.

"What do you mean, your schedule changed?"

Link dropped his notebook onto the desk next to me and shrugged. "I don't know. One minute Savannah sits down next to me, then Ridley comes in and sits on the other side, and the next thing I know, *World History*'s printed on my schedule. Rid's, too. She shows the teacher, and we get kicked right outta class."

"How did you manage that?" I asked as Ridley settled into her seat.

"Manage what?" She looked at me innocently, clicking and un-clicking her creepy scorpion belt buckle.

Lena wasn't letting her off that easy. "You know what he's talking about. Did you take a book from Uncle Macon's study?"

"Are you actually accusing *me* of reading?"

Lena lowered her voice. "Were you trying to Cast? It's not safe, Ridley."

"You mean not safe for me. Because I'm a stupid Mortal."

"Casting is dangerous for Mortals, unless you've had years of training, like Marian. Which you haven't." Lena wasn't trying to rub it in, but every time she said the word "Mortal," Ridley cringed. It was like pouring gasoline on a fire.

Maybe it was too hard to hear from a Caster. I jumped in. "Lena's right. Who knows what could happen if something went wrong?"

Ridley didn't say a word, and for a second it seemed like I had single-handedly put out the flames. But as she turned to face me, her blue eyes blazing as bright as her yellow ones ever had, I realized how wrong I was.

"I don't remember anyone complaining when you and your little British Marian-in-training were Casting at the Great Barrier."

Lena blushed and looked away.

Ridley was right. Liv and I had Cast at the Great Barrier. It was how we freed Macon from the Arclight, and why Liv would never be a Keeper. And it was a painful reminder of a time when Lena and I were as far away from each other as two people could be.

I didn't say anything. Instead I stumbled over my thoughts, crashing and burning in the silence while Mr. Littleton tried to convince us how fascinating World History was going to be. He failed. I tried to come up with something to say that would rescue me from the awkwardness of the next ten seconds. I failed.

Because even though Liv wasn't at Jackson, and she spent all her days in the Tunnels with Macon, she was still the elephant in the room. The thing Lena and I didn't talk about. I had only seen Liv once since the night of the Seventeenth Moon, and I missed her. Not like I could tell anyone that.

I missed her crazy British accent, and the way she mispronounced Carolina so it sounded like Carolin-er. I missed her selenometer that looked like a giant plastic watch from thirty years ago, and the way she was always writing in her tiny red notebook. I missed the way we joked around and the way she made fun of me. I missed my friend.

The sad part was, she probably would have understood.

I just couldn't tell her.

Off Route 9

After school, Link stayed to play basketball with the guys. Ridley wouldn't leave without him as long as the cheer squad was in the gym, even though she wouldn't admit it.

I stood inside the gym doors and watched Link dribble down the court without breaking a sweat. I watched him sink the ball from the paint, from the top of the key, from the three-point mark, from center court. I watched the other guys stand there with their mouths hanging open. I watched Coach sit back on the bleachers with his whistle still stuck in his mouth. I enjoyed every minute, almost as much as Link.

"You miss it?" Lena was watching me from the doorway.

I shook my head. "No way. I don't want to hang out with the rest of those guys." I smiled. "And for once, no one's looking at us." I held out my hand and she took it. Hers was warm and soft.

"Let's get out of here," she said.

Boo Radley was sitting at the corner of the lot by the stop sign, panting like there wasn't enough air in the world to cool him off. I wondered if Macon was still watching us and everyone else through the Caster dog's eyes. We pulled up next to him and opened the door. Boo didn't even hesitate.

We drove up Route 9, where Gatlin's houses disappeared and turned into rows of fields. This time of year, those fields were usually a mix of green and brown — corn and tobacco. But this year there was nothing but black and yellow, as far as the eye could see — dead plants, and lubbers eating their way right onto the road. You could hear them crunching beneath the tires. It looked wrong.

It was the other thing we didn't like to talk about. The apocalypse that had settled over Gatlin in place of fall. Link's mom was convinced that the heat wave and the bugs were the results of the wrath of God, but I knew she was wrong. At the Great Barrier, Abraham Ravenwood had promised that Lena's choice would affect both the Caster and Mortal worlds. He wasn't kidding.

Lena stared out the window, her eyes locked on the ravaged fields. There was nothing I could say that would make her feel any better, or less responsible. The only thing I could do was try to distract her. "Today was crazy, even for the first day of school."

"I feel bad for Ridley." Lena pushed her hair up off her shoulders, twisting it into a messy knot. "She's not herself."

"Which means she's not an evil Siren secretly working for Sarafine. How sorry should I be?"

"She seems so lost."

"My prediction? She's gonna mess with Link's head again."

40

Lena bit her lip. "Yeah, well. Ridley still thinks she's a Siren. Messing with people is part of the job description."

"I bet she'll bring down the whole cheer-amid before she's done."

"Then she'll get expelled," Lena said.

I pulled off at the crossroads, turning off Route 9 and onto the road to Ravenwood. "Not before she burns Jackson to the ground."

The oak trees grew and arched over the road leading up to Lena's house, bringing the temperature down a degree or two.

The breeze from the open window blew through Lena's dark curls. "I don't think Ridley can stand being in the house. My whole family is acting crazy. Aunt Del doesn't know if she's coming or going."

"That's nothing new."

"Yesterday Aunt Del thought Ryan was Reece."

"And Reece?" I asked.

"Reece's powers have been all over the place. She's always complaining about it. Sometimes she looks at me and freaks out, and I don't know if it's because of something she's read in my face or because she can't read anything at all."

Reece was already cranky enough, under normal circumstances.

"At least you have your uncle."

"Sort of. Every day Uncle Macon disappears into the Tunnels, and he won't say what he's doing down there. Like he doesn't want me to know."

"How is that weird? He and Amma never want us to know anything." I tried to act like I wasn't worried even as the tires rolled over more lubbers.

41

"He's been back for weeks now, and I still don't know what kind of Caster he is. I mean, except Light. He won't talk about it, not to anyone." *Not even me.* That's what she was saying.

"Maybe he doesn't know himself."

"Forget it." She looked out the window, and I took her hand. We were both so hot I could barely feel the burn of her touch.

"Can you talk to your grandma?"

"Gramma spends half her time in Barbados, trying to figure things out." Lena didn't say what she really meant. Her family was trying to find a way to restore the Order—banish the heat and the lubbers and whatever we had to look forward to in the Mortal world. "Ravenwood has more Binding spells on it than a Caster prison. It's so claustrophobic that I feel as Bound as the house. It gives new meaning to being grounded." Lena shook her head. "I keep hoping Ridley doesn't feel it, now that she's a Mortal."

I didn't say anything, but I was pretty sure Ridley felt it, because I did. As we got closer to the great house, I could feel the magic—buzzing like it was a live power line, the weight of a thick fog that had nothing to do with the weather.

The atmosphere of Caster magic, Dark and Light.

I had been able to sense it ever since we came back from the Great Barrier. And when I pulled up to the crooked iron gates that marked the boundaries of Ravenwood, the air around us crackled, almost as charged as an electrical storm.

The gates themselves weren't the real barrier. Ravenwood's gardens, so overgrown while Macon was gone, were the one place in the whole county that was a refuge from the heat and the bugs. Maybe it was a testament to the power of Lena's family, but as we passed through the gates, I could feel the energy from outside pulling one way while Ravenwood pulled the other.

Ravenwood was standing its ground—you could tell by the way the endless brown outside its grounds gave way to green within, the way the gardens remained uneaten, untouched. Macon's flower beds were blooming and brilliant, his trees trimmed and orderly, the broad green lawns clipped close and clean, stretching down from the great house to the Santee River. Even the paths were lined with new gravel. But the outside world was pushing against the gates and the Casts and Bindings keeping Ravenwood safe. Like waves crashing on the rocks, battering the same reef over and over, eroding a few grains of sand at a time.

Eventually, waves always get their way. If the Order of Things was really broken, Ravenwood couldn't remain the only outpost of a lost world for long.

I pulled the hearse up to the house, and before I could say a word, we were out of the car and into the damp air outside. Lena threw herself onto the cool grass, and I dropped down next to her. I'd been waiting for this moment all day, and I felt sorry for Amma and my dad and the rest of Gatlin, trapped in town beneath the burning blue sky. I didn't know how much more of this I could take.

I know.

Crap. I didn't mean—

I know. You're not blaming me. It's all right.

She moved closer, reaching for my face with her hand. I braced myself. My heart didn't just race anymore when we touched. Now I could feel the energy draining from my body, as if it was being sucked out. But she hesitated and let her hand drop. "This is my fault. I know you don't feel like you can say it, but I can."

43

"L."

She rolled onto her back and stared at the sky. "Late at night I lie in bed, close my eyes, and try to break through it. Try to pull the clouds in and push the heat away. You don't know how hard it is. How much it takes from all of us to keep Ravenwood like this." She picked a blade of green grass. "Uncle Macon says he doesn't know what will happen next. Gramma says it's impossible to know, because this has never happened before."

"Do you believe them?"

When it came to Lena, Macon was about as forthcoming as Amma was with me. If there was something she could have done differently, he'd be the last person to tell her.

"I don't know. But this is bigger than Gatlin. Whatever I did, it's affecting other Casters outside of my family. Everyone's powers are misfiring like mine."

"Your powers have never been predictable."

Lena looked away. "Spontaneous combustion is a little more than unpredictable."

I knew she was right. Gatlin was teetering dangerously on the edge of an invisible cliff, and we had no idea what was at the bottom. But I couldn't say that to her—not when she was the one responsible for putting it there. "We'll figure out what's going on."

"I'm not so sure." She held one hand up to the sky, and I thought back to the first time I followed her into the garden at Greenbrier. I had watched her tracing clouds with her fingertips, making shapes in the sky. I hadn't known then what I was getting myself into, but it wouldn't have mattered.

Everything had changed, even the sky. This time there wasn't a cloud to trace. There was nothing but the threatening blue heat.

Lena raised her other hand and looked over at me. "This isn't going to stop. Things are going to keep getting worse. We have to be ready." She pulled on the sky with her hands absentmindedly, twisting the air slowly, like taffy between her fingers. "Sarafine and Abraham aren't going to just walk away."

I'm ready.

She looped her finger through the air. "Ethan, I want you to know that I'm not afraid of anything, anymore."

I'm not either. Not as long as we're together.

"That's the thing. If something happens, it will be because of me. And I'll have to be the one to fix it. Do you understand what I'm saying?" She didn't take her eyes off her fingers.

No. I don't.

"You don't? Or you don't want to?"

I can't.

"You remember when Amma used to tell you not to pick a hole in the sky or the universe would fall through?"

I smiled. "C. O. N. C. O. M. I. T. A. N. T. Eleven down. As in, you go ahead and pull on that thread and watch the whole world unravel like a sweater, Ethan Wate."

Lena should've been laughing, but she wasn't. "I pulled on the thread when I used *The Book of Moons.*"

"Because of me." I thought about it all the time. She wasn't the only one of us who had pulled on the one piece of yarn that tied up all of Gatlin County, above and below the surface.

"I Claimed myself."

"You had to. You should be proud of that."

"I am." She hesitated.

"But?" I watched her carefully.

"But I'm going to have to pay a price, and I'm ready to."

I closed my eyes. "Don't talk like that."

"I'm being realistic."

"You're waiting for something bad to happen." I didn't want to think about it.

Lena played with the charms on her necklace. "It's not really a question of *if* but *when*."

I'm waiting. That's what the notebook said.

What notebook?

I didn't want her to know, but now I couldn't stop it. And I couldn't pretend we could go back to the way things were.

The wrongness of everything came crashing down on me. The summer. Macon's death. Lena acting like a stranger. Running away with John Breed, and away from me. And then the rest of it, the part that happened before I met Lena—my mom not coming home, her shoes sitting where she'd left them, her towel still damp from the morning. Her side of the bed not slept in, the smell of her hair still on her pillow.

The mail that still came addressed in her name.

The suddenness of it all. And the permanence. The lonely reality of the truth—that the most important person in your life suddenly ceased to exist. Which on a bad day meant maybe she had never existed at all. And on a good day, there was the other fear. That even if you were a hundred percent sure she had been there, maybe you were the only one who cared or remembered.

How can a pillow smell like a person who isn't even on the same planet as you anymore? And what do you do when one day the pillow just smells like any old pillow, a strange pillow? How can you bring yourself to put away those shoes?

But I had. And I had seen my mother's Sheer at Bonaventure Cemetery. For the first time in my life, I believed something actually happened when you died. My mom wasn't alone in the dirt in His Garden of Perpetual Peace, the way I'd always been afraid she was. I was letting her go. At least, I was close.

Ethan? What's going on?

I wished I knew.

"I'm not going to let anything happen to you. No one will." I said the words even though I knew I wasn't capable of protecting her. I said them because I felt like my heart was going to rip itself to shreds all over again.

"I know," she lied. Lena didn't say anything else, but she knew what I was feeling.

She pulled down the sky with her hands, as hard as she could, like she wanted to rip it away from the sun.

I heard a loud cracking sound.

I didn't know where it came from, and I didn't know how long it would last, but the blue sky broke open, and though there wasn't a cloud in sight, we let the rain fall on our faces.

I felt the wet grass, and the raindrops in my eyes. They felt real. I felt my sweaty clothes dampening instead of drying. I pulled her close and held her face in my hands. Then I kissed her until I wasn't the only one who was breathless, and the ground beneath us dried and the sky was harsh and blue again.

Dinner was Amma's prizewinning chicken potpie. My portion alone was the size of my plate, or maybe home plate. I punctured the biscuit crust with my fork, letting the steam escape. I could smell the good sherry, her secret ingredient. Every potpie in our county had a secret ingredient: sour cream, soy sauce, cayenne pepper, even parmesan cheese straight out of the shaker. Secrets and piecrust went hand in hand around here. Slap a piecrust up top and all the folks in town will kill themselves trying to figure out what's hiding underneath.

"Ah. That smell still makes me feel about eight years old." My dad smiled at Amma, who ignored both the comment and his suspiciously good mood. Now that the semester had started up again at the university, and he was sitting there in his collared teaching shirt, he looked downright normal. You could almost forget the year he spent sleeping all day, holed up in his office all night "writing" a book that amounted to nothing more than hundreds of pages of scribble. Barely speaking or eating, until he started the steep, slow climb back to sanity. Or maybe it was the smell of the pies going to work on me, too. I dug deep.

"You have a good first day of school, Ethan?" my dad asked, his mouth full.

I examined the pie on my fork. "Good enough."

Everything was chopped up real small, underneath the dough. You couldn't tell diced chicken from diced vegetables in the tiny chaos of mashed-up pie guts. Crap. When Amma had her cleaver out, it was never a good sign. This potpie was evidence of some kind of furious afternoon I didn't want to imagine. I felt sorry for her scarred cutting board. I looked over at her empty plate and knew she wasn't about to sit down and make small talk tonight. Or explain why not.

I swallowed. "How about you, Amma?"

She was standing at the kitchen counter tossing a salad so hard I thought she was going to shatter our cracked glass bowl. "Good enough."

My dad calmly raised his glass of milk. "Well, my day was unbelievable. I woke up with an incredible idea, out of the blue. Must have come to me last night. During my office hours, I wrote up a proposal. I'm going to start a new book."

"Yeah? That's great." I picked up the salad bowl, concentrating on an oily-looking wedge of tomato.

"It's about the Civil War. I might even find a way to use some of your mom's old research. I have to talk to Marian about it."

"What's the book called, Dad?"

"That's the part that hit me out of nowhere. I woke up with the words in my head. *The Eighteenth Moon*. What do you think?"

The bowl slipped out of my hands, hitting the table and shattering on the floor. Torn-up leaves mixed with jagged pieces of broken glass, sparkling across my sneakers and the floorboards.

"Ethan Wate!" Before I could say another word, Amma was there, scooping up the soggy, slippery, dangerous mess. Like always. As I got down on my own hands and knees, I could hear her hissing at me under her breath.

"Not another word." She might as well have slapped an old piecrust right across my mouth.

What do you think it means, L?

I lay in bed, paralyzed, my face hidden in the pillow. Amma had shut herself up in her room after dinner, which I was pretty sure meant she didn't know what was going on with my dad either.

I don't know.

Lena's Kelting came to me as clearly as if she was sitting next to me on the bed, as usual. And as usual, I wished she really was.

How would he come up with that? Did we say something about the songs in front of him? Have we messed something up?

Something else. That was the part I didn't say and tried not to think. The answer came quickly.

No, Ethan. We never said anything.

So if he's talking about the Eighteenth Moon...

The truth hit us at the same time.

It's because someone wants him to.

It made sense. Dark Casters had already killed my mom. My dad, just getting back on his feet, was an easy mark. And he had been targeted once already, the night of Lena's Sixteenth Moon. There was no other explanation.

My mother was gone, but she had found a way to guide me by sending the Shadowing Songs, *Sixteen Moons* and *Seventeen Moons*, which stayed stuck in my head until I finally started to listen. But this message wasn't coming from my mom.

L? You think it's some kind of warning? From Abraham?

Maybe. Or my wonderful mother.

Sarafine. Lena almost never said her name, if she could avoid it. I didn't blame her.

It has to be one of them, right?

Lena didn't answer, and I lay there in my bed in the dark silence, hoping it was one of the two. One of the devils we knew, from somewhere in the known Caster world. Because the devils we didn't know were too terrifying to think about—and the worlds we didn't know, even worse.

Are you still there, Ethan?

I'm here.

Will you read me something?

I smiled to myself and reached under my bed, pulling out the first book I found. Robert Frost, one of Lena's favorites. I opened to a random page. *"We make ourselves a place apart / Behind light words that tease and flout, / But oh, the agitated heart / Till someone really find us out..."*

I didn't stop reading. I felt the reassuring weight of Lena's consciousness leaning against mine, as real as if her head was leaning against my shoulder. I wanted to keep her there as long as I could. She made me feel less alone.

Every line felt like it was written about her, at least to me.

As Lena drifted off, I listened to the hum of the crickets until I realized it wasn't the crickets at all. It was the lubbers. The plague, or whatever Mrs. Lincoln wanted to call it. The longer I listened, the more it sounded like a million buzz saws in the distance, destroying my town and everything around it. Then the lubbers faded into something else—the low chords of a song I would recognize anywhere.

I'd been hearing the songs since before I met Lena. *Sixteen Moons* had led me to her, the song only I could hear. I couldn't escape them, any more than Lena could run from her destiny or I could hide from mine. They were warnings from my mom— the person I trusted most, in any world.

Eighteen Moons, eighteen spheres,
From the world beyond the years,
One Unchosen, death or birth,
A Broken Day awaits the Earth...

I tried to make sense of the words, the way I always did. "The world beyond the years" ruled out the Mortal world. But what was coming from this other world—the Eighteenth Moon or the "One Unchosen"? And who could that be?

The only person it ruled out was Lena. She'd made her choice. Which meant there was another choice to be made—by someone who had yet to make one.

But the last line was the one that made me sick. "A Broken Day?" That pretty much covered every day now. How could things possibly get more broken than this?

I wished I had more than a song and that my mom was here to tell me what it meant. More than anything, I wished I knew how to fix everything we had broken.

⊰ 9.12 ⊱

Glass Houses and Stones

A whole catfish stared at me with glassy eyes, its tail giving a final flop. On one side of the fish was a massive plate piled with slabs of fatty, uncooked bacon. A platter of raw shrimp, translucent and gray, sat on the other side, next to a bowl of dry instant grits. A plate of runny eggs, with bleeding yolks in thick white sauce, was the best of the worst. It was weird, even for Ravenwood, where I sat across from Lena in the formal dining room. Half the food looked like it was ready to get up and run or swim its way off the table. And there wasn't one thing on the table that anyone in Gatlin would ever eat for breakfast. Especially not me.

I looked back at my empty plate, where chocolate milk had appeared in a tall crystal glass. Sitting next to the runny eggs, the milk wasn't appealing.

Lena made a face. "Kitchen? Seriously? Again?" I heard an

indignant clanging from the other room. Lena had irritated Ravenwood's mysterious cook, who I'd still never seen. Lena shrugged, looking at me. "I told you. Everything is out of whack around here. It gets worse every day."

"Come on. We can grab a sticky bun at the Stop & Steal." I'd lost my appetite around the time I saw the uncooked bacon.

"Kitchen's doing her best. Life is hard enough lately, I'm afraid. Last night Delphine was pounding on my door in the middle of the night, insisting the British were coming." A familiar voice, the soft shuffling of slippers, a scraping chair—and there he was. Macon Ravenwood, holding an armful of rolled newspapers, lifting a teacup that was suddenly full of what probably was supposed to be tea but looked like some kind of soupy green muck. Boo stalked in after him and curled up at his master's feet.

Lena sighed. "Ryan's crying. She won't admit it, but she's afraid she'll never completely come into her powers now. Uncle Barclay can't Shift anymore. Aunt Del says he can't even turn a frown into a smile."

Macon raised his cup, nodding in my direction. "That can all wait until after breakfast. 'How do you rate the morning sun,' Mr. Wate?"

"Excuse me, sir?" It sounded like a trick question.

"Robbie Williams. Quite the songwriter, don't you think? And quite a relevant question as of late." He glanced down at his tea before taking a sip, and put the cup down. "My way of saying good morning, I suppose."

"Morning, sir." I tried not to stare. He was wearing a black satin robe. At least I thought it was a robe. I'd never seen a robe with a handkerchief sticking out of the chest pocket. It didn't look anything like my dad's ratty checkered bathrobe.

Macon caught me staring. "I believe the term you're searching for is *smoking jacket*. I find, now that I have whole days of sunshine ahead of me, I've discovered there is more to life than formal haberdashery."

"Huh?"

"Uncle M likes to lounge around in his pajamas. That's what he means." Lena gave him a kiss on the cheek. "We have to get going or we'll miss out on the sticky buns. Be nice and I'll bring you one."

He sighed. "Hunger is such an incredible inconvenience."

Lena picked up her backpack. "I'll take that as a yes."

Macon ignored her, smoothing open the first of his newspapers. "Earthquakes in Paraguay." He snapped open the next, which appeared to be written in French. "The Seine is drying up." Another. "The polar ice cap is melting at ten times the predicted rate. If one is to believe the Helsinki press." A fourth paper. "And the entire southeastern coast of the United States appears to be afflicted by a curious plague of pestilence."

Lena closed his newspaper, revealing a plate of white bread sitting directly in front of him. "Eat. The world will still be on the brink of disaster when you finish your breakfast. Even in your smoking jacket."

The darkness in Macon's expression lifted, the green eyes of an Incubus-turned-Light-Caster blazing a bit lighter at her touch. Lena gave him a smile, the one she saved only for him. The smile that said she had noticed all of it—every minute of their life together. What they had, they knew. Since Macon had basically come back to her from the dead, Lena hadn't taken a minute they shared for granted. I never doubted that, though I envied it.

It was what I'd had with my mom—and now I didn't. I

wondered if I had smiled differently when I looked at her. I wondered if she'd known that I had noticed it all, too. That I knew she'd read every book I was reading, just so we could talk about it over dinner at our old oak table. That I knew she'd spent hours at the Blue Bicycle bookstore in Charleston, trying to find the right book for me.

"Come on!" Lena motioned, and I shook loose the memory and picked up my backpack. She gave her uncle a quick hug. "Ridley!" she called up the stairs. A muffled groan floated down from one of the bedrooms. "Now!"

"Sir." I folded my napkin and stood up.

Macon's relaxed expression vanished. "Be careful out there."

"I'll keep an eye on her."

"Thank you, Mr. Wate. I know you will." He lowered his cup. "But you be careful yourself. Things are a bit more complicated than they might seem." The town was falling apart, and we'd pretty much broken the whole world. I wasn't sure how things could get any more complicated than that.

"Careful of what, sir?" The table was quiet between us, even though I could hear Lena and Gramma arguing with Ridley in the hallway.

Macon looked down at his pile of newspapers, smoothing open the last one, in a language I'd never seen and yet somehow recognized.

"I wish I knew."

After breakfast at Ravenwood, if you could call it that, the day only got weirder. We were late for school because when we got to Link's house to pick him up, his mom caught him dumping his breakfast in the trash and made him sit through a second one. Then, when we drove by the Stop & Steal, Fatty, Jackson's faithful truant officer, wasn't sitting in his car eating a sticky bun and reading the paper. And there were half a dozen buns left in the bakery section. That had to be the first sign of the apocalypse. But even more unbelievable, we walked into the administration building twenty minutes late, and Miss Hester wasn't at the front desk to give us detention. Her purple nail polish sat in front of her office chair, unopened. Like the whole world had somehow rotated five degrees in the wrong direction.

"This is our lucky day." Link put up his fist, and I tapped his knuckles against mine. I would have gone with freaky.

It was confirmed when I caught a glimpse of Ridley wandering toward the bathroom. I could've sworn she had changed into a regular girl, wearing weirdly regular-girl clothes. And finally, when I slid into my seat next to Lena, on what should have been Mrs. English's Good-Eye Side, I found myself in the Twilight Zone of classroom seating charts.

I was sitting where I always did. It was the room that had changed, or Mrs. English, who spent the whole period grilling students on the wrong side of the room.

" 'This is a sharp time, now, a precise time—we live no longer in the dusky afternoon when evil mixed itself with good and befuddled the world.' " Mrs. English looked up. "Miss Asher? How dusky a time would Arthur Miller think we live in today?"

Emily stared at her, shocked. "Ma'am? Don't you mean to be asking—them?" Emily looked over at Abby Porter, Lena, and me, the only people who ever sat on the Good-Eye Side.

"I *mean* to be asking anyone who expects to pass my class, Miss Asher. Now answer the question."

Maybe she put her glass eye in the wrong side this morning.

Lena smiled without looking up from her paper.

Maybe.

"Um, I think Arthur Miller would be majorly psyched that we aren't all so messed up anymore."

I peeked over my copy of *The Crucible*. And as Emily stammered to condemn a witch hunt not much different from the one she had all but led herself, that glass eye was staring straight at me.

As if it could not only see me but see right through me.

_____ ᘓ

By the time school let out, things were starting to feel more normal. Ethan-Hating Emily hissed when I walked by, trailed by Eden and Charlotte, third and fourth in command, like the good old days. Ridley figured out that Lena had Cast a *Facies Celata* on her, Charming her Siren clothes so they appeared to be regular clothes. Now Ridley was back to her old self, black leather and pink stripes—revenge, vendettas, and all. Worse, as soon as the bell rang, she dragged both of us to basketball practice to watch Link's scrimmage.

This time there was no hanging out in the doorway of the gym. Ridley wasn't happy until we were sitting front and center. It was painful. Link wasn't even on the court, and I had to watch my old teammates screwing up plays I used to run. But Lena and Ridley were bickering like sisters, and there was more going on in the stands than on the court. At least, until I saw Link get up from the bench.

"You Cast a *Facies* on *me*? Like I was some kind of *Mortal*?" Ridley was practically shrieking. "Like I wouldn't know? So now you think I'm not only powerless but stupid?"

"It wasn't my idea. Gramma told me to do it after she saw what you were wearing at the house." Lena looked embarrassed.

Ridley's face was as pink as the streaks in her hair. "It's a free world. At least, it is outside of Gat-Dung. You can't use your powers to dress people however you want. Especially not like *that*." She shuddered. "I'm not one of Savannah Snow's Barbie dolls."

"Rid. You don't have to be like them. But you don't have to try so hard to be *so* different."

"Same thing," Ridley snapped.

"It's not."

"Look at that herd and tell me why I should care what those *people* think of me."

Ridley had a point. As Link moved up and down the court, the eyes of the entire cheer squad were glued to him as if they were one person. Which, basically, they were. I didn't even watch the court after a while. I already knew Link could probably hit a jumper from the stands, with his superstrength.

Ethan, he's jumping too high.

By about three feet. Lena was stressing, but I knew Link had been fantasizing about this moment his entire life.

Yep.

And running too fast.

Yep.

Aren't you going to say something?

Nope.

Nothing was going to stop him. Word had gotten around

that Link had kicked up his game over the summer, and it seemed like half the school had shown up at practice to see for themselves. I couldn't decide if it was further proof of how boring life was in Gatlin, or how bad our new Linkubus was at Mortal camouflage.

Savannah had the cheerleaders up and moving. To be fair, it was their practice, too. But to be fair to the rest of us, we weren't exactly expecting Savannah's new routines. From the looks of it, Emily, Eden, and Charlotte weren't expecting them either. Emily didn't even get off the bench.

From the sidelines, Savannah was jumping almost as high as Link. "Give me an L!"

"You're not serious." Lena almost spit out her soda.

You could hear Savannah across the gym. "Give me an I!"

I shook my head. "Oh, she's serious. There's nothing ironic about Savannah Snow."

"Give me an N!"

"We are never going to hear the end of this." Lena looked at Ridley. She was chewing gum like Ronnie Weeks slapping on nicotine patches when he quit smoking. The more Savannah jumped, the harder Ridley chewed.

"Give me a K!"

"Give me a break." Ridley spit out her gum and stuck it underneath the bench. Before we could stop her, she was climbing over the aluminum bleachers, down to the court—superhigh sandals, pink-striped hair, black miniskirt, and all.

"Oh no." Lena started to get up, but I pulled her back down.

"You can't stop it from happening, L."

"What is she doing?" Lena couldn't bear to look.

Ridley was talking to Savannah, tightening the low-slung

belt with the poisonous insect trapped in it, like a gladiator gearing up for battle. At first I strained to listen, but within seconds they were shouting.

"What's your problem?" Savannah snapped.

Ridley grinned. "Nothing. Oh, wait...you."

Savannah dropped her pom-poms on the gym floor. "You're a skank. If you want to lure some other guy into your skanky trap, be my guest. But Link is one of us."

"Here's the thing, Barbie. I've already trapped him, and since I'm trying to play nice, this is me giving you fair warning. Back off before you get hurt."

Savannah crossed her arms over her chest. "Make me."

It looked like they needed a ref.

Lena covered her eyes. "Are they fighting?"

"Uh—more like cheering, I think." I pulled Lena's hand from her eyes. "You have to see this for yourself."

Ridley had one thumb hooked over her belt, the other shaking a lone, borrowed pom-pom like it was a dead skunk. The squad was next to her, climbing into their standard pyramid formation—Savannah leading the way.

Link stopped running down the court. Everyone did.

L, I don't know if this is the right time for payback.

Lena didn't take her eyes off Ridley.

I'm not doing anything. But someone is.

Savannah was smiling from the base. Emily scowled as she climbed to the top. The other girls followed almost mechanically.

Ridley waved a drooping pom-pom over her head.

Link dribbled the ball in place. Waiting, like the rest of us who knew Ridley, for the terrible thing that hadn't happened yet but would any second now.

L, you think Ridley—?

It's impossible. She's not a Caster anymore. She doesn't have any powers.

"Give me an"—Ridley shook her pom-pom halfheartedly—"R."

Emily wobbled at the top of the pyramid.

Ridley called out again. "Um, and an I?"

A shudder went through the team, like they were doing the wave in pyramid formation.

"And then, let's go with a D." Ridley dropped the pom-pom. Emily's eyes widened. Link held the ball in one hand. "What does it spell, Cheerlosers?" Ridley winked.

Lena—

I started to move before I saw it happen.

"Rid?" Link shouted at her, but she didn't look back at him.

Lena was halfway over the bench, on her way down to the court.

Ridley, no!

I was right behind her, but there was no way to stop it.

It was too late.

The pyramid collapsed on top of Savannah.

Everything happened really quickly after that, like Gatlin wanted to fast-forward the whole story from breaking news to ancient history. An ambulance picked up Savannah and took her to the hospital, over in Summerville. People were saying it was a miracle Emily hadn't been killed, falling all the way from the top. Half the school kept repeating the words *spinal injury*, which was only a rumor, because Emily seemed about as full of backbone as ever. Apparently Savannah cushioned her fall, as if she had selflessly martyred herself for the greater good of the team. That was the story, anyway.

Link went to the hospital to check on her. I think he felt as guilty as if he'd beaten Savannah up himself. But the official diagnosis, according to Link's call from the lobby, was "good an' banged up," and by the time Savannah sent her mom home for her makeup, everyone involved was feeling better. It probably helped that, the way Link told it, the whole cheer squad was there asking him who he thought had been friends with Savannah the longest.

Link was still relaying the details. "The girls'll be all right. They've sorta been takin' turns sittin' on my lap."

"Yeah?"

"Well, everyone's pretty upset. So I'm doin' my part to comfort the squad."

"How's that going?"

I had a feeling both Link and Savannah were enjoying the afternoon, in their own ways. Ridley was nowhere to be found, but when she figured out where Link had gone, things would probably get even worse. Maybe it was a good thing Link was familiarizing himself with the county hospital.

By the time Link hung up, Lena and I were back in her room, and Ridley was moping around downstairs. Lena's bedroom was about as far as you could get from Jackson High, and being there made everything that happened in town seem about a million miles away. Her room had changed since she came back from the Great Barrier. Lena said it was because she needed to see the world through her gold and green eyes. And Ravenwood had changed to mirror her feelings, the way it had always changed for her and Macon.

Her room was now entirely transparent, like some kind of weird tree house made of glass. From the outside it still looked exactly the same, with its weather-beaten shutters covered in vines. I could see remnants of her old room. There were still windows where there had been windows, doors where there had been doors. But the ceiling was open, with sliding panels of glass shoved to one side to let in the night air. In the afternoon, the wind scattered leaves across her bed. Her floor was a mirror that reflected the changing sky. When the sun beat down on us—as it always did now—the light refracted and broke and scattered over so many different surfaces, it was impossible to tell which sun was the real one. They all burned equally, with a blinding glare.

I lay back on her bed, closing my eyes and letting the breeze roll over me. I knew it wasn't real, just another version of Lena's Casting Breeze, but I didn't care. My body felt like it was breathing for the first time today. I pulled my damp shirt off and tossed it onto the floor. Better.

I opened an eye. Lena was writing on the glass wall closest to her bed, and the words hung in the air like spoken sentences. Inked in Sharpie.

no light no dark no you no me
know light know dark know you know me

It made me feel better, seeing the handwriting I remembered from before the Sixteenth Moon.

so goes the hard way — the (fall a)part way —
the (break a)heart day

I rolled onto my side. "Hey. What does that mean, 'the break a heart day'?" I didn't like the sound of that one.

She looked over at me and smiled. "It's not today."

I pulled her down on the bed next to me, my hand on the back of her neck. My fingers tangled in her long hair, and I ran my thumb down her collarbone. I loved the way her skin felt, even if it burned. I pressed my lips against hers, and I heard Lena's breath catch. I was losing mine, but I didn't care.

Lena ran her hand down my back, her fingers trailing along my bare skin.

"I love you," I whispered into her ear.

She held my face in her hands and leaned back so she could look at me. "I don't think I could ever love anything the way I love you."

"I know I couldn't."

Lena's hand rested on my chest. I knew she could feel my heartbeat thudding beneath it. She sat up, grabbing my shirt off the floor. "You'd better put this back on, or you're going to get me grounded for the rest of my life. It's not like Uncle M sleeps all day. He's probably down in the Tunnels with—" She caught herself, which is how I knew who she was talking about. "He's in his study, and he'll expect to see me any minute now."

I sat up, holding my shirt in my hands.

"Anyway, I don't know why I write the things I do. They sort of come into my head."

"Like my father and his new bestseller, *The Eighteenth Moon?*" I hadn't been able to stop thinking about it, and Amma was avoiding me. Maybe Macon would have the answer.

"Like Savannah and her supercool new Link cheer." Lena leaned against me. "It's a mess."

"Give me an M. Give me an E-S-S."

"Shut up," Lena said, kissing my cheek. "Shirt on."

I pulled my shirt back over my shoulders, pausing midway. "You sure about that?" She bent to kiss my stomach, yanking my shirt back down over it. I felt the stabbing pain disappear as quickly as it came — but I reached for her anyway.

She ducked out of my arms. "We should tell Uncle Macon about what happened today."

"Tell him what? That Ridley's starting fights? And even though she's completely powerless, bad things happen to cheerleaders when she's around?"

"Just in case. She could be up to something. Maybe you should tell him about your dad's new book." Lena held out her hand, and I took it, the energy draining out of me slowly.

"You mean, because the last book turned out so well? We don't even know if there is a book." I didn't want to think about my dad and his books any more than I wanted to think about Ridley and Savannah Snow.

We were halfway down the hall before I realized we had stopped talking. The closer we got, the more I sensed Lena's pace slowing. She didn't mind going back down into the Tunnels. She just didn't want me going down there.

Which had nothing to do with the actual Tunnels and everything to do with Macon's favorite exchange student.

Adam and Eve

Lena stopped in front of a black lacquered door. A handmade flyer for the Holy Rollers — WHAT'S ROCK WITHOUT THE ROLL? — hung skewed to one side. She knocked on Ridley's door. "Rid?"

"Why are we looking for Ridley?" I had seen enough of her today.

"We aren't. There's a shortcut to the Tunnels in her room. Uncle Macon's secret passageway, remember?"

"Right. Because now his bedroom is…" I looked at the door, trying to imagine how Ridley had massacred Macon's old room. I hadn't been in it since the day Lena and I broke up.

Lena shrugged. "He didn't want to keep his old room. And he sleeps in his study in the Tunnels most of the time, anyway."

"Good choice for Ridley's room. Because she's *not* the kind of girl who would sneak out a secret passageway in the middle of the night," I said.

Lena paused, her hand on the doorway. "Ethan. She's the least magical person in the house. She's got more to be afraid of going down there than any of—"

Before she could finish her sentence, I heard an unmistakable sound. The sound of the sky ripping, and an Incubus slipping out of sight.

Traveling.

"Did you hear that?"

Lena frowned at me. "What?"

"It sounded like someone was ripping."

"Uncle Macon doesn't rip anymore. And Ravenwood is completely Bound. There's no way any Incubus, no matter how powerful, could get in here." She looked worried, though, even as she said the words.

"It must have been something else. Maybe Kitchen is experimenting again." I touched her hand on the door, my breath catching. "Open up."

Lena pushed, but nothing happened. She pushed again. "That's weird. The handle's jammed."

"Let me try." I threw my weight against the door. It didn't budge, which was kind of humiliating, so I tried it again, even harder. "It's not jammed. It's—you know."

"What?"

"Whatever the Latin is for using magic to lock your door."

"You mean a Cast? That's not possible. Ridley couldn't use an *Obex* Cast, even if she found one in a book. They're too difficult."

"Are you kidding me? After the stunt she pulled with the cheer squad?"

Lena looked at the door, her green eye glowing and her gold eye darkening. Her black curls began to blow around her shoulders, and before I heard her speak the Cast, the door blew open with such force it went flying off the hinges and into Ridley's bedroom. Which seemed like the Caster way of saying "Screw you."

I flipped on the lights inside Ridley's room.

Lena wrinkled her nose as I picked up a pink lollipop stuck to the long blond hairs wrapped around a giant hot roller. There was a mess of clothes and shoes and nail polish and makeup and candy—on every surface, in the sheets, hidden in the pink retro shag carpet.

"Make sure you put that back where you found it. She'll have a fit if she finds out we were in here. She's been really weird about her room lately." Lena nudged an open bottle of nail polish that was oozing onto the dresser. "But there are no signs of Casting. No books or charms."

I flipped back the pink carpet to reveal the smooth lines of the hidden Caster door in the floor.

"Nothing except—" Lena held up a nearly empty bag of Doritos. "Ridley hates Doritos. She likes sweet, not salty."

I stared down into the darkness at the stairs I only half believed were there. "I'm looking at an invisible stairwell, and you're telling me the chips are weird?"

Lena held up a second bag, a full one. "Pretty much. Yes."

I held out my foot, feeling around until I found the solid footing in the air. "I used to like chocolate milk. Now it makes me sick. Does that mean I have magic powers, too?"

I stepped into the darkness before I could hear her answer.

At the base of the stairs that led into Macon's private study, we could see him standing at a desk, staring at the pages of an enormous book. Lena took a step—

"Seven." A girl's voice.

We froze at the sound of the familiar voice. I put my hand on Lena's arm.

Wait.

So we stood in the shadows of the passage, at the edge of the door. They hadn't seen us.

"Seven what, Miss Durand?" Macon asked.

Liv appeared in the doorway, holding a stack of books. Her blond hair spilled over her favorite Pink Floyd T-shirt, her blue eyes catching the light. In the darkness of the underground, Liv looked like she was made of sunshine.

Marian's former assistant, my former friend. But that wasn't quite right, and we all knew it. She had felt like more than a friend. While Lena was gone, that had been one thing. But Lena wasn't gone anymore, which left us where? Liv would always be my friend, even if she couldn't be. She had helped me find my way back to Lena, and to the Great Barrier, the seat of both Dark and Light power. She had given up her future as a Keeper for me and Lena. We both knew we would always owe Liv for that.

There was more than one kind of way to be Bound to a person. I had learned that myself, the hard way.

Liv let the books drop onto the desk in front of Macon. Dust rose from the ancient bindings. "There are only five instances of mixed Caster bloodlines powerful enough to result in this combination. I've been cross-referencing every Caster family tree I can find on both sides of the Atlantic, including your own."

Mixed supernatural blood. Ethan, they're looking for John.

Lena could barely stand to Kelt it. Even her thoughts were quiet.

Macon was mumbling into his book. "Ah, yes. Well. All in the interest of science, of course."

"Of course." Liv opened her familiar red notebook.

"And? Have you found anything like him in any of the Kept family records? Anything that could explain the existence of our mysterious hybrid, the elusive John Breed?"

I guess you're right.

Liv spread out two sheets of parchment that I recognized immediately. The Duchannes and Ravenwood Family Trees. "There are only four likely occurrences—at least, according to the Council of the Far Keep."

The council of what?

Later, Ethan.

Liv was still talking. "One of which is Sarafine Duchannes' parents: Emmaline Duchannes, a Light Caster, and your father, Silas Ravenwood, a Blood Incubus. Lena's grandparents." Liv looked up, her cheeks reddening.

Macon dismissed the possibility. "Emmaline is an Empath, a Caster gift certainly not capable of resulting in a hybrid Incubus that can walk in the daylight. And obviously our hybrid is too young to be a result of that particular union."

Lena shuddered, and I squeezed her hand.

They're looking at all those crazy family trees, L. None of it means anything.

Not yet.

Lena rested her head against my shoulder, and I leaned closer to the door to listen.

DUCHANNES FAMILY TREE

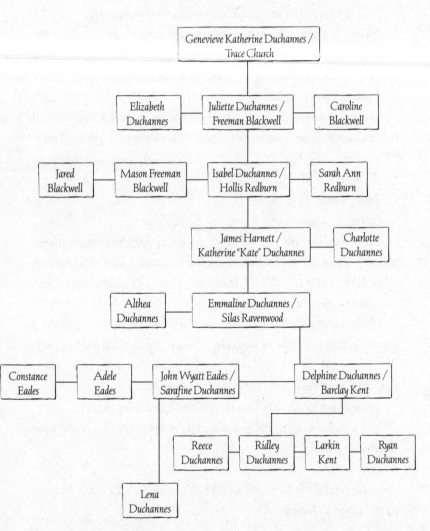

Genevieve Katherine Duchannes / Trace Church

Elizabeth Duchannes — Juliette Duchannes / Freeman Blackwell — Caroline Blackwell

Jared Blackwell — Mason Freeman Blackwell — Isabel Duchannes / Hollis Redburn — Sarah Ann Redburn

James Harnett / Katherine "Kate" Duchannes — Charlotte Duchannes

Althea Duchannes — Emmaline Duchannes / Silas Ravenwood

Constance Eades — Adele Eades — John Wyatt Eades / Sarafine Duchannes — Delphine Duchannes / Barclay Kent

Reece Duchannes — Ridley Duchannes — Larkin Kent — Ryan Duchannes

Lena Duchannes

RAVENWOOD FAMILY TREE

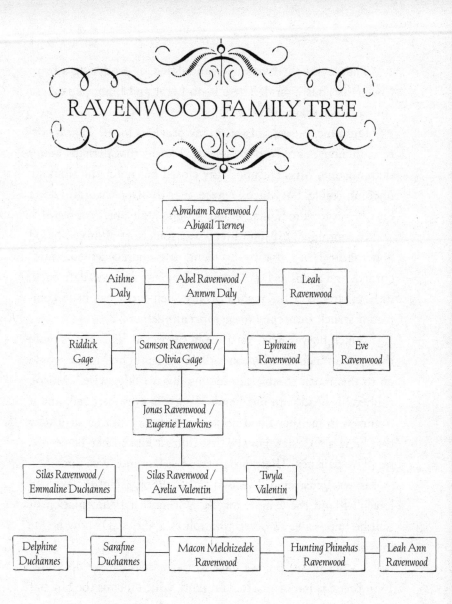

"That leaves three possible candidates for producing a Dark Caster-Incubus hybrid. There is no Light and Light pairing, of course, since there are no..."

"Light Incubuses, as I was in my previous form? That is correct. Incubuses are Dark by nature. I know that perhaps better than anyone, Miss Durand." Liv closed her notebook, looking uncomfortable, but Macon waved her off. "Don't worry. I don't bite. Never took to human blood. I found it all a bit *distasteful*."

Liv continued. "If John Breed was some sort of mixed-blood Supernatural, it's not by accident. It's unprecedented, unrecorded, and as far as Dr. Ashcroft's Keeping archives date back, unKept. It's as if the record of any such birth has been completely struck from the *Lunae Libri* altogether."

"Which proves what we already suspected. This boy is more than just an Incubus who can walk in the sunlight. No one would go to this much trouble to hide his lineage otherwise." Macon rubbed his head with one hand. His green eyes were red, and it occurred to me that I had no idea whether or not he slept now that he was a Caster. For the first time, it looked like he needed to. "Five pairings. That's progress, Miss Durand. Well done."

Liv was frustrated. I recognized the look. "Hardly. We still haven't found the genetic match. Without that information, it will be impossible to determine John's abilities. Or how he fits into all this."

"A valid point. But we have to focus on what we do know. John Breed is important to Abraham, which means the boy has a significant role in whatever he is planning."

Liv held out her arm, the dials of her strange-looking homemade watch spinning on her wrist. Her selenometer, which gave her the only answers she trusted. "Truthfully, sir, I don't know how much time we have to figure that out. I've never seen readings like these. I hate to say it—but it's like the moon is about to come crashing down on Gatlin."

Macon stood, clasping a heavy hand on her shoulder. I'd felt that pressure—a part of me could feel it now. "Never be afraid to speak the truth, Miss Durand. We're a little past the point of pleasantries. We must simply press on. It's all we can do."

She straightened under his hand. "I'm not sure I know the protocol when facing the potential annihilation of the Mortal world."

"I believe, dear girl, that's entirely the point."

"What?"

"Look at the facts. It appears that since the Claiming the Mortal world has been altered. Or, as you said yourself, the sky is falling. Hell on Earth, our charming Mrs. Lincoln might say. And the Caster world has been presented with a new species of Caster-Incubus we've never seen before. An Adam of sorts. Whatever purpose the hybrid boy serves, it's not an accident. The timing is too perfect. It's all part of a grand design—or, considering Abraham is undoubtedly involved, a grandiose design."

Lena looked pale, and I grabbed her arm, propping her up next to me.

Let's go.

She held her finger to her lips.

He's the Adam?

L—

Ethan. If he's the Adam…

Liv stared at Macon, her eyes wide. "You think Abraham somehow *engineered* this?"

Macon scoffed. "Hunting certainly doesn't have the intellect

75

for this sort of endeavor, and Sarafine alone doesn't have the power. The boy, however indeterminate his origin, is Lena's age? A little older?"

I don't want to be the Eve.

You're not.

You don't know that, Ethan. I think I am.

You're not, L.

I pulled her into my arms, and I could feel the heat of her cheek through the thin cotton of my shirt.

I think I was supposed to be.

Macon continued, but he seemed farther and farther away with every word. "Unless John Breed was pulled out of some other realm, he evolved here in the Mortal or Caster world. Which necessitates more than a decade and a half of ruthless cunning, at which Abraham excels." Macon fell silent.

"Are you saying John was born in a Caster laboratory? Like some kind of supernatural test-tube baby?"

"In broad terms, yes. Perhaps not so much born as *bred*, one assumes. Which would explain why he is so important to Abraham." Macon paused. "That sort of dull wit I would expect from my brother, not Abraham. I'm disappointed."

"John *Breed*," Liv said slowly. "Oh my God. It was right there in front of us, all along." Liv sunk onto the ottoman across from Macon's desk.

I held Lena tighter. When her thoughts came, they were a whisper.

It's sick. He's sick.

I didn't know if she meant John or Abraham, but it didn't matter. She was right. It was all sick.

Abraham's gone, L.

76

Even as I thought the words, I knew I was lying. John might have been gone, but Abraham wasn't.

"So we're left with two questions, Miss Durand. How and, more important, why?"

"If John Breed is gone, it doesn't matter." Liv's face was pale, and it occurred to me that she looked as exhausted as Macon did.

"Is he? I'm not entirely willing to make assumptions without a body."

"Shouldn't we turn our research to the more pressing issues— the infestations, the climate change? How to stop these plagues that Lena's Seventeenth Moon seems to have brought on the Mortal world?"

Macon leaned forward in his chair. "Olivia, do you have any idea how old this library is?"

She shook her head doubtfully.

"Do you know how old any of the Caster libraries are? Across the pond and beyond? In London? Prague? Madrid? Istanbul? Cairo?"

"No. I suppose not."

"In any of these libraries, many of which I've visited myself in the past few weeks, do you imagine there is one reference to how to restore the Order of Things?"

"Of course. There has to be. This must have happened at least once before."

He closed his eyes.

"Never?" She was trying to say the word, but from where we stood, we almost couldn't hear it.

"Our only clue is the boy. How did he come to be, and for what purpose?"

"Or the girl?" Liv asked.

"Olivia. That's enough."

But Liv wasn't deterred that easily. "Perhaps you already know? How did she come to be, and for what purpose? Scientifically speaking, it would be relevant."

Lena shut me out, willing her mind apart from mine, until I was alone in the passageway even as we clung to each other.

Macon shook his head. When he spoke, his voice was harsh. "Don't say anything to the others. I want to be absolutely certain."

"Before you tell Lena what she's done," Liv said flatly. It was a fact, but somehow she didn't say it that way.

Macon's green eyes held all the emotion his black ones never had. Fear. Anger. Resentment. "Before I tell her what she has to do."

"You might not be able to stop this." She looked down at her selenometer out of habit.

"Olivia, it's not only the universe that could be destroyed. It's my niece. Who is, as far as I am concerned, more important than a thousand lost universes."

"Believe me, I know." If Liv was bitter, she didn't let on.

It felt like my heart stopped beating. Lena slipped out of my arms before I even realized she was gone.

I found Lena in her room. She didn't cry, and I didn't try to console her. We sat in silence, holding hands until it hurt, until the sun fell away — behind the words, behind the glass and the trees and the river. The night slid across her bed, and I waited for the darkness to erase everything.

Izabel

Are you sure we're going the right way?" We had turned off the highway, south of Charleston. But the houses had changed from traditional Victorians with wraparound porches and white turrets stretching toward the clouds to—nothing. The houses were gone, replaced with miles of tobacco fields and an occasional weather-beaten barn.

Lena glanced at the sheet of notebook paper in her lap. "This is the way. Gramma said there weren't a lot of other houses near my old...where my house used to be." When Lena told me she wanted to see the house where she was born, it made sense—for about ten seconds. Because it wasn't just the house where she took her first steps and scribbled on the walls with crayon. It was also the place where her father died. Where Lena could have died, when her mother set fire to the house, right before Lena's first birthday.

But Lena insisted, and there was no talking her out of it. We hadn't said a word to each other about what we'd overheard in Macon's study, but I knew this had to be another piece of the puzzle. Macon thought Lena's and John's pasts held some kind of key to what was happening in the Caster and Mortal worlds. Which was the reason we were driving through the backwoods right now.

Aunt Del leaned forward from the backseat of the Volvo. Lucille was sitting in her lap. "It doesn't look familiar to me, but I could be wrong." That was an understatement. Aunt Del was the last person I would ask for directions, unless we were in the Tunnels. And lately I wasn't sure if she could find her way around down there either. If visiting the charred remains of Lena's birthplace had been a bad idea, bringing Aunt Del with us was an even worse one. Since Lena's Claiming, no one seemed to be turned inside out as much as Lena's aunt.

Lena pointed at my window. "I think it's up here. Uncle M said to look for a driveway on the left." A fence, with white paint peeling down the sides, guarded the road. There was a break in the fence a few yards ahead. "That's it."

As I turned between the crooked posts, I heard Lena's breath catch. I took her hand, and my pulse quickened.

Are you sure you want to do this?

No. But I need to know what happened.

L, you know what happened.

This is where it all started. Where my mother held me as a baby. Where she decided to hate me.

She was a Dark Caster. She wasn't capable of love.

Lena leaned against my shoulder as I drove down the dusty driveway.

Part of me is Dark, too, Ethan. And I love you.

I stiffened. Lena wasn't Dark, not like her mother.

It's not the same. You're also Light.

I know. But Sarafine isn't gone. She's out there somewhere, with Abraham, waiting. And the more I know about her, the more prepared I'll be to fight her.

I wasn't sure if that's what this trip was really about. But it didn't matter. Because when I pulled up to what was left of the house, it was suddenly about something different.

Reality.

"My stars," Aunt Del whispered.

It was worse than the yellowed photos in my mom's archive—the ones that captured what was left of the plantations after the Great Burning—black skeletons of enormous homes reduced to nothing but charred framework, as empty and hollow as the towns the Union soldiers left in their wake.

This house, Lena's old house, was nothing more than a cracked foundation floating in a sea of blackened earth. Nothing had grown back. It was as if the ground itself had been scarred by what happened here.

How could Sarafine have done this to her family?

We didn't matter to her. This proves it.

Lena dropped my hand and walked toward the rubble.

Let's go, L. You don't have to do this.

She looked back at me, green and gold eyes determined.

Yes, I do.

Lena turned to Aunt Del. "I need to see what happened here. Before…this." She wanted her aunt to use her powers to peel away the layers of the past so Lena could see the house that once stood here—and, more important, see inside it.

Aunt Del looked more nervous than usual, her hair coming loose from her bun as we walked over to Lena. "My powers have been misfiring a bit. I may not be able to find exactly the moment you're looking for, sweetheart." What moment was that? The fire? I didn't know if I could stand to see it—if Lena could. "They may not even work at all."

I put my hand on the back of Lena's neck gently. Her skin was hot.

"Can you try?"

Her face pained, Aunt Del looked at the burnt wood scattered around the base of the house. She nodded and held out her hand. The three of us sat on the black ground and joined hands, the heat beating down on us like a fire of its own.

"All right." Aunt Del stared at the crumbling foundation intently, preparing to use her powers as a Palimpsest to show us the history of what was left of this place.

The air began to shift around us, slowly at first. Just as the world started to spin around me—I saw it for a split second. The shadow that always moved too fast for me to see. The one I felt in English class, the one following me. The one I couldn't escape. It was watching, as if somehow it could see whatever we saw in the layers of Aunt Del's perception.

Then a door opened into the past, and I was looking into a bedroom—

The walls are painted a pale, shimmering silver, and strands of white lights hang across the ceiling like stars in a magical sky. A girl with long black curls is standing by the window, staring out at the real sky. I know those curls and that beautiful profile—it's Lena. But the girl turns, holding a bundle in her

82

arms, and I realize it isn't Lena. It's Sarafine, her golden eyes shining. She stares at the baby, whose tiny hands are reaching. Sarafine holds out her finger, and the baby grabs it. She looks down at the baby, smiling. *"You are such a special girl, and I will always take care of you—"*

The door slams shut.

I waited for another to open, the way the doors always did, opening and closing like a chain reaction. But there was no point. The sky swirled back into view, and for a minute I was seeing double. Both Aunt Dels looked flustered.

"I—I'm sorry. Nothing like this has ever happened before. It doesn't make sense." Only it did. Aunt Del's powers were out of whack, like everyone else's. Usually, she could stand anywhere and see the pieces of the past, present, and future, like the pages of a flip-book. Now there were pages missing, and she had only caught a single glimpse of the past.

Aunt Del was visibly shaken and looked more confused than ever. I took her arm to help her up. "Don't worry, Aunt Del. Macon's going to figure out how to...fix the Order." Which seemed like the right thing to say, even though it was clear that Gatlin—maybe the whole world—was pretty broken.

Lena looked broken, too. She pushed herself up and walked closer to what was left of the house, as if she could still see the bedroom. Rain pelted down without warning, and heat lightning flashed across the sky. The grasshoppers scattered, and within seconds I was drenched.

L?

Standing there in the rain reminded me of the first night we met, in the middle of Route 9. She looked almost the same, and yet so different.

83

Am I crazy, or did it look like Sarafine cared about me?

You're not crazy.

But, Ethan, that's not possible.

I pushed the wet hair out of my eyes.

Maybe it is.

The rain stopped instantly, from a downpour back to sunshine in the span of a few seconds. It happened all the time now — Lena's powers fluctuating between extremes she couldn't control.

"What are you doing?" I jogged to catch up with her.

"I want to see what's left." She wasn't talking about the stones and burnt wood. Lena wanted a feeling to hold on to, proof of the one happy moment she had experienced here.

I followed her to the edge of the foundation, which was more of a wall now. I don't know if it was my imagination, but the closer we got to the charred remains, the more it smelled like ash. You could see where the steps that led up to the porch had burned away. I was tall enough to see over the side of the wall. There was nothing but a hole filled with cracked concrete, splintered pieces of rotted black wood littering the ground.

Lena was kneeling in the mud. She reached for something about the size of a shoe box.

"What is it?" Even when I got closer, it was hard to tell.

"I'm not sure." She wiped the mud off with her hand, revealing rust and dented metal. There was a melted keyhole on one side. "It's a lockbox." Lena handed me the box. It was heavier than it looked.

"The lock is melted, but I think I can open it." I looked around and picked up a piece of broken rock. I lifted the rock to get some leverage, when suddenly the metal hinges scraped open. "What the—?" I looked up at Lena, and she shrugged.

"Sometimes my powers still work the way I want them to." She kicked at a puddle. "Other times, not so much."

Even though the box was burnt and dented on the outside, it had protected the contents: a silver bracelet with an intricate design, a worn paperback copy of *Great Expectations*, a photo of Sarafine in a blue dress, with a dark-haired boy at a school dance. There was a cheesy backdrop behind them, like the one Lena and I had posed in front of at the winter formal. There was another photo, tucked under the bracelet—a baby picture of a little girl. I knew it was Lena because the child looked exactly like the baby Sarafine had been holding in her arms.

Lena touched the edge of the baby picture and lifted it above the box. The world around us started to fade, the sunlight quickly turning to darkness. I knew what was happening, but this time it wasn't happening to me. I was following Lena into the vision, the way she had followed me the day I sat in church with the Sisters. Within seconds the muddy ground turned to grass—

Izabel was shaking violently. She knew what was happening, and it had to be a mistake. It was her deepest fear, the nightmares that had haunted her since she was a child. This wasn't supposed to happen to her—she was Light, not Dark. She had tried so hard to do the right things, to be the person everyone wanted her to be. How could she be anything but Light, after all that? But as the devastating cold tore through her veins, Izabel knew she was wrong; it wasn't a mistake. She was going Dark.

The moon, her Sixteenth Moon, was full and luminous now. As she stared at it, Izabel could feel the rare gifts her family was so sure she possessed—the powers of a Natural—being twisted into something else. Soon her thoughts and heart would not be her own. Sorrow, destruction, and hate would force everything else out. Everything good.

Izabel's thoughts tortured her, but the physical pain was unbearable, as if her body was tearing itself to shreds from the inside. But she forced herself to her feet and ran. There was only one place she could go. She blinked hard, her vision clouded by a golden haze. Tears burned her skin. It couldn't be true.

By the time she made it to her mother's house, her breath was ragged. Izabel reached above the door and touched the lintel. But for the first time it didn't open. She pounded on the door until her hands were cut and bleeding, then she slid to the ground, her cheek resting against the wood.

When the door opened, Izabel fell, her face slamming against the marble floor of the hallway. Even that didn't compare to the pain raging through her body. A pair of black lace-up boots was barely inches from her face. Izabel clutched at her mother's legs frantically.

Emmaline pulled her daughter up from the floor. "What happened? What is it?"

Izabel tried to hide her eyes, but it was impossible. "It's a mistake, Mamma. I know how it looks, but I'm still the same. I'm still me."

"No. It can't be." Emmaline grabbed Izabel's chin so she could see her daughter's eyes. They were as yellow as the sun.

A girl not much older than Izabel came down the winding staircase, taking the steps two at a time. "Mamma, what's going on?"

Emmaline whirled around, pushing Izabel behind her. "Go back upstairs, Delphine!"

But there was no way to hide Izabel's glowing yellow eyes. Delphine froze. "Mamma?"

"I said go upstairs! There's nothing you can do for your sister!" Their mother's voice was defeated. "It's too late."

Too late? Her mother didn't mean that—she couldn't. Izabel wrapped her arms around her mother, and Emmaline jumped as if she'd been stung. Izabel's skin was as cold as ice.

Emmaline turned, holding Izabel by the shoulders. Tears already marked the woman's face. "I can't help you. There's nothing I can do."

Lightning streaked across the black sky. A bolt tore down, splitting the huge oak that shaded their house. The splintered trunk crashed down, taking out part of the roof with it. A window shattered upstairs, and the sound of glass breaking echoed through the house.

Izabel recognized the unfamiliar look on her mother's face.

Fear.

"It's a mistake. I'm not—" Dark. Izabel couldn't bring herself to say the word.

"There are no mistakes, not where the curse is concerned. You are Claimed Light or Dark; there is no in between."

"But Mamma—"

Emmaline shook her head, pushing Izabel across the threshold. "You can't stay here. Not now."

Izabel's eyes went wild. "Gramma Katherine isn't going to let me live there anymore. I have nowhere else to go." She was sobbing uncontrollably. "Mamma, please help me. We can fight this together. I'm your daughter!"

"Not anymore."

Delphine had been silent, but she couldn't believe what her mother was saying. She couldn't turn her sister away. "Mamma, it's Izabel! We have to help her!"

Emmaline looked at Izabel, remembering the day she was born. The day Emmaline had silently chosen her child's true name. She had imagined the moment she would share it with Izabel—staring into her daughter's green eyes and tucking her black curls behind her ear as she whispered the name.

Emmaline stared into her daughter's glowing yellow eyes, then turned away.

"Her name isn't Izabel anymore. It's Sarafine."

The real world came into focus slowly. Lena was standing a few feet away, still holding the box. I could see it shaking in her hands, her eyes wet with tears. I couldn't imagine what she was feeling.

In the vision, Sarafine was just a girl whose fate was decided for her. There wasn't a trace of the monster she was now. Was that how it happened? You opened your eyes and your whole life changed?

L? Are you okay?

Our eyes met, and for a second she didn't answer. When she did, her voice was quiet in my mind.

She was just like me.

The City That Care Forgot

I looked down at my sneakers in the darkness. I could feel the moisture seeping through the canvas, then my socks, until my skin was numb with cold. I was standing in some kind of water. I could hear it moving, not so much rushing as rippling. Something brushed against my ankle and then moved away. A leaf. A twig.

A river.

I could smell the rot, mixed with mud. Maybe I was in the swamp near Wader's Creek. The dark fringe in the distance could be swamp grass, and the tall forms, cypress trees. I reached up with one hand. Fluttering feathers, tickling long and light. Spanish moss. This was definitely the swamp.

I crouched low and felt the water with my hand. It felt thick and heavy. I scooped a handful and held it to my nose, letting it trickle through my fingers. I listened.

It didn't sound right.

Despite everything I knew about pond rot and bacteria and larvae, I stuck one of my fingers in my mouth.

I knew the taste. I'd know it anywhere. Like sucking on the handful of coins I'd stolen from the fountain in Forsyth Park when I was nine.

It wasn't water.

It was blood.

Then I heard the familiar whispering and felt the pressure of another body knocking into mine.

It was him again. The me who wasn't me.

I'M WAITING.

I heard the words as I fell. I tried to respond, but when I opened my mouth, I began to choke on the river. So I thought the words, though I could barely even think.

What are you waiting for?

I felt myself sinking to the bottom. Only there was no bottom, and I kept falling and falling—

I woke up thrashing. I could still feel his hands around my neck, and the dizziness—the overwhelming feeling that the room was closing in on me. I tried to catch my breath, but the feeling wouldn't go away. My sheets were smeared with blood, and my mouth still tasted like dirty pennies. I wadded up the top sheet and hid it under my bed. I'd have to throw it away. I couldn't let Amma find a blood-soaked sheet in my hamper.

Lucille jumped onto the bed, her head cocked to one side.

Siamese cats had a way of looking at you like they were disappointed. Lucille had it down.

"What are you staring at?" I pushed my sweaty hair out of my eyes, the salt from my sweat mixing with the salt from the blood.

I couldn't make sense of the dreams, but I wasn't going to be able to go back to sleep.

So I called the one person I knew who would be awake.

Link climbed through my window twenty minutes later. He hadn't worked up the nerve to try Traveling yet, ripping through space and materializing wherever he wanted, but he was still pretty stealth.

"Man, what's with all the salt?" A trail of white crystals fell from the windowsill as Link swung his leg over. He scratched his hands. "Is that supposed to hurt me or somethin'? 'Cause it's really annoyin'."

"Amma's been crazier than usual." An understatement. The last time I found this many bundles of herbs and tiny handmade dolls around, she was trying to keep Macon out of my room. I wondered who she was trying to keep out this time.

"Everyone's crazier than usual. My mom started talkin' about buildin' a bunker again. She's buyin' up every can at the Stop & Steal, like we're gonna hole up in the basement until the Devil gives up or somethin'." He dropped into the swivel chair next to my desk. "I'm glad you called. I usually run outta stuff to do by one or two in the morning."

"What do you do all night?" I'd never asked him before.

Link shrugged. "Read comics, watch movies on my computer, hang out in Savannah's room. But tonight I sat around listenin' to my mom on the phone with the pastor and Mrs. Snow all night."

"Is your mom really upset about what happened to Savannah?"

Link shook his head. "Not as upset as she is about the lake dryin' up. She's been cryin' and prayin' and tyin' up the phone lines tellin' everyone it's one a the seven signs. I'll be in church all day after this."

I thought about the dream and the bloody sheets. "What do you mean, the lake dried up?"

"Lake Moultrie. Dean Wilks went out there to go fishin' this afternoon, and the lake was dry. He said it looked like a crater, and he walked right out to the middle."

I grabbed a T-shirt. "Lakes don't just dry up." It was getting worse—the heat and bugs and crazy Caster power surges. And now this. What was next?

"I know, dude. But I can't tell my mom that your girlfriend broke the whole universe." He picked up an empty bottle of unsweetened tea that was sitting on my desk. "Since when do you drink tea? And where did you get the unsweet kind?"

He was right. I had been drinking my weight in chocolate milk since sixth grade. But over the last few months, everything seemed sweeter, and I could barely stand more than a sip of chocolate milk. "The Stop & Steal orders it for Mrs. Honeycutt because she's diabetic. I just can't drink anything too sweet. Something's going on with my taste buds."

"You're not lyin'. First you're eatin' the sloppy joes at school, and now you're drinkin' tea. Maybe the lake dryin' up isn't that crazy."

"It's not a—"

Lucille jumped off the bed, and Link spun the chair toward the door. "Shh. Someone's up."

I listened, but I didn't hear anything. "It's probably my dad. He has a new project."

Link shook his head. "No. It's comin' from downstairs. Amma's awake." Hybrid Incubus or not, his hearing was pretty impressive.

"Is she in the kitchen?"

Link held up his hand so I would be quiet. "Yeah, stuff's rattlin' around in there." He paused for a minute. "Now she's by the back door. I can hear that squeaky hinge on the screen door." What squeaky hinge?

I rubbed the rest of the blood off my arm and climbed out of bed. The last time Amma left the house in the middle of the night, it was to meet Macon and talk about Lena and me. Were they meeting again?

"I need to see where she's going." I put on my jeans and grabbed my sneakers. I followed Link down the stairs, hitting every creaky board. He didn't make a sound.

The kitchen lights were off, but I could see Amma standing by the curb in the moonlight. She was wearing her pale yellow church dress and white gloves. She was definitely headed for the swamp. Just like my dream.

"She's going to Wader's Creek." I looked for the keys to the Volvo, in the dish on the counter. "We have to follow her."

"We can take the Beater."

"We have to drive with the headlights off. It's harder than you think."

"Dude, I practically have X-ray vision. Let's roll."

94

We waited for the 1950s Studebaker to pull up to the curb, like I knew it would. Sure enough, five minutes later, Carlton Eaton's truck drove down Cotton Bend.

"Why is Mr. Eaton pickin' up Amma?" Link let the Beater roll in neutral before he turned the ignition.

"He drives her out to Wader's Creek in the middle of the night sometimes. That's all I know. Maybe she bakes him pies or something."

"That's the only thing I miss eatin'. Amma's pie."

Link wasn't joking about not needing headlights. He left a few car lengths between the Beater and the pickup, but it wasn't because he was concentrating on the road. He spent most of the ride complaining about Ridley, who he couldn't seem to stop talking about, or playing me songs from his band's new demo. The Holy Rollers sounded as bad as ever, but even way out here, the hum of the lubbers drowned them out. I couldn't stand the hum.

The Holy Rollers hadn't finished their fourth song when the truck reached the unmarked path that led to Wader's Creek. It was the spot where Mr. Eaton had dropped Amma off the last time I had followed them. But tonight the truck didn't stop.

"Dude, where's he goin'?"

I had no idea, but it didn't take long to figure it out.

Carlton Eaton's truck practically coasted onto the mile-wide stretch of dust that had served as a parking lot only a few months before. The dusty expanse backed up to an enormous field, probably as dead and scorched as the grass in the rest of the county. But even without the heat wave, the grass here wouldn't have recovered yet—from the carts and tent poles, cigarette butts, and the weight of the metal structures that had left black scars in the earth.

"The fairgrounds? Why's he bringin' Amma here?" Link pulled over near a clump of dead bushes.

"Why do you think?" There was only one thing out here now that the fair was gone. An Outer Door to the Caster Tunnels.

"I don't get it. Why would Mr. Eaton take Amma into the Tunnels?"

"I don't know."

Mr. Eaton killed the engine and walked around to the passenger side to open the door for Amma. She swatted at him as he tried to help her down. He should've known better. Amma was barely five feet tall and a hundred pounds, but there was nothing frail about her. She followed him toward the field and the Outer Door, her white gloves glowing in the darkness.

I opened the door to the Beater as quietly as I could. "Hurry up, or we'll lose them."

"Are you kiddin'? I can hear them yappin' all the way from here."

"Seriously?" I knew Link had powers, but I guess I didn't expect them to be so *powerful*.

"I'm not one a those lame superheroes like Aquaman." Link wasn't impressed with my abilities as a Wayward. Aside from being pretty good with a map and the Arclight, it wasn't too clear what I could do, or why. So, yeah, Aquaman was about right.

Link was still talking. "I'm thinkin' Magneto or Wolverine."

"Had any luck bending metal with your mind or shooting knives out of your knuckles?"

"No. But I'm workin' on it." Link stopped walking. "Hold on. They're talkin'."

"What are they saying?"

"Mr. Eaton's lookin' for his Caster key to open the door, and Amma's givin' him an earful about misplacin' his stuff." That sounded like Amma. "Wait. He found his key, and he's openin' the door. Now he's helpin' Amma down." Link paused.

"What's happening?"

Link took a few steps forward. "Mr. Eaton's leavin'. Amma went down alone."

I shouldn't have been worried. Amma had been in the Tunnels by herself lots of times, usually to find me. But I had a bad feeling. We waited until Mr. Eaton was headed back to his truck, and then we bolted for the Outer Door.

Link was there first, which was hard not to notice, because he gave new meaning to fast. I bent down next to him, studying the outline of the door—one you'd never notice unless you were looking for it. "So, how do we get in? I'm guessing you don't have your garden shears with you." The last time we were here, Link had pried the door open with a gigantic pair of garden shears he'd stolen from the Jackson bio lab.

"Don't need 'em. I've got a key." I stared at the crescent-shaped key. Even Lena didn't have one.

"Where did you steal that?"

Link punched me in the shoulder, lightly. I flew backward and landed in the dirt.

"Sorry, man. I don't know my own strength." He pulled me back up and worked the key into the lock. "Lena's uncle gave it to me so I can meet him in his creepy study and learn how to be the good kind a Incubus." It sounded like Macon, who had

97

spent years teaching himself the restraint necessary to feed off Mortal dreams instead of blood.

I couldn't help but think of the alternative—Hunting and his Blood Pack, and Abraham.

The key worked, and Link heaved the round door open proudly. "See—Magneto. Told you."

Usually I would've made a joke, but tonight I didn't. Link was a whole lot closer to being Magneto than I was.

—⟳

This Tunnel reminded me of a dungeon in an old castle. The ceiling was low, and the rough rock walls were wet. The sound of dripping water echoed through the passageway, although there was no sign of the source. I had been in this Tunnel before, but somehow it felt different tonight—or maybe it was me that had changed. Either way, the walls felt close, and I wanted to get to the end.

"Hurry up or we'll lose her." I was actually the one slowing us down, tripping in the darkness.

"Relax. She sounds like a horse walkin' through gravel. There's no way we'll lose her." It wasn't an analogy Amma would appreciate.

"You can really hear her footsteps?" I couldn't even hear his.

"Yeah. I can smell her, too. Follow the pencil lead and Red Hots."

So Link followed the smell of Amma's crossword puzzles and her favorite candy, and I followed him until he stopped at the base of a crude set of stairs that led back up to the Mortal world. He inhaled deeply, the way he used to when one of

Amma's peach cobblers was baking in the oven. "She went up there."

"You sure?"

Link lifted an eyebrow. "Can my mom preach to a preacher?"

—◠

Link pushed open the heavy stone door, and light flooded into the Tunnel. We were behind some old building, the door etched into the chipped brick. The air was thick and sticky with the distinct stench of beer and sweat. "Where the hell are we?"

Nothing looked familiar. "No clue."

Link walked around to the front of the building. The smell of beer was even stronger. He peered into the window. "This place is some kind of pub."

There was a cast-iron placard next to the door: LAFITTE'S BLACKSMITH SHOP.

"This doesn't look like a blacksmith's shop."

"That's because it isn't." An elderly man in a Panama hat, like the one Aunt Prue's last husband used to wear, walked up behind Link. He leaned heavily on his cane. "You are standin' in front a one a Bourbon Street's most infamous buildin's, and the hist'ry a this place is as famous as the Quarter itself."

Bourbon Street. The French Quarter. "We're in New Orleans."

"Right. Of course we are." After this summer, Link and I knew the Tunnels could lead anywhere, and time and distance didn't operate the same way within them. Amma knew it, too.

The old man was still talking. "Folks say Jean and Pierre Lafitte opened a smithy here in the late seventeen hundreds as a front for their smugglin' operation. They were pirates who looted Spanish galleons and smuggled what they stole into N'awlins, sellin' everything from spices and furniture to flesh and blood. But these days, most folks come for the ale."

I cringed. The man smiled and tipped his hat. "You kids pass a good time in the City That Care Forgot."

I wasn't betting on it.

The old man bent further over his cane. Now he was holding his hat out in front of us, shaking it expectantly.

"Oh, sure. Okay." I fumbled in my pocket, but all I had was a quarter. I looked at Link, who shrugged.

I leaned closer to drop the coin into the hat, and a bony hand grabbed my wrist. "Smart boy like you. I'd be gettin' myself outta this town and back down into that Tunnel." I pulled my arm free. He smiled big, pulling his lips wide over yellowed, uneven teeth. "Be seein' you."

I rubbed my wrist, and when I looked up, he was gone.

It didn't take long for Link to pick up Amma's trail. He was like a bloodhound. Now I understood why it had been so easy for Hunting and his Pack to find us when we were searching for Lena and the Great Barrier. We walked through the French Quarter toward the river. I could smell the murky brown water mixed with sweat and the scent of spices from nearby restaurants. Even at night, the humidity hung in the air, heavy and wet, a jacket you couldn't take off, no matter how badly you wanted to.

"Are you sure we're going the right—?"

Link threw his arm out in front of me, and I stopped. "Shh. Red Hots."

I searched the sidewalk ahead of us. Amma was standing under a streetlamp, in front of a Creole woman sitting on a plastic milk crate. We walked to the edge of the building with our heads down, hoping Amma wouldn't notice us. We stuck to the shadows close to the wall, where the streetlamp threw out a pale circle of light.

The Creole woman was selling beignets on the sidewalk, her hair styled in hundreds of tiny braids. She reminded me of Twyla.

"*Te te* beignets? You buy?" The woman held out a small bundle of red cloth. "You buy. Lagniappe."

"Lan-yap what?" Link mumbled, confused.

I pointed at the bundle, whispering back, "I think that woman's offering to give Amma something if she buys some beignets."

"Some what?"

"They're like doughnuts."

Amma handed the woman a few dollars, accepting the beignets and the red bundle in her white-gloved hand. The woman looked around, her braids swinging over her shoulder. When she seemed satisfied no one was listening, she whispered something quickly in what sounded like French Creole. Amma nodded and put the bundle in her pocketbook.

I elbowed Link. "What did she say?"

"How should I know? I may have supersonic hearin', but I don't speak French."

It didn't matter. Amma was already walking back in the opposite direction, her expression unreadable. But something was wrong.

This night was wrong. I wasn't following Amma out to the swamp in Wader's Creek to meet Macon. What would send her a thousand miles from home in the middle of the night? Who did she know in New Orleans?

Link had a different question. "Where's she goin'?"

I didn't have an answer to that one either.

———⟡———

By the time we caught up with Amma on St. Louis Street, it was deserted. Which made sense, considering where we were standing. I stared at the tall wrought iron gates of St. Louis Cemetery No. 1.

"It's a bad sign when there are so many cemeteries they've gotta number 'em." Even though he was part Incubus, Link didn't look crazy about wandering around the cemetery at night. It was the seventeen years of God-fearing Southern Baptist in him.

I pushed open the gate. "Let's get this over with."

St. Louis Cemetery No. 1 was unlike any cemetery I'd ever seen. There were no sprawling lawns dotted with headstones and bent oaks. This place was a city for the dead. The narrow alleyways were lined with ornate mausoleums in various stages of decay, some as tall as two-story houses. The more impressive mausoleums were surrounded by black wrought iron fences, with enormous statues of saints and angels staring down from the rooftops. This was a place where people honored their dead. The proof was carved into the face of every statue, every worn name that had been touched hundreds of times.

"This place makes His Garden of Perpetual Peace look like a landfill." For a minute, I thought of my mom. I understood wanting to build a marble house for someone you loved, which was exactly what this whole place seemed like.

Link was unimpressed. "Whatever. When I die, just throw some dirt over me. Save your money."

"Right. Remind me of that in a few hundred years when I'm at your funeral."

"Well, then I guess I'll be throwin' some dirt on you—"

"Shh! Did you hear that?" I heard the sound of gravel cracking. We weren't the only ones here.

"Of course—" Link's voiced faded into the background as a shadow blurred past me. It had the same hazy quality as a Sheer, but it was darker and lacked the features that made Sheers look almost human. As it moved around me, even through me, I felt the familiar panic from my dreams crushing me. I was cornered in my own body, unable to move.

Who are you?

I tried to focus on the shadow, to see something more than the blur of dark air, but I couldn't.

What do you want?

"Hey, man. You okay?" I heard Link's voice, and the pressure dissipated, as if someone had been kneeling on my chest and suddenly got up. Link was staring at me. I wondered how long he'd been talking.

"I'm okay." I wasn't, but I didn't want to tell him that I was—what? Seeing things? Having nightmares about rivers of blood and falling off water towers?

As we made our way deeper into the cemetery, the intricately detailed tombs and the sparse, crumbling ones gave way to alleys lined with mausoleums in complete disrepair. Some were actually made of wood, like the dilapidated shacks that lined parts of the swamp in Wader's Creek. I read the surnames that were still visible: Delassixe, Labasiliere, Rousseau, Navarro. They were Creole names. The last one in the row stood apart from the rest, a narrow stone structure, not more than a few feet wide. It was a Greek Revival, like Ravenwood. But while Macon's house was like a picture you'd find in a South Carolina photography book, this tomb was nothing much to look at. Until I stepped closer.

Strands of beads, knotted with crosses and red silk roses, hung next to the door, and the stone itself was etched with hundreds of crude Xs in various shapes and sizes. There were other strange drawings, clearly made by visitors. The ground was littered with gifts and mementos: Mardi Gras dolls and religious candles with the faces of saints painted on the glass, empty bottles of rum and faded photographs, tarot cards, and more strands of brightly colored beads.

Link bent down and flipped one of the dirty cards between his fingers. The Tower. I didn't know what it meant, but any card with people falling out of the windows probably wasn't good. "We're here. This is it."

I looked around. "What are you talking about? There's nothing here."

"I wouldn't say that." He pointed at the door of the mausoleum with the water-stained card. "Amma went in there."

"You're joking, right?"

"Dude, would I joke about goin' into a creepy tomb at night, in the most haunted city in the South?" Link shook his head. " 'Cause I know that's what you're about to tell me we're gonna do." I didn't want to go in there either.

Link tossed the card back into the pile, and I noticed a brass placard at the base of the door. I bent down and read what I

could make out in the moonlight: MARIE LAVEAU. THIS GREEK
REVIVAL TOMB IS REPUTED BURIAL PLACE OF THIS NOTORIOUS
"VOODOO QUEEN."

Link took a step back. "A voodoo queen? Like we don't have
enough problems."

I was only half listening. "What would Amma be doing
here?"

"I don't know, man. Amma's dolls are one thing, but I don't
know if my Incubus powers work on dead voodoo queens. Let's
bail."

"Don't be an idiot. There's nothing to be afraid of. Voodoo is
just another religion."

Link looked around nervously. "Yeah, one where people
make dolls and stab them with pins." It was probably something
he'd heard from his mom.

But I had spent enough time with Amma to know better.
Voodoo was part of her heritage, the mix of religions and mysticism that was as unique as Amma's cooking. "Those are people
who are trying to use dark power. That's not what it's about."

"I hope you're right. Because I don't like needles."

I put my hand on the door and pushed. Nothing. "Maybe it's
Charmed, like a Caster door."

Link slammed his shoulder against it, and the door scratched
across the stone floor as it opened into the tomb. "Or maybe not."

I stepped inside cautiously, hoping to see Amma bent over
some chicken bones. But the tomb was dark and empty except
for the raised cement casement that held the coffin, and the dirt
and cobwebs. "There's nothing here."

Link walked to the back of the small crypt. "I'm not so sure
about that." He ran his fingers along the floor. There was a

square carved into the stone, with a metal ring in the center. "Check this out. Looks like some kinda trapdoor."

It was a trapdoor, leading under a cemetery—in the tomb of a dead voodoo queen. This was beyond going dark, even for Amma.

Link had his hand on the metal ring. "Are we doin' this or what?" I nodded, and he lifted the door open.

⊰ 9.15 ⊱

Wheel of Fate

When I saw the rotting wooden stairs, illuminated by a dim yellow light from below, I knew they didn't lead to a Caster Tunnel. I had stepped onto my share of stairs that twisted down from the Mortal world into those Tunnels, and rarely saw them when I did. They were usually veiled with protective Casts, so it looked like you could fall to your death if you dared to make the leap.

This was a different kind of leap, and somehow it felt more dangerous. The stairway was crooked, the railing nothing more than a few boards haphazardly nailed together. I could've been staring down into the Sisters' dusty basement, which was always dark because they never let me replace the exposed bulb above the door. Except this wasn't a basement, and it didn't smell dusty. Something was burning down there, and it gave off a thick, noxious odor.

"What's that smell?"

Link inhaled, then coughed. "Licorice and gasoline." Yeah, that was a combination you encountered every day.

I reached out for the railing. "You think these stairs will hold?"

He shrugged. "They held Amma."

"She weighs a hundred pounds."

"Only one way to find out."

I went first, each board groaning beneath my weight. My hand tightened on the railing, tiny splinters digging into my skin. There was a huge room off to the side of the staircase, the source of both the light and the nauseating fumes.

"Where the hell are we?" Link whispered.

"I don't know." But I knew this was a dark place, a place Amma would never ordinarily go. It stank of more than gas and licorice. There was death in the air, and when we entered the room, I understood why.

It was some kind of shop, the walls lined with shelves that housed cracked leather volumes and glass jars filled with both dead and living things. One jar held bat wings, fully intact but no longer attached to the bodies. Another container was brimming with animal teeth; others, claws and snakeskin. Smaller, unlabeled bottles held murky liquids and dark powders. But the living creatures imprisoned here were even more disturbing. Huge toads pushed themselves against the walls of glass jars, desperate to get out. Snakes slid over one another, piled inside terrariums coated with thick layers of dust. Live bats hung from the tops of rusty wire cages.

There was something more than wrong about this place—from the scratched steel table in the center of the room to the strange altar in the corner, surrounded by candles, carvings, and a stick of black incense that reeked of licorice and gasoline.

Link elbowed me, pointing at a dead frog floating in a jar. "This place is worse than summer school in the bio lab."

"Are you sure Amma's down here?" I couldn't imagine her in this twisted version of my great-aunts' basement.

Link nodded toward the back of the room, where a yellow light flickered. "Red Hots."

We walked between the rows of shelves, and within seconds I could hear Amma's voice. At the end of the aisle, two low bookcases flanked a narrow walkway into the back of the store—or whatever this place was called. We dropped down onto our hands and knees and hid behind the bookcases. Chicken feet floated in a bottle next to my shoulder.

"I need to see the langiappe." It was a man's voice, gravelly and heavily accented. "You would be surprised how many people find their way here and are not who they claim to be."

I dropped down onto my stomach and pulled myself forward so I could see around the side of the bookcase. Link was right. Amma was standing in front of a black wooden table, clutching her pocketbook with both hands. The legs of the table formed the feet of a bird, its talons inches from Amma's tiny orthopedic shoes. She was in profile, her dark skin glowing in the yellow light, her bun tucked neatly beneath her flowered church hat, her chin up and her back straight. If she was afraid, I couldn't tell. Amma's pride was as much a part of who she was as her riddles, biscuits, and crossword puzzles.

"I imagine so." She opened her purse and took out the red bundle the Creole woman had given her.

Link was on his stomach, too. "Is that the thing the lady with the doughnuts gave her?" he whispered. I nodded, and gestured for him to be quiet.

The man behind the table leaned into the light. His skin was ebony, darker and smoother than Amma's. His hair was twisted into rough, careless braids tied together at the base of his neck. String and tiny objects I couldn't see clearly were woven into the braids. He traced the line of his goatee as he watched Amma intently.

"Give it to me." He reached out his hand, the cuff of his dark tunic sliding down his arm. His wrist was bound in thin strands of string and leather, laden with charms. His hand was scarred — the skin warped and shiny, as if it had been burned more than once.

Amma dropped the bundle into his hand without touching him.

He noticed her caution and smiled. "You island women are all the same, practicin' the art to ward against my magic. But your herbs and powders are no match for the hand of a bokor."

The art. Voodoo. I'd heard it called that before. And if women like Amma provided protection from his magic, that could mean only one thing. He performed black magic.

He opened the bundle and held up a single feather. He examined it closely, turning it over in his hands. "I see you're not a trespasser, so what do you require?"

Amma tossed a handkerchief onto the desk. "I'm not a trespasser, or one a the island women you're used to seein'."

The bokor lifted the delicate fabric, examining the embroidery. I knew what the design was, even though I couldn't see it from here — a sparrow.

The bokor looked at the handkerchief, then back at Amma.

"The mark a Sulla the Prophet. So you're a Seer, one a her descendants?" He smiled broadly, his white teeth gleaming in the darkness. "Now, that makes this little visit even more unexpected. What would bring a Seer to my workshop?"

Amma watched him closely, as if he was one of the snakes slithering around in the shop's terrarium. "This was a mistake. Got no business with your kind. I'll be seein' myself out." She shoved her purse into the crook of her arm and turned on her heel to go.

"Leaving so soon? Don't you want to know how to change the cards?" His menacing laughter echoed through the room.

Amma stopped in her tracks. "I do." Her voice was quiet.

"Yet you know the answer yourself, Seer. That's why you're here."

She spun around to face him. "You think this is a social visit?"

"You can't change the cards once they're dealt. Not the cards we're talkin' about. Fate is a wheel that turns without our hand."

Amma slammed her hand down on the table. "Don't try to sell me the silver linin' from a cloud as black as your soul. I *know* it can be done."

The bokor tapped on a bottle of crushed eggshells near the edge of the table. Again, his white teeth shone in the darkness. "Anything can be done for a price, Seer. Question is, what are you willin' to pay?"

"Whatever it takes."

I shuddered. There was something about the way Amma said it, even the shifting sound of her voice, that made it seem like an invisible line between the two of them was disappearing. I wondered if that line ran deeper than the one she crossed the night of the Sixteenth Moon, when she and Lena used *The Book of Moons* to bring me back from the dead. I shook my head. We had all crossed too many lines already.

The bokor watched Amma intently. "Let me see the cards. I need to know what we're dealin' with."

Amma took a stack of what looked like tarot cards out of her purse, but the images on the cards weren't right. They weren't tarot cards — these were something else. She arranged them on the table carefully, re-creating a spread. The bokor watched, flipping the feather between his fingers.

Amma dropped the last card. "There it is."

He balked, muttering in a language I didn't understand. But I could tell he wasn't happy. The bokor swept clean his rickety wooden table, bottles and vials shattering on the ground. He leaned as close to Amma as I'd ever seen anyone dare to get. "The Angry Queen. The Unbalanced Scale. The Child of Darkness. The Storm. The Sacrifice. The Split Twins. The Bleeding Blade. The Fractured Soul."

He spit, shaking the feather at her, his version of the One-Eyed Menace. "A Seer from the line a Sulla the Prophet is smart enough to know this is not just any spread."

"Are you sayin' you can't do it?" It was a challenge. "That I've come all this way for cracked eggshells and dead swamp frogs? Can get those from any fortune-teller."

"I'm sayin' you can't pay the price, old woman!" His voice rose, and I stiffened. Amma was the only mother I had left. I couldn't stand to hear anyone talk to her that way.

Amma looked up at the ceiling, muttering. I was willing to bet she was talking to the Greats. "Not a bone in my body wanted to come to this godforsaken nest a evil—"

The bokor picked up a long staff wrapped in the crisp skin of a snake, and circled Amma like an animal waiting to strike. "And yet you came. Because your little dolls and herbs can't save the *ti-bon-age*. Can they?"

Amma stared at him defiantly. "Someone is gonna die if you don't help me."

"And someone will die if I do."

"That's a discussion for another day." She tapped one of the cards. "This here is the death I care about."

He examined the card, stroking it with his feather. "Interestin' you would choose the one who is already lost. Even more interestin' you would come to me instead a your precious Casters. This concerns them, does it not?"

The Casters.

My stomach dropped. Who was already lost? Was he talking about Lena?

Amma drew a heavy breath. "The Casters can't help me. They can barely help themselves."

Link looked at me, confused. But I didn't understand any more than he did. How could the bokor help Amma with something the Casters couldn't?

The images crashed down on me before I could stop them. The unbearable heat. The plague of insects infesting every inch of town. The nightmares and the panic. Casters who couldn't control their powers, or use them all. A river of blood. Abraham's voice echoing through the cavern after Lena Claimed herself.

There will be consequences.

The bokor circled around to face Amma, measuring her expression. "You mean the Light Casters can't."

"No other kind I'd ask for help."

He seemed pleased with her answer, but not for the reason I thought. "Yet you came to me. Because I can do something they can't—the old magic our people carried across the ocean with us. Magic that can be controlled by Mortals and Casters alike." He was talking about voodoo, a religion born in Africa and the Caribbean. "They don't understand the *ti-bon-age*."

Amma stared at him like she wished she could turn him to stone, but she didn't leave.

She needed him, even if I didn't know why.

"Name your price." Her voice wavered.

I watched as he calculated the cost of both Amma's request and her integrity. They were opposing forces, working the extremes of a shared mysticism that was as black and white as the Light and Darkness in the Caster world. "Where is it now? Do you know where they've hidden it?"

"Hidden what?" Link mouthed silently. I shook my head. I had no idea what they were talking about.

"It's not hidden." For the first time, Amma met his eyes. "It's free."

At first he didn't react, as if she might have misspoken. But when the bokor realized Amma was serious, he circled back to the table and pored over the spread. I could hear broken bits of French Creole in his gnarled voice. "If what you say is true, old woman, there is only one price."

Amma ran her hand over the cards, pushing them into a pile. "I know. I'll pay it."

"You understand, there is no turnin' back? No way to undo what will be done. If you tamper with the Wheel a Fate, it will continue to turn until it crushes you in its path."

Amma stacked the cards and put them back in her purse. I could see her hand shaking, jerking in and out of shadow.

"Do what you need to do, and I'll do the same." She snapped shut her purse and turned to go. "In the end, the Wheel crushes us all."

The Far Keep

And then Link and I bolted like Amma was chasing us with the One-Eyed Menace. I was so scared she would know we'd followed her, I didn't get out of bed until morning." I left out the part where I woke up on the floor, the same way I always did after one of the dreams.

By the time I finished telling Marian the story, her tea was cold. "What about Amma?"

"I heard the screen door close as the sun was coming up. By the time I came downstairs, she was making breakfast as if nothing happened. Same old cheese grits, same old eggs." Except neither one tasted right anymore.

We were in the archive in the Gatlin County Library. It was Marian's private sanctuary, one she had shared with my mom. It was also the place where Marian looked for answers to questions that most folks in Gatlin didn't even know to ask, which was why I was here. Marian Ashcroft had been my mom's best friend, but she had always felt more like my aunt than my real one. Which I guess was the other reason I was here.

Amma was the closest thing I had left to a mother. I wasn't ready to assume the worst of her, and I didn't want anyone else to either. But still, I didn't exactly feel comfortable with the idea of her running around with a guy who was on the wrong side of everything Amma believed in. I had to tell someone.

Marian stirred her tea, distracted. "You're absolutely sure of what you heard?"

I nodded. "It wasn't really the kind of conversation you forget." I'd been trying to wipe the image of Amma and the bokor out of my mind ever since I saw them. "I've watched Amma freak out before when she didn't like what the cards were telling her. When she knew Sam Turley was going to drive off the bridge at Wader's Creek, she locked herself in her room and didn't say a word for a week. This was different."

"A Seer never tries to change the cards. Especially not the great-great-great-granddaughter of Sulla the Prophet." Marian stared into her teacup, thinking. "Why would she try now?"

"I don't know. The bokor said he could do it, but it would cost her. Amma said she'd pay the price. No matter what. It didn't make any sense, but it has something to do with the Casters."

"If he was a bokor, that's not idle talk. They use voodoo to hurt and destroy rather than enlighten and heal."

I nodded. For the first time in as long as I could remember, I was actually scared for Amma. Which made about as much sense as a kitten being scared for a tiger. "I know you can't interfere in the Caster world, but the bokor's a Mortal."

117

"Which is why you came to me." Marian sighed. "I can do some research, but the one question I won't be able to answer is the only one that matters. What would send Amma to a person who opposes everything she believes in?" Marian held out a plate of cookies, which meant she didn't have the answer.

"HobNobs?" I winced. They weren't just any cookies—Liv's suitcase had been full of them when she arrived in South Carolina at the beginning of the summer.

Marian must have noticed, because she sighed and put the plate down. "Have you talked to Olivia about what happened?"

"I don't know. Not about—well, no." I sighed. "Which really sucks, because Liv is...you know, Liv."

"I miss her, too."

"Then why didn't you let her keep working with you?" After Liv broke the rules and helped free Macon from the Arclight, she had disappeared from the Gatlin County Library. Her training as a Keeper had ended, and I'd expected her to go back to the U.K. Instead, she started spending her days in the Tunnels with Macon.

"I couldn't. It would be improper. Or, if you prefer, forbidden. Until everything is sorted out, we aren't to see each other. Not officially."

"You mean she's not staying with you?"

Marian sighed. "She's moved into the Tunnels for now. She may be happier there. Macon's seen to it that she has a study of her own." I couldn't picture Liv spending so much time in the darkness of the Tunnels, when all she reminded me of was sunshine.

Marian turned in her seat, pulled a folded letter from her desk, and handed me the paper. It was heavy in my hands, and I

118

realized the weight came from a thick waxen seal at the bottom of the page. Not the kind of letter you get in the mail.

"What's this?"

"Go on. Read it."

" 'The Council of the Far Keep finds, in the grave matter of Marian Ashcroft of the *Lunae Libri*...' " —I started skimming—" '...suspension of responsibilities, with regard to the Western Keep...trial date forthcoming.' " I looked up from the paper in disbelief. "You were fired?"

"I prefer *suspended*."

"And there's a trial?"

She set her teacup on the table between us and closed her eyes. "Yes. At least, that's what they are choosing to call it. Don't think Mortals have a monopoly on hypocrisy. The Caster world is not exactly a democracy, as you might have noticed. The whole free will bit gets a little sidelined in the interest of the rule of law."

"But you had nothing to do with that. Lena broke the Order."

"Well, I appreciate your version of events, but you've lived in Gatlin long enough to know how versions have a way of changing. Nevertheless, I expect you'll have your day on the stand." The lines on Marian's face had a habit of deepening from lines into shadows when she was really worried. Like now.

"But you weren't involved." It was our longest running battle. From the moment I learned Marian was a Keeper—like my mother before her—I knew the one rule that mattered. Whatever was happening, Marian stayed out of it. She was an observer, responsible for keeping the records of the Caster world and marking the place that world intersected with the Mortal one.

Marian kept the history; she didn't make it.

That was the rule. Whether her heart would allow her to follow it was a different story. Liv had learned the hard way that she couldn't follow the rule, and now she could never be a Keeper. I was pretty sure my mom had felt the same way.

I picked up the letter again. I touched the thick black wax seal—the same as the seal of the state of South Carolina. A Caster moon over a palmetto tree. As I touched the crescent moon, I heard the familiar melody and stopped to listen. I closed my eyes.

> *Eighteen Moons, eighteen Sheers,*
> *Feeding off your deepest fears,*
> *Vexed to find as Darkness nears,*
> *Secret eyes and hidden ears…*

"Ethan?" I opened my eyes to see Marian looming over me.

"It's nothing."

"It's never nothing. Not with you, EW." She smiled a little sadly at me.

"I heard the song." I was still tapping my fingers against the sides of my jeans, the melody stuck in my head.

"Your Shadowing Song?"

I nodded.

"And?"

I didn't want to tell her, but I didn't see how I was going to get out of it, and I couldn't manage to make up another version in the space of three seconds. "Nothing good. The usual. A Sheer, a Vex, secrets and darkness."

I tried not to feel anything, not the lurching in my stomach or the chill spreading through my body while I said it. My mom was trying to tell me something. And if she was sending the song, it meant it was something important. And dangerous.

"Ethan. This is serious."

"Everything's serious, Aunt Marian. It's hard to figure out what I'm supposed to do."

"Talk to me."

"I will, but right now I don't even know what to tell you." I stood up to leave. I shouldn't have said anything. I couldn't make sense of what was happening, and the more Marian pushed, the faster I wanted to get away. "I'd better get going."

She followed me to the door of the archive. "Don't be gone so long this time, Ethan. I've missed you."

I smiled and hugged her, looking over her shoulder into the Gatlin County Library—and almost jumped out of my skin.

"What happened?"

Marian looked as surprised as I did. The library was a catastrophic, floor-to-ceiling disaster. It looked like a tornado had struck while we were in the archive. Stacks were leveled, and books were thrown open everywhere, along the tabletops, the checkout counter, even the floor. I'd only seen something like this once before, last Christmas, when every book in the library opened to a quote that had to do with Lena and me.

"This is worse than last time," Marian said quietly. We were thinking the same thing. It was a message meant for me. Just as it had been then.

"Uh-huh."

"Well. There we go. Are you feeling Vexed yet?" Marian reached for a book sitting on top of the card catalog. "Because I certainly am."

"I'm starting to." I pushed my hair out of my eyes. "Wish I

knew the Cast for reshelving books without actually having to pick them all up."

Marian bent and handed me the first. "Emily Dickinson."

I opened it as slowly as a person can open a book, and found a random page.

" 'Much Madness is divinest Sense...' "

"Madness. Great." What did it mean? And, more important, what did it mean for me? I looked at Marian. "What do you think?"

"I think the Disorder of Things has finally reached my stacks. Go on." She opened another book and handed it to me. "Leonardo da Vinci."

Great. Another famous crazy person. I handed it back to her. "You do it."

" 'While I thought that I was learning how to live, I've been learning how to die.' " She closed the book softly.

"Madness and now death. Things are looking up."

She put one hand around my neck and let the book slide from her other. *I'm here with you.* That's what her hands said. My hands didn't say anything except that I was terrified, which I was pretty sure she could tell from how hard they were shaking. "We'll take turns. One reads while the other cleans."

"I call cleaning."

Marian gave me a look, handing me another book. "You're calling the shots in my library now?"

"No, ma'am. That wouldn't be very gentlemanly." I looked down at the title. "Oh, come on." Edgar Allan Poe. He was so dark he'd make the other two look cheerful in comparison. "Whatever he has to say, I don't want to know."

"Open it."

"'Deep into that darkness peering, long I stood there wondering, fearing / Doubting, dreaming dreams no mortal ever dared to dream before...'"

I snapped the book shut. "I get it. I'm losing it. I'm going crazy. This whole town is cracked. The universe is one big nuthouse."

"You know what Leonard Cohen says about cracks, Ethan?"

"No, I don't. But I get the feeling I could open a few more books in this library and tell you."

"'There is a crack in everything.'"

"That's helpful."

"It is, actually." She put her hands on my shoulders. "'There is a crack in everything. That's how the light gets in.'"

She was pretty much exactly right—or at least the Leonard Cohen guy was. I felt happy and sad at the same time, and I didn't know what to say. So I dropped to my knees on the carpet and started stacking books.

"Better get going on this mess."

Marian understood. "Never thought I'd hear you say that, EW." She was right. The universe really must be cracked, and me right along with it.

I hoped somehow the light was finding a way in.

⊰ 9.19 ⊱

The Devil You Know

I was dreaming. Not *in* a dream — so real I could feel the wind as I fell, or smell the metallic stench of blood in the Santee — but actually dreaming. I watched as whole scenes played out in my mind, only something was wrong. The dream felt wrong — or didn't, because I couldn't feel anything. I might as well have been sitting on the curb watching everything as it passed by....

The night Sarafine had called the Seventeenth Moon.

The moon splitting in the sky above Lena, its two halves forming the wings of a butterfly — one green, one gold.

John Breed on his Harley, Lena's arms wrapped around him.

Macon's empty grave in the cemetery.

Ridley holding a black bundle, light escaping from beneath the fabric.

The Arclight resting on the muddy ground.

124

A single silver button, lost in the front seat of the Beater, one night in the rain.

The images floated on the periphery of my mind, just out of reach. The dream was soothing. Maybe my every subconscious thought wasn't a prophecy, a warped piece of the puzzle that would form my destiny as a Wayward. Maybe *that* was the dream. I relaxed into the gentle tug-of-war as I drifted on the edge of sleep and wakefulness. My mind groped for more concrete thoughts, trying to sift through the haze the way Amma sifted flour for a cake. Again and again, I kept coming back to the image of the Arclight.

The Arclight in my hands.

The Arclight in the grave.

The Arclight and Macon, in the sea cave at the Great Barrier.

Macon turning to look at me. "Ethan, this isn't a dream. Wake up. Now!"

Then Macon caught fire and my mind seized up and I couldn't see anything, because the pain was so intense I couldn't think or dream anymore.

A shrill sound cut through the rhythmic buzz of the lubbers outside my window. I bolted upright, and the sound intensified as I fought myself awake.

It was Lucille. She was on my bed hissing, the hair on her arched back standing up in a stiff line. Her ears were flattened against her head, and for a second I thought she was hissing at me. I followed her eyes across my room, through the darkness. There was someone standing at the foot of my bed. The polished handle of his cane caught the light.

125

My mind hadn't been groping for concrete thoughts.

Abraham Ravenwood had.

"Holy crap!"

I scrambled backward, slamming into the wooden headboard behind me. There was nowhere to go, but all I wanted to do was get away. Instinct took over—fight or flight. And there was no way I was going to try to fight Abraham Ravenwood.

"Get out. Now." I pressed my hands against my temples, as if he could still reach me through the dull ache in my head.

He watched me intently, measuring my reactions. "Evening, boy. I see, like my grandson, you haven't learned your place yet." Abraham shook his head. "Little Macon Ravenwood. Always such a disappointing child." Involuntarily, my hands slid into fists. Abraham looked amused and flicked his finger.

I dropped to the floor in front of him, gasping. My face smashed against rough floorboards, and all I could see were his cracked leather boots. I struggled to raise my head.

"That's better." Abraham smiled, his white beard framing even whiter canines. He looked different from the last time I'd seen him, at the Great Barrier. His white Sunday suit was gone, replaced by a darker, more imposing one, his signature black string tie fastened neatly under his shirt collar. The illusion of the friendly Southern gentleman was gone. This *thing* standing in front of me was nothing like a man, and even less like Macon. Abraham Ravenwood, father of every Ravenwood Incubus who came after, was a monster.

"I wouldn't say monster. But then, I don't see as how it matters much what you think of me, boy."

Lucille hissed more loudly.

I tried to push myself up from the floor and keep my voice from shaking. "What the hell were you doing in my head?"

He lifted an eyebrow. "Ah, you sensed me feeding. Not bad for a Mortal." He leaned forward. "Tell me, what does it feel like? I've always wondered. Is it more like a blade or a bite? When I cut loose the thoughts you hold most dear? Your secrets and your dreams?"

I staggered to my feet slowly, but I could barely carry my own weight. "It feels like you should stay out of my mind, Psycho."

Abraham laughed. "I would be happy to. There's not much to see in there. Seventeen years and you've barely lived. Aside from a few meaningless trysts with trifling Caster trash."

I flinched. I wanted to grab him by the collar and hurl him out my window. Which I would've, if I could have moved my arms.

"Yeah? If my brain's so useless, why are you creeping into my room fishing around in it?" My whole body was shaking. I could talk a good game, but I was concentrating on trying not to pass out in front of the most powerful Incubus any of us had ever known.

Abraham walked over to the window and ran his finger along the ledge and the trail of salt Amma had dutifully left there. He licked the crystals off his finger. "I can never get enough salt. Gives the blood a savory note." He paused, looking out my window at the scorched lawn. "But I do have a question for you. Something of mine has been taken from me. And I think you know where to find it."

He flicked his finger against the window, and the glass shattered in the panes.

I took a slow step toward him. It was like dragging my feet through cement. "What makes you think I'd tell you anything?"

"Let's see. Fear, for starters. Take a look." He leaned out the window, looking down into my front yard. "Hunting and his dogs didn't come all this way for nothing. They love a midnight snack."

My heart pounded in my ears. They were outside—Hunting and his Blood Pack.

Abraham turned back to face me, his black eyes shining. "Enough talk, boy. Where is John? I know my worthless grandson didn't kill him. Where is Macon hiding him?"

There it was. Someone had finally said it. John was alive.

I knew it was true. I felt like I'd known all along. We had never found John's body. All this time he had probably been in the Caster Tunnels, hanging out at some club like Exile, waiting.

The anger welled up inside me, and I could barely force the words out. "The last time I saw him, he was in the cave at the Great Barrier, helping you and Sarafine destroy the world."

When he wasn't busy running away with my girlfriend.

Abraham looked smug. "I'm not sure you understand the gravity of the situation, so let me enlighten you. The Mortal world—your world, including this pathetic little town—is being destroyed, thanks to Macon's niece and her ridiculous behavior, not me."

I fell back onto my bed as if Abraham had punched me. It felt like he did. "Lena did what she had to do. She Claimed herself."

"She destroyed the Order, boy. And she made the wrong choice when she chose to walk away from us."

"Why do you care? You don't seem like you're concerned about anyone but yourself."

He laughed, once. "A good point. Although we find ourselves in a dangerous state, it does provide me with certain *opportunities.*"

Aside from John Breed, I couldn't imagine what he meant, and I didn't want to. But I tried not to let him see how scared I really was. "I don't care if John has something to do with your opportunities. I told you, I don't know where he is."

Abraham watched me carefully, like a Sybil who could read every line in my face. "Imagine a crack that runs deeper than the Tunnels. A crack that runs into the Underground, where only the darkest of Demons dwell. Your girlfriend's youthful *rebelliousness* and her gifts have created such a crack." He paused, flipping casually through the World History textbook on my desk. "I am not young, but with age comes power. And I have gifts of my own. I can call Demons and creatures of Darkness, even without *The Book of Moons.* If you don't tell me where John is, I'll show you." He smiled, in his own deranged way.

Why was John Breed so important to him? I remembered the way Macon and Liv had talked about John in Macon's study. *John was the key.* The question was — to what?

"I told you —"

Abraham didn't let me finish. He ripped, reappearing at the foot of my bed. I could see the hate in his black eyes. "Don't lie to me, boy!"

Lucille hissed again, and I heard another rip.

I didn't have time to see who it was.

Something heavy fell on top of me, slamming down onto the bed like a bag of bricks dropped from the ceiling. My head hit the wooden frame behind me, and I bit through my bottom lip.

The sickening metallic taste of blood from the dream filled my mouth.

Over Lucille's gnarled cries, I heard the sound of the hundred-year-old mahogany splintering beneath me. I felt an elbow jab me in the ribs, and I knew. A bag of bricks hadn't dropped on me.

It was a person.

There was a loud crack as the bed frame broke and the mattress crashed to the floor. I tried to throw them off. But I was pinned.

Please don't let it be Hunting.

An arm flew out in front of me, the way my mom's always did when I was a kid and she hit the brakes of the car unexpectedly. "Dude, chill!"

I stopped fighting. "Link?"

"Who else would risk disintegratin' into a million pieces to save your sorry ass?"

I almost laughed. Link had never Traveled before, and now I knew why. Ripping must be harder than it looked, and he sucked at it.

Abraham's voice cut through the darkness. "Save him? You? I think it's a little late for that." Link almost jumped out of the broken pile of bed at the sound of Abraham's voice. Before I could answer, my bedroom door flew open so hard it almost came off the hinges. I heard the click of the light switch, and black splotches blurred everything as my eyes adjusted to the light.

"Holy—"

"What the devil is goin' on in here!" Amma was standing in the doorway, wearing the rose-patterned bathrobe I bought her for Mother's Day, with her hair wrapped in rollers and her hand wrapped around her old wooden rolling pin.

"—hell," Link whispered. I realized he was practically sitting in my lap.

But Amma didn't notice. Her eyes zeroed in on Abraham Ravenwood.

She pointed the rolling pin at him, her eyes narrowing. She circled him like a wild animal, only I couldn't tell who was the predator and who was the prey.

"What are *you* doin' in this house?" Her voice was angry and low. If she was afraid, she sure didn't show it.

Abraham laughed. "Do you actually think you can chase me off with a rolling pin, like a lame dog? You can do better than that, Miss Treadeau."

"You get outta my house or, the Good Lord as my witness, you'll wish you were a lame dog." Abraham's face hardened. Amma turned the rolling pin so that it pointed at Abraham's chest, like the tip of a sword. "Nobody messes with my boy. Not Abraham Ravenwood, not the Serpent or Old Scratch himself, you hear?"

Now the rolling pin was pushing into Abraham's jacket. With every inch, the thread of tension between the two of them pulled tighter. Link and I moved closer to Amma on either side.

"This is the last time I'm going to ask," Abraham said, his eyes bearing down on Amma. "And if the boy doesn't answer me, your Lucifer will seem like a welcome reprieve from the hell I will rain down on this town."

He paused and looked at me. "Where is John?"

I recognized the look in his eye. It was the same look I had seen in the visions, when Abraham killed his own brother and fed from him. It was vicious and sadistic, and for a second I considered naming a random place so I could get this monster out of my house.

But I couldn't think fast enough. "I swear to God, I don't—"

The wind blew in through the broken window, hard, whipping around us and scattering papers all over the room. Amma staggered back, and her rolling pin went flying. Abraham didn't move, the wind blowing past him without so much as rustling his jacket, as if it was as terrified of him as the rest of us.

"I wouldn't swear, boy." He smiled, a terrible, lifeless smile. "I would pray."

⊰ 9.19 ⊱

Winds of Hell

The wind rushed through my window with a force so powerful it took everything on top of my desk with it. Books and papers, even my backpack, twisted in the air, swirling like a tornado trapped in a bottle. The towers of shoe boxes that lined my walls crashed to the floor, sending everything from comic books to my bottle cap collection from first grade flying through the air. I grabbed hold of Amma, who was so tiny I was worried she might get picked up with everything else.

"What's happenin'?" I could hear Link yelling from somewhere behind me, but I couldn't see him.

Abraham was standing in the center of the room, his voice calling into the churning black vortex. "To those who have brought destruction into my house, I invite chaos into yours." The wind circled around him without even catching his coattails.

He was commanding it. "The Order is Broken. The Door is Open. Arise, Ascend, Destroy!" His voice grew louder. *"Ratio Fracta est! Ianua Aperta est! Sugite, Ascendite, Exscindite!"* Now he was shouting. *"Ratio Fracta est! Ianua Aperta est! Sugite, Ascendite, Exscindite!"*

The swirling air darkened and began to take shape. The hazy black forms jerked out of the spiral, as if they were climbing their way out of the vortex and hurling themselves over the edge, into the world. Which seemed pretty disturbing, considering what they were hurling themselves into was the middle of my bedroom.

I knew what they were. I'd seen them before. I never wanted to see them again.

Vexes—the Demons that inhabited the Underground, void of soul and shape—erupted from the wind, curling into dark forms that moved across my plain blue ceiling, growing until it seemed like they would suck all the air from the room itself. The creatures of shadow moved like a thick, churning fog, shifting in the air. I remembered the one that had almost attacked us outside Exile—the terrifying scream when it reared back and opened its jaws. As the shadows grew into beasts in front of us, I knew the screaming wouldn't be far behind.

Amma tried to wrestle free from my arms, but I wouldn't let go. She would have attacked Abraham with her bare hands if I'd let her. "Don't you come into my house thinkin' you can bring a world a evil through one tiny crack in the sky."

"Your house? This seems more like the Wayward's house to me. And the Wayward is exactly the person to show my friends the way in, through your tiny crack in the sky."

Amma closed her eyes, murmuring to herself. "Aunt Delilah,

Uncle Abner, Grandmamma Sulla...." She was trying to call the Greats, her ancestors in the Otherworld, who had protected us from the Vexes twice before. They were their own force to be reckoned with.

Abraham laughed, his voice carrying above the hissing wind. "No need to call up your ghosts, old woman. We were just leaving." I could hear the rip begin before he dematerialized. "But don't worry. I'll see you soon. Sooner than you'd like."

Then he ripped open the sky and stepped through it. Gone.

Before any of us could say a word, the Vexes shot out my open window, a single streak of black moving above the sleeping houses on Cotton Bend. At the end of the street, the line of Demons divided in different directions, like the fingers of a dark hand wrapping itself around our town.

My room was strangely quiet. Link tried to navigate around the papers and comic books settling on the floor. But he could barely stand still. "Man, I thought they were gonna drag us down to hell, or wherever they came from. Maybe my mom is right and it is the End a Days." He scratched his head. "We're lucky they're gone."

Amma walked over to the window, rubbing the gold charm she wore around her neck. "They're not gone and we're not lucky. Only a fool would think either."

The lubbers buzzed underneath the window, the broken symphony of destruction that had become the sound track of our lives. Amma's expression was just as broken, a mix of fear and sorrow and something I'd never seen before.

Unreadable, inscrutable Amma. Staring out at the night.

"The hole in the sky. It's gettin' bigger."

There was no way we could go back to sleep, and there was no way Amma was letting us out of her sight, so the three of us sat around the scarred pine table in the kitchen listening to the clock tick. Luckily, my dad was in Charleston, like he was most weeknights now that he was teaching at the university. Tonight would've sent him back to Blue Horizons for sure.

I could tell Amma was distracted because she cut Link a slice of chocolate pecan pie when she cut one for me. He made a face and slid it onto the china plate next to Lucille's water dish. Lucille sniffed it and walked away, curling up quietly under Amma's wooden chair. Not even Lucille had an appetite tonight.

By the time Amma got up to put on the water for tea, Link was so restless he was banging out a tune on the place mat with his fork. He looked at me. "Remember the day they served that nasty chocolate pecan pie in the cafeteria, and Dee Dee Guinness told everyone that you were the one who gave Emily the Valentine's Day card no one signed?"

"Yeah." I picked at the dried glue on the table from when I was a kid. My pie sat untouched. "Wait, what?" I hadn't been listening.

"Dee Dee Guinness was pretty cute." Link was smiling to himself.

"Who?" I had no idea who he was talking about.

"Hello? You got so mad you stepped on a fork and crushed it? And they didn't let you back in the cafeteria for a whole six months?" Link examined his fork.

"I remember the fork, I think. But I don't remember anyone named Dee Dee." It was a lie. I couldn't even remember the fork. Come to think of it, I couldn't remember the valentine either.

Link shook his head. "We've known her our whole lives, and she totally ratted you out in third grade. How could you forget her?" I didn't answer, and he went back to tapping his fork.

Good question.

Amma brought her teacup to the table, and we sat in silence. It was like we were waiting for a tidal wave to crash down over us, and it was too late to pack or panic or run. When the phone rang, even Amma jumped.

"Who'd be calling this late?" I said late, but I meant early. It was almost six in the morning. We all were thinking the same thing: Whatever was happening, whatever Abraham had let loose on the world—this would be it.

Link shrugged, and Amma picked up the black rotary phone that had been on the wall since my dad was a kid. "Hello?"

I watched as she listened to the caller on the other end of the line. Link rapped on the table in front of me. "It's a lady, but I can't tell who it is. She's talkin' too fast."

I heard Amma's breath catch, and she hung up the phone. For a second, she stood there holding the receiver.

"Amma, what's wrong?"

She turned around, her eyes watering. "Wesley Lincoln, do you have that car a yours?" My dad had taken the Volvo to the university.

Link nodded. "Yes, ma'am. It's a little dirty, but—"

Amma was already halfway to the front door. "Hurry up. We've got to go."

♦ ♦ ♦

Link pulled away from the curb a little slower than usual, for Amma's sake. I'm not sure she would've noticed or cared if he'd skidded down the street on two wheels. She sat in the front seat, staring straight ahead, clutching the handles of her pocketbook.

"Amma, what's wrong? Where are we going?" I was leaning forward from the backseat, and she didn't even yell at me about not wearing my seat belt. Something was definitely wrong.

When Link turned onto Blackwell Street, I saw just how wrong.

"What the he—" He looked at Amma and coughed. "Heck?"

There were trees all over the road, torn from the ground, roots and all. It looked like a scene from one of the natural disaster shows Link watched on the Discovery Channel. Man vs. Nature. But this wasn't natural. It was the result of a supernatural disaster—Vexes.

I could feel them, the destruction they carried with them, bearing down on me. They had been here, on this street. They had done this, and they'd done it because of me.

Because of John Breed.

Amma wanted Link to turn down Cypress Grove, but the road was blocked, so he had to turn down Main. All the streetlights were out, and daylight was just beginning to cut through the darkness, turning the sky from black to shades of blue. For a minute, I thought Main Street might have made it through Abraham's tornado of Vexes, until I saw the green. Because that's all it was now—a green. Forget about the stolen tire swing across the street. Now the ancient oak itself was gone. And the statue of General Jubal A. Early wasn't standing proudly in the center, sword drawn for battle.

The General had fallen, the hilt of his sword broken.

The black sheath of lubbers that had covered the statue for weeks was gone. Even they had abandoned him.

I couldn't remember a time when the General wasn't there, guarding his green and our town. He was more than a statue. He was part of Gatlin, woven into our untraditional traditions. On the Fourth of July, the General wore an American flag across his back. On Halloween, he wore a witch's hat, and a plastic pumpkin full of candy hung from his arm. For the Reenactment of the Battle of Honey Hill, someone always put a real Confederate frock coat over his permanent bronze one. The General was one of us, watching over Gatlin from his post, generation after generation.

I had always hoped things would change in my town, until they started changing. Now I wanted Gatlin to go back to the boring town I'd known all my life. The way things were when I hated the way things were. Back when I could see things coming, and nothing ever came.

I didn't want to see this.

I was still staring at the fallen General through the back window when Link slowed down. "Man, it looks like a bomb went off."

The sidewalks in front of the stores that lined Main were covered with glass. The windows had blown out of every one of them, leaving the stores nameless and exposed. I could see the painted gold L and I from the Little Miss window, separated from the other letters. Dirty hot-pink and red dresses littered the sidewalk, thousands of tiny sequins reflecting the bits and pieces of our everyday lives.

"That's no bomb, Wesley Lincoln."

"Ma'am?"

Amma was staring out at what was left of Main. "Bombs drop from the heavens. This came from hell." She didn't say another word as she pointed toward the end of the street. *Keep driving.* That's what she was saying.

Link did, and neither one of us asked where we were going. If Amma hadn't told me by now, she wasn't planning to. Maybe we weren't going anywhere specific. Maybe Amma just wanted to see which parts of our town had been spared and which had been forsaken.

Then I saw the red and white flashing lights at the end of the street. Huge pillows of black smoke poured into the air. Something was on fire. Not just something in town, but the heart and soul of our town, at least for me.

A place where I thought I would always be safe.

The Gatlin County Library—everything that meant anything to Marian, and all that was left of my mother—was engulfed in flames. A telephone pole was wedged in the middle of its crushed roof, orange flames eating away at the wood on both sides. Water was pouring from the fire hoses, but as soon as they put out the fire in one place, another ignited. Pastor Reed, who lived down the street, was throwing buckets of water around the perimeter, his face coated in ash. At least fifteen members of his congregation had gathered to help, which was ironic, considering most of them had signed one of Mrs. Lincoln's petitions to have books banned from the library they were trying to save. "Book banners are no better than book burners." That's what my mom used to say. I never thought there would come a day when I'd actually see books burning.

Link slowed down, weaving between the parked cars and fire

engines. "The library! Marian's gonna freak. You think those things did this?"

"You think they didn't?" My voice sounded far away, like it wasn't mine. "Let me out. My mom's books are in there."

Link started to pull over, but Amma put her hand on the wheel. "Keep drivin'."

"What?" I figured she was bringing us here because the volunteer firemen needed help pouring water on the rest of the roof so it didn't catch fire. "We can't leave. They might need our help. It's Marian's library."

It's my mom's library.

Amma wouldn't look away from the window. "I said keep driving, unless you want to pull over and let me drive. Marian's not in there, and she's not the only one needin' our help tonight."

"How do you know?" Amma tensed. We both knew I was questioning her abilities as a Seer, the gift that was as much a part of her as the library was a part of my mom.

Amma stared straight ahead, her knuckles turning white as she clutched the handles of her pocketbook. "They're only books."

For a second, I didn't know what to say. It was like she'd slapped me in the face. But like a slap, after the initial sting, everything was clearer. "Would you say that to Marian—or Mom if she was here? They're a piece of our family—"

"Take a look before you lecture me about your family, Ethan Wate."

When I followed her eyes past the library, I knew Amma hadn't been taking stock. She already knew what we'd lost. I was the last one to figure it out. Almost.

My heart was hammering and my fists were clenched by the

time Link pointed down the street. "Oh, man. Isn't that your aunts' place?"

I nodded, but I didn't say anything. I couldn't find the words.

"It was." Amma sniffed. "Keep drivin'."

I could already see the red glare of the ambulance and fire engine parked on the lawn of the Sisters' house—or what used to be their house. Yesterday, it had been a proud, white, two-story Federal, with a wraparound porch and a makeshift ramp for Aunt Mercy's wheelchair. Today, it was half a house, cut down the center like a child's dollhouse. But instead of perfect arrangements of furniture in every room, everything in the Sisters' house was upturned and torn apart. The blue crushed-velvet sofa was lying on its back, end tables and rocking chairs pushed up against it, as if the contents of the house had slid to one side. Frames were piled on top of beds, where they had fallen off the walls. And the eerie cutout faced a mountain of rubble: wooden boards, sheets of plaster, unidentifiable pieces of furniture, a porcelain claw-foot tub—the half of the house that hadn't survived.

I stuck my head out the car window, staring up at the house. I felt like the Beater was rolling in slow motion. In my head, I counted what had been rooms. Thelma's was downstairs, in the back, closest to the screen door. Her room was still there. Aunt Grace and Aunt Mercy shared the darkest room, behind the stairs. And I could still see the stairs. That was something. I ticked them off in my head.

Aunt Grace and Aunt Mercy and Thelma.

Aunt Prue.

I couldn't find her room. I couldn't find her pink flowered bedspread with all the little tiny balls on it, whatever they were called. I couldn't find her mothball-smelling closet and her mothball-smelling dresser and her mothball-smelling rag rug.

It was all gone, as if some giant fist had come down from the sky and pulverized it into dust and debris.

The same giant fist had spared the rest of the street. The other houses on Old Oak Road were untouched, without so much as a fallen tree or broken roof shingle in their yards. It looked like the result of a real tornado, the way it touched down randomly, destroying one house while leaving the one next door perfectly intact. But this wasn't the random result of a natural disaster. I knew whose giant fist it was.

It was a message for me.

Link guided the Beater to the curb, and Amma was out of the car before it even stopped. She headed right for the ambulance, as if she already knew what we were going to find. I froze, my stomach churning.

The phone call. It hadn't been the greater Gatlin gossip grapevine, reporting that a twister had destroyed most of town. It had been someone calling to tell Amma that my ancient great-aunts' house had caved in and—what? Link grabbed my arm and pulled me across the street. Practically everyone on the block was crowded around the ambulance. I saw them without seeing any of them, because it was all so surreal. None of it could possibly be happening. Edna Haynie was in her pink plastic hair curlers and fuzzy bathrobe, despite the ninety-degree heat, while Melvin Haynie was still wearing the white undershirt and shorts he had slept in. Ma and Pa Riddle, who ran the dry cleaner's out of their garage, were dressed for disaster. Ma Riddle was madly spinning her hand-cranked radio, even though the power didn't seem to be going out and reception didn't seem to be coming in. Pa Riddle wouldn't let go of his shotgun.

"Excuse me, ma' am. Sorry." Link elbowed his way through the crowd, until we were on the other side of the ambulance. The metal doors were open.

Marian was standing on the brown grass outside the open doors, next to someone wrapped in a blanket. Thelma. Two tiny figures were propped up between them, skinny whitish-blue ankles peeking out from under long, frilly white nightgowns.

Aunt Mercy was shaking her head. "Harlon James. He doesn't like messes. He won't like this one bit."

Marian tried to wrap a blanket around her, but Aunt Mercy shrugged it off. "You're in shock. You need to warm up. That's what the firemen said." Marian handed me a blanket. She was in emergency mode, trying to protect the people she loved and minimize the damage—even though her whole world was burning up a few blocks away. There was no way to minimize that kind of damage.

"He's run off, Mercy," Aunt Grace mumbled. "I told you, that dog's no good. Prudence must a left the dog door open again." I couldn't help but look to where the dog door had been, and now the whole wall was missing.

I shook out the blanket and tucked it gently around Aunt Mercy's shoulders. She was clinging to Thelma like a child. "We have ta tell Prudence Jane. You know she's crazy 'bout that dog. We have to tell her. She'll be angrier than a June wasp if she hears it from someone else first."

Thelma gathered them in her arms. "She'll be fine. Just some complications, like the ones you had a few months back, Grace. You remember."

144

Marian looked at Thelma for a long time, like a mother checking out a child coming in from the yard. "You feeling all right, Miss Thelma?"

Thelma looked almost as confused as the Sisters usually did. "I don't know what happened. One minute, I was dreamin' about a fat piece a George Clooney and a hot date with some brown sugar pound cake, and the next thing I knew, the house was comin' down around us." Thelma's voice was shaky, like she couldn't find a way to make sense of the words she was saying. "Barely had time to get to the girls, and when I found Prudence Jane..."

Aunt Prue. I didn't hear anything else. Marian looked at me. "She's with the paramedics. Don't worry, Amma's with her."

I pushed past Marian, feeling my arm slide through her fingers when she tried to grab it. Two paramedics leaned over someone lying on a stretcher. Tubes hung from metal poles and disappeared into my aunt's frail body in places I couldn't see, covered with white tape. The paramedics were hooking bags of clear fluid onto more metal poles, their voices impossible to hear over the chaotic chatter of voices, sobs, and sirens. Amma knelt next to her, holding her limp hand and whispering. I wondered if she was praying or talking to the Greats. Probably both.

"She's not dead." Link came up behind me. "I can smell her—I mean, I can tell." He inhaled again. "Copper and salt and red-eye gravy."

I smiled, in spite of everything, and let out the breath I was holding. "What are they saying? Is she gonna be okay?"

Link listened to the paramedics leaning over Aunt Prue. "I don't know. They're sayin' when the house fell she had a stroke, and she's unresponsive."

I turned back to look at Aunt Mercy and Aunt Grace. Amma and Thelma helped them into wheelchairs, waving off the volunteer firefighters as if they didn't know the men were really Mr. Rawls, who filled their prescriptions at the Stop & Steal, and Ed Landry, who pumped their gas at the BP.

I bent down and picked up a piece of glass from the rubble at my feet. I couldn't tell what it had been, but the color of the glass made me think it was Aunt Prue's green glass cat, the one she'd kept proudly on display next to her glass grapes. I turned it over and saw it had a round red sticker on it. Marked, like everything in the Sisters' house, for one relative or another, when they died.

A red sticker.

The cat was meant for me. The cat, the rubble, the fire—all of it was meant for me. I stuck the broken green glass in my pocket and watched helplessly as my aunts were wheeled toward the only other ambulance in town.

Amma shot me a look, and I knew what it meant. *Don't say a word and don't do a thing.* It meant go home, lock the doors, and stay out of it. But she knew I couldn't.

One word kept fighting its way back into my mind. *Unresponsive.* Aunt Grace and Aunt Mercy wouldn't understand what it meant when the doctors told them Aunt Prue was unresponsive. They would hear what I heard when Link said it.

Unresponsive.

As good as dead.

And it was my fault. Because I couldn't tell Abraham how to find John Breed.

John Breed.

Everything snapped into focus.

146

The mutant Incubus who had led us into Sarafine and Abraham's trap—who had tried to steal the girl I loved, and had Turned my best friend—was destroying my life one more time. My life and the people I loved.

Because of him, Abraham had unleashed the Vexes. Because of him, my town was destroyed and my aunt was nearly dead. Books were burning, and for the first time, it wasn't because of small minds or small people.

Macon and Liv were right. It was all about him.

John Breed was the one to blame.

I made a fist. It wasn't a giant fist, but it was mine. So was this. My problem. I was a Wayward. If I was supposed to find the way—to be there for some great and terrible purpose, or whatever it was Marian and Liv had said the Casters would need me to lead them into or out of—I had found it. And now I had to find John Breed.

There was no going back, not after today.

One ambulance pulled away. Then another. The sirens echoed down the street, and as they disappeared in front of me, I started to run. I thought about Lena. I ran faster. I thought about my mom and Amma and Aunt Prue and Marian. I ran until I couldn't catch my breath, until the fire trucks were so far behind me that I couldn't hear the sirens anymore.

I stopped when I reached the library, and stood there. The flames were gone, for the most part. Smoke was still streaming into the sky. The way the ash swirled in the air, it looked like snow. Boxes of books, some black, others soaking wet, were piled in front of the building.

It was still standing, a good half of it. But it didn't matter, not to me. It would never smell the same again. My mother, what was left of her in Gatlin, was finally gone. You couldn't unburn the books. You could only buy new ones. And those pages would never have been touched by her hands, or bookmarked with a spoon.

A part of her had died tonight, all over again.

I didn't know much about Leonardo da Vinci. What had the book said? Maybe I was learning how to live, or maybe I was learning how to die. After today, it could go either way. Maybe I should listen to Emily Dickinson and let the madness begin to make sense. Either way, it was Poe who stuck with me.

Because I had the feeling I was deep into that darkness peering, about as deep as a person could be.

I pulled the piece of green glass out of my pocket and stared at it, as if it could tell me what I needed to know.

Ladies of the House

Ethan Wate, can you fetch me some sweet tea?" Aunt Mercy called from the living room.

Aunt Grace didn't miss a beat. "Ethan, don't you be gettin' her any sweet tea. She'll have ta use the powder room if she drinks any more."

"Ethan, don't you listen ta Grace. She's got a mean streak a mile long and ten powder rooms wide."

I looked at Lena, who was holding a plastic pitcher of sweet tea in her hand. "Was that a yes or a no?"

Amma slammed the door shut and held out her hand for the pitcher. "Don't you two have some homework to do?" Lena arched an eyebrow and smiled back, relieved. Since Aunt Prue had gone to County Care and the Sisters had moved in with us, I felt like I hadn't been alone with Lena in weeks.

I took Lena's hand and pulled her toward the kitchen door.

You ready to make a run for it?

I'm ready.

We rushed into the hall as fast as we could, trying to make it to the stairs. Aunt Grace was bundled up on the couch, her fingers hooked through the holes of her favorite crocheted afghan, which was about ten different shades of brown. It matched our living room perfectly, now stacked floor to ceiling with brown cardboard boxes full of everything the Sisters had made my dad and me haul out of their house last week.

They hadn't been satisfied with the things that had actually survived: almost everything from Aunt Grace and Aunt Mercy's bedroom, a brass spittoon that all five of Aunt Prue's husbands had used (and never cleaned), four of the spoons from Aunt Grace's Southern spoon collection and the wooden display rack, a stack of dusty photo albums, two mismatched dining room chairs, the plastic fawn from their front yard, and hundreds of unopened miniature jelly jars they had swiped from Millie's Breakfast 'n' Biscuits. But the things that had survived weren't enough. They had henpecked us until we dragged the broken stuff out, too.

Most of it had stayed in the boxes, but Aunt Grace had insisted that decorating would help ease their "sufferin'," so Amma let them put some of their things around the house. Which was the reason Harlon James I, Harlon James II, and Harlon James III—all preserved thanks to what Aunt Prue called the *delicate* Southern art of taxidermy—were staring at me right now. Harlon James I sitting, Harlon James II standing, and Harlon James III sleeping. It was the sleeping Harlon James that really disturbed me; Aunt Grace kept it—him—next to the couch, and one way or another, someone stubbed a toe on him every time they walked by.

It could be worse, Ethan. He could be on the couch.

Aunt Mercy was sulking in her wheelchair in front of the television, clearly agitated she'd lost this morning's battle over the couch. My dad was sitting next to her, reading the paper. "How are you kids doing today? It's nice to see you, Lena." His expression said, *Get out while you can.*

Lena smiled at him. "You, too, Mr. Wate."

He had been taking a day off here and there when he could, to keep Amma from losing her mind.

Aunt Mercy was gripping the remote, even though the television wasn't on, and waved it at me. "Where do you two lovebirds think you're off ta?"

Head for the stairs, L.

"Ethan, don't tell me you're thinkin' a takin' a young lady upstairs. That wouldn't be proper." Aunt Mercy clicked the remote at me, as if she could put me on pause before I made it to my room. She looked over at Lena. "You keep your cute little fanny out a boys' rooms, Chickadee."

"Mercy Lynne!"

"Grace Ann!"

"I don't want ta hear that kinda dirty talk comin' from you."

"What, fanny? Fanny fanny fanny!"

Ethan! Get me out of here.

Don't stop.

Aunt Grace sniffed. " 'Course he's not takin' her upstairs. His daddy would roll over in his grave."

"I'm right here." My dad waved at her.

"His mamma," Aunt Mercy corrected.

Aunt Grace waved her handkerchief, the one that was permanently glued to the inside of her curled hand. "Mercy Lynne, you must be goin' senile. That's what I said."

"You most certainly did not. I heard you clear as a bell, with my good ear. You said his daddy'd be—"

Aunt Grace tossed the afghan aside. "You couldn't hear a bell if it crept up behind you and bit you in the sweet—"

"Sweet tea, ladies?" Amma appeared with a tray, just in time. Lena and I snuck up the stairs while Amma blocked the view from the living room. There was no getting past the Sisters, even without Aunt Prue. And there hadn't been for days now. Between getting them settled in our house, and getting everything that was left out of theirs, my dad and Amma and I had been doing nothing but waiting on them hand and foot since they moved in.

Lena disappeared into my room, and I closed the door behind me. I slid my arms around her waist, and she leaned her head against me.

I've missed you.

I know. Chickadee.

She punched me playfully.

"Don't you close that door, Ethan Wate!" I couldn't tell if the voice was Aunt Grace's or Aunt Mercy's, but it didn't matter. On this point they were in perfect agreement. "There're more chickens than people in this world, an' that sure as summer ain't no accident!"

Lena smiled and reached behind me, pushing the door back open.

I groaned. "Don't do that."

Lena touched my lip. "When's the last time the Sisters walked up the stairs?"

I leaned closer to her, our foreheads touching. My pulse started racing the second we touched. "Now that you mention it, Amma's going to be pouring sweet tea until that pitcher runs dry."

I picked Lena up and carried her over to my bed, which was really just a mattress on my floor now, thanks to Link. I dropped down next to her, purposely ignoring my broken window, my open door, or what was left of my bed.

It was just the two of us. She stared back up at me, one green eye and one gold, black curls splayed out on the mattress around her, like a black halo. "I love you, Ethan Wate."

I propped myself up on my elbow and looked down at her. "I've been told I'm very lovable."

Lena laughed. "Who told you that?"

"Lots of girls."

Her eyes clouded over for a second. "Yeah? Like?"

"My mom. My Aunt Caroline. And Amma." I poked her in the ribs, and she started to squirm, giggling into my shirt. "I love you, L."

"You better. Because I don't know what I would do without you." Her voice was raw and as honest as I'd ever heard it.

"There's no me without you, Lena." I leaned down and kissed her, lowering myself until my body fit perfectly against hers, like they were made to be together. Because we were—no matter what the universe or my pulse had to say about it. I could feel the energy seeping from me, but it only made my mouth seek out hers again.

Lena pulled away before my heart began to pound dangerously. "I think we'd better stop, Ethan."

I sighed and rolled onto my back next to her, my hand still tangled in her hair. "We didn't even get started."

"Until we figure out why it's getting worse—more intense between us—we have to be careful."

I grabbed for her waist. "What if I said I don't care?"

"Don't say that. You know I'm right. I don't want to accidentally set you on fire, too."

"I don't know. Still might be worth it."

She punched me in the arm, and I smiled up at the ceiling. I knew she was right. The only people who still seemed in control of their powers were the Incubuses. Ravenwood was a mess, and so was everyone in it.

But that didn't make it any better. I needed to touch her, like I needed to breathe.

I heard a meow. Lucille was kneading the bottom of my mattress. Ever since she lost her bed to Harlon James IV, she had taken over mine. My dad had rushed back from Charleston the night of the so-called twister, and he'd found Aunt Prue's dog the next day, cowering in a corner of the kindergarten yard. Once Harlon James arrived at our house, he wasn't much different from the Sisters. He made himself right at home in Lucille's bed. Eating Lucille's chicken dinners off her china plate. Even scratching Lucille's cat post.

"Aw, come on, Lucille. You've lived with them longer than I have." But it didn't matter. As long as the Sisters were living with us, Lucille was living with me.

Lena gave me a quick kiss on the cheek and leaned over the side of the bed to dig through her bag. An old copy of *Great Expectations* slipped out. I recognized it right away.

"What's that?"

Lena picked it up, avoiding my eyes. "It's called a book." She knew what I was really asking.

"Is it the one you found in Sarafine's box?" I already knew it was.

"Ethan, it's just a book. I read lots of them."

"It's not just a book, L. What's going on?"

Lena hesitated, then flipped through the tattered pages. When she reached a dog-eared page, she started to read: "'And could I look upon her without compassion, seeing her punishment in the ruin she was, in her profound unfitness for this Earth on which she was placed....'" Lena stared into the book, as if there were answers inside that only she could see. "That passage was underlined."

I knew Lena was curious about her mother—not Sarafine, but the woman we had seen in the vision—the one who had cradled Lena in her arms as a baby. Maybe Lena believed the book or the metal box of her mother's things held the answers. But it didn't matter what was underlined in any old copy of Dickens.

Nothing in that box was free of the blood on Sarafine's hands.

I reached out and grabbed the book. "Give it to me." Before Lena could say a word, my bedroom faded away—

It had started to rain, as if the sky was matching Sarafine tear for tear. By the time she reached the Eades house, she was drenched. She climbed the white trellis under John's window and hesitated. She pulled the sunglasses she stole from Winn-Dixie out of her pocket and put them on before knocking lightly on the glass.

Too many questions were tangled up in her mind. What was she going to tell John? How could she make him understand she was still the same person? Would a Light Caster still love her now that she was...this?

"Izabel?" John was half asleep, his dark eyes staring back at her. "What are you doing out there?" He grabbed her hand before she could answer, and pulled her inside.

"I—I needed to see you."

John reached for the lamp on his desk.

Sarafine grabbed his hand. "Don't. Leave it off. You'll wake up your parents."

He looked at her more closely, his eyes adjusting to the dark. "Did something happen? Are you hurt?"

She was beyond hurt, beyond hope, and there was no way to prepare John for what she was about to tell him. He knew about her family and the curse. But Sarafine had never told John the date of her real birthday. She had made up a date, one that was several months away, so he wouldn't worry. He didn't know that tonight was her Sixteenth Moon—the night she had been dreading for as long as she could remember.

"I don't want to tell you." Sarafine's voice broke as she choked back tears.

John pulled her into his arms, resting his chin on her head. "You're so cold." He rubbed his hands over her arms. "I love you. You can tell me anything."

"Not this," she whispered. "Everything's ruined."

Sarafine thought about all the plans they had made. Going off to college together, John next year and

Sarafine the year after. John was going to study engineering, and she planned to major in literature. She had always wanted to be a writer. After they graduated, they would get married.

There was no point thinking about it. None of it would happen now.

John squeezed her tighter. "Izabel, you're scaring me. Nothing could ruin what we have."

Sarafine pushed him away and pulled off the sunglasses, revealing the golden-yellow eyes of a Dark Caster. "Are you sure about that?"

For a second, John only stared. "What happened? I don't understand."

She shook her head, the tears burning the skin on her icy cheeks. "It was my birthday. I never told you because I was sure I would go Light. I didn't want you to worry. But at midnight—"

Sarafine couldn't finish. He knew what she was going to say. He could see it in her eyes.

"It's a mistake. It has to be." She was talking to herself as much as to John. "I'm still the same person. They say you feel different when you go Dark—you forget about the people you care about. But I haven't. I never will."

"I think it happens gradually...." John's voice trailed off.

"I can fight it! I don't want to be Dark. I swear." It was too much—her mother turning her away, her sister calling for her, losing John. Sarafine couldn't face any more heartbreak. She crumpled, her body sinking to the floor.

*John knelt beside her, gathering her into his arms.
"You're not Dark. I don't care what color your eyes are."*

*"No one believes that. My mother wouldn't even let
me in the house." Sarafine choked.*

*John pulled her up. "Then we'll leave tonight." He
grabbed a duffel bag and started shoving clothes into it.*

"Where are we going to go?"

*"I don't know. We'll find somewhere." John zipped
the bag and pulled her face into his hands, looking into
her gold eyes.*

"It doesn't matter. As long as we're together."

We were in my bedroom again, in the bright afternoon heat.
The vision faded, taking the girl who seemed nothing like
Sarafine with it. The book dropped to the floor.

Lena's face was streaked with tears, and for a second she looked
exactly like the girl in the vision. "John Eades was my dad."

"Are you sure?"

She nodded, wiping her face with her hands. "I've never seen
a picture of him, but Gramma told me his name. He seemed so
real, like he was still alive. And they really seemed to love each
other." She reached down to pick up the book where it had
fallen, open, with the cover faceup, the worn cracks in its spine
proof of how many times it had been read.

"Don't touch it, L."

Lena picked it up. "Ethan, I've been reading it. That's never
happened before. I think it was because we were touching it at
the same time."

She opened the book again, and I could see dark lines where someone had underlined sentences and circled phrases. Lena noticed me trying to read over her shoulder. "The whole book is like this, marked up like some kind of map. I just wish I knew where it led."

"You know where it leads." We both did. To Abraham and the Dark Fire—the Great Barrier and darkness and death.

Lena didn't take her eyes away from the book. "This line is my favorite. 'I have been bent and broken, but—I hope—into a better shape.' "

We had both been bent and broken by Sarafine.

Was the result a better shape? Was I better for what I'd been through? Was Lena?

I thought about Aunt Prue lying in a hospital bed, and Marian sifting through boxes of burnt books, charred documents, waterlogged photographs. Her life's work destroyed.

What if the people we loved were bent until they broke and were left with no shape at all?

I had to find John Breed before they were too broken to put back together.

Visiting Hours

The next day, Aunt Grace figured out where Mercy was hiding her coffee ice cream in the icebox. The day after that, Aunt Mercy found out Grace had been eating it, and pitched a three-alarm fit. The day after the day after that, I played Scrabble with the Sisters' nonsense words all afternoon, until I was so beaten down I didn't challenge *YOUBET* as a single word, *COTTON* as a verb, *SKUNKED* as an adjective, and *IFFEN* as the long form of *if.*

I was done.

There was one person who wasn't there, though. A person who smelled like copper and salt and red-eye gravy. A person who might have played the tiles to spell *DURNED-FOOL*— while she was the farthest thing from one. A person who could single-handedly map out most of the Caster Tunnels in the South.

A few days later, I couldn't take it anymore. So when Lena insisted on going to see Aunt Prue, I didn't refuse. The truth was, I wanted to see her. I wasn't sure what Aunt Prue was going to be like. Would she look like she was sleeping—the way she did when she fell asleep on the sofa? Or would she look the way she had in the ambulance? There was no way to tell, and I felt guilty and scared.

More than anything, I didn't want to feel alone.

_____ ⌒ᓭ

County Care was a rehab facility—a cross between a nursing home and a place where you went after a hard-core ATV accident. Or when you flipped a dirt bike, crashed a truck, got side-swiped by a big rig. Some folks thought you were lucky if that happened, since you could make a lot of money if the right truck hit you. Or you could end up dead. Or both, as in the case of Deacon Harrigan, who ended up with the nicest headstone in town, while his wife and kids got all new siding and an in-ground trampoline, and started eating out at Applebee's in Summerville five nights a week. Carlton Eaton told Mrs. Lincoln, who told Link, who told me. The checks came every month straight from the capitol building over in Columbia, rain or shine. That's what you got when the trash truck ran you down, anyway.

Walking inside County Care didn't make me feel like Aunt Prue was lucky, though. Even the strange, sudden quiet and the hospital-strength air conditioning didn't make me feel better. The whole place smelled like something sickly sweet, almost powdery. Something bad trying to smell like something good.

161

Even worse, the lobby, the hallways, and the bumpy cottage cheese ceiling were painted Gatlin peach. Sort of like a whole tub of Thousand Island dressing poured over a salad bar's worth of cottage cheese and slapped up on the ceiling.

Maybe French dressing.

Lena was trying to cheer me up.

Yeah? Either way I feel like puking.

It's okay, Ethan. Maybe it won't be so bad once we see her.

What if it's worse?

It was worse, about ten feet farther in. Bobby Murphy looked up from the desk. Last time I'd seen him, he'd been on the basketball team with me, hassling me for getting dumped at that dance by Ethan-Loving turned Ethan-Hating Emily Asher. I let him do it, too. He had been varsity point guard three years running, and nobody messed with him. Now Bobby was sitting behind the reception desk in a peach-colored orderly's uniform, and he didn't look so tough. He also didn't look all that happy to see me. Probably didn't help that his laminated nametag said BOOBY.

"Hey, Bobby. Thought you were over at Summerville Community College."

"Ethan Wate. Here you are, an' here I am. Don't know which one a us I feel sorrier for." His eyes flickered over to Lena, but he didn't say hello. Talk was talk, and I was sure he was up on all the latest, even way out here at County Care, where half the folks couldn't make a sound.

I tried to laugh, but it came out more like a cough, and the silence swept back in between us.

"Yeah. 'Bout time you showed up, anyway. Your Aunt Prudence has been askin' for you." He grinned, shoving a clipboard across the counter.

"Really?" I froze up for a minute, though I should have known better.

"Nah. Just pullin' your leg. Here, give me your John Hancock and you can head on down to the garden."

"Garden?" I handed him back the clipboard.

"Sure. Out back in the residential wing. Where we grow all the good vegetables." He smiled, and I remembered him back in the locker room. *Man up, Wate. Letting a freshman skirt push you around? You're makin' us all look bad.*

Lena leaned over the counter. "That line ever get old, Booby?"

"Not as old as that one." He stood up out of his chair. "How about, 'I'll show you mine, you show me yours'?" He stared at the place where Lena's shirt dove into a V at her chest. My hand clenched into a fist.

I could see her hair curling around her shoulders as she leaned even closer to him. "I'm thinking now would be a great time for you to stop talking."

Bobby opened and shut his mouth like he was a catfish stuck wriggling on the bottom of dried-up Lake Moultrie. He didn't say a word.

"That's more like it." Lena smiled and picked up our visitor badges from the counter.

"So long, Bobby," I said as we headed out back.

The farther we made it down the hall, the sweeter the air and the thicker the smell. I looked in the doors of the rooms we passed, each one like some kind of messed-up Norman Rockwell painting—where only crappy things were happening, frozen into little snapshots of pathetic life.

163

An old man sat in a hospital bed, his head wrapped in white bandages that made it appear gigantic and surreal. He looked like some kind of alien, flipping a little yo-yo on a metal track, back and forth. A woman sat in the chair across from him, stitching something inside a wood hoop. Probably part of some needlepoint he would never see. She didn't look up, and I didn't slow down.

A teenage boy lay in another bed, his hand moving across some paper on top of a fake wood-grain tray table. He was staring off into space, drooling, but his hand kept writing and writing, as if it couldn't help itself. The pen didn't seem to be moving across the paper; it was more like the letters were writing themselves. Maybe every word he'd ever written was in that one big pile of letters, each one stacked up on top of the next. Maybe it was his whole life story. Maybe it was his masterpiece. Who knew? Who cared? Not Bobby Murphy.

I resisted the urge to go take the paper and try to decode it.

Motorcycle accident?

Probably. I don't want to think about it, L.

Lena squeezed my hand, and I tried not to remember her, barefoot and helmetless, on the back of John Breed's Harley.

I know it was stupid.

I pulled her away from that door.

A little girl at the end of the hall had a roomful of folks, but it was the saddest birthday party I'd ever seen. She had a Stop & Steal cake and a table covered with cups of what looked like cranberry juice, covered with plastic wrap. That was about it. The cake had a number five on it, and the family was singing. The matches weren't lit.

Probably can't light them in here, Ethan.

What kind of crappy birthday is that?

The thick sweetness of the air grew worse, and I glanced through an open doorway that led into some kind of hallway kitchen. Cases of Ensure, liquid food, were piled from floor to ceiling. That was the smell—the food that wasn't food. For these lives that weren't lives.

For my Aunt Prue, who had slipped away into the vast unknown when she was supposed to be asleep in her bed. My Aunt Prue, who had charted unknown Caster Tunnels with the precision of Amma working on one of her crossword puzzles.

It was all too horrible to be real. But it was. All of it was happening, and not in some Tunnel where space and time was different than in the Mortal world. This was happening in Greater Gatlin County. It was happening in my own hometown, to my own family.

I didn't know if I could face it. I didn't want to see Aunt Prue this way. I didn't want to remember her like this.

Sad doorways and an open can of Ensure, in a puke-peach hall.

I almost turned around, and I would have—but then I reached the other side of the doorway, and the smell of the air changed. We were there. I knew because the doorway was open, and the particular scent of the Sisters crept out. Rose water and lavender, from those little bundles the Sisters kept in their drawers. It was distinctive, that smell, the one I hadn't paid much attention to all the times I listened to their stories.

"Ethan." Lena stepped in front of me. I could hear the distant hum of machines beyond her, in the room.

"Come on." I stepped toward her, but she put her hands on my shoulders.

"You know, she might not be—there."

I tried to listen, but I was distracted by the sounds of the unknown machines, doing unknown things to my entirely known aunt.

"What are you talking about? Of course she's there. It says her name, right there on the door." Which it did, on the kind of whiteboard you'd find in a college dorm, in faded black dry-erase marker.

STATHAM, PRUDENCE.

"I know her body is there. But even if she's there, your Aunt Prue, with all the things that make her your Aunt Prue—she might not be *there*."

I knew what she was saying, even if I didn't want to. Which, a thousand times more than anything, I didn't.

I put my hand on the door. "Are you saying you can tell? The way Link could smell her blood and hear her heart? Would you be able to—find her?"

"Find what? Her soul?"

"Is that something a Natural can do?" I could hear the hope in my voice.

"I don't know." Lena looked like she was about to cry. "I'm not sure. I feel like there's something I'm supposed to do. But I don't know what."

She looked away, down to the other end of the hall. I could see a watery streak work its way down the side of her jaw.

"You're not supposed to know, L. It's not your fault. This whole thing is my fault. Abraham came looking for me."

"He didn't come for you. He came for John." She didn't say it, but I heard the rest. *Because of me. Because of my Claiming.* She changed the subject before I had a chance to say anything.

166

"I asked Uncle Macon what happens to people when they're in a coma."

I held my breath, in spite of all the things I did or didn't believe. "And?"

She shrugged. "He wasn't sure. But Casters believe the spirit can leave the body under certain circumstances, like Traveling. Uncle M described it as a kind of freedom, like being a Sheer."

"That wouldn't be so bad, I guess." I thought back to the teenage boy, mindlessly writing, and the elderly man with the yo-yo. They weren't Traveling. They weren't Sheers. They were stuck in the most Mortal of all conditions. Trapped in broken-down bodies.

No matter what, I couldn't handle that. Not for Aunt Prue. Especially not for my Aunt Prue.

Without another word, I stepped past Lena and into my aunt's room.

My Aunt Prudence was the smallest person in the world. As she liked to put it, she bent with every passing year and shrunk with every passing husband—and so she barely came up to my chest, even if she could stand up straight in her thick-soled Red Cross shoes.

But lying there, smack in the middle of that big hospital bed, with every possible kind of tube snaking in and out of her, Aunt Prue looked even smaller. She barely made a dent in the mattress. Slits of light broke through the plastic blinds on one side of her room, painting bars across her motionless face and body.

The combined effect looked like a prison hospital ward. I couldn't look at her face. Not at first.

I took a step closer to her bed. I could see the monitors, even if I didn't know what they were for. Things were beeping, lines were moving. There was only one chair in the room, peach-upholstered and hard as a rock, with a second, empty bed next to it. After what I'd seen in the other rooms, the bed looked like a waiting trap. I wondered which variety of broken-down person would be caught in there the next time I came to see Aunt Prue.

"She's stable. You don't need to worry. Her body's comfortable. She's just not with us right now." A nurse was pulling shut the door behind her. I couldn't see her face, but a shock of dark hair twisted out from beneath her ponytail. "I'll leave you for a minute, if you'd like. Prudence hasn't had a visitor since yesterday. I'm sure it would be good for her to spend some time with you."

The nurse's voice was comforting, even familiar, but before I could get a good look at her, the door clicked shut. I saw a vase of fresh flowers on the table next to my aunt's bed. Verbena. They looked like the flowers Amma had resorted to growing inside. "Summer Blaze," that's what she called them. "Red as fire itself."

On a hunch, I walked over to the window and pulled up the blinds. Light came flooding in, and the prison disappeared. There was a thick line of white salt lining the edge of the glass.

"Amma. She must have come yesterday while we were with Aunt Grace and Aunt Mercy." I smiled to myself, shaking my head. "I'm surprised she only left salt."

"Actually —" Lena pulled a mysterious-looking burlap bundle, tied with twine, from under Aunt Prue's pillow. She smelled it and made a face. "Well, it's not lavender."

168

"I'm sure it's for protection."

Lena pulled the chair closer to the bed. "I'm glad. I'd be scared, lying here all by myself. It's too quiet." She reached for Aunt Prue's hand, hesitating. The IV was taped across her knuckles.

Spotted roses, I thought. Those hands should be holding a hymnal, or a hand of gin rummy. A cat's leash or a map.

I tried to shake the slow-sinking wrongness. "It's okay."

"I'm not sure—"

"I think you can hold her hand, L."

Lena took Aunt Prue's tiny hand in both of her own. "She looks peaceful, like she's sleeping. Look at her face."

I couldn't. I reached out for her, awkwardly, and let my hand grab what I guess was her toe, where the lump of her foot poked the blanket up like a pup tent.

Ethan, you don't have to be afraid.

I'm not afraid, L.

You think I don't know how it feels?

How what feels?

To worry if someone I love is going to die.

I looked at her hovering over my aunt like some kind of Caster nurse.

I do worry, L. All the time.

I know, Ethan.

Marian. My dad. Amma. Who's next?

I looked at Lena.

I worry about you.

Ethan don't—

Let me worry about you.

"Ethan, please." There it was. The talking. The talking that

169

came when the Kelting became too personal. It was one step back from thinking, and one step away from changing the subject entirely.

I didn't let it drop. "I do, L. From the second I wake up until I fall asleep, and then in my dreams every second in between."

"Ethan. Look at her."

Lena moved next to me and put her hand on mine, until both of us were touching the tiny bandaged hand that belonged to Aunt Prue. "Look at her eyes."

I did.

She looked different. Not happy, not sad. Her eyes were milky, unfocused. She looked gone, like the nurse said.

"Aunt Prue isn't like the others. I bet she's far away exploring, like she always wanted to. Maybe she's finishing her map of the Tunnels right now." Lena kissed me on the cheek and stood up. "I'm going to see if there's somewhere to get a drink. Do you want something? Maybe they have chocolate milk."

I knew what she was really doing. Giving me time alone with my aunt. But I didn't tell her that, or that I couldn't stand the taste of chocolate milk anymore. "I'm okay."

"Let me know if you need me." She pulled the door closed behind her.

Once Lena left, I didn't know what to do. I stared at Aunt Prue lying in the hospital bed with tubes threaded in and out of her skin. I lifted her hand gently in mine, careful not to disturb her IV. I didn't want to hurt her. I was pretty sure she could still feel pain. I mean, she wasn't dead—that's what I kept reminding myself.

I remembered hearing somewhere that you're supposed to

talk to people in comas because they can hear you. I tried to think of something to tell her. But the same words kept playing over and over in my mind.

I'm sorry. It's my fault.

Because it was true. And the weight of it—the guilt—was so heavy I could feel it bearing down on me all the time.

I hoped Lena was right. I hoped Aunt Prue was somewhere making maps or stirring up trouble. I wondered if she was with my mom. Could they find each other, wherever they were?

I was still thinking about it when I closed my eyes for a second....

I could feel Aunt Prue's bandaged hand in mine. Only when I looked down at the bed, Aunt Prue was gone. I blinked, and the bed was gone, then the room. And I was nowhere, looking at nothing, hearing nothing.

Footsteps.

"Ethan Wate, that you?"

"Aunt Prue?"

She came shuffling out of the absolute nothingness. She was there and not there, flickering in and out of sight in her best housedress, the one with the loud flowers and the pearly-looking snaps. Her slippers were crocheted in the same rainbow of browns as Aunt Grace's favorite afghan.

"Back so soon?" She waved the handkerchief in her curled hand. "Told you last night, I got things ta do while I'm out an' about like this. Can't keep runnin' ta me every time you need the answer ta some durned question I don't know."

"What? I didn't visit you last night, Aunt Prue."

She frowned. "You tryin' ta play tricks on a old woman?"

"What did you tell me?" I asked.

"What did you ask?" She scratched her head, and I realized with a rising panic that she was beginning to fade away.

"Are you coming back, Aunt Prue?"

"Can't say just yet."

"Can you come with me now?"

She shook her head. "Don't you know? That's up ta the Wheel a Fate."

"What?"

"Sooner or later, it crushes us all. That's what I told you, remember? When you asked 'bout comin' over here. Why're you askin' so many questions today? I'm bone tired, an' I need ta get me some rest."

She was almost gone now.

"Leave me be, Ethan. Don't ya be lookin' ta come downside. The Wheel ain't done with you."

I watched as her brown crocheted slippers disappeared.

———— ᘓ

"Ethan?" I could hear Lena's voice and feel her hand on my shoulder, shaking me awake.

My head felt heavy, and I opened my eyes slowly. Bright light poured in from the unblinded window. I had fallen asleep in the chair next to Aunt Prue, the way I used to fall asleep on my mom's chair, waiting for her to finish up in the archive. I looked down, and Aunt Prue was lying on her bed, milky eyes open as if nothing had happened. I dropped her hand.

I must have looked spooked, because Lena looked worried. "Ethan, what is it?"

"I—I saw Aunt Prue. I talked to her."

"While you were asleep?"

I nodded. "Yeah. But it didn't feel like a dream. And she wasn't surprised to see me. I had already been there."

"What are you talking about?" Lena was watching me carefully now.

"Last night. She said I came to see her. Only I don't remember." It was becoming more common, and more frustrating. I was forgetting things all the time now.

Before Lena could say anything, the nurse rapped on the door, opening it just a crack.

"I'm sorry, but visiting hours are over. You'll have to let your aunt have some rest now, Ethan."

She sounded friendly, but the message was clear. We were out the door and into the empty hall before my heart had time to stop pounding.

—ᘓ

On the way out, Lena realized she had left her bag in Aunt Prue's room. While I waited for her to get it, I walked through the hallway slowly, stopping at a doorway. I couldn't help it. The boy in the room was about my age, and for a minute I found myself wondering what it would be like to be in his place. He was still sitting up at the table, and his hand was still writing. I looked up and down the hall, then slipped into his room.

"Hey, man. Just passing through."

I sat down on the edge of the chair in front of him. His eyes didn't even flicker in my direction, and his hand didn't stop moving. Over and over, he had written a hole into his paper, even into the sheet underneath.

I tugged on the paper, and it moved, an inch or so.

The hand stopped. I looked at his eyes.

Still nothing.

I tugged the paper again. "Come on. You write. I'll read. I want to hear it, whatever you have to say. Your masterpiece."

The hand began to move. I pulled the paper, a millimeter at a time, trying to match the speed of the writing.

this is the way the world ends this is the way the world ends this is the way the world ends on the eighteenth moon the eighteenth moon the eighteenth moon this is the way the world

The hand stopped, a thin line of drool spilling across the pen and the paper.

"I got it. I hear you, man. The Eighteenth Moon. I'll figure it out."

The hand began to write again, and this time I let the words write over themselves until the message was lost once again.

"Thanks," I said quietly. I looked past him, to where his name was written in dry-erase marker on the little whiteboard that was not and would never be on the door of anyone's dorm room.

"Thanks, John."

End of Days

It's some kind of sign." I was driving Lena home, and we were tearing down Route 9. She kept glancing at the speedometer.

"Ethan, slow down." Lena was as spooked as I was, but she was doing a good job of hiding it.

I couldn't get away from County Care fast enough, the peach walls and sickening smell, the broken bodies and empty eyes. "His name was John, and he was writing 'the world ends on the Eighteenth Moon' over and over. And his chart said he was in a motorcycle accident."

"I know." Lena touched my shoulder, and I could see her hair curling in the breeze. "But if you don't slow down, I'm going to do it for you."

The car slowed, but my mind was still racing. I took my hands off the wheel, and it didn't even swerve. "You want to drive? I can pull over."

"I don't want to drive, but if we end up in County Care, we won't be able to figure this out." Lena pointed at the road. "Watch where you're going."

"But what does it mean?"

"Well, let's think about what we know."

I dragged my mind back to the night Abraham showed up in my room. The first time I really believed John Breed was still alive. The night that started it all. "Abraham comes looking for John Breed. Vexes destroy the town and put Aunt Prue in the hospital. And I meet some guy named John there, who warns me about the Eighteenth Moon. Maybe it's some kind of warning."

"It's like the Shadowing Song." She was right. "And then there's your father's book."

"I guess." I still couldn't bring myself to think about how my dad fit into any of this.

"So the Eighteenth Moon and John Breed are connected somehow." Lena was thinking out loud.

"We need to know when the Eighteenth Moon is. How do we figure that out?"

"Well, that depends. Whose Eighteenth Moon are we talking about?" Lena looked out the window, and I said the one thing she didn't want to hear.

"Yours?"

She shook her head. "I don't think it's mine."

"How do you know?"

"My birthday is a long way off. And Abraham seems pretty desperate to find John." She was right. Abraham wasn't looking for her this time. He wanted John. Lena was still talking. "And that guy's name wasn't Lena."

I wasn't listening anymore.

His name wasn't Lena. It was John. And he was scribbling messages about the Eighteenth Moon.

I almost swerved off the road. The hearse righted itself, and I gave up, taking my hands back off the wheel. I was too freaked out to drive. "Do you think it could be about John Breed's Eighteenth Moon?"

Lena twisted her charm necklace around her finger, thinking. "I don't know, but it fits."

I took a deep breath. "What if everything Abraham said was true, and John Breed is still alive? What if something even worse is going to happen on his Eighteenth Moon?"

"Oh my God," Lena whispered.

The car jerked to a stop in the middle of Route 9. A truck horn blared, and I saw a blur of faded red metal spin around us. For a minute, neither one of us said a word.

The whole world was spinning out of control, and there was nothing I could do to stop it.

—⁀ᒡ

After I dropped Lena off at Ravenwood, I wasn't ready to go home. I had some thinking to do, and I couldn't do it there. Amma would take one look at me and know something was wrong. I didn't want to walk into the kitchen and pretend everything was okay—that I hadn't seen Amma making some kind of deal with the voodoo equivalent of a Dark Caster. That I hadn't spoken to Aunt Prue while she was lying, unresponsive, in her peach-colored prison. Or watched a random guy named John send me a message saying the end of the world was coming.

177

I wanted to face the truth—all the heat and the bugs and the dried-up lake, the broken houses and busted roofs and cosmic Orders I couldn't fix. The consequences Lena's Claiming had brought on the Mortal world and Abraham's wrath had brought on my town. As I drove down Main, it looked a hundred times worse in the daylight than it had a few nights ago in the dark.

The shop windows were all boarded up. You couldn't see Maybelline Sutter chatting up her customers while she cut their hair too short or dyed it a shade of bluish white at the Snip 'n' Curl. You couldn't see Sissy Honeycutt stuffing vases full of carnations and baby's breath at the counter of Gardens of Eden, or Millie and her daughter serving up biscuits and red-eye gravy a few doors down.

They were in there, but Gatlin wasn't a town of glass windows anymore. It was a town of locked doors and stockpiled pantries, a town full of folks waiting for the next twister or the end of the world, depending on who you asked.

So I wasn't surprised to see Link's mom standing in front of the Evangelical Baptist Church when I turned down Cypress Grove. Close to half the folks in Gatlin were there, Methodists and Baptists alike—on the sidewalk, the lawn, anywhere they could elbow themselves a spot. Reverend Blackwell was standing in front of the chapel doors, underneath the words ONLY ROOM FOR THE RIGHTEOUS IN HEAVEN. The sleeves of his white button-down were rolled up, his shirt wrinkled and untucked. He looked like he hadn't slept in days.

He was holding a bullhorn—not that he needed it. He called out into the crowd of people, who were waving their own cardboard signs and crosses as if he was Elvis back from the dead.

178

"The Bi-ah-ble"—he always gave the word three syllables—"tells us there will be signs. Seven seals to mark the End a Days."

"Amen! Praise the Lord!" the crowd shouted back. One voice stood out above the rest, of course. Mrs. Lincoln was standing at the base of the steps, her DAR lackeys huddled around her, arm in arm. She was carrying her own homemade sign, with the words THE END IS NEAR written in bloodred marker.

I pulled over next to the curb, the heat smacking me in the face the second the car stopped moving. The crooked oak shading the church was swarming with lubbers, the sun shining off the armor of their black backs.

"Conflict! Drought! Pestilence!" Reverend Blackwell paused, looking up at the pathetic, dying oak. " 'Fearful sights and great signs from heaven.' That's the Gospel a Luke." He bowed his head respectfully for a second, then lifted it with a renewed sense of determination in his eyes. "Now, I have seen some fearful sights!"

The crowd nodded in agreement.

"A few nights ago, a tornado came down from the heavens like the finger a God! And it touched us, crushed the very framework a this fair town! A fine family lost their home. Our town library, home to the words a God and man, burned to the ground. You think that was an accident?" The reverend defending the library? That was a first. I wished my mom was here to see it.

"No!" Folks were shaking their heads, at rapt attention.

He pointed out into the crowd, moving his finger across the sea of faces as if he was speaking to each person individually. "Then I ask you, was it a great sign from heaven?"

"Amen!"

"It was a sign!" someone else shouted.

Reverend Blackwell clutched the Bible to his chest like a life preserver. "The Beast is at the gates, with his army a deee-mons!" I couldn't help but remember what John Breed had called himself. A Demon Soldier. "And he's comin' for us. Will you be ready?"

Mrs. Lincoln thrust her flimsy sign into the air, and the other disturbingly distinguished ladies of the DAR did the same in a show of solidarity. THE END IS NEAR knocked into HONK FOR THE HOLY GHOST and nearly ripped I BRAKE FOR REDEMPTION right off its taped-up yardstick handle.

"I'll be ready to fight the Devil back to his own door with my bare hands if I have to!" she shouted. I believed her. If we were actually dealing with the Devil, we may have stood a chance with Mrs. Lincoln leading the charge.

The reverend held the Bible over his head. "The Bi-ah-ble promises there will be more signs. Earthquakes. Persecution an' tortures a the e-lect." He closed his eyes in rapture, a sign of his own. " 'And when these things begin to come to pass, then look up, an' lift up your heads, for your re-demption draweth nigh.' Luke 21:28." He dropped his head dramatically, his message delivered.

Mrs. Lincoln couldn't contain herself any longer. She grabbed the bullhorn in one hand, waving her sign in the other. "The demons are comin', and we have to be ready! I've been sayin' it for years! Lift your heads up and watch for them. They may be standin' at your back door! They may be walkin' among us now!"

It was ironic. For once, Link's mom was right. The Demons

were coming, but the folks in Gatlin weren't prepared for this kind of fight.

Even Amma—with her dolls that weren't dolls and her tarot cards that weren't tarot cards, her salt-lined windowsills and bottle trees—she wasn't ready for this fight. Abraham and Sarafine, with an army of Vexes? Hunting and his Blood Pack? John Breed, who was nowhere and everywhere?

Because of him, the end was near, and Demons were walking among us. It was all about him. He was the one to blame.

And if there was one thing I had become so intimately acquainted with that I could feel it crawling around under my skin, the way lubbers were crawling all over that oak, it was blame.

Jeopardy

It was getting late when I finally made it home. Lucille was waiting on the front porch, her head tilted to the side as if she was waiting to see what I was going to do. When I opened the door and headed down the hall toward Amma's room, I finally knew. I wasn't ready to confront her, but I needed her help. John Breed's Eighteenth Moon was too big for me to face on my own, and if anyone would know what to do, it was Amma.

Her bedroom door was closed, but I could hear her rummaging around in there. She was muttering, too, but her voice was too soft for me to make out anything she was saying.

I knocked on the door lightly, my head pressed against the cool wood.

Please let her be okay. Just tonight.

She opened the door far enough for her to peek through the crack. She was still wearing her apron, and she held a threaded needle in one hand. I looked past her into the dim light of her bedroom. Her bed was covered with scrap material, spools of thread, and herbs. She was making her dolls, no doubt. But something was off. It was the smell—that awful combination of gasoline and licorice I remembered from the bokor's shop.

"Amma, what's going on?"

"Nothin' you need to worry about. Why don't you get on upstairs and do some a your schoolwork?" She didn't look me in the eye, and she didn't ask where I'd been.

"What's that smell?" I searched the room, looking for the source. There was a thick black candle on her dresser. It looked exactly like the one the bokor had been burning. There were tiny hand-sewn bundles piled up around it. "What are you making in there?"

She was flustered for a second, but then she pulled herself together and shut her door behind her. "Charms, same as I always do. Now you get on upstairs and worry about what's goin' on in that mess you call a room."

Amma had never burned what smelled like toxic chemicals in our house before, not when she was making her dolls or any kind of charms. But I couldn't tell her I knew where that candle had come from. She would skin me alive if she knew I'd been in that bokor's shop, and I needed to believe there was a reason for all this—one I just didn't understand. Because Amma was the closest thing I had to a mother, and like my mother, she had always protected me.

Still, I wanted her to know I was paying attention—that I knew something was wrong. "Since when do you burn candles that smell like they belong in a science lab when you make your dolls? Horsehair and—"

My mind was completely blank.

I couldn't remember what else she stuffed inside those dolls—what was inside the jars that lined her shelves. Horsehair, I could picture that jar. But what were in the other ones?

Amma was watching me. I didn't want her to realize that I couldn't remember. "Forget it. If you don't want to tell me what you're really doing in there, fine."

I stormed down the hall and out the front door. I leaned against one of the porch beams, listening to the sound of the lubbers eating away at our town—the way something was eating away at my mind.

Out on my front porch, the growing dark was equal parts warm and sad. Through the open window, I could hear pans clattering, floorboards complaining as Amma beat the kitchen into submission. She must have given up on the charms for tonight. The familiar rhythm of her sounds didn't cheer me up like it usually did, though. It made me feel guiltier, which made my heart pound harder, which made me pace faster, until the floorboards on the porch were groaning almost as loud as the ones in the kitchen.

On either side of the wall, we were both full of secrets and lies.

I wondered if the worn wooden floor in Wate's Landing was the only place in Gatlin that knew all the skeletons in my family's closet. I'd ask Aunt Del to take a look, if her powers ever started working again.

It was dark now, and I needed to talk to someone. Amma wasn't an option anymore. I pressed number three on my speed dial. I didn't want to admit that I couldn't remember the number I'd called a hundred times.

I was forgetting things all the time now, and I didn't know why. But I knew it wasn't good.

I heard someone pick up. "Aunt Marian?"

"Ethan? Are you all right?" She sounded surprised to hear my voice on the other end of the line.

I'm not all right. I'm scared and confused. And I'm pretty sure none of us are going to be all right.

I forced the words out of my head, lowering my voice. "Yeah. I'm fine. How are you holding up?"

She sounded tired. "You know, Ethan, your mom would be proud of this town. I've had more people come in and volunteer to help rebuild the library than ever came in the whole time it was standing."

"Yeah, well. I guess that's the thing about burning books. It all depends on who burns them."

Her voice lowered. "Any luck with the answer to that? Who burned them?" The way she said it, I could tell it was all she'd thought about—and this time, she knew Mrs. Lincoln wasn't the culprit.

"That's why I'm calling. Can you do me a favor?"

Can you make everything the way it used to be, when my biggest problem was getting stuck reading car magazines at the Stop & Steal with the guys?

"Anything."

Anything that doesn't get me involved in a way I can't be. That's what she meant.

"Can you meet me at Ravenwood? I need to talk to you and Macon—and everyone, I guess."

Silence. The sound of Marian thinking. "About this?"

"Sort of."

More silence. "Things aren't good for me right now, EW. If the Council of the Far Keep thought I was violating the rules again—"

"You're going to visit a friend at his house. That can't be against the rules." Could it? "I wouldn't ask if it wasn't important. It's about more than the library, the heat—what's happening in town. It's about the Eighteenth Moon."

Please. You and Amma are all I have, and she's gone darker than she ever has. And I can't talk to my mom. So it has to be you.

I knew the answer before she said a word. If there was one thing I loved about Marian, it was how she always heard what was being said, even if no one was saying it. "Give me a few minutes."

I snapped my phone shut and tossed it onto the step next to me. Time for another call, no phone required. I stared up at the sky. The stars were starting to come out, the moon already waiting.

L? Are you there?

There was a long pause, and I could feel Lena slowly begin to relax her mind into mine until we were connected again.

I'm here, Ethan.

We need to figure this out. After what happened at County Care, we can't waste any more time. Find your uncle. I already called Marian, and I'll pick up Link on my way over.

What about Amma?

I wanted to tell her what happened tonight, but it hurt too much.

She's in a bad place right now. Can you ask your gramma?

She's not here. But Aunt Del is. And it will be hard to leave Ridley out.

That wasn't going to help the situation, but if Link was coming, it was going to be impossible to keep her away.

You never know, we might get lucky. Maybe Rid will be too busy sticking pins in little cheerleader voodoo dolls.

Lena laughed, but I didn't. I couldn't imagine dolls that didn't smell like the poison burning in Amma's room. I felt a kiss on my cheek, even though I was alone on the porch.

On my way.

I didn't bring up the name of the other person who would be there. Then again, neither did Lena.

Back inside, Aunt Grace and Aunt Mercy were watching *Jeopardy!*, which I hoped would be a good distraction, since Amma knew all the answers and pretended she didn't. And the Sisters knew none and insisted they did.

"It sleeps for three years? Well, conchashima, Grace. I sure as sin know that one, and I ain't tellin' ya the answer." *Conchashima* was Aunt Mercy's made-up curse word, which she saved for occasions when she really wanted to irritate one of her sisters, since she refused to tell them what it meant. I was pretty sure she didn't know either.

Aunt Grace sniffed. "Conchashima yourself, Mercy. What did all a Mercy's husbands do when they were supposed ta be makin' a livin'? That's the answer they're lookin' for."

"Now, Grace Ann, I think they're really askin' how long you slept through the sermon last Easter Sunday. Droolin' under my good cabbage rose hat."

"It said three years, not three hours. And if the good rev'rend didn't like ta hear his own voice so much, maybe it'd be easier for the rest a us ta hear it. You know I can't see anythin' but feathers an' flowers sittin' behind Dot Jessup in that big old Easter bonnet, anyhow."

"Snails." They looked at Amma blankly. She untied her apron. "How long can a snail sleep? Three years. And how long are you girls going to make me wait to have my supper? And where on God's green earth do you think you're goin', Ethan Wate?"

I froze at the door. There was no distracting Amma, ever.

True to form, Amma had no intention of letting me go out alone at night—not after Abraham and the fire at the library and Aunt Prue. She hauled me into the kitchen so fast you would've thought I'd sassed her.

"Don't you think I don't know when you're full a blue mud." She looked around the kitchen for the One-Eyed Menace, but I had beaten her to it and stuck it in the back pocket of my jeans. She didn't have a pencil either, so she was unarmed.

I made my move. "Amma, it's nothing. I told Lena I'd have dinner with her family." I wished I could tell her the truth, but I couldn't. Not until I figured out what she was doing with that bokor in New Orleans.

She cocked a hip and let me have it. "On pulled pork night? My own three-time blue-ribbon-winnin' Carolina Gold, and you're expectin' me to believe that claptrap?" She sniffed and shook her head. "You'd settle for a peacock patty on a gold plate over *my* pulled pork?" Amma didn't think much of Kitchen's cooking, and she had a point.

"No. I just forgot." It was the truth, even though she had mentioned dinner this morning.

"Hmm." She didn't believe me. Which was understandable, considering that on a normal night this would be my idea of heaven.

"D. I. S. S. E. M. B. L. I. N. G. Eleven across. As in, you're up to somethin', Ethan Wate, and it's not dinner."

She was up to something, too. But I didn't have a crossword for that.

I leaned down and put my arms around her. "I love you, Amma. You know that?" It was true.

"Oh, I know plenty. I know you're about as far from the truth as Wesley's mamma is from a bottle a whiskey, Ethan Wate." She pushed me off, but I'd gotten to her. Amma, standing in this sweltering kitchen, scolding me whether I deserved it or not and whether she meant it or not.

"You don't have to worry about me. You know I'll always come home."

She softened for a moment, putting her hand on my face, shaking her head. "That peach you're peddlin' sure smells sweet, but I'm still not buyin' it."

"Be back by eleven." I grabbed the car keys off the counter and gave her a peck on the cheek.

"Not a hair past ten or you'll be givin' Harlon James a bath tomorrow—and I mean all a them!" I backed out of the kitchen before she could stop me. And before she noticed I had taken the One-Eyed Menace with me.

———⌒℈

"Check it out." Link was hanging out the window of the Volvo, and the car started tilting in his direction. "Whoa."

189

"Sit down."

He flopped back down into his seat. "See those black ditches? It looks like someone set off napalm or shot a flamethrower all the way up the road, heading straight for Ravenwood. And then it stopped."

Link was right. Even in the moonlight, I could see the deep grooves, at least four feet wide, on both sides of the dirt road. A few feet from the gates of Ravenwood, they disappeared.

Ravenwood was untouched, but the full scale of the attack on Lena's house the night Abraham unleashed the Vexes must have been massive. She never said it was this bad, and I hadn't asked. I was too worried about my own family, and my house, and my library. My town.

Now I was staring at the damage, and I hoped this was the worst of it. I pulled over to the side of the road, and we both got out. It was a given that pyrotechnics on this scale were worth a closer look.

Link squatted next to the black trail in front of the gate. "It's thickest when you get up close to the house. Right before it disappears."

I picked up a black branch, and it crumbled in my hand. "This isn't what Aunt Prue's house looked like. That was more like a tornado. This was some kind of fire, more like the library."

"I don't know, man. Maybe Vexes do different things to different—people, or whatever."

"Casters are people."

Link picked up another branch, inspecting it. "Yeah, yeah. We're all people, right? All I know is, this thing is fried."

"Do you think it was Sarafine? Fire is sort of her thing." I hated to consider it, but it was possible. Sarafine wasn't dead. She was out there somewhere.

"Yeah, she's hot, all right." He noticed me staring at him like he was nuts. "What? I can't call it like I see it?"

"Sarafine's the Queen of Darkness, dumbass."

"Seen a movie lately? The Queen a Darkness is always totally hot. Third Degree Burns." He wiped the ash from the crumbling branch off his hands. "Let's get outta here. Somethin' around here is givin' me a headache. You hear that buzzin' sound, like a whole bunch a chainsaws or somethin'?"

The Binding Casts. He could feel them now.

I nodded, and we started the car. The rusty, crooked gates opened into the shadows, as if they were expecting us.

You here, L?

I shoved my hands into my pockets and looked up at the great house. I could see the windows, the splintering wood shutters overgrown with ivy, as if Lena's room hadn't changed at all. I knew it was an illusion, and from where Lena stood in her bedroom she could see me through the glass walls.

I'm trying to get Reece to stay upstairs with Ryan, but she's being as cooperative as usual.

Link was looking up at the portico to the window opposite Lena's.

What happened with Ridley?

I asked her if she wanted to come. I figured she's going to notice everyone showing up. She said she would, but who knows? She's been acting so weird lately.

If Ravenwood had a face, Lena's room would be one blinking eye, and Ridley's window, the other. The ramshackle shutters were open, though they hung unevenly, and the window behind them was filthy. Before I turned away, a shadow passed behind Ridley's window. At least I thought it was a shadow; in the moonlight it was hard to tell.

I couldn't see who it was. They were too far away. But the window began to rattle, harder and harder, until the shutter swung off its hinge and slid down beneath the window entirely. Like someone was trying really hard to yank it open, even if it meant bringing the whole house down. For a second, I thought it was an earthquake, but the ground wasn't moving. Only the house was.

Weird.

Ethan?

"Did you see that?" I looked at Link, but he was staring up at the chimney now.

"Look. The bricks are fallin'," he said.

The shudder grew stronger, and some kind of energy surged through the entire house. The front door shook.

Lena!

I took off running for the door. I could hear things crashing and breaking inside. I reached up and pushed on the lintel, the Caster carving hidden above the door. Nothing happened.

Hold on, Ethan. Something's wrong.

Are you okay?

We're fine. Uncle Macon thinks something is trying to get in.

From out here, it looked more like someone was trying to get out.

The door opened, and Lena pulled me inside. I felt the thick

192

curtain of power as I moved across the threshold. Link dove in after me, and the door slammed behind us. After what I had experienced outside, I was relieved to be in the house. Until I looked around.

By now I was used to the constantly changing interior of Ravenwood Manor. I had seen everything from historic plantation antiques to classic horror-movie Gothic in this room, but I was completely unprepared for this.

It was some sort of supernatural bunker, the Caster equivalent of Mrs. Lincoln's cellar, where she stored supplies for everything from hurricanes to the apocalypse. The walls were covered in what looked like armor—sheets of dull silver metal from floor to ceiling, and the furniture was gone. Stacks of books and velvet armchairs had been replaced by huge plastic drums and cases of candles and scotch. There was a bag of dog food that was obviously for Boo, though I had never seen him eat anything but steaks.

A row of white jugs looked suspiciously like the supply of bleach Link's mom kept around to "prevent infection from spreading." I walked over and picked up one of the jugs. "What's this? Some kind of Caster disinfectant?"

Lena took it out of my hand and lined it up next to the others. "Yeah, it's called bleach."

Link knocked on one of the plastic drums. "My mom would love this place. It would definitely score some points for your uncle. Forget about your thirty-six-hour pack and your seventy-two-hour pack. Those are for lightweights. This is some serious disaster prep. I'd say you've got enough for a good three weeks here. Except you don't have a crowbar."

I looked at him blankly. "A crowbar?"

"For diggin' the bodies out a the rubble."

"Bodies?" Mrs. Lincoln was crazier than I thought.

Link looked back at Lena. "And you guys don't have any food."

"That is where Casters differ, Mr. Lincoln." Macon was standing in the doorway to the dining room, looking perfectly relaxed. "Kitchen is quite capable of supplying whatever we need. But it is important to be prepared. This afternoon is certainly evidence of that."

He gestured toward the dining room, and we followed him in. The black claw-foot table was gone, replaced by a shiny aluminum one that looked like something from a medical research lab. Link and I must have been the last to arrive, because there were only two empty seats at the table.

If I ignored the weird lab table and sheet metal on the walls, it reminded me of the Gathering, when I met Lena's family for the first time. Back when Ridley was still Dark and had tricked me into bringing her into Ravenwood. It seemed almost funny now. A world where Ridley was the biggest threat.

"Please, take a seat, Mr. Wate and Mr. Lincoln. We're trying to determine the origin of the tremors."

I slipped into one of the two empty chairs beside Lena, and Link took the other. Judging from the number of people around the table, I wasn't the only one with something on my mind, but I didn't say that. Not to Macon.

I know. It's like he was expecting us. When I told him you were coming, he didn't seem surprised. And everyone started showing up.

Marian leaned forward, into the pool of light that fell to the table from the nearest candle. "What happened out there? We could feel it inside."

I heard a voice behind me. "I don't know, but we could feel it outside, too."

In the shadows, I could see Macon gesture at the table. "Leah, why don't you take the seat on Ethan's left?" By the time I turned, an empty chair had appeared between Link and me, and Leah Ravenwood was in it.

"Hey, Leah." Link saluted her. Her eyes widened as she noticed the change in him. I wondered if she could sense her own kind.

"Welcome, brother." Her black hair fell out of the ponytail at her neck, and for a second I remembered the nurse at County Care.

"Leah. It was you with Aunt Prue."

"Shh. We have more important things to discuss." She squeezed my hand and winked, which was her way of answering the question. It had been Leah watching over my aunt for me.

"Thank you."

"It's nothing. I just do as I'm told." She was lying. Leah was as independent as Lena.

"You never do what you're told."

She laughed. "Fine, then I do as I like. And I like to keep an eye on my family. My family, your family, it's all the same."

Before I could say anything else, Ridley burst into the room, wearing something that looked more like underwear than clothes. The candles flamed up for a second; Ridley still managed to have an effect on this room.

"I don't see my name on any of the place cards. But I know I was invited to the party. Right, Uncle M?"

"You're more than welcome to join us." Macon sounded calm. He was probably used to Ridley's outbursts by now.

"What exactly are you wearing, sweetheart?" Aunt Del raised a hand to her eye, as if she was having trouble seeing any clothes on Ridley's body at all.

Ridley unwrapped a piece of gum, tossing the wrapper onto the table. "So, which is it? Welcome or invited? I like to know the size of the snub. I sulk better that way."

"Ravenwood is your home now, Ridley." Macon tapped his fingers impatiently but smiled as if he had all the time in the world.

"Actually, Ravenwood belongs to my *cousin*, Uncle M. Since you gave it to her and blew off the rest of us." She was on a serious rampage tonight. "What, no grub? Oh, that's right. Kitchen isn't herself. None of you supernatural types are. Ironic, isn't it? I'm in a room full of all these über-powerful people, and you can't manage to get dinner on the table."

"The mouth on that girl." Aunt Del shook her head.

Macon gestured for Ridley to sit down. "I would appreciate it if you could be respectful of the minor . . . issues we all seem to be having."

"Whatever." Ridley dismissed Macon with a wave of her hot-pink nails. "Let's get this party started." She hitched up the strap of whatever it was she had on. Even by Ridley's standards, she wasn't wearing much.

"Aren't you cold?" Aunt Del whispered.

"It's *vintage*," Ridley snapped.

"From what? The Moulin Rouge?" Liv stood in the doorway, her arms full of books.

Ridley flicked Liv's braid as she stepped past Liv to the nearest open seat. "As a matter of fact, Pippi—"

"Please." Macon silenced both of them with a look. "I'm impressed with the theatrics, Ridley. A bit less so with the costume. Now, if you'd take a seat." Macon sighed. "Olivia, thank you for joining us."

Ridley squeezed into the chair that had appeared next to Link, ignoring him as attentively as possible. He winked. "Don't know what kinda store Moo Landrews is, but if they get one at the mall in Summerville, I'm gettin' your birthday present there." Ridley kept her eyes fixed in front of her, pretending not to notice him noticing her.

Macon began. "Olivia, did you feel the tremors?"

I kept my eyes trained on Macon's face. But I heard Liv sit down and toss what I imagined was her red notebook onto the table and begin winding the gears on her selenometer. I knew all of her sounds, the way I knew Link's or Amma's or Lena's.

"If you don't mind, Sir Macon." Liv pushed a stack of books and papers across the table toward him. "With that last one, I wanted to make sure I had the exact measurements."

"Go on, Olivia." Lena tensed when Macon said Liv's name. I could feel it, coming in waves at me from her direction.

Liv kept talking, oblivious. "Basically, it's getting worse. If the numbers are accurate, there's a singular energy attracted to this house." Great. All I needed was for Liv to start talking about attraction.

"Interesting." Macon nodded. "So it is growing stronger, as we suspected?"

The "we" must have gotten to Lena.

I'm so tired of her.

"Liv?" Crap. I accidentally said her name out loud. What was wrong with me? I couldn't even keep Kelting and talking straight. Lena stared at me, stunned.

"Yes, Ethan?" Liv was waiting for me to ask her a question.

The whole table turned in my direction. I had to come up with something. What were we talking about?

Attraction.

"I was wondering…"

"Yes?" Liv looked at me expectantly. I was glad Reece wasn't in the room, even if her powers were out of whack. A Sybil would see what I was feeling.

And I didn't need a selenometer to prove it or measure it for me. Even though we would never be anything more than friends, Liv and I would always mean something to each other.

My stomach contracted. This time, it wasn't killer bees. More like Vexes gnawing on my internal organs.

"Vexes," I said out of nowhere. Everyone was still staring at me.

Liv nodded patiently, waiting for me to say something that made sense. "Yes. There has been a great deal more than the usual amount of activity lately."

"No. I mean, what if we're assuming something's trying to get into Ravenwood because of everything Abraham has been throwing at us?"

Marian looked at me blankly. "My library was nearly burned to the ground. Your aunts' house was destroyed. It's a fairly safe assumption, wouldn't you say?"

Everyone in the room looked at me like I was an idiot, but I kept going. "What if we're wrong? What if someone is doing this from the inside?"

Liv lifted an eyebrow.

Ridley threw up her hands. "That's the stupidest—"

"It's brilliant, actually," Liv said.

"Of course *you* think so, Mary Poppins." Ridley rolled her eyes.

"I do. And unless you have more convincing math, you'll have to shut up and listen to me for once." Liv turned to Macon. "Ethan could be right. There's an anomaly in the numbers I haven't been able to explain. But if I were to flip everything, it makes perfect sense."

"Why would someone be doing this from the inside?" Lena asked.

I kept my eyes focused on the red notebook on the table— the rows of numbers, the things that were safe and known.

"The question isn't why." Macon's voice sounded strange. "It's who."

Lena glanced at Ridley. We were thinking the same thing.

Ridley jumped out of her chair. "You think it's me? I'm always the one who gets blamed for everything that goes wrong around here!"

"Ridley, calm down," Macon said. "No one—"

But she cut him off. "Did you ever consider that the numbers on Little Miss Perfect's crappy watch could be wrong? No, that would be impossible, because she has all of you eating out of her hand!"

Lena smiled.

It's not funny, L.

I'm not laughing.

Macon raised his hand. "Enough. It's quite possible something isn't trying to get into Ravenwood at all. It may already be here."

"Don't you think we'd notice if one of Abraham's Dark creatures had breached the Bindings?" Lena sounded unconvinced.

Macon rose from his seat, his eyes fixed on me. He was looking at me the same way he had the first night we met, when I showed him Genevieve's locket at this table. "A valid point, Lena. Assuming we are dealing with a breach."

Leah Ravenwood studied her brother. "Macon, what are you thinking?"

Macon walked around the table until he was standing directly across from me. "I'm more interested in what Ethan is thinking." Macon's green eyes started to glow. They reminded me of the luminescent color from the Arclight.

"What's going on?" I whispered to Leah, who looked shocked.

"I knew Macon's powers changed when he became a Caster. But I had no idea he could Mindhunt."

"What does that mean, exactly?" It didn't sound good, considering that Macon was completely focused on me.

"The mind is a labyrinth, and Macon can navigate his way through it."

It sounded like one of Amma's answers, the kind that doesn't really tell you anything. "You mean he can read minds?"

"Not the way you're thinking. He can sense disturbances and anomalies, things that don't belong." Leah was staring at Macon.

His green pupils were glowing and sightless now, yet I knew he was watching me. It was disturbing to be seen without being seen. Macon stared at me for a long minute. "You, of all people."

"I what?"

"It seems you have brought something—no, *someone*—here with you this evening. An uninvited guest."

"Ethan would never do that!" Lena sounded as surprised as I was.

Macon ignored her, still watching me. "I can't quite put my finger on it, but something has changed."

"What are you talking about?" A sick feeling was building inside me.

Marian stood up slowly, as if she didn't want to startle him. "Macon, you know the Order is affecting everyone's powers. You aren't immune. Is it possible you are perceiving something that isn't there?"

The green light faded from Macon's eyes. "Anything is possible, Marian."

My heart was pounding in my chest. A second ago he was accusing me of bringing someone into Ravenwood, and now he had what—changed his mind?

"Mr. Wate, it seems you are not yourself. Something quite significant is missing. Which explains why I sensed a stranger in my house, even if the stranger is you."

Everyone was staring at me. I felt my stomach lurch, as if the ground was still moving beneath my feet. "Missing? What do you mean?"

"If I knew, I would tell you." Macon started to relax. "Unfortunately, I'm not entirely sure."

I didn't know what Macon was talking about, and I didn't care anymore. I wasn't going to sit here and be accused of things I hadn't done, because his powers were all screwed up and he was too arrogant to deal with it. My world was collapsing around me, and I needed answers. "I hope you had fun hunting, or whatever you call it. But that's not what I came to talk about."

"What did you come to talk about?" Macon sat back down

at the head of the table. He said it like I was the one wasting everyone's time, which only made me angrier.

"The Eighteenth Moon isn't about Ravenwood or Lena. It's about John Breed. But we don't know where he is or what's going to happen."

"I think he's right." Liv chewed on the end of her pen.

"I thought you might want to know so we can find him." I stood up. "And I'm sorry if I don't seem like myself. Maybe it has something to do with the fact that the world is falling apart."

Ethan, where are you going?

This is bullshit.

"Ethan, calm down. Please." Marian started to get up.

"Tell that to the Vexes that destroyed the whole town. Or Abraham and Sarafine and Hunting." I looked right at Macon. "Why don't you turn your X-ray vision on them?"

Ethan!

I'm done here.

He doesn't mean—

I don't care what he means, L.

Macon was watching me.

"There are no coincidences, right? When the universe warns me about something, it's usually my mom talking. So I'm going to listen." I walked out before anyone could say anything. I didn't need to be a Wayward to see who was lost.

⊰ 10.04 ⊱

Rubbery Chicken

All I could see was fire. I felt the heat and saw the color of the flames. Orange, red, blue. Fire was so many more colors than people thought.

I was in the Sisters' house, and I was trapped.

Where are you?

I looked down at my feet. I knew he would be there any minute. Then I heard the voice, through the flames below me.

I'M WAITING.

I ran down the stairs, toward the voice, but the staircase crumbled under my feet, and suddenly I was falling. As the floor gave way, I hit the basement beneath me, my shoulder crashing through the burning wood below.

I saw orange, red, blue.

I realized I was in the library, when I should have been in Aunt Prue's basement. Books were burning all around me.

Da Vinci. Dickinson. Poe. And another one.

The Book of Moons.

And I saw a flash of gray that wasn't part of the fire at all.

It was him.

The smoke swallowed me, and I blacked out.

I woke up on the floor. When I looked in the bathroom mirror, my face was black with soot. I spent the rest of the day trying not to cough up ash.

I had been sleeping even worse than usual since my argument with Macon, or whatever you'd call it. Fighting with Macon usually led to fighting with Lena, which was more painful than fighting with everyone I knew combined. But now everything was different, and Lena didn't know what to say any more than I did.

We tried to avoid thinking about what was happening around us—the things we couldn't stop and the answers we couldn't find. But it was always lurking in the back of our minds, even if we didn't admit it. We tried to focus on things we could control, like keeping Ridley out of trouble and the lubbers out of our houses. Because when every day is the End of Days, after a while they feel pretty much like every other day, even though you know that's crazy. And nothing is the same.

The bugs got hungrier, the heat got hotter, and the whole town got crazier. But more than anything, it was still the heat we all noticed. It was proof that no matter who was scoring or dating or lying in a bed at County Care—underneath everything, from the minute you woke up in the morning to the minute you fell asleep, and all the minutes in between—something was wrong and it wasn't getting better. It was getting worse.

But I didn't need to feel the heat outside to prove it to me. I had all the proof I needed inside—in our kitchen. Amma was practically connected to our old stove on a cellular level, and when something was going on in her head, it found its way into the kitchen. I couldn't figure out what was going on with her, and she sure wasn't going to tell me. I could only piece it together from the few clues she left, in the language she used the most—cooking.

Clue number one: rubbery chicken. Rubbery chicken was useful, mostly in terms of establishing a state of mind and a timeline, like rigor mortis on a cop show. For Amma, who was famous in three counties for her chicken 'n' dumplings, rubbery chicken meant two things: a) she was distracted, and b) she was busy. She didn't just forget to take the chicken out of the oven. She didn't have time to deal with it once it was out. So the chicken sat too long in the heat, and even longer on the cooling rack. Waiting for Amma to come around, like the rest of us. I wanted to know where she was and what she was up to all that time.

Clue number two: a general lack of pie. Pie was gone, and when it wasn't, there was no sign of Amma's famous lemon meringue. Which meant a) she wasn't speaking to the Greats, and b) she definitely wasn't speaking to Uncle Abner. I hadn't checked the liquor cabinet, but a lack of Jack Daniels would seal the deal for Uncle Abner, too.

I wondered if her little trip to the bokor had anything to do with that.

Clue number three: the sweet tea was unspeakably sweet, which meant a) the Sisters were sneaking into the kitchen and dumping sugar in the pitcher, the way they did with salt in the gravy, b) Amma was so out of it she couldn't keep track of how many cups of sugar she was dumping in, or c) something was wrong with me.

Maybe all three, but Amma was up to something, and I was determined to find out what. Even if I had to ask that bokor myself.

Then there was the song. With every passing day, I heard it with greater frequency, like one of those Top 40 songs that plays on the radio so much that it's always stuck in your head.

Eighteen Moons, eighteen fears,
The cries of Mortals fade, appear,
Those unknown and those unseen
Crushed in the hands of the Demon Queen...

The Demon Queen? Seriously? After the literal translation of the Vex verse, I didn't want to imagine what a run-in with a Demon Queen could mean. I hoped my mom had confused it with homecoming queen.

But the songs were never wrong.

I tried not to think about the cries of Mortals or the hands of the Demon Queen. But the thoughts I refused to think, the conversations that remained unspoken, the fears I never confessed, the dread building inside me—I couldn't escape them. Especially not at night, when I was safe in my room.

Safe, and the most vulnerable.

I wasn't the only one.

Even within the Bound walls of Ravenwood, Lena was just as vulnerable. Because she had something from her mother, too. And I knew she was touching one of the things in that dented metal box when I saw the orange glow of the flames—

The fire ignited, flames curling around the gas burner one by one, until they created a single, beautiful blazing circle on the stovetop. Sarafine watched, fascinated. She forgot about the pot of water on the counter. She forgot about dinner most nights now. She couldn't think about anything but the flames. Fire had energy—power that defied even the laws of science. It was impossible to control, leveling miles of forest in minutes.

Sarafine had been studying fire for months. Watching theoretical ones on the science channel, and real ones on the news. The television was on all the time. The second there was a mention of a fire, she would stop whatever she was doing and rush to watch. But that wasn't the worst part. She had started using her powers to set small fires. Nothing dangerous, only tiny ones in the woods. They were like campfires. Harmless.

Her fascination with fire had started around the same time as the voices. Maybe the voices drove her to watch things burn; it was impossible to know. The first time Sarafine heard the low voice in her mind, she had been doing the laundry.

This is a miserable, worthless life—a life equal to death. A waste of the greatest gift the Caster world has to offer. The power to kill and destroy, to use the very air we breathe to fuel your weapon. The Dark Fire offers itself. It offers freedom.

The laundry basket dropped, and clothes spilled out onto the floor. Sarafine knew the voice wasn't her own. It didn't sound like her, and the thoughts were not her own. Yet they were in her mind.

The greatest gift the Caster world has to offer. *The gifts of a Cataclyst—that's what it meant. It's what happened when a Natural went Dark. And no matter how much Sarafine wanted to pretend it wasn't true, she was Dark. Her yellow eyes reminded her every time she looked in the mirror. Which wasn't often. She couldn't stand the sight of herself, or the possibility that John might see those eyes again.*

Sarafine wore dark sunglasses all the time, even though John didn't care what color her eyes were. "Maybe they'll brighten up this dump," he said one day, looking around the tiny apartment. It was a dump—peeling paint and broken tiles, heat that never worked and electricity that shorted out all the time. But Sarafine would never admit it, because it was her fault they were living there. Nice places didn't rent to teenagers who were obviously runaways.

They could've afforded a better place. John always came up with plenty of money. It wasn't hard to find things to pawn, when you could make objects disappear right out of people's pockets or store windows. He was an Evanescent, like most of history's great magicians—and thieves. But he was also Light, using his gift in this vile way to keep them alive.

To keep her alive.

The voices reminded her of that every day.

If you leave, he can use his parlor tricks to impress Mortal girls, and you can do what you were born for.

She shook the voices out of her head, but the words left a shadow, a phantom image that never entirely disappeared. The voices were the strongest when she was watching things burn—the way she was now.

Before she realized it, the kitchen towel was smoking, blackened edges curling inward like an animal recoiling in fear. The smoke alarm screamed.

Sarafine slapped the towel against the floor until the flames turned into a sad trail of smoke. She stared at the charred towel, crying. She had to throw it away before John saw it. She could never tell him about this. Or the voices.

It was her secret.

Everyone had secrets, right?

A secret couldn't hurt anyone.

I sat up with a start, but my room was still. My window was shut, even though the heat was so stifling that the sweat running down my neck felt like the slow crawl of spiders. I knew a closed window couldn't keep Abraham out of my room, but somehow it made me feel better.

I was overwhelmed by an irrational panic. With every settling board, every creaking stair, I expected to see Abraham's face emerge from the darkness. I looked around, but the dark in my room was simply the dark.

I kicked off the sheet. I was so hot, I'd never be able to fall back to sleep. I grabbed the glass from my nightstand and poured some water on my neck. For a second, cool air swept over me, before the heat swallowed me back up again.

"You know, it's going to get worse before it gets better."

When I heard the voice, I almost jumped out of my skin.

I looked over and my mom was sitting in the chair in the corner of my room. In the chair I had laid out my clothes on the day of her funeral, then never sat in again. She looked the way she had in the cemetery the last time I saw her—kind of blurry around the edges—but she was still my mom in all the important ways.

"Mom?"

"Sweetheart."

I crawled out of bed and sat on the floor next to her, my back against the wall. I was afraid to get too close, afraid I was dreaming and she would disappear. I just wanted to sit by her for a minute, like we were in the kitchen talking about my day at school or something trivial. Whether or not it was real.

"What's going on, Mom? I've never been able to see you like this before."

"There are..." She hesitated. "Certain circumstances that allow you to see me. I don't have time to explain. But this isn't like before, Ethan."

"I know. Everything is worse."

She nodded. "I wish things were different. I don't know if there is a happy ending this time. You need to understand that."

I felt a lump in my throat, and I tried to swallow it away.

"I can't figure this out. I know it has something to do with John Breed's Eighteenth Moon, but we can't find him. I don't know what we're supposed to be fighting. The Eighteenth Moon? Abraham? Sarafine and Hunting?"

She shook her head. "It's not that simple, or that easy. Evil doesn't always have one face, Ethan."

"Yes, it does. We're talking about Light and Dark. Things don't get any more black and white than that."

"I think we both know that isn't true." She was talking about Lena. "You're not responsible for the whole world, Ethan. You aren't the judge of it all. You're just a boy."

I reached up and threw myself at my mom, into her lap. I expected my hands to pass right through her. But I could feel her, as if she was really there, as if she was still alive, even though when I looked at her she was still hazy. I clung to her until my fingers dug into her soft, warm shoulders.

It felt like a miracle to touch her again. Maybe it was.

"My little boy," she whispered.

And I smelled her. I smelled everything—the tomatoes frying, the creosote she used to cover her books with in the archive. The smell of freshly cut graveyard grass, from the nights we spent there, watching those light-up crosses.

For a few minutes she held me, and it felt like she had never left at all. Then she let go, but I was still holding on to her.

For a few minutes, what we had, we knew.

Then I started to sob. I cried in a way I hadn't since I was a kid. Since I fell down the stairs racing Matchbox cars on the banister, or off the top of the jungle gym in the schoolyard. This fall hurt more than any physical one ever could.

Her arms encircled me, as if I was a kid. "I know you're angry at me. It takes a while to feel the truth."

"I don't want to feel it. It hurts too much."

211

She hugged me tighter. "If you don't feel it, you won't be able to let it go."

"I don't want to let go."

"You can't fight fate. It was my time to go." She sounded so sure, so at peace. Like Aunt Prue, when I was holding her hand at County Care. Or Twyla, when I saw her slipping away to the Otherworld on the night of the Seventeenth Moon.

It wasn't fair. The people who were left behind never got to feel that sure of anything.

"I wish it wasn't."

"Me too, Ethan."

"Your time to go. What does that mean, exactly?"

She smiled at me as she rubbed my back. "When the time comes, you'll know."

"I don't know what to do anymore. I'm afraid I'm going to screw things up."

"You'll do the right thing, Ethan. And if you don't, the right thing will find you. The Wheel of Fate is like that."

I thought about what Aunt Prue said to me. *The Wheel of Fate...It crushes us all.*

I looked my mom in the eye and noticed her face was streaked with tears, just like mine. "What is it, Mom?"

"Not it, my sweet boy." She touched my cheek as she began to fade softly back into the warm darkness. "Who."

⊰ 10.09 ⊱

Catfight

A few days later, I was sitting in the good booth at the Dar-ee Keen, which unofficially belonged to Link now. Some nervous freshmen actually cleared out when we got there. I remembered my freshman year when that was Link and me. He was nodding at girls as they walked by our booth, and I was eating my weight in Tater Tots.

"They must be buying a different kind or something. These are actually good." I popped another Tater Tot into my mouth. I hadn't touched one in years. But today, they'd looked good up on the grimy menu board.

"Dude, I think you're losin' it. Even I never ate those things."

I shrugged as Lena and Ridley slid into the booth with two malts. Ridley started drinking both of them. "Mmm. Raspberry."

"Is that a first for you, Rid?" Link looked happy to see her. They were speaking again. I gave it five minutes until the bickering set in.

"Mmm. Oreo. Oh my God." She stuck the straws into her mouth and started drinking both malts at the same time.

Lena looked disgusted and pulled out a bag of french fries. "What are you doing?"

"I wanted raspberry Oreo," Ridley mumbled, the straws slipping out of her mouth.

I pointed at the sign over the register that read: ANYTHING YOU WANT, ANY WAY WE GOT IT. "You know you can order it like that."

"I'd rather do it my way. It's more fun. What are we talking about?"

Link tossed a wad of folded-up flyers onto the table. "The big deal is Savannah Snow's party after the game against Summerville."

"Well, have fun." I stole one of Lena's fries.

Link made a face. "Aw, man, first the Tater Tots, now this? How can you eat that crap? Smells like dirty hair and old oil." He sniffed again. "And a rat or two."

Lena dropped the bag.

I grabbed another fry. "You used to eat this crap all the time. And you were a lot more fun."

"Well, I'm about to get more fun, because I scored you guys invites to Savannah's party. We're all going." He unfolded the orange flyers, and there they were: four orange invites, each cut in a circle and decorated to look like a basketball.

Lena picked up one by the corner as if it was actually covered in dirty hair and old oil. "The golden ticket. Guess that makes us the cool kids now."

Link didn't pick up on her sarcasm. "Yeah, I hooked y'all up."

Ridley slurped her malts. She had drained both of them down to the dregs. "Actually, I did."

"What?" I couldn't have heard her right.

"Savannah invited the whole squad, and I told them I needed to bring my entourage. You know, for security or whatever." She put down the glasses. "You can thank me later. Or now."

"Say that again?" Lena looked at her cousin like she was crazy.

Ridley seemed confused. "You're my entourage?"

Lena shook her head. "The other part."

"Security?"

"Before that."

Rid thought for a second. "Squad?"

"That." Lena said it like it was a four-letter word.

It had to be a joke. I looked at Link, who was purposely not looking at me.

Ridley shrugged. "Yeah, whatever. Team thingy. I forget the name. I like the skirts. Besides, this gig is the closest I can get to being a Siren, as long as I'm trapped in this lame Mortal body." She gave us her best fake smile. "Go, Wildcats."

Lena was speechless. I could feel the windows of the Dar-ee Keen begin to rattle as if a gale force wind was hitting them. Which it probably was.

I crumpled up my napkin. "Are you kidding? You're one of them now?"

"What?"

"The Savannah Snows and Emily Ashers—the kind of girls

who harassed us all the time in school," Lena snapped. "The ones we hate."

"I don't see what you're getting so worked up about."

"Oh, I don't know. Maybe it's because you joined the same squad that started a club to get me kicked out of school last year. You know, the Jackson High cheer-slash-death squad?"

Ridley yawned. "Whatever. Tell me something that has to do with me."

I looked at the windows out of the corner of my eye. They were still rattling. A tree branch flew against one, as if it had been tossed up out of the ground like a weed. I pulled one of Lena's curls straight between my fingers.

Calm down, L.

I'm calm.

She doesn't mean to hurt you.

No. Because she doesn't notice, or care.

I turned to Link, who was sitting with his arms behind his head, enjoying our reactions. "Did you know about this?"

Link grinned. "Haven't missed a practice." I stared him down. "Aw, come on. She looks pretty hot in those short skirts. Third Degree Burns, Baby."

Ridley smiled.

I was pretty sure Link had lost his mind. "And you think this is a good idea?"

He shrugged. "I don't know. Whatever floats her boat. And you know what they say: Keep your friends close and your enemies' clothes.... Wait, how does that go?"

I looked at Lena.

This I gotta see.

The windows rattled harder.

The next afternoon, we went to see for ourselves. The girl had moves. You had to give her that. Even if Ridley wore her cheerleading skirt with a metallic tank top instead of the standard gold and blue uniform, you couldn't deny it.

"I wonder if she's good at this because she was a Siren." I watched as Ridley pulled back handsprings down the length of the basketball court.

"Yeah. I wonder." Lena didn't look too convinced.

"What, you think there's some kind of cheer Cast? Is there a Latin word for cheerleader?"

Lena watched Ridley nail another handspring. "I'm not sure, but I'm going to find out."

We watched from the highest bleacher, and after the first ten minutes of practice, it was obvious what was really going on. The real reason Ridley joined the squad. She was replacing Savannah, in every possible way. Rid was the base, holding up the team during the pyramid. She was leading the cheers and, in a few cases, making them up on the fly, as far as I could tell. The rest of the squad was stumbling behind her, trying to copy her seemingly random moves.

When Ridley cheered, her shouts were so loud she actually distracted the guys on the court. Or maybe it was the metallic tank top. "Give it to me, Wildcat boys! You can be my Wildcat toys! Bounce your balls and shoot 'em high. Ridley's come to Jackson High."

The guys on the team started laughing, except for Link. He looked like he wanted to chuck a basketball at her. Only

217

someone else was going to beat him to it. Savannah jumped off the bench, her arm still in a sling, and made a beeline for Ridley.

"I'm guessing that's not one of their approved cheers."

Lena put her head in her hands. "I'm guessing, between Ridley and Savannah, we'll all be kicked out of school by the end of the season." We both knew what happened when you took on women like Mrs. Snow. Not to mention Savannah Snow.

"Well, you've got to give Ridley credit for one thing. It's October, and she's still at Jackson. She made it longer than three days."

"Remind me to bake her a cake when I get home." Lena was annoyed. "The last time we went to school together, I spent half my time doing her homework. Otherwise, she would've gotten every boy in school to do it for her. That's the only way she knows how to operate."

Lena rested her head on my chest. Our fingers intertwined, and I felt a jolt. Even though my skin would start to burn in a few minutes, it was worth it. I wanted to remember that feeling—not the jolt, but the touch before it. The way her hand felt in mine.

I never thought there would be a time when I'd need to remember. When she would be anywhere but in my arms. Until last spring, when she left me, and the memories—some too painful to remember, some too painful to forget—were all I had. Those were the things I held on to.

Sitting next to her on my front steps.

Kelting with her while I was lying in bed and she was in hers.

The way she twisted her charm necklace when she was lost in thought, like she was doing right now, while she watched the game.

The nothing-out-of-the-ordinary between us that was so unbelievable and so extraordinary. It wasn't because she was a Caster. It was because she was Lena and I loved her.

So I watched her as she watched Ridley and Savannah. Until the drama courtside grew louder, and nothing was silent—even though you didn't need to hear what they were saying to know what was going on.

"Okay, that's a rookie mistake." Lena narrated the action for me as Savannah got into Ridley's face. Ridley was snarling like an alley cat. "See what I mean? You can't come at Rid like that without expecting to get your face clawed off." Lena tensed up. I could tell she was debating going down there before things got ugly.

Emory beat her to it, luring Ridley over to the sidelines. Savannah tried to look angry, but she was obviously relieved.

So was Lena. "That almost makes me like Emory."

"You can't solve all of Ridley's problems for her."

"I can't solve any of them. I've spent my whole life not solving Ridley's problems."

I nudged her with my shoulder. "That's why they're Ridley's problems."

She relaxed and settled back on the bleacher. "When did you get so Zen?"

"I'm not Zen." Was I? In the back of my mind, all I could think about was my mom and the beyond-the-grave wisdom that was uniquely hers. Maybe it was creeping into the front of my mind. "My mom came to see me." I regretted saying it as soon as the words came out of my mouth.

Lena sat up so fast my arm went flying. "When? Why didn't you tell me? What did she say?"

"A few nights ago. I didn't feel like talking about it." Especially not after I'd watched Lena's mother plunge further into Darkness in the vision that same night. But it was more than that. I was coming unglued—talking to my unconscious aunt in my sleep, forgetting things when I was awake—and the impossibly heavy weight of doom lurking in the back of my mind. I didn't want to admit how bad it was getting—to Lena or to myself.

Lena turned back to the basketball court. Her feelings were hurt. "Well, you're full of information today."

I wanted to tell you, L. But it was a lot to take in.

You could have told me like this.

I was trying to sort some things out. I think I've been mad at her all this time, like I blamed her for dying. How crazy is that?

Ethan, think about how I acted when I thought Uncle Macon was dead. I went crazy.

It wasn't your fault.

I'm not saying it was. Why is everything about fault with you? It wasn't your mom's fault she died, but a part of you still blames her. It's normal.

We sat next to each other on the bench without talking. Watching the cheerleaders cheer and the basketball players play below us.

Ethan, why do you think we found each other in our dreams?

I don't know.

It's not the way people usually meet.

I guess not. Sometimes I wonder if this is all one of those psychotic coma dreams. Maybe I'm lying in County Care right now.

I almost laughed, but I remembered something.

County Care.

The Eighteenth Moon. I asked my mom about it.

About John Breed?

I nodded.

All she said was something about evil having a lot of faces, and that it wasn't up to me to judge.

Ah. The judging thing. See? She agrees with me. I knew your mom would like me.

I had one more crazy question.

L, have you ever heard of the Wheel of Fate?

No. What is it?

According to my mom, it's not a thing. It's a person.

"What?" I caught Lena off guard, and she stopped Kelting.

"The weird thing is, I keep hearing that phrase—the Wheel of Fate. Aunt Prue mentioned it, too, when I fell asleep in her room. It must have something to do with the Eighteenth Moon, or my mom wouldn't have brought it up."

Lena stood up and held out her hand. "Come on."

I got up after her. "What are you doing?"

"Leaving Ridley to solve her own problems. Let's go."

"Where are we going?"

"To solve yours."

⊰ 10.09 ⊱

Good-Eye Side

Apparently Lena believed the answer to my problems was waiting at the Gatlin County Library, because five minutes later we were there. A chain-link fence surrounded the building, which looked more like a construction site than a library now. The missing half of the roof was covered with enormous blue plastic tarps. The doorway was flanked by the carpet that had been ripped up from the concrete floor, destroyed as much by the water as the fire. We stepped over the charred boards and walked inside.

The opposite side of the library was sealed off with heavy plastic. It was the one that had burned. I didn't want to know what it looked like over there. The side where we were standing was just as depressing. The stacks were gone, replaced by boxes of books that looked like they'd been sorted into piles.

The destroyed. The partly destroyed. The salvageable.

Only the card catalog sat there, untouched. We would never get rid of that thing.

"Aunt Marian! You here?" I wandered past the boxes, expecting to see Marian in her stocking feet, walking around with an open book.

Instead, I saw my dad, sitting on a box behind the card catalog, talking enthusiastically to a woman.

There was no way.

Lena stepped in front of me so they wouldn't notice me looking like I was going to puke. "Mrs. English! What are you doing here? And Mr. Wate! I didn't know that you knew our teacher." She even managed a smile, as if running into them here was a pleasant coincidence.

I couldn't stop staring.

What the hell is he doing here with her?

If my dad was flustered, it didn't show. He looked excited— happy, even, which was worse. "Did you know Lilian knows almost as much about the history of this county as your mom did?"

Lilian? My mom?

Mrs. English looked up from the books scattered on the floor around her, and our eyes locked. For a second, her pupils looked slit-shaped, like a cat's. Even the glass eye that wasn't real.

L, did you see that?

See what?

But now there was nothing to see—only our English teacher blinking over her glass eye as she watched my father with her good one. Her hair was a graying mess that matched the lumpy gray sweater she was wearing over her shapeless dress. She was the toughest teacher at Jackson, if you ignored the loophole

223

most people chose to exploit—the Bad-Eye Side. I never imagined that she existed outside the classroom. But here she was, existing all over my dad. I felt sick.

My dad was still talking. "She's helping me with my research for *The Eighteenth Moon*. My book, remember?" He turned back to Mrs. English, grinning. "They don't hear a word we say anymore. Half my students are listening to their iPods or talking on their cell phones. They might as well be deaf."

Mrs. English looked at him strangely and laughed. I realized I'd never heard her laugh before. The laugh itself wasn't disturbing. Mrs. English laughing at my father's jokes was. Disturbing and gross.

"That's not entirely true, Mitchell."

Mitchell?

It's his name, Ethan. Don't panic.

"According to Lilian, the Eighteenth Moon could be viewed as a powerful historical motif. The phases of the moon could coordinate with—"

"Nice to see you, ma'am." I couldn't stand to hear my dad's theories on the Eighteenth Moon, or listen to him share them with my English teacher. I walked past them, toward the archive. "Be home by dinner, Dad. Amma's making pot roast." I had no idea what Amma was cooking, but pot roast was his favorite. And I wanted him home for dinner.

I wanted him to exist away from my English teacher.

She must have understood what my dad didn't, that I really didn't want to see her as anything but my teacher, because as soon as I tried to go, Lilian English disappeared and Mrs. English took her place. "Ethan, don't forget I need the outline for your essay on *The Crucible*. On my desk by the end of class tomorrow, please. You, too, Miss Duchannes."

"Yes, ma'am."

"I expect you have a thesis already?"

I nodded, but I had completely forgotten an essay was due, let alone an outline. English wasn't high on my list of priorities lately.

"And?" Mrs. English looked at me expectantly.

You gonna help me out here, L?

Don't look at me. I haven't thought about it.

Thanks.

I'll be hiding in the mess in the reference section until they leave.

Traitor.

"Ethan?" She was waiting for an answer.

I stared at her, and my father stared at me. Everyone was watching me. I felt like a goldfish trapped in a bowl.

What was the life span of a goldfish? It was one of the Sisters' *Jeopardy!* questions a few nights ago. I tried to think.

"Goldfish." I didn't know why I said it. But lately I was blurting out things without even thinking.

"I beg your pardon?" Mrs. English looked confused. My dad scratched his head, trying not to act embarrassed.

"I mean, what it's like living in a goldfish bowl—with other goldfish. It's complicated."

Mrs. English wasn't impressed. "Enlighten me, Mr. Wate."

"Judgment and free will. I think I'm going to write about judgment. Who has the power to decide what's good and what's evil, you know? Sin and all that. I mean, does it come from some kind of higher order, or does it come from the people you live with? Or your town?"

It was my dream talking, or my mom.

"And? Who has that power, Mr. Wate? Who is the ultimate judge?"

"I guess I don't know. Haven't written the paper yet, ma'am. But I'm not sure us goldfish have the right to judge each other. Look where it got those girls in *The Crucible*."

"Would someone *outside* the community have done a better job?"

A cold feeling crept over me, as if there actually was a right or wrong answer to the question. In English class, there were no right or wrong answers as long as you could find evidence to back up your opinion. But it didn't feel like we were talking about an English assignment anymore.

"Guess I'll be answering that in my paper." I looked away, feeling stupid. In class, it would've been a good answer, but standing in front of her now, it was something else.

"Am I interrupting?" It was Marian to the rescue. "I'm sorry, Mitchell, but I have to lock the library up early today. What's left of it. I'm afraid I've got some—official library business to attend to."

She looked at Mrs. English with a smile. "Please do come back. With any luck, we'll be back on our feet and open by the summer. We love having educators use our resources."

Mrs. English started collecting her papers. "Of course."

Marian had them out the door before my dad could ask why I wasn't leaving with him. She flipped the sign and twisted the lock—not that there was anything left to steal.

"Thanks for the save, Aunt Marian."

Lena stuck her head out from behind a stack of boxes. "Are they gone?" She was holding a book, wrapped in one of her

scarves. I could see the title, only partially covered by the sparkly gray fabric. *Great Expectations.*

Sarafine's book.

As if the afternoon hadn't been bad enough.

Marian pulled out a handkerchief and rubbed her glasses. "It
wasn't a save entirely. I am expecting some official visitors, and
I'm fairly certain it would be best if you two weren't here when
they arrive."

"I just need a minute. I have to grab my bag." Lena disappeared back into the boxes, but I was right behind her.

"What are you doing with that?" I grabbed the book, and
the second I touched it, the broken shelves faded into darkness—

*It was late, the first time she met him. Sarafine knew
she shouldn't be walking alone this late at night. Mortals were no threat to her, but she knew there were other
things out there. But the voices had started whispering
to her, and she had to get out of the house.*

*When she saw the figure at the corner, her heart
started to pound. But as the man moved closer, Sarafine
realized he was no threat. His long beard was white, the
same color as his hair. He was wearing a dark suit and a
string tie, leaning against a polished black cane.*

*He was smiling, as if they knew each other. "Good
evening, child. I've been waiting for you."*

*"Excuse me? I think you've mistaken me for some-
one else." She smiled. He was probably senile.*

*The old man laughed. "There's no mistaking you. I
know a Cataclyst when I see one."*

Sarafine felt the icy blood pumping through her veins.

He knew.

The fire flared up along the sidewalk, only a few feet from the old man's cane. Sarafine closed her eyes, trying to control it, but she couldn't.

"Let it burn. It is on the cold side tonight." He smiled, unaffected by the flames.

Sarafine was shaking. "What do you want?"

"Came to help you. You see, we're family. Maybe I should introduce myself." He held out his hand. "I'm Abraham Ravenwood."

She knew the name. She'd seen it on her half brothers' family tree. "Hunting and Macon said you were dead."

"Do I look dead?" He smiled. "Couldn't die just yet. I've been waiting for you."

"Me? Why?" Sarafine's own family wouldn't speak to her. It was hard to believe someone had been waiting for her.

"You don't understand what you are yet, do you? Are you hearing the call? The voices?" He looked into the flames. "I can see you've already found your gift."

"It's not a gift. It's a curse."

His head snapped back in her direction, and she could see his black eyes. "Now, who's been telling you that? Casters, I imagine." He shook his head. "Doesn't surprise me. Casters are liars, only one step removed from Mortals. But not you. A Cataclyst is the most powerful Caster in our world, and born from the Dark Fire. Too powerful to be considered a Caster at all, the way I see it."

Was it possible? Could she possess the most power-

ful gift in the Caster world? Part of her yearned for it to be true—to be special, rather than cast aside. A part of her that wanted to give in to the urges.

To burn everything in her path.

To make all the people who had hurt her pay.

No!

She forced the thoughts from her mind. John. She focused on John and his beautiful green eyes.

Sarafine was shaking. "I don't want to be Dark."

"Too late for that. You can't fight what you are." Abraham laughed, a sinister sound. "Now let's see those pretty yellow eyes of yours."

Abraham had been right. Sarafine couldn't fight what she was, but she could hide it. She had no other choice. She was two souls, battling for the same body. Right and wrong. Good and evil. Light and Dark.

John was the only thing that tethered her to the Light. She loved him, although sometimes that love was starting to feel more like a memory. Something far away she could see but never reach.

Still, she reached.

The memory was easiest to see when they were lying in bed, tangled up in each other.

"Do you know how much I love you?" John whispered, his lips barely grazing her ear.

Sarafine moved closer, as if his warmth could somehow soak into her cold skin and change her from the outside in. "How much?"

"More than anything or anyone. More than myself."

"I feel the same way." Liar. She could hear the voice even now.

John leaned down until their foreheads were touching. "I'm never going to feel this way about anyone else. It will always be you." His voice was low and raspy. "You're eighteen now. Marry me."

Sarafine could hear another voice in the back of her mind, a voice that came into her thoughts and dreams late at night. Abraham. You think you love him, but you don't. You can't love someone who doesn't know who you are. You're not really a Caster; you're one of us.

"Izabel?" John was staring back at her, searching in her eyes for the girl he'd fallen in love with. A girl who was being consumed little by little.

How much of her was left?

"Yes." Sarafine wrapped her arms around John's neck, tethering herself once more. "I'll marry you."

Lena opened her eyes. She was lying on the dirty concrete floor next to me, the toes of our sneakers almost touching. "Oh my God, Ethan. It started when she met Abraham."

"Your mom was already going Dark."

"You don't know that. Maybe she could have fought it, like Uncle Macon."

I knew how badly Lena wanted to believe there was some good in her mother. That she wasn't destined to be the murderous monster we both knew.

Maybe.

We stood up as Marian turned the corner. "It's getting late. As much as I've missed having you lounge around on the floor, I really need you to leave. This isn't pleasant business, I'm afraid."

"What do you mean?"

"The Council is paying me a visit."

"The Council?" I wasn't sure which one she was talking about.

"The Council of the Far Keep."

Lena nodded, and smiled sympathetically. "Uncle Macon told me. Is there anything we can do? Write letters or sign a petition? Hand out flyers?"

Marian smiled, looking tired. "No. They're just doing their job."

"Which is?"

"Making sure the rest of us follow the rules. I think this falls into the category of taking one's lumps. I am prepared to take responsibility for anything I've done. But nothing more. 'The price of greatness is responsibility.'" She looked at me expectantly.

"Um, Plato?" I guessed hopefully.

"Winston Churchill." She sighed. "That's all they can ask of me, and all I can ask of myself. Now it's time for you to go."

Now that Mrs. English and my dad were gone, I noticed that Marian was dressed in clothes that were very un-Marian. Instead of a brightly colored dress, she was wearing a black robe over a black dress. As if she was going to a funeral. Which was just about the last place I was going to let Marian go without me.

"We're not going anywhere."

She shook her head. "Except home."

"No."

"Ethan, I'm not sure that's a good idea."

"When Lena and I were the ones in front of the firing squad,

231

you walked right into the line of fire—you and Macon. There's no way I'm going anywhere."

Lena dropped down into one of the few remaining chairs and made herself comfortable. "Me neither."

"You're very kind, both of you. But I intend to keep you all out of this. I think it's better for everyone."

"Haven't you noticed whenever someone says that, it's never better for anyone, especially not the person saying it?" I looked at Lena.

Go get Macon. I'll stay here with Marian. I don't want her to go through this alone.

Lena was at the door, the lock unbolting itself, before Marian could say a word.

I'm on it.

I put my arm around Marian's shoulders and gave her a squeeze. "Isn't this one of those times when we should pull out a book that magically tells us everything is going to be okay?"

She laughed, and for a second she sounded like the old Marian, the Marian who wasn't on trial for things she didn't do, who wasn't worrying about things she couldn't help. "I don't recall the books we've found lately saying anything of the sort."

"Yeah. Let's stay away from the Ps. No Edgar Allan Poe for you today."

She smiled. "The Ps aren't all bad. There is always, for example, Plato." She patted my arm. 'Courage is a kind of salvation,' Ethan." She rummaged in a box and pulled out a blackened book. "And you'll be happy to know, Plato survived the Gatlin County Library's own Great Burning."

Things might be bad, but for the first time in weeks, I actually felt better.

⊰ 10.09 ⊱

Reckoning

W e were sitting in the archive, in the flickering candlelight. The room was relatively undamaged, which was a miracle. The archive had been soaked, not burned—thanks to the automatic sprinklers in the ceiling. The three of us waited at the long table in the center of the room, having tea from a Thermos.

I stirred mine absentmindedly. "Shouldn't the Council be visiting you in the *Lunae Libri*?"

Marian shook her head. "I'm not even sure if they want me back there. This is the only place they'll speak to me."

"I'm sorry," Lena said.

"There's nothing to be sorry about. I only hope—"

The cracking sound of lightning filled the room, then the rumble of thunder, and blinding flashes of light. Not the ripping sound of Traveling, but something new. The book appeared first.

The Caster Chronicles.

That was the name inscribed on the front. It landed on the table between us. The book was so massive that the table groaned under its weight.

"What's that?" I asked.

Marian put her finger to her lips. "Shh."

Three cloaked figures appeared, one after the next. The first, a tall man with a shaved head, held up his hand. The thunder and lightning stopped instantly. The second, a woman, flung a hood back over her shoulder to reveal an unnatural and overwhelming whiteness. White hair, white skin, and irises so white she appeared to be made of nothing at all. The last, a man the size of a linebacker, appeared between the table and my mother's old desk, disrupting her papers and books in the process. He was holding a large brass hourglass. But it was empty. There wasn't a single grain of sand inside.

The only thing the three of them had in common was what they had on. Each wore a heavy, hooded black robe and a strange pair of glasses, as if it was some kind of uniform.

I looked at the glasses more closely. They seemed to be made of gold, silver, and bronze, twisted together into one thick braid. The glass in the lenses was cut into facets, like the diamond in my mother's engagement ring. I wondered how they could see.

"*Salve*, Marian of the *Lunae Libri*, Keeper of the Word, the Truth, and the World Without End." I almost jumped out of my skin, because they spoke in perfect unison, as if they were one person. Lena grabbed my hand.

Marian stepped forward. "*Salve*, Great Council of the Far Keep. Council of the Wise, the Known, and That Which Cannot Be Known."

"You know for what purpose we have come to this place?"

"Yes."

"Have you anything to say other than that which we know?"

Marian shook her head. "I do not."

"You admit to taking action inside the Order of Things, in violation of your sacred oath?"

"I allowed one who was in my charge to do so, yes."

I wanted to explain, but between the perfectly hollow sound of their choral voices and the white eyes of the woman, I could barely breathe.

"Where is the one?"

Marian pulled her own robe tighter around her body. "She isn't here. I sent her away."

"Why?"

"To keep her from harm," Marian answered.

"From us." They said it without even the slightest hint of emotion.

"Yes."

"You are wise, Marian of the *Lunae Libri*."

Marian didn't look as wise right now. She looked terrified. "I have read about *The Caster Chronicles*—the stories and records of the Casters you keep. And I know what you've done to Mortals who have transgressed as she has. And to Casters."

They studied Marian like an insect under glass. "You care for this one? The Keeper who is not to be? A girl child?"

"Yes. She is like a daughter to me. And she is not for you to judge."

The voices rose. "You do not speak to us of our powers. We speak to you of yours."

Then I heard another voice, one I had heard so many times

before when I'd felt this helpless. "Now, gentlemen, madam, that's not the way we speak to ladies of good report here in the South." Macon was standing behind us, with Boo Radley at his feet. "I'm going to have to ask you to conduct yourselves with a little more respect for Dr. Ashcroft. She is a *beloved* Keeper of this community. Beloved by many, who possess great power in the Caster and Incubus worlds alike."

Macon was impeccably dressed. I was pretty sure he was in the same suit he wore to the Disciplinary Committee Meeting, when he showed up to rescue Lena from Mrs. Lincoln and her lynch mob.

Leah Ravenwood materialized next to him in her black coat, holding her staff. Bade, her mountain lion, growled, pacing in front of Leah. "My brother speaks the truth. Our family supports him, and the Keeper. You should know that before you continue down this road. She doesn't stand alone."

Marian looked at Macon and Leah gratefully.

Someone stepped through the doorway behind Leah. "And if there's anyone to blame, it's me." Liv walked past Leah and Macon. "Aren't I the one you've come to punish? I'm here. Have at it."

Marian grabbed Liv's hand, refusing to let her go any farther.

The Council regarded her solemnly. "The Incubus and the Succubus are of no concern to us."

"They're standing in for my family," Liv said. "I have no one else except Professor Ashcroft."

"You are brave, child."

Liv didn't move or let go of Marian's hand. "Thank you."

"And foolish."

"So I've been told. Quite often, actually." Liv looked at them as if she wasn't the least bit afraid, which I knew was impossible. But her voice didn't waver. Like she was relieved this moment was finally happening, and she could stop dreading it.

The Council wasn't finished with her. "You held a sacred trust and chose to break it."

"I chose to help a friend. I chose to save a life. I'd do it again," Liv answered.

"Those were not your decisions to make."

"I accept the consequences of my actions. Like I said, I'd do it all again if I had to. That's what you do for the people you love."

"Love is not our concern," the voices answered as one.

"'All you need is love.'" Liv was quoting the Beatles to the Council of the Far Keep. If she was going down, she was going down in style.

"You understand what it is you say?"

Liv nodded. "Yes."

The Council members looked around the room, their eyes moving from Liv and Marian to Macon and Leah.

Lightning cracked, and the room filled with heat and energy. *The Caster Chronicles* radiated light.

The tall man spoke to the other two, his voice deeper without theirs blending into it. "We will take what has been spoken to the Far Keep. There is a price to be paid. It shall be paid."

Macon bowed. "Have a safe journey. Be sure to visit us if you're ever passing through our fair town again. I do hope you can stay longer next time and try some of our famous buttermilk pie."

The woman with the milky white eyes removed her glasses and stared in Macon's direction. But it was impossible to tell what she was really looking at, because her eyes didn't move at all.

The lightning cracked again, and they were gone.

Thunder rumbled while the book lingered on the table for another second. Then it disappeared, following the dark figures into the light.

"Bloody hell!" Liv collapsed into Marian's arms.

I stood frozen in place.

Hell didn't begin to cover it.

Once Macon was satisfied that the Keepers were gone, he moved toward the door. "Marian, I hate to leave you, but there are a few things I want to look into. Or rather, look up."

Liv recognized her cue and started to follow him.

But Macon wasn't looking at Liv. "Lena, I'd like you to come with me if you don't mind."

"What?" Lena looked confused.

But not as confused as Liv, who was already gathering her notebook. "I can help. I know where all the books are—"

"That's quite all right, Olivia. The sort of information I'm looking for is not in the books you've read. The Far Keep doesn't provide other Keepers with access to information regarding the origins of the Council. Those records are kept by Casters." He nodded at Lena, who was already shoving her things into her bag.

"Of course. Yes." Liv looked hurt. "I can only imagine."

Macon paused at the door. "Leah, would you mind leaving Bade? I believe Marian could use her company tonight." Which really meant he didn't want to leave Marian alone, without a two-hundred-pound bodyguard on the premises.

Leah scratched the big cat's head. "Not at all. I have to get back to County Care anyway, and they aren't partial to animals."

Bade circled the table where we were sitting, finally settling on a spot beside Marian.

Lena looked at me, and I could tell she didn't want to leave me alone with Liv and Marian, but she didn't want to let Macon down either. Especially not when he was asking for her help, instead of Liv's.

Go on, L. It's fine. I don't mind.

Her answer was a very public kiss and a meaningful look at Liv. Then they were gone.

After they left, I sat in the archive with Liv and Marian, drawing out the moment as long as we could. I couldn't remember the last time the three of us were alone together, and I missed it. Liv and Marian tossing around quotes, and me always coming up with the wrong answer.

Liv finally stood up. "I have to go. I don't want you to get in any more trouble."

Marian stared into the bottom of her teacup. "Olivia, don't you think I could have stopped you if I'd wanted to?"

Liv looked like she couldn't decide whether to laugh or cry. "You weren't even there when I helped Ethan release Macon from the Arclight."

"I was there when you took off into the Tunnels with Ethan and Link. I could've stopped you then." Marian took a shaky breath. "But I had a friend once, too. And if I could turn back the clock—if there was anything I could've done to save her—I would have done it. Now she's gone, and there's nothing I can do to get her back."

I squeezed Marian's hand.

"I'm sorry," Liv said. "And I'm sorry I got you into so much trouble. I wish I could persuade them to leave you alone."

"You can't. No one can. Sometimes everyone does the right thing and there's still a mess left to clean up. Someone has to take responsibility for it."

Liv stared at a water-stained box on the floor. "It should be me."

"I disagree. This is my chance to help another friend, one I love very much." Marian smiled and reached for Liv's hand. "And there has to be at least one librarian in this town—Keeper or not."

Liv threw her arms around Marian and hugged her like she was never going to let go. Marian gave Liv one last squeeze and looked over at me. "EW, I'd appreciate it if you would see Liv back to Ravenwood. If I gave her my car, I'm afraid it would end up on the wrong side of the road."

I hugged Marian, whispering to her as I did. "Be careful."

"I always am."

We had to make a lot of detours to get anywhere in Gatlin now. So five minutes later, I was driving past my own house, with Liv in the passenger seat—like we were on our way to deliver library books or stop at the Dar-ee Keen. Like it was last summer.

But the overwhelming brown of everything and the buzzing of ten thousand lubbers reminded me it wasn't.

"I can almost smell the pie from here," Liv said, looking toward my house longingly.

I glanced at the open window. "Amma hasn't made a pie in a while, but you can probably smell her pecan fried chicken."

Liv groaned. "You've no idea what it's like living in the

Tunnels, especially when Kitchen is out of sorts. I've been living on my stash of HobNobs for weeks now. If I don't get another package soon, I'm doomed."

"You know, there is a little thing called the Stop & Steal around here," I said.

"I know. There's also a little thing called Amma's homemade fried chicken."

I knew where this conversation was heading all along and was halfway to the curb by the time she said it. "Come on. I bet you ten bucks she made biscuits, too."

"You had me at 'fried.'"

Amma gave Liv all the thighs, so I knew she was still feeling sorry for Liv after last summer. Luckily, the Sisters were asleep. I didn't feel like answering questions about why there was a girl at my house who wasn't Lena.

Liv stuffed her face faster than Link in his prime. By the time I was on my third piece, she was on her second plateful.

"This is the second-best piece of fried chicken I've ever tasted in my life." Liv was actually licking her fingers.

"Second best?" I was the one who said it, but I saw Amma's face when I did. Because by Gatlin standards, those two words alone were blasphemy. "What's better?"

"The piece I'm about to have. And possibly the piece after that." She slid her empty plate across the table.

I could see Amma smiling to herself as she added more Wesson oil to her five-gallon pot. "Wait till you taste a batch right outta the fryer. Can't say you've tried that, have you, Olivia?"

"No, ma'am. But I also haven't had any homemade food since the Seventeenth Moon." There it was again. The familiar cloud settled back over the kitchen, and I pushed my plate away. The extra-crispy crust was choking me.

Amma dried the One-Eyed Menace with a dishrag. "Ethan Lawson Wate. You go get our friend some a my best preserves. Back a the pantry. Top shelf."

"Yes, ma'am."

Amma called after me before I made it to the hall. "And none a that pickled watermelon rind. I'm savin' that for Wesley's mamma. It turned out sour this year."

The basement door was across from Amma's room. The wooden stairs were scarred with black marks, like a burnt marshmallow, from the time me and Link put a hot pot on the stairs when we were trying to make Rice Krispies Treats on our own. We almost burned a hole in one step, and Amma gave me stinkeye for days. I made sure to step on the mark every time I went down those stairs.

Going down into a basement in Gatlin wasn't all that different from going through a Caster Doorwell. Our basement wasn't the Tunnels, but I'd always thought of it as some kind of mysterious underworld. Under beds and in basements—that's where all the best secrets were kept in our town. The treasure might be stacks of old magazines in the furnace room, or a week's worth of icebox cookies from Amma's industrial freezer. Either way, you were going back up with an armload or a stomach full of something.

At the bottom of the stairs was a doorway framed in two-by-fours. No door, just a string hanging on the other side of the doorframe. I yanked the string as I had a thousand times before, and there was Amma's prized collection. Every house around here had a pantry, and this was one of the finest pantries in three counties. Amma's mason jars held everything from pickled watermelon rinds and the skinniest green beans to the roundest onions and the most perfectly green tomatoes. Not to mention the pie fillings and preserves—peach, plum, rhubarb, apple, cherry. The rows stretched back so far your teeth started to ache just from looking at them.

I ran my hand along the top shelf, where Amma kept all her prizewinners, the secret recipes and jars she saved for company. Everything in here was rationed, as if we were in the army and these jars were filled with penicillin or ammunition—or maybe land mines, because that's how carefully you had to hold them.

"It's quite a sight." Liv was standing in the doorway behind me.

"I'm surprised Amma let you down here. This is her secret stash."

She picked up a jar, holding it in front of her. "It's so shiny."

"You want your jelly to sparkle and your fruit not to float. You want your pickles cut to the same size, your carrots nice and round, your pack even."

"My what?"

"How it goes in the jar, see?"

"Of course." Liv smiled. "How would Amma feel if she knew you were sharing the secrets of her kitchen?"

If anyone knew them, it was me. I'd been by Amma's side in the kitchen longer than I could remember, burning my hands on everything I wasn't supposed to touch, sneaking rocks and twigs and all kinds of things into unsuspecting pans of preserves. "You want the liquid to cover the top of whatever's inside."

"Are bubbles good or bad?"

I laughed. "You'll never see a bubble in one of Amma's jars."

She pointed to the bottom shelf. There was a jar so full of bubbles you'd think the bubbles themselves were what Amma was trying to bottle, instead of the cherries. I knelt down in front of the shelf and pulled it out. It was an old mason jar covered in cobwebs. I had never noticed it before.

"That can't be Amma's." I rotated the jar in my hand. FROM THE KITCHEN OF PRUDENCE STATHAM. I shook my head. "It's my Aunt Prue's. She must have been crazier than I thought." Nobody ever gave Amma anything that came out of another kitchen. Not if they knew what was good for them.

As I slid the jar back in place, I noticed a dirty loop of rope hanging back in the shadow of the bottom shelf.

"Hold on. What's that?" I pulled on the rope, and the shelves made a groaning sound, like they were about to fall over. I felt around with my hand until I found the place where the rope met the wall. I pulled again, and the wood began to give way. "There's something back here."

"Ethan, be careful."

The shelves swung forward slowly, revealing a second space. Behind the pantry was a secret room, with crude brick walls and a dirt floor. The room stretched back into a dark tunnel. I stepped inside.

"Is that one of the Tunnels?" Liv looked into the darkness behind me.

"I think this is a Mortal tunnel." I glanced at Liv from the shadows of the tunnel. She looked safe and small inside the pantry, surrounded by Amma's old rainbows caught in a jar.

I realized where I was standing. "I've seen pictures of hidden rooms and tunnels like these. Runaway slaves used them to leave houses at night without being seen."

"Are you saying—?"

I nodded. "Ethan Carter Wate, or someone in his family, was part of the Underground Railroad."

⊰ 10.09 ⊱

Temporis Porta

Who is Ethan Carter Wate again, exactly?" Liv asked.

"My great-great-great-great-uncle. He fought in the Civil War, then deserted because he didn't believe it was right."

"I remember now. Dr. Ashcroft told me the story of Ethan and Genevieve and the locket."

For a moment, I felt guilty that Liv was here instead of Lena. Ethan and Genevieve were more than a story to me and Lena. She would've felt the weight of this moment.

Liv ran her hand along the wall. "And you think this could be part of the Underground Railroad?"

"You'd be surprised how many old houses in the South have a room like this."

"If that's true, then where does this tunnel go?" Now she was right next to me. I took an old lantern down from a nail that had been hammered between the crumbling bricks of the wall. I turned the key, and the lantern filled with light.

"How can there still be oil in there? This thing has to be a hundred and fifty years old."

A rickety wooden bench lined one of the walls. The remains of what looked like an army-issue canteen, some kind of canvas sack, and a wool blanket were stacked neatly beneath it. They were all coated with a thick layer of dust.

"Come on. Let's see where it leads." I held the lantern out in front of me. All I could see was the twisting tunnel and an occasional patch of brick built into the dirt.

"Waywards. You think you can go wherever you want." She reached up with one hand and touched the ceiling over our heads. Brown dirt rained down, and she ducked, coughing.

"Are you scared?" I nudged her with my shoulder.

Liv leaned back and yanked on the twisted loop of rope. The false door behind us closed with a sharp bang, and it was dark. "Are you?"

The tunnel dead-ended. I wouldn't have seen the trapdoor over our heads if Liv hadn't noticed a slice of light above us. The door hadn't been opened in a long time, because when we pushed our way up, whole shovelfuls of dirt caved into the tunnel—and all over us.

"Where are we? Can you see?" Liv called up from below. I couldn't get a solid foothold in the side of the dirt wall, but I managed to haul myself aboveground.

"We're in a field on the other side of Route 9. I can see my house from here. I think this used to be my family's field before they built the road."

"So Wate's Landing must have been a safe house. It would have been easy enough to sneak food into that tunnel right from the pantry." Liv was looking at me, but I could tell she was a thousand miles away.

"Then at night, when it was safe, you ended up out here." I let myself fall back down to the ground, pulling the trapdoor back into place. "I wonder if Ethan Carter Wate knew. If he was part of it." After seeing him in the visions, it felt like something he would do.

"I wonder if Genevieve knew," Liv said.

"How much do you know about Genevieve?"

"I read the files." Of course she did.

"Maybe they did it together."

"Maybe it had something to do with that." Liv was looking past me.

"What?"

She pointed behind me. There were planks hammered into an awkward X. But the boards were rotting, and you could see a doorway behind them.

"Ethan. Am I imagining—"

I shook my head. "No. I see it, too."

It wasn't a Mortal doorway. I recognized the symbols carved into the old wood, even if I couldn't read them. Across from the trapdoor that led into the Mortal world was a second doorway, which led into the Caster one.

"We'd better go," Liv said.

"You mean go in there." I set the lantern down on the ground.

Liv already had her red notebook out and was sketching, but she still sounded worried. "I mean go back to your house." She sounded annoyed, but I could tell she was as interested in what lay beyond the doorway as I was.

"You know you want to go in there." Some things never changed.

The first board splintered, coming off in my hands as soon as I pulled it loose.

"What I want is for you to stay out of the Tunnels, before this somehow manages to get us both into trouble."

The last of the boards fell away. In front of me was a carved wooden doorway that framed massive double doors. The bottom seemed to disappear into the dirt floor. I bent down to take a closer look. There were actual roots connecting the doors to the earth. I ran my hands along the length of them. They were rough and solid, but I didn't recognize the wood.

"It's ash. And rowan, I think," Liv said. I could hear her scribbling in her notebook. "There isn't a single ash or rowan tree within miles of Gatlin. They're supernatural trees. They protect creatures of Light."

"Which means?"

"Which means these doors are probably from somewhere far away. And they could lead to somewhere equally far away."

I nodded. "Where?"

She pressed her hand into a design along the carved lintel. "I haven't a clue. Madrid. Prague. London. We have rowan trees in the U.K." She started copying the symbols from the doors onto a page.

I pulled on the handle with both hands. The iron latch groaned, but the doors didn't open. "That's not the question."

"Oh, really?"

"The question is, what are we doing here? What are we supposed to see?" I pulled on the handle again. "And how do we get on the other side?"

"That's three questions." Liv studied the doors. "I think it's like the lintel at Ravenwood. The carvings are a kind of access code to get inside."

"Figure it out. We have to find a way in."

"I'm afraid it may not be that easy. Wait. Is that a word up there?" She brushed the dust off the doorway. Some kind of inscription was carved into the frame.

"If it's a Caster doorway, I wouldn't be surprised." I rubbed the wood with my hand, and it splintered beneath my fingers. Whatever it was, it was ancient.

" '*Temporis Porta.*' Time Door? What does that mean?" Liv asked.

"It means we don't have time for this." I leaned my forehead against the doors. I could feel a surge of heat and energy where the ancient wood touched my face. It was vibrating.

"Ethan?"

"Shh."

Come on. Open. I know there's something I'm supposed to see.

I focused my mind on the doors in front of me, the way I had on the Arclight the last time we were trying to find our way through the Tunnels.

I'm the Wayward. I know I am. Show me the way.

I heard the distinct sound of wood beginning to crack and splinter.

The wood shook as if the doors were going to collapse.

Come on. Show me.

I stood back as they swung open, split by light. Dust fell from their seal as if this entrance hadn't been opened in a thousand years.

"How did you do that?" Liv was staring at me.

"I don't know, but it's open. Let's go."

We stepped inside, and the dust and the light dissolved around us. Liv reached out her hand, and before I could take it, I disappeared—

I was standing alone in the center of a huge hall. It looked the way I imagined Europe, maybe England or France or Spain— somewhere old and timeless. But I couldn't be sure. The farthest the Tunnels had ever taken me was the Great Barrier. The room was as big as the inside of a ship, tall and rectangular, made entirely of stone. I don't think it was a church, but something like a church or a monastery—vast and holy and full of mystery.

Massive beams crossed the ceiling, surrounded by smaller wood squares. Inside each square was a gold rose, a circle with petals.

Caster circles?

That didn't seem right.

Nothing about this place was familiar. Even the power in the air—buzzing, like a downed electrical wire—felt different.

There was an alcove across the room, with a small balcony. Five windows ran the length of the wall, stretching higher than the tallest houses in Gatlin, framing the room with soft light that crept through the billows of sheer fabric hanging over them. Thick golden drapes hung at their sides, and I couldn't tell if the breeze blowing through the windows was a Caster or a Mortal one.

The walls were paneled and curved into low benches near the floor. I had seen pictures like these in my mom's books. Monks and acolytes sat on benches like this to pray.

Why was I here?

When I looked up again, the room was suddenly full of people. They were wedged onto the entire length of the bench, filling the space in front of me, crowding and pushing from all sides. I couldn't see their faces; half of them were cloaked. But all of them were buzzing with anticipation.

"What's going on? What are we waiting for?"

No one answered. It was as if they couldn't see me, which didn't make sense. This wasn't a dream. I was in a real place.

The crowd moved forward, murmuring, and I heard the banging of a gavel. *"Silentium."*

Then I saw familiar faces, and I realized where I was. Where I had to be.

The Far Keep.

At the end of the hall, Marian was hooded and robed, her hands tied with a golden rope. She stood in the balcony above the room, next to the tall man who showed up in the library archive. The Council Keeper, I heard people around me whisper. The albino Keeper was standing behind him.

He spoke in Latin, and I couldn't understand him. But the people around me did, and they were going crazy. *"Ulterioris Arcis Concilium, quod nulli rei—sive homini, sive animali, sive Numini Atro, sive Numini Albo—nisi Rationi Rerum paret, Marianam ex Arce Occidentali Perfidiae condemnat."*

The Council Keeper repeated the words in English, and I understood why the people around me were reacting this way.

"The Council of the Far Keep, which answers only to the Order of Things, to no man, creature, or power, Dark or Light, finds Marian of the Western Keep guilty of Treason."

There was a piercing pain in my stomach, as if my whole body had been sliced with a giant blade.

"These are the Consequences of her inaction. The Consequences shall be paid. The Keeper, though Mortal, will return to the Dark Fire from which all power comes."

The Council Keeper removed Marian's hood, and I could see her eyes, ringed with darkness. Her head was shaved, and she looked like a prisoner of war. "The Order is broken. Until the New Order comes forth, the Old Law must be upheld, and the Consequences paid."

"Marian! You can't let them—" I tried to push through the crowd, but the more I tried, the faster people surged forward, and the farther away she seemed.

Until I hit something, someone unmoving and unmovable. I looked up into the glassy stare of Lilian English.

Mrs. English? What is she doing here?

"Ethan?"

"Mrs. English. You have to help me. They have Marian Ashcroft. They're going to hurt her, and it's not her fault. She didn't do anything!"

"What do you think of the judge now?"

"What?" She wasn't making any sense.

"Your paper. It's due on my desk tomorrow."

"I know that. I'm not talking about my paper." Didn't she understand what was happening?

"I think you are." Her voice sounded different, unfamiliar.

"The judge is wrong. They're all wrong."

"Someone must be at fault. The Order is broken. If not Marian Ashcroft, then who is to blame?"

I didn't have the answer. "I don't know. My mom said—"

"Mothers lie," Mrs. English said, her voice void of emotion. "To allow their children to live the great lie that is Mortal existence."

I could feel my anger building. "Don't talk about my mom. You don't know her."

"The Wheel of Fate. Your mother knows about that. The future is not predetermined. Only you can stop the Wheel from crushing Marian Ashcroft. From crushing them all."

Mrs. English disappeared, and the room was empty. There was a smooth rowan doorway in front of me, recessed into the wall as if it had always been there. The *Temporis Porta*.

I reached for the handle. The second I touched it, I was on the other side again, standing in the Mortal tunnel, staring at Liv.

"Ethan! What happened?" She hugged me, and I felt a flicker of the connection that would always be between us.

"I'm fine, don't worry." I pulled back. Her smile faded, her cheeks turning bright pink as she realized what she had done. She swung her arms behind her back, clutching them awkwardly, like she wished she could make them disappear.

"What did you see? Where did you go?"

"I'm not exactly sure, but I know it was the Far Keep. I recognized two of the Keepers who came to the library. But I think it was the future."

"The future? How do you know?" The wheels were already spinning in Liv's mind.

"It was Marian's trial, which hasn't happened yet."

Liv was twisting the pencil tucked behind her ear. "*Temporis Porta* means 'Time Door.' It could be possible."

"Are you sure?" After what I'd seen, I hoped it was more of a warning—some sort of possible future that wasn't set in stone.

"There's no way to know, but if the *Temporis Porta* is some kind of portal, which seems likely, then you could have been seeing something that hasn't happened yet. The actual future." Liv started scribbling in her red notebook. I knew she wanted to remember every detail of this conversation.

"After what I saw, I hope you're wrong."

She stopped writing. "I suppose it wasn't good, then?"

"No." I stopped. "If that really was the future, we can't let Marian go to that trial. Promise me. If they come again, you'll help me keep her away from the Council. I don't think she knows—"

"I promise." Her face was dark and her voice cracked, and I knew that she was trying not to cry.

"Let's hope there's some other explanation." But even as I said it, I knew there wasn't. And so did Liv.

We retraced our steps, through the dirt, the heat, and the darkness, until I couldn't feel anything except the weight of my world collapsing.

⊰ 10.13 ⊱

Golden Ticket

That night, after the visit from the Far Keep, Marian went into her house and didn't come out again, as far as I could tell. The next day, I stopped by to see if she was okay. She didn't answer the door, and she wasn't at the library either. The day after that, I brought her mail up to the porch. I tried to look in her windows, but her shades were drawn, and the curtains, too.

I rang the bell again today, but she didn't answer. I sat down on her front steps and leafed through her mail. Nothing out of the ordinary—bills. A letter from Duke University, probably about one of her research grants. And some kind of returned letter, but I didn't recognize the address. Kings Langley.

Why was that familiar? My head felt foggy, like there was something at the edge of my memory I couldn't reach.

"That would be mine, I believe." Liv sat down on the step

next to me. Her hair was braided, and she was wearing cutoff jeans and a periodic table T-shirt.

On the surface, Liv seemed the same. But I knew the summer had changed things for her. "I never asked you if you were okay after that scene at the library, with the Council. Are you—all right, I mean?"

"I suppose. But what happened at the *Temporis Porta* scared me more." She looked scared, and faraway.

"Me, too."

"Ethan, I think it was the future. You walked through the door, and you were transported to another physical place. That's the way a time portal operates."

The Far Keep hadn't felt like a dream, or even a vision. It was like stepping into another world. I just wished that world wasn't the future.

Liv's face clouded over. Something else was bothering her.

"What is it?"

"I've been thinking." Liv twisted her selenometer nervously. "The *Temporis Porta* only opened for you. Why didn't it let me through?"

Because bad things keep happening to me. That's what I was thinking, but I didn't say it. I also didn't mention that I'd seen my English teacher in the future. "I don't know. So what do we do?"

"The only thing we can. We make sure Marian doesn't go to the Far Keep."

I looked up at her door. "Maybe we should be glad she won't come out of the house. Guess I should've known nothing good would come out of sneaking around in Amma's pantry."

"Except the preserves." Liv smiled weakly. She was trying to distract me from the one thing I could never get away from—myself.

"Cherry?"

"Strawberry." She said it in two syllables. Straw-bry. "With a spoon, straight out of the jar."

"You sound like Ridley. All sugar, all the time." She smiled when I said it.

"I meant to ask you. How are Ridley and Link and Lena?"

"Aw, you know. Ridley's tearing up the school. She's a cheer-leader now."

Liv laughed. "Siren, cheerleader. I'm not up on American culture, but even I appreciate the similarities."

"I guess. Link is the biggest big man on campus you've ever seen. The girls hang all over him. He's a real chick magnet."

"How is Lena? Happy to have her uncle back, I bet. And you."

She didn't look at me, and I didn't look at her. When she finally spoke, she looked up into the blazing sun, instead of at me. That's how much she didn't want to say it to my face. "It's hard for me, you know? I find myself thinking about you, things I want to tell you, things I think are funny or odd, but you aren't there."

I wanted to drop Marian's mail and bolt down the steps.

Instead, I took a deep breath. "I know. The rest of us are all still together, and you're alone. After everything we went through, we bailed on you. It sucks." I finally said it. It had been bother-ing me since the day we came home to Gatlin, the day Liv dis-appeared into the Tunnels with Macon.

"I have Macon. He's been wonderful to me, almost like a

257

father." She twisted the bits of string that were always tied to her wrist. "But I miss you and Marian, and not being able to talk to either of you is horrible, actually. I don't want to get her into any more trouble. But it's like being told you have to give up ice cream, or prawn crisps, or Ovaltine."

"I know. I'm sorry it's all so weird." What was weird was this conversation. It was so much like Liv to be the one brave enough to have it.

She looked sideways at me, and half smiled. "I was thinking, after I saw you yesterday. It's not like I can't speak to you without trying to kiss you. You're not *that* irresistible."

"Tell me about it."

"I wish I could print up a sign and tape it to my forehead. I OFFICIALLY DO NOT WANT TO KISS ETHAN WATE. NOW PLEASE LET ME BE FRIENDS WITH HIM."

"Maybe we could make T-shirts that say PLATONIC."

"Or NOT DATING."

"UNATTRACTED."

Liv took the returned letter out of the pile with a sigh. "This was me feeling sorry for myself a few weeks ago. I wrote home and asked if they'd have me back."

I realized I knew next to nothing about Liv's family. "*Home* home? Your family?"

"Just my mother. My father's long gone. You know, the glamorous life of a theoretical physicist. But no, this was a feeble attempt to get her to send me to Oxford, actually. I turned the university down to come here. And it seemed like it was time for me to go, or at least it did then."

"And now?" I didn't want her to leave.

"Now I feel like I can't leave Marian until this whole mess is sorted out."

I nodded, picking at my shoelaces. "I'd be happy if she would just come out of her house." But I didn't want to think about the future she might be facing if she did.

"I know. She isn't at the library either. Maybe she needs some time." Of course, Liv had been making the same rounds I had. We were so alike, in more ways than one. More than being the only Mortals in the equation.

"You know, you were pretty brave back there in the library."

She smiled. "Wasn't it amazing? I was quite proud. Then I got in bed and cried for about ten hours straight."

"I don't blame you. It was hard-core." And she'd only seen the half of it. The Far Keep was so much worse.

"Last night—" I started in, just as she said, "You know, I have to go—"

My timing was off, as usual, and our sentences tripped over each other. We sat there for a minute while the awkwardness set in. Still, I couldn't bring myself to leave.

She stood up, brushing off her shorts. "I'm glad we had a chance to catch up."

"Me, too."

As she walked down the carefully kept path that led to Marian's gate, I had an idea. Not a perfect idea, but a decent one.

"Wait up." I pulled a folded orange flyer out of my pocket. "Take it."

Liv unfolded it. "What's this?"

"An invitation to Savannah Snow's party, after the basket-ball game against Summerville on Saturday night. It's the hottest ticket in town." That was hard to say with a straight face.

"How did you and Lena get invited to a party at Savannah's house?"

"You underestimate the combined powers of a former Siren and a Linkubus."

She put the paper in her pocket. "So, you want to add an expelled Keeper-in-Training into the mix?"

"I'm not sure we'll actually go, but Link and Ridley definitely will. You should come, too, and hang out, like old times."

She hesitated. "I'll think about it."

"Think about it?"

"Won't it be a little awkward if you and Lena are there?"

Of course it would.

"Why would it be awkward?" I tried to sound convincing.

"Why do people say things like that? I don't know how comfortable Lena will feel around me." She searched the sky, as if the answer was hidden in the unbroken blue universe. "Which is why we need those T-shirts, I suppose."

I jammed my hands into my pockets, trying to come up with an answer to that. "You brought Macon back. You stood up for Marian. Lena respects you and what you did to help both of us. You practically live at Ravenwood—under it, at least. You're like family."

She narrowed her eyes, studying my face as if she didn't quite believe me. Which made sense, since part of it wasn't true. "Maybe. Possibly. That's the best I can do, under the circumstances."

"I'll take that as a yes."

"I have to get back. Macon's waiting for me. But I'll consider going to the party." She took a key out of her pocket and held it up. It was a crescent key, like the one Marian had. Now Liv could open the Outer Doors that connected the Mortal and Caster worlds. There was something right about that. She waved and disappeared around the corner while I turned back to the dark house. Shades still drawn.

I left the mail in a pile on the rocker by Marian's door and hoped it would be gone in the morning. I hoped my memories of the *Temporis Porta* would be gone even sooner.

———— ❧

"You did what? Please tell me you're joking."

We were at the Cineplex, standing in line for popcorn. Lena wasn't as happy about the whole making peace with Liv thing as I had hoped. Actually, she was exactly as unhappy about it as I'd predicted. But if Liv decided to come to the party, Lena was going to find out that I was the one who had invited her. It was better to take the hit now. An angry girlfriend was one thing. An angry Caster girl meant you could lose a limb or step off a cliff.

I had planned to tell Lena about finding the *Temporis Porta* with Liv last night. But considering her reaction to the party invite, it seemed better to wait on that one.

So I had to come clean about the rest.

I sighed and repeated my argument, even though it was going to get me nowhere. "If you had anything to worry about, would I invite Liv somewhere I might be going with you? Don't you think I'd make some kind of secret plans?"

"What kind of secret plans?"

I shrugged. "I don't know. Because I don't have any."

"But let's say that you did."

"But I don't." This was going downhill fast.

"Ethan, this is hypothetical."

"This is a trap." I knew better than to engage in hypothetical questions with a girl.

We reached the counter, and I pulled out my wallet. "Well?"

Lena looked at me like I was crazy. "The usual."

The usual? What was the usual? My mind was totally blank.

"The usual," I repeated dumbly.

She gave me a look and then turned to the cashier. "Popcorn and Milk Duds, please."

Are you okay?

Yeah, I just blanked. I don't know.

The cashier slid Lena's popcorn over the counter and looked at me. I scanned the list on the wall. "And how about…popcorn and Hot Tamales?"

Hot Tamales?

They don't have Red Hots, L.

You thinking about someone I know?

I shrugged. Of course I was. Amma wasn't making egg rolls with her cleaver, or pie filling with the One-Eyed Menace. Her sharp #2 pencils were in the drawer, and I hadn't seen a crossword puzzle on the kitchen table in weeks.

Ethan, don't worry about Amma. She'll come out of it.

Amma's never gone dark for this long before. We have a bottle tree in our front yard.

Since Abraham showed up at your house?

More like since school started.

Lena dumped her Milk Duds into the popcorn tub.

If you're this worried about it, why don't you ask her?

You ever try to ask Amma something?

Yeah. No. Maybe we need to go see this bokor for ourselves.

No offense, L, but he's not the kind of guy you want to take your girlfriend to see. And I'm not sure an actual Caster would be safe there.

The whole cheer squad passed by us. Ridley was walking with some guy I didn't know, who had his hand in the back pocket of her stretchy skirt. He wasn't from Jackson; Summerville was my guess. Savannah was hanging on Link, who was staring at Ridley while she pretended not to notice him. Emily walked behind them with Charlotte and Eden, and you could see the rage on Savannah's face. She wasn't the one holding up the pyramid anymore.

"You sittin' with us?" Link called out as he passed.

Savannah smiled and waved. Lena looked at the two of them as if they were walking down the street in their underwear.

"I'm never going to get used to that," she said.

"Me neither."

"Did you explain to Rid about the last four rows of the Cineplex?"

"Oh, no—"

———— ৎ১

So we ended up wedged between Link and Savannah and Ridley and the guy from Summerville, in the last four rows. The credits had barely started before Savannah was whispering and giggling into Link's neck, which as far as I could tell was just an excuse to get her mouth up near his. I elbowed him as hard as I could.

"Ow!"

"Ridley's sitting right there, man."

"Yeah. With that tool."

"You want her crawling all over him like that?" Ridley wasn't the kind of girl who got mad. She got even.

Link leaned forward, looking past Lena and me to where Ridley was sitting. The Summerville Tool already had his hand on her leg. When she saw Link watching, she snaked her arm through the guy's and tossed her pink and blond hair. Then she pulled out a lollipop and began unwrapping it.

Link shifted in his seat. "Yeah. You're right. I'm gonna have to kick his—"

Lena grabbed the sleeve of his shirt before Link got up. "You're not doing anything. Just behave, and she will, and then maybe you can actually start dating like normal people and stop this stupid game."

"Shh!" The Summerville Tool shot us a look. "Shut up. Some of us are tryin' to watch the movie."

"Yeah, right," Link yelled back at him. "I know what you're tryin' to watch."

Link gave me a pleading look. "Please let me go outside and beat the crap outta him, before I miss any a the good parts. You know I'm gonna end up doin' it anyway."

He had a point. But he was a Linkubus, and the rules were different now.

"You ready to let Ridley beat the crap out of Savannah? Because you know she'll do it."

He shook his head. "I don't know how much more a this I can take. Rid's drivin' me nuts." For a second, the old Link was back, hung up on the girl who would always be out of his league.

Maybe that was it. Maybe he would always think Ridley was out of his league, even though his league had changed.

"You have to ask her to Savannah's party, as your date." It was the only way to defuse this particular bomb.

"You kiddin' me? That's like askin' for an open war with the whole squad. Savannah already has me doin' all this extra stuff—comin' over early to set up an' everythin'."

"I'm just calling it like I see it." I dug into my Hot Tamales popcorn. My mouth was burning, which seemed like a sign. Time to keep it shut.

I wasn't giving out any more advice.

By the end of the night, Link had beaten the crap out of the Summerville Tool in the parking lot. Ridley called Link every name in the book, and Savannah stepped in. For a minute, it looked like there was going to be a serious catfight, until Savannah remembered her arm was still in a sling, and pretended the whole thing was a big misunderstanding.

When I got home, there was a note taped to my front door. It was from Liv.

I changed my mind. See you at the party. XO Liv

XO.

That was just something girls wrote at the end of notes, right?

Right.

I was dead.

A Real Bad Girl

It took more than a little convincing to get Amma to let me go to Savannah Snow's party. And it wasn't like she wouldn't notice if I tried to sneak out. Amma never went anywhere anymore. She hadn't gone home to Wader's Creek once since she pulled the tarot spread that sent her into a voodoo queen's crypt. She wouldn't admit it, but when I asked her why she never went back home anymore, she got defensive.

"You think I can leave the Sisters to keep an eye on themselves? You know Thelma hasn't been the least bit clear herself, since the accident."

"Oh, Miss Amma. Quit your fussin'. I only get the eensiest bit confused, now an' again," Thelma called from the next room, where she was straightening the couches just so. Aunt Mercy liked one pillow and two blankets. Aunt Grace liked two pillows and one blanket. Aunt Mercy didn't like used blankets, which meant you had to wash them before she'd let them near her. Aunt Grace didn't like pillows that smelled like hair, even if it was her own. The sad thing was, since "the accident" I knew more about their pillow preferences and hiding places for coffee ice cream than I ever wanted to know.

The accident.

"The accident" used to mean my mom's car crash. Now it was polite Southern code for Aunt Prue's condition. I didn't know if it made me feel better or worse, but once Amma started invoking "the accident," there was no getting her to change her mind.

Still, I tried. "They don't stay up past eight o'clock. How about we all hang out and play Scrabble together, and then I'll go out once everyone is asleep?"

Amma shook her head as she pulled trays of cookies in and out of the oven. Snickerdoodles. Molasses. Shortbread. Cookies, not pie. Cookies were for delivery. She never fed cookies to the Greats. I don't know why, but the Greats weren't much for cookies. Which meant she still wasn't talking to them.

"Who are you baking for tonight, Amma?"

"What, you're too good for my cookies now?"

"No, but you took the paper doilies out, which means these aren't for me."

Amma started arranging the cookies on the tray. "Well, aren't you a smart one. Takin' these down to County Care. Thought those nice nurses might want a cookie or two to keep 'em company, these long nights."

"So, can I go?"

"You're simpler than I thought, if you're thinkin' Savannah Snow wants you anywhere near her place."

"It's just a regular old high school party."

She lowered her voice. "There's no such thing as a regular old high school party when you're takin' a Caster and an Incubus and a worn-out Siren with you." Turns out, Amma could even whisper a pretty fierce scolding. Then she slammed the oven door and stood there with an oven-mitted hand on each hip.

"Quarter Incubus," I whispered back. Like that changed anything. "It's at the Snows' house. You know what they're like." I did my best impression of Reverend Blackwell. "Fine, God-fearin' folk. Keep a Bi-ah-ble right next to the bed." Amma glared at me. I gave it up. "Nothing's gonna happen."

"If I had a nickel for every time you've said that, I'd be livin' in a castle." Amma covered the cookies in plastic wrap. "If the party's at the Snows' house, why are you goin' anyhow? Didn't even invite you last year, as I recollect."

"I know. But I thought it would be fun."

I met Lena on the corner of Dove Street because she'd had even less luck with her uncle and ended up sneaking out of her house. She was so afraid Amma would see her and send her back home that she parked the hearse a block away. Not like her car was hard to miss.

Macon had made it clear no one was going to any parties, not while the Order was still broken—especially not at the Snows'. Ridley had made it equally clear she was going. *How did they expect her to fit in as a Mortal if she wasn't allowed to do normal things with her new Mortal friends?* Things were thrown. In the end, Aunt Del caved, even if Macon didn't.

So Ridley had walked right out the front door, while Lena was left to find a way to sneak out.

"He thinks I'm in my room, sulking because he wouldn't let me go out." Lena sighed. "Which is where I was until I figured out my exit strategy."

"How did you get out?" I asked.

"I had to use, like, fifteen different Casts: Hiding, Blinding, Forgetting, Disguising, Duplicating."

"Duplicating? You mean you cloned yourself?" That was a new one.

"Just my scent. Anyone who Casts a Revelation on the house might be fooled, for a minute or two." She sighed. "But there's no fooling Uncle Macon. I'm dead when he finds out I'm gone. You think it's bad living with a Seer? All Uncle Macon wants to do is practice his Mindhunting skills."

"Awesome. So we have all night." I pulled her closer to me, and she leaned her back up against her car.

"Umm. Maybe longer. There's probably no way I'll get back inside tonight. The place is Bound a thousand times over."

"You can stay with me if you want to." I kissed her neck, working my way up to her ear. My mouth was already burning, but I didn't care. "Why are we going to this stupid party again when we have a perfectly good car right here?"

She pushed up onto her toes, kissing me until my head was pounding as hard as my heart. Then she pulled back, ducking away. "Aunt Mercy and Aunt Grace would really love that, wouldn't they? It would almost be worth it to see the looks on their faces when I came down to breakfast in the morning. Maybe I could wear one of your towels." She started to laugh, and I pictured it all right, only the shrieking in my head was so loud, I gave up.

"Let's just say, the language could get a whole lot stronger than 'fanny.' "

"I bet they'd call the 'durned po-lice.' " She was right.

"Yeah, but I'm the one they'd have arrested for compromising your virtue."

"Then I guess we better pick up Link, before you have the chance."

I couldn't remember the last time I'd set foot in Savannah's house, but I started to feel uncomfortable the minute we walked up to the stairs. There were pictures of her everywhere—wearing sparkly tiaras and all kinds of MISS AREN'T-I-BETTER-THAN-YOU? sashes, posing with her cheer uniform and pom-poms—and a whole row of what I guess were supposed to be modeling head shots, featuring Savannah in bathing suits, with fake eyelashes and too much lipstick. From the looks of it, she'd been wearing lipstick since she got out of diapers.

Turns out, the Snows didn't really need party decorations. Past the table covered with a hundred basketball cupcakes, past the punch bowl with little plastic basketballs frozen into the ice ring, past the chicken salad sandwiches made into basketballs with little round cookie cutters, Savannah was the biggest decoration of all. She was still wearing her cheer uniform, but she had written Link's name on one cheek and drawn a giant pink heart on the other. She stood in the middle of the backyard—waiting, smiling, generally lighting up the place as if she was the Christmas tree at a Christmas party. And the minute Savannah saw Link, it was like someone had flipped the switch that turned on all her lights.

"Wesley Lincoln!"

"Hey there, Savannah."

Savannah was hoping for some serious sparks between them, but she didn't have a chance. When it came to Link, there was only one girl who could cause that kind of spark, and it was only a matter of minutes until she arrived and really lit up the place.

More like an hour.

That's when Ridley got there and ratcheted things up a notch or two — or two hundred. "Evening, boys."

Link's head whipped around when he saw her, and he broke into a smile about a mile wide, confirming what I knew all along. Ridley was still under his skin, and pretty much everywhere else. I knew what that kind of radar felt like. It was the way I felt about Lena.

Uh-oh. This isn't good, L.

I know.

"Come on. I think it's going to get ugly." I took Lena's hand and turned to leave, and there was Liv. Lena shot me a look.

Crap.

With everything else going on, I'd forgotten all about giving Liv the invitation.

"Lena." Liv smiled.

"Liv." Lena sort of smiled. "I didn't know if you were coming."

"Really? I left Ethan a note." Liv smiled at me pointedly.

"Really." Lena shot me a look that said I'd be hearing about this later.

Liv shrugged. "Well, you know Ethan." *Don't you?* That's what Lena heard.

"Yeah, I do." Lena wasn't smiling anymore.

I started to panic and noticed the punch table, a good fifteen feet away. That seemed like a safe distance. "I'm going to get something to eat. Anybody want anything?"

"Nope." Liv smiled at me like everything was fine.

"Not a thing." Lena smiled at me like she was about to kill me.

I escaped as quickly as I could.

Mrs. Snow was standing by the punch bowl talking to two men I'd never seen before. They were both wearing university caps and collared shirts. "It's a surprise," Mrs. Snow told them. "That's why my daughter wanted to throw this little get-together. She wanted you to be able to talk to Wesley in a casual environment."

"That sure was kind of your daughter, ma'am."

"Savannah's a very thoughtful girl. Always puttin' others first. And her boyfriend, Wesley, is a real talented basketball player. That's why my husband asked y'all to come up. And Wesley comes from a good, churchgoing family. His mother's got a hand in everythin' that goes on in this town."

I froze at the table, a chocolate basketball jammed halfway into my mouth. They were college scouts. And they were here to meet Link.

I looked across the yard to where Link and Savannah were dancing and Ridley was circling like a shark. Rid would make her move any minute now, striking so fast that there would be nothing left but blood in the water.

I took off, nearly knocking over the punch bowl in the process.

"Sorry, Savannah. I need to talk to Link for a minute." I grabbed Link and hauled him out Savannah's back gate.

"What the hell?" Link looked at me like I was crazy.

"There are scouts in there, from the university. Mrs. Snow

set this whole thing up for you. And if you let Ridley get near Savannah tonight, you're going to blow everything."

"What are you talkin' about?" He looked confused.

"Basketball. College recruiters. It's your ticket out of here."

He shook his head. "Nah, dude. You've got it all wrong. I don't want a ticket out of this town. I just wanna a ticket outta this party."

"You what?"

He was already shaking his head and walking back to the party. "It's not Savannah. It never was. It's Ridley, good or bad." He looked at me like he was telling me he had a fatal disease or something. "I can't shake it."

"Shake what, Shrinky Dink?" Ridley was standing with her back against the gate. Unlike the rest of the girls on the squad, she wasn't wearing her cheer uniform. Her green dress was so tight in some places and slit so high in others, you weren't exactly sure where to look.

Link moved closer to her. "Come on, Rid. I want to talk to you."

"That's not what your little girlfriend said. She said you didn't want to talk to me. In fact, she told me to get the hell off her property."

"Savannah's not my girlfriend."

I tried to pretend I didn't know what was about to happen. I tried not to listen, or care.

But I could hear the desperation in Link's voice. "It's never been anyone but you."

"What are you talking about?" She froze, but it was too late.

Link couldn't stop himself. "Sometimes I think crazy things, like I want to be with you forever. We could live in an RV and see the world. I mean, the parts you can drive to. And you could write songs, and I could play them at gigs. Can't you see it?"

Ridley's face looked like it was about to crack into a thousand tiny pieces. "I — don't know what to say."

"Say you'll be my girl, the way it used to be."

I could see her wavering, and I realized how hard it must be to be her right now. Because she wasn't the Ridley she used to be, any more than he was the Link he used to be. Nothing was the same. Not for anyone.

Then she noticed Lena and Liv, watching from one side — and me, standing there on the other. Her face clouded over. Ridley wasn't going to crack, especially not in front of us. "What are you on, Shrinky Dink?"

"Come on, Rid. You're my girl. Stop pretending you don't feel the same way about me."

"I'm a Siren. I'm nobody's girl. I don't *feel* anything. And I don't fall in love. I can't." She started to back away. "It's always been just a gig."

"Rid, you're not a Siren anymore. You're never gonna be one again."

Ridley spun around, her blue eyes raging. "That's where you're wrong. I'm not going to be stuck in this pathetic excuse for a town forever. And there's no way I'm traveling the world in some crappy trailer with you. I have plans."

"Ridley —" Link sounded miserable.

"Big plans. And I can tell you right now, they have nothing to do with you!" She turned to face the rest of us. "Any of you!"

Link looked like she'd slapped him in the face. For a guy who spent most of his time joking around, I'd never heard him lay it out like that to a girl.

As Ridley walked toward the gate, Link kicked the lawn chair next to him, sending it flying.

Across the yard, Savannah saw her chance, and took it. She smoothed her blond hair and pushed her way through the crowd to Link. She slid her hands up his T-shirt. "Come on, Link. Let's dance."

The next minute they were dancing and Savannah was all over him. Lena, Liv, and I stared as if we were watching a three-car pile-up on Route 9. You couldn't turn away.

Liv scrunched up her nose. "Should we be letting this happen?"

Lena shrugged. "I don't see what we can do to stop it. Unless you want to go over there."

"No, thanks."

That's when Savannah—who clearly didn't realize she was dancing with a heartbroken guy whose hopes and dreams of true love and record deals and RV parks across the country had just been shattered—moved in for the kill.

The three of us collectively held our breath.

Right there under the twinkling lights, Savannah took Link's face in her hands and pulled him toward her.

"Bollocks." Liv hid her face.

"This is bad." Lena didn't want to look either.

"We're screwed." I braced myself.

The kiss lasted for a full twenty seconds.

Until Ridley happened to look over her shoulder.

You could probably hear the sound a half a mile away. Ridley was standing behind the gate at the edge of Savannah's back-yard, screaming so loud that everyone at the party stopped dancing. She was holding her scorpion belt, her lips moving as if she was Casting.

"She can't be—" Lena whispered.

I grabbed Lena's hand. "We have to stop her. She's lost it."

But it was too late.

A minute later, everything turned into complete and total chaos.

I felt the Cast rip through the party like a wave. And you could almost see it, hitting one person and moving on to the next. You could tell where it had hit, from the angry expressions and the shouting left in its wake. One minute, couples were dancing—the next, they were fighting. Guys were shoving each other while unsuspecting victims tried to move out of the way. Until the Cast hit them, and then they were the ones doing the pushing and yelling.

I heard the punch bowl shatter on the floor, but I couldn't see it through the crowd of cheerleaders pulling each other's hair and basketball players tackling each other. Even Mrs. Snow was screaming at the college scouts, giving them enough pieces of her mind to keep them from ever crossing the county line again.

Lena's eyes went dark. "I can feel it—a *Furor*!" She grabbed Liv and me, pulling us toward the gate, but it was too late.

I knew as soon as it hit, because Liv turned and slapped Lena across the face as hard as she could.

"Have you lost your mind?" Lena held her cheek, which was already turning an angry shade of red.

Liv pointed at her, the heavy black selenometer turning on her wrist. "That is for all the whining, Princess."

"What?" Lena's hair started to curl, her green and gold eyes narrowing.

Liv went on. "Poor, beautiful me. My gorgeous boyfriend is so in love with me, but my heart is broken because—hey—that's how beautiful emo girls like me are supposed to act."

"Shut up!" Lena looked like she was about to punch Liv in the face. I heard thunder rumble in the sky.

"Instead of being happy that a great guy loves me, I'm going to slap on some more black nail polish and run off with some other gorgeous guy."

"That's not what happened!" Lena swung at Liv, but I caught her arm. Rain started to fall.

Liv kept talking. "And—wait for it—I'm the most powerful Caster in the universe. In case the rest of you lowly Mortals didn't already feel like total crap."

"Are you crazy?" Lena screamed at her, but it was hard to hear over all the chaos. "My uncle died. I thought I was going Dark."

"Do you know what it feels like to hang out with a guy when you have feelings for him? Help him look for his girlfriend who doesn't want to be found? Watch him break his own heart, and yours, over some stupid Caster girl who doesn't give a rat's ass about him?"

Lightning ripped across the sky, the rain pelting us like hailstones. Lena lunged for Liv. I moved in front of Lena, holding her back.

"Liv. That's enough. You're wrong." I had no idea what Liv was doing, but I wanted her to shut up.

"Feelings for him? At least you finally admit it!" Lena was screaming.

"I don't admit anything except that you're a bloody little bitch who thinks the world orbits around your pretty little curls."

That was it. Lena wrenched her arms free and slammed her hands into Liv's shoulders. Liv fell backward, hitting the ground hard. Lena wasn't going to let her have the last word. Or the last hit.

"Okay, little Miss I'm-Not-Here-to-Steal-Your-Boyfriend." Lena imitated Liv's voice. "Really, we're just friends, even though I'm smarter and blonder than the rest of you combined. And did I mention my cute little British accent?"

Liv kicked mud at her, but Lena moved out of the way just in time. Lena didn't stop there. "And if that's not enough, let me martyr myself, so you can spend the rest of your life feeling guilty. Or maybe I can spend all my time with your uncle, so he can think of me as the daughter he never had. Oh, wait—he already has one of those! But who cares. Because if Lena has it, I'm going to try to take it!"

Liv scrambled to her feet and tried to slip past me. I held on to her. "Stop it! You're acting like idiots. It's a Cast! You don't even realize who you should be mad at!"

"And you do?" Lena screamed, trying to reach around me to grab Liv's hair.

"Of course I do. But the only person I'm angry at isn't here." I bent down and picked up Ridley's scorpion belt from the muddy grass. I handed it to Lena. "It's Ridley. And she's gone. So I have no one to yell at."

I heard the Beater's engine gunning. I pointed out the gate, and we watched the Beater peel away from the curb. "Actually, I think there's someone even angrier at her than I am. And it looks like he's taking off to find her."

"You really think this is some kind of Cast?" Lena looked at Liv.

"No. I think we always fight like stray dogs in the street when we try to socialize at parties." Liv rolled her eyes.

"See? There you go, having to be the smart one all the time."

Lena tried to pull free, but I clamped down harder on both of their arms.

"It's a *Furor*, you moron," Liv snapped.

"I'm a moron? I said *Furor* before this whole thing started."

I pushed them both through the gate in front of me. "You're both acting like morons. And now we're gonna get in the car and go up to Ravenwood. And if you two can't say something nice to each other, don't say anything."

But I didn't have to worry, because if there was one thing I had figured out about girls, it was that pretty soon they would give up trashing each other. They'd be too busy trashing me.

"That's because he's afraid to make a decision," Liv said.

"No, it's because he doesn't want to upset anyone," Lena snapped.

"How would you know? He never says what he's thinking."

"That's not it. He never thinks about what he's saying," Lena fired back.

"Enough!" I pulled through the crooked iron gates of Ravenwood, furious at both of them. Furious at Ridley. Furious at how the year was turning out. *Furor*, that was the right name for it, whatever this was. I hated feeling this way, and I hated it even more because I knew the feelings were real, even if it took a spell to bring them out into the open.

Lena and Liv were still fighting when we got out of the car. Even though they knew they were under the influence of a Cast, they couldn't help themselves. Or maybe they didn't want to. The three of us walked toward the front door, and I stayed between them. Just in case.

"Why don't you give us some space?" Lena pushed in front of Liv. "Ever heard of a third wheel?"

Liv pushed her back. "Like I wanted to come here? So once again, I'm supposed to clean up your mess? Then you'll forget all about me, until next time—"

I wasn't listening anymore. I was looking at Ridley's window. I saw a shadow pass in front of it, behind the curtains. All I could see was a silhouette, but I could tell it wasn't Ridley.

Link must have gotten here first, except I didn't see the Beater. "I think Link's in there."

"I don't care. Ridley has a lot of explaining to do." Lena was halfway up the staircase when I crossed the threshold. I sensed the change immediately—the air itself felt different. Lighter, somehow. I looked back at Liv.

Her expression looked the way I felt. Confused. Disoriented. "Ethan, does something feel weird to you?"

"Yeah—"

"It's the *Furor*," Liv said. "It's broken. The magic can't pass the Bindings."

"Ridley! Where are you?" Lena was steps from her cousin's door. When she reached it, she threw open the door without knocking. She didn't seem to care if Link was in there or not. But it didn't matter.

The guy in Ridley's room wasn't Link.

Hostage

W hat the hell?" I heard his voice before I saw him. Because he probably wasn't expecting to see me in Ridley's room any more than I was expecting to find him here.

John Breed was sprawled out on Ridley's pink shag carpet, with a video-game controller in one hand and a bag of Doritos in the other.

"John?" Lena was as surprised as I was. "You're supposed to be dead."

"John Breed? Here? It's not possible." Liv was shocked.

John dropped the bag and jumped to his feet. "Sorry to disappoint you."

I stepped in front of Lena and Liv protectively. "I know I'm disappointed."

Lena didn't need protecting. She pushed past me. "How dare you come into my house after everything you did? You pretended

281

to be my friend, when all you wanted to do was take me to Abraham." Thunder rumbled outside. "Every word you said to me was a lie!"

"That's not true. I didn't know what they were gonna do. Bring me the Bible. *The Book of Moons*, whatever you want. I'll swear on it."

"We can't do that. Since Abraham has it." I was pissed off, and I didn't want to listen to John play dumb. It was a new tactic, and I was still trying to adjust to the fact that he was hanging out in Ridley's bedroom eating Doritos.

Lena wasn't finished. "If that wasn't bad enough, you turned Link into—you." Lena's hair was curling, and I hoped the room wasn't about to catch fire.

"I couldn't help it. Abraham can make me do things." John was pacing. "I—I can't even remember most of what happened that night."

I crossed the room, until I was standing right in front of him. I didn't care if he could kill me. "Do you remember dragging Lena up to that altar and tying her down? Do you remember that part?"

John stopped pacing and stared at me, his green eyes searching mine. When he spoke, I could barely hear him. "No."

I hated him. The memory of his hands on Lena—of almost losing her that night. But he looked like he was telling the truth.

John dropped down on the bed. "I black out sometimes. It's been that way since I was a kid. Abraham says it's because I'm different, but I don't believe him."

"Are you saying you think he has something to do with it?" Liv pulled out her red notebook.

282

John shrugged. "I don't know."

Lena looked at me.

What if he's telling the truth?

What if he's not?

"None of that explains why you're in Ridley's bedroom," Lena said. "Or how you got into Ravenwood."

John stood up and walked over to the window. "Why don't you ask that manipulative cousin of yours?" He sounded pissed off for a guy who had just been caught breaking and entering.

Lena's expression darkened. "What does Ridley have to do with this?"

John shook his head, kicking a pile of dirty clothes. "I don't know. How about everything? She's the one who trapped me here."

I don't know if it was the way he said it, or because we were talking about Ridley, but part of me believed him. "Back up. What do you mean, she trapped you?"

He shook his head. "Technically, she trapped me twice. First in the Arclight, and then in here, when she let me out."

"Let you out?" Lena looked stunned. "But we buried the Arclight—"

"And your cousin dug it up and brought it here. She released me, and I've been stuck in this house ever since. This place is Bound so tight, I can't get any farther than the kitchen."

The Bindings. It wasn't keeping something out of Ravenwood; it was keeping someone in. Just like I thought.

"When did she let you out?"

"Sometime in August, I guess."

I remembered the day Lena and I came in here to go down into the Tunnels—the rip I thought I'd heard.

"August? You've been in here for two months?" Lena was losing it. "You're the one who's been helping Ridley. That's how she's Casting!"

John laughed, but it sounded like bitterness more than anything. "Helping her? Thanks to your uncle's library, she's been using me as her own personal genie. Consider this dump my bottle."

"But how did she keep Macon from finding you?" Liv was writing down every word.

"An *Occultatio*, a Concealment Cast. Of course, she made me do it." He banged the wall with his fist, revealing the black tattoo that snaked its way around his upper arm. Another reminder that he was Dark, no matter what color his eyes were. "Lena's uncle has a book about almost everything—except how to get out of this place."

I didn't want to listen to him complain about the way he'd been treated. I'd hated John since the first time I saw him last spring, and now he had shown up to ruin our lives again. I looked over at Lena, whose face was unreadable, her thoughts closed off.

Was this the way she felt about Liv?

Except Liv hadn't tried to kidnap my girlfriend and lead most of my friends to their deaths. "That's funny, because I've got a few bottles hanging on a tree in my front yard, and I'd love to stuff you into one of them," I said.

John appealed to Lena. "I'm trapped. I can't get out of here, and your nutbag cousin promised to help me. But she needed me to do a few things for her first."

He ran his hand through his hair, and I noticed he didn't look as cool as I remembered. In his wrinkled black T-shirt and five o'clock shadow, he looked like he'd been watching soap operas and eating a lot of Doritos. "Ridley's not a Siren—she's an extortionist."

"But how have you been helping her if you can't leave Ravenwood?" Liv asked. It was a good question. "Have you been teaching her to Cast?"

John laughed. "Are you kidding? I turned cheerleaders into zombies and some party into a rumble. You think Ridley could pull off a *Furor*? She can barely tie her own shoes as a Mortal. Who do you think has been doing her math homework all year?"

"Not me." Lena was softening, I could tell, and it was killing me. He was like a painful, nasty infection that wouldn't go away. "Then how is she Casting, if you didn't teach her?"

John pointed to the belt around Lena's waist. "That thing." He yanked on an empty belt loop, at the top of his jeans. "It acts as a conduit. Ridley wears the belt, and I do the Casting."

The creepy scorpion belt. No wonder she never took it off. It was her lifeline to the Caster world and John Breed—the only way she could have any power of her own.

Liv shook her head. "I hate to say it, but it all makes sense now."

It did make sense, but that didn't change anything for me. People lied. And John Breed was a liar, as far as I was concerned. I turned to Lena. "You don't actually believe any of this? There's no way we can trust him."

Lena looked from Liv to me. "What if he's telling the truth? He knew about the cheerleaders. And the party. I think I agree with Liv. It all makes sense."

You two are going to start agreeing now?

285

Ethan. It was a Cast. A Furor Cast makes people uncontrol-lably angry.

Sure seemed real to me.

I looked at John, skeptical. "There's no way to know for sure."

John sighed. "I'm still in the room, you know."

Lena glanced at the door. "Well, there is one way."

Liv looked at her, nodding. "Are you thinking what I'm thinking?"

"Hello?" John looked at me. "Are they always like this?"

"Yes. No. Shut up."

—⌒⊱

Reece was standing in the middle of Ridley's room, her arms crossed disapprovingly. In her sweater set and pearls, she looked like she had been shipped in from some other, more proper Southern family. She wasn't happy about being used as a human lie detector, and seemed even more annoyed to see John Breed in her sister's room. Maybe Reece had some misguided fantasy that Ridley was going to become a Girl Scout like her, now that she was Mortal. But once again, her sister was bringing her down by association. Come to think of it, it was too bad the DAR had the whole bloodline requirement. Reece could have founded her own chapter.

"If you think I'm keeping this a secret, you two are crazier than my sister. This is *so* over the line."

Neither one of us wanted a lecture from Reece, but Lena didn't give up. "We aren't asking you to keep it a secret. We want to know if he's telling the truth before we tell Uncle Macon what's been going on." Lena was probably hoping John was lying—that Ridley hadn't been hiding a dangerous Incubus stolen from the grave and channeling his powers.

It wasn't clear which was worse.

"Because you're about to be grounded for the rest of your life?" Reece asked.

"Something along those lines."

Reece tapped her foot impatiently. "As long as we're clear. You *are* telling Uncle Macon. Or I will." Of course she would. She couldn't pass up a good grounding.

I was worried about more than her ratting us out. "Are you sure this will work, since—"

"Since what?" Reece snapped. "Since my powers have been a little inconsistent? Is that what you're trying to say?" *Great.* An angry Reece was never a good thing.

"I—I just meant, are you sure you'll know if he's lying?" It was too late to backpedal now.

Reece looked like she wanted to tear my head off. "Not that it's any of your business, but I'm still a Sybil. Whatever I see in his face is the truth. If my powers are *off*, I won't see anything."

Lena slid between us.

You're in over your head. I've got this.

Thanks.

I've been dealing with Reece the Beast a lot longer than you have. It's an acquired skill.

"Reece." Lena took her hand, and I could see her hair begin to curl. I winced. Casting at a Caster was almost never a good idea. "You're the most powerful Sybil I've ever met."

"Don't try that on me." Reece pulled her hand away. "I'm the only Sybil you've ever met."

"But you know I trust you, no matter what." Lena smiled encouragingly at her cousin. Reece frowned at both of us.

I looked away. Misfiring powers or not, I wasn't looking into the eyes of a Sybil if I could help it. I noticed Liv hadn't said a word or looked in Reece's direction either.

"One shot. Then you're telling Uncle Macon, either way. Because this whole thing shows, once again, why you should *not* be allowed to Cast when you're underage." She folded her arms again. It took me a while to figure out that was a yes.

John hopped off the bed and walked over to where Reece was standing. "Let's get this over with. What do I have to do?"

Reece stared into John's green eyes, studying his face as if it held all the answers we were looking for. "You're doing it."

John didn't move. He stared back at Reece, letting her absorb his thoughts and memories. Reece turned away before he did, shaking her head as if she didn't like what she'd seen.

"It's true. He didn't know what Abraham and Sarafine were planning, and he doesn't remember what happened that night. Ridley let him out of the Arclight, and he's been here ever since, doing my sister's dirty work."

John looked at me. "Satisfied?"

"Wait? How is that possible?"

Reece shrugged. "Sorry to disappoint you. He's not evil. He's just a jerk. Sometimes it's a fine line."

"Hey." John looked less smug now. "I thought you were supposed to be the nice one. Where's that famous Ravenwood hospitality?"

Reece ignored him.

I should've been relieved, but Reece was right. I was disappointed. I didn't want John to be one of Sarafine and Abraham's pawns. I wanted him to be one of the bad guys. That's how I saw him—how I would always see him.

More than anything, I wanted Lena to see him that way.

Lena wasn't thinking about John. "We have to talk to my uncle. We have to find Ridley before she does anything stupid."

Right. If I knew Ridley, she was probably hitchhiking her way out of Summerville by now. After the stunt she pulled tonight, she knew Lena would go straight to Macon. And Ridley wasn't big on facing the music. "I think it's a little too late for that."

Lena bent down and flipped back the corner of the pink shag carpet. "Let's go."

"You sure about this? I don't want to, you know, wake him up or something." I also didn't want to see the look on his face when we told him that Ridley had turned Savannah Snow's house into a thirty-on-thirty boxing match, using the Charmed belt of an Incubus we were all looking for—who just happened to be living in Ridley's bedroom.

Lena opened the trapdoor. "I doubt he's asleep."

Liv shook her head. "Lena's right. We have to tell Macon. Immediately. You don't understand, we've been—" She faltered, looking at Lena. "Your uncle has been trying to find John Breed for months."

Lena nodded. It wasn't a smile, but it was something. "Let's go."

John ripped open another bag of Doritos. "While you're down there, can you ask him to let me out of here?"

"Ask him yourself," Lena said. "You're coming with us."

John looked down into the darkness that led into the Tunnels below us, then back at me. "Never thought you'd be rescuing me, Mortal."

I wanted to kill him or punch him in the face. I wanted to make him pay for everything he'd done to Lena and Link, all the trouble Abraham had caused because of him. But I would leave that to Macon.

"Trust me, I'm not."

He smiled, and I stepped into the air, feeling for the rough solidity of the steps I would never see.

⊰ 10.19 ⊱

The Ultimate Weapon

I knocked on the door of Macon's study, and it swung open. I didn't need to worry about waking him up, though. A miserable-looking Link was already sitting at the table.

Macon waved me in. "Link has filled me in on everything. Luckily, he came straight here, before he hurt anyone." I hadn't considered the damage a raging Incubus could inflict.

"What part of *everything* do you know?" I stepped inside.

"That my niece snuck out of the house." He looked at me pointedly. "Not a wise decision."

"No, sir." Macon was already angry, and I didn't want to tell him something that was going to make him even angrier.

He crossed his arms. "And that Ridley somehow managed to Cast a *Furor?*"

A whole lot angrier.

"I know you're upset, but there's something more important

I need to tell you." I glanced at the door. "Or maybe you should see for yourself."

"John Breed." Macon loomed over him. "This is quite an unexpected turn of events. All things considered."

John was standing just inside the door of the study, as if he was going to make a break for it, Mortal-style. In Macon's presence, his smart-ass attitude was gone.

Link was staring at John like he wanted to tear him apart. "What the hell is he doin' here?" I felt bad for Link, being stuck in the same room with John. He had to hate John even more than I did, if that was possible.

Lena couldn't look at her uncle or Link. She was ashamed of Ridley, and herself for not figuring it out sooner. But more than anything, I knew she was worried about her cousin, no matter what she'd done. "Ridley stole the Arclight out of Uncle Macon's grave after we buried it. She freed John, and she's been using his belt as a conduit to channel his powers until now."

"Belt?"

Liv pulled out her little red notebook. "The one Lena's wearing. The disgusting belt with the scorpion trapped inside."

Macon held out his hand. Lena unclicked the buckle and handed the belt to him.

Link turned on John. "What did you do to her?"

"Nothing. Ridley's been ordering me around since she let me out of the Arclight."

"Why would you agree?" Even Macon was incredulous. "You don't strike me as particularly selfless."

"I didn't have a choice. I've been stuck in this house for months now, trying to get out." John slumped against the wall. "Ridley wouldn't help me unless I found a way for her to Cast. So I did."

"You expect us to believe that a powerful hybrid Incubus allowed a Mortal girl to trap him in her bedroom?"

John shook his head, frustrated. "This is Ridley we're talking about. I think you all have a bad habit of underestimating her. When she wants something, she finds a way to get it." We all knew he was right.

"He's telling the truth, Uncle Macon," Reece said, from where she was standing by the fireplace.

"You're absolutely sure?"

Reece wasn't about to bite Macon's head off, the way she had done to me. "I'm sure."

John looked relieved.

Liv stepped forward, her notebook in hand. She had no interest in why Ridley may or may not have done something. She wanted the facts. "You know, we've been looking for you," she told John.

"Yeah? Bet you're not the only ones."

Liv and Macon convinced John to sit down at the table with the rest of us, which meant Link refused to. He leaned against the wall next to the fireplace, sulking. All the Linkubus hype aside, John had changed Link in ways I would never really understand. And I knew something else John didn't know.

As much as Link loved driving all the girls crazy, it didn't really matter. There was only one girl Link wanted, and none of us knew where to find her.

"Abraham has gone to great lengths to locate your where-abouts, literally tearing this town apart. What I need to know is why. Abraham doesn't do anything without a reason." Macon was asking the questions, while Liv wrote down John's responses. Reece was sitting across from John, watching for any trace of a lie.

John shrugged. "I'm not really sure. He found me when I was a kid, but he's not exactly a father figure, if you know what I mean."

Macon nodded. "You said he found you. What happened to your parents?"

John shifted uncomfortably in his seat. "I don't know. They disappeared. I'm pretty sure they ditched me because I was… you know, different."

Liv stopped writing. "All Casters are different."

John laughed. "I'm not a regular Caster. My powers didn't manifest when I was a teenager." Liv stared at him. He pointed at her notebook. "You're going to want to write this part down."

She raised an eyebrow. *Subject displays combative attitude.* I could imagine it on the page.

"I was born this way, and my powers have only gotten stron-ger. Do you know what it's like to be able to do things no one else your age can?"

"Yes." There was a trace of something in Liv's voice, a mix of sadness and sympathy. She had always been smarter than every-one around her, designing devices to measure the pull of the moon, or some other thing no one else cared about or understood.

Macon was studying John, and you could see the former Incubus in him sizing up this strange new one. "And exactly what sort of powers do you have, aside from being impervious to the effects of sunlight?"

294

"Standard Incubus stuff—amplified strength, hearing, sense of smell. I can Travel. And girls are pretty into me." John stopped and looked at Lena as if they shared a secret. She looked away.

"Not as much as you think," I said. He smiled at me, enjoying Macon's protective custody.

"I can do other things, too."

Liv searched his face. "Like what?"

Link's arms were crossed, and he was staring at the door, pretending he wasn't listening. But I knew he was. Like it or not, he and John would always be connected now. The more Link knew about John, the more he would be able to figure out about himself.

John looked at Reece, then at Lena. Whatever it was, he didn't want to say. "Random stuff."

Macon's eyes flickered. "What *random stuff*? Perhaps you could elaborate."

John gave up. "It sounds like a bigger deal than it is. But I can absorb other Casters' powers."

Liv stopped writing. "Like an Empath?" Lena's grandma could borrow the powers of other Casters temporarily, but she never described it as "absorbing" anything.

John shook his head. "No. I keep them."

Liv's eyes widened. "Are you saying you can steal the powers of other Casters?"

"No. They still have their powers, but I have them, too. Sort of like a collection."

"How is that even possible?" Liv asked.

Macon leaned back in his chair. "I would be very interested in hearing the answer to that question, Mr. Breed."

John glanced at Lena again. I wanted to jump across the table. "All I have to do is touch them."

"What?" Lena looked like he had slapped her in the face. Is that what he'd been doing with his hands all over her on the dance floor at Exile? Or when she had climbed onto the back of his stupid motorcycle that day at the lake? Siphoning her powers, like a parasite?

"It's not like I do it on purpose. It just happens. I don't even know how to use most of the powers I have."

"But I'm sure Abraham does." Macon poured himself a glass of dark liquor from a decanter that had appeared on the table. Never a sign things were going well.

Liv and Macon looked at each other, a silent exchange.

I could see the wheels in Liv's mind turning. "What could Abraham be planning?"

"With a hybrid Incubus who can collect the powers of other Casters?" Macon answered. "I'm not entirely sure, but with those capabilities at his side, Abraham would have the ultimate weapon. And Mortals wouldn't stand a chance against that sort of power."

John whipped around to face Macon. "What did you say?"

"Would you care for me to repeat—"

"Wait." John cut Macon off before he could finish. He closed his eyes as if he was trying to remember something. " 'Casters are an imperfect race. Polluting our bloodlines and using their powers to oppress us. But the day will come when we wield the ultimate weapon and eradicate them from the Earth.' "

"What kinda crap is that?" John had Link's attention.

"Abraham and Silas used to say it all the time when I was a

296

kid. I had to memorize it. Sometimes when I got in trouble, Silas made me write it over and over for hours."

"Silas?" Macon stiffened at the mention of his father's name. I remembered the things my mom had said about Silas in the Arclight visions. He sounded like a monster, abusive and racist, trying to pass his hatred on to his sons—and apparently to John.

Macon looked at John, his eyes darkening to a green so deep it was nearly black. "How did you know my father?"

John raised his empty green eyes to meet Macon's. His voice was different when he finally answered—not powerful or cocky, not John Breed at all.

"He raised me."

The One Who Is Two

After that, Macon and Liv spent most of their time grilling John about Abraham and Silas, and who knows what else, while Lena and I pored over every book in Macon's study. There were also old letters from Silas, encouraging Macon to join his father and brother in the battle against the Casters. But aside from that there were no clues to John's past, no mentions of any Caster or Incubus capable of anything close to John's abilities.

The few times we were allowed to join the inquisition, Macon watched Lena and John's interactions carefully. I think he was worried that the strange pull John had wielded over Lena in the past might return. But Lena was stronger now, and John annoyed her as much as the rest of us. I was more worried about Liv. I had witnessed the reaction of the Mortal girls in Gatlin the first time John walked into the Dar-ee Keen. But Liv seemed immune.

I was used to the ups and downs of living in the place between the Caster and Mortal worlds, but these days were all downs. The same week John Breed turned up at Ravenwood, Ridley's clothes disappeared out of her room, like she was gone for good. And a few days later, Aunt Prue took a turn for the worse.

I didn't ask Lena to come with me the next time I went to County Care. I felt like being alone with Aunt Prue. I don't know why, just like I didn't know much about anything that was going on with me these days. Maybe I was going crazy. Maybe I'd been crazy all along, and I didn't even know it.

———

The air was freezing cold, as if they found a way to suck the Freon and the power from all the air conditioners in Gatlin County and pipe it into County Care. I wished it was this cold anywhere but here, where the cold wrapped itself around the patients like corpses in a refrigerator.

This kind of cold never felt good, and it definitely never smelled good. At least sweating made you feel kind of alive, and that smell was about as human as you could get. Maybe I'd spent too much time considering the metaphysical implications of heat.

Like I said, crazy.

Bobby Murphy didn't say a word when I walked up to the front desk, didn't even look me in the eye. Just handed me the clipboard and a pass. I wasn't sure if Lena's Shut-the-Hell-Up Cast still affected him all the time, or only when I was around. Either way was fine with me. I didn't feel like talking.

I didn't look in the other John's room or the Unseen

Needlepoint Room, and I walked right past the Sad Birthday Party Room. I held my breath as I passed the Food That Wasn't Food Room, before the smell of Ensure hit.

Then I smelled the lavender, and I knew my Aunt Prue was there.

Leah sat in a chair by her bed, reading a book in some kind of Caster or Demon language. She wasn't in the standard County Care peach uniform. Her boots were propped up on a hazardous waste disposal container in front of her. She'd obviously given up trying to pass for a nurse.

"Hey there."

She looked up, surprised to see me. "Hey, yourself. It's about time. I've been wondering where you've been."

"I don't know. Busy. Stupid stuff."

Freaking out and chasing down hybrid Incubuses and Ridley, my mother and Mrs. English, and some crazy thing about some crazy Wheel...

She smiled. "Well, I'm glad to see you."

"Me, too." That was all I could manage. I gestured at her boots. "They don't give you a hard time for all that?"

"Nah. I'm not really the kind of girl people give a hard time."

I couldn't make any more small talk. Talking was getting harder and harder every day, even with people I cared about. "Do you mind if I spend some time with Aunt Prue? You know, alone?"

"Of course not. I'm going to run out and check on Bade. If I don't get her house-trained soon, she'll have to sleep outside, and she's really an indoor cat." She tossed her book onto the chair and ripped out of the room.

I was alone with Aunt Prue.

She had gotten even smaller since the last time I was here. Now there were tubes where there hadn't been, as if she was turning into a piece of machinery an inch at a time. She looked like an apple baking in the sun, wrinkling in ways that seemed impossible. For a while, I listened to the rhythmic pulsing of the plastic ankle cuffs on her legs, expanding and contracting, expanding and contracting.

As if they could make up for not walking, not being, not watching *Jeopardy!* with her sisters, not complaining about everything while loving it all.

I took her hand. The tube that ran into her mouth bubbled with her every breath. It sounded wet and croupy, like a humidifier with water inside it. Like she was choking on her own air.

Pneumonia. I overheard Amma talking to the doctor in the kitchen. Statistically speaking, when coma patients died, pneumonia was the Grim Reaper. I wondered if the sound of the tube in her throat meant Aunt Prue was getting closer to a statistically predictable end.

The thought of my aunt as another statistic made me want to throw the hazardous waste bin through the window. Instead, I grabbed Aunt Prue's tiny hand, her fingers as small as bare twigs in winter. I closed my eyes and took her other hand, twisting my strong fingers together with her frail ones.

I rested my forehead against our hands and closed my eyes. I imagined lifting my head up and seeing her smiling, the tape and tubes gone. I wondered if wishing was the same thing as praying. If hoping for something badly enough could make it happen.

I was still thinking about it when I opened my eyes, expecting to see Aunt Prue's room, her sad hospital bed and her depressing peach walls. But I found myself standing in the sunshine, in front of a house I'd been to a hundred times before....

The Sisters' house looked exactly the way I remembered it, before the Vexes tore it apart. The walls, the roof, the section where Aunt Prue's bedroom had been—they were all there, not a white pine board or a roof shingle out of place.

The walk leading up to the wraparound porch was lined with hydrangea, the way Aunt Prue liked. Lucille's clothesline was still stretched across the lawn. There was a dog sitting on the porch—a Yorkshire terrier that looked suspiciously like Harlon James, except it wasn't. This dog had more gold in his coat, but I recognized him and bent down to pet him. His tag read HARLON JAMES III.

"Aunt Prue?"

The three white rocking chairs were sitting on the porch, with little wicker tables between them. There was a tray on one of them, with two glasses of lemonade. I sat in the second rocking chair, leaving the first one empty. Aunt Prue liked to sit in the one closest to the walk, and I figured she would want that chair if she was coming.

It felt like she was coming.

She'd brought me here, hadn't she?

I gave Harlon James III a scratch, which was strange, since he was sitting in our living room, stuffed. I looked at the table again.

"Aunt Prue!" She startled me, even though I was expecting her. She didn't look any better than she had lying in her hospital bed, in real life. She coughed, and I heard the familiar noise of the rhythmic compressions. She was still wearing the plastic cuffs around her ankles, expanding and contracting, as if she was still in her bed at County Care.

She smiled. Her face looked transparent, her skin so pale and thin that you could see the bluish purple of the veins beneath it.

"I've missed you. And Aunt Grace, Aunt Mercy, and Thelma are going out of their minds without you. Amma, too."

"I see Amma most days and your daddy on the weekends. They come by ta talk a lot more regular than some people." She sniffed.

"I'm sorry. Things have been all wrong."

She waved her hand at me. "I'm not goin' anywhere. Not just yet. They got me on house arrest, like one a them criminals from the TV." She coughed and shook her head.

"Where are we, Aunt Prue?"

"Don't reckon I know. But I don't have much time. They keep you pretty busy 'round here." She unhooked her necklace and took something off it. I hadn't seen her wearing the necklace in the hospital, but I recognized it. "From my daddy, from his daddy's daddy, from way before you were even a thought in the mind a the Good Lord."

It was a rose, hammered out of gold.

"This is for your girl. Ta help me keep an eye on her for ya. Tell her ta keep it with her."

"Why are you worrying about Lena?"

"Now, don't you go worryin' 'bout that. You just do as I tell you." She sniffed again.

"But Lena's fine. I'll always take care of her. You know that." The thought that Aunt Prue was worried about Lena scared me more than anything that had happened in the last few months.

"All the same, you give it ta her."

"I will."

But Aunt Prue was gone, leaving only half a glass of lemonade and an empty rocking chair, still rocking.

I opened my eyes, squinting into the brightness of my aunt's room, and I realized the sun was coming in sideways, much lower than when I'd arrived. I checked my cell. Three hours had passed.

What was happening to me? Why was it easier to slip into Aunt Prue's world than to have a simple conversation in my own? The first time I spoke to her, it didn't seem like any time had passed at all, and I couldn't have done it without a powerful Natural at my side.

I heard the door open behind me.

"You all right, kid?" Leah was standing in the doorway.

I looked down at my hand, uncurling my fingers around a tiny gold rose. *This is for your girl.* I wasn't all right. I was pretty sure nothing was.

I nodded. "Fine. Just tired. I'll see you around, Leah." She waved me off, and I left the room with the weight of a backpack full of rocks on my shoulders.

When I got into the car and the radio started playing, I wasn't surprised to hear the familiar melody. After seeing Aunt Prue, I was relieved. Because there it was, as right as the rain that hadn't fallen in months. My Shadowing Song.

> *Eighteen Moons, eighteen nears,*
> *The Wheel of Fate herself appears,*
> *Then the One Who Is Two*
> *Will bring the Order back anew....*

The *One Who Is Two*, whatever that meant, was tied to fixing the Order.

And what did it have to do with the Wheel of Fate—the Wheel that was a *she*? Who could be powerful enough to control the Order of Things and take human form?

There were Light and Dark Casters, Succubuses and Sirens, Sybils and Diviners. I remembered the previous verse of the song—the one about the Demon Queen. Possibly one who could take human form, like stepping into a Mortal's body. There was only one Demon Queen I knew who could do that. Sarafine.

Finally, a piece of information I could wrap my mind around. Even though Liv and Macon had spent every day of the last week with John—treating him like Frankenstein, visiting royalty, or a prisoner of war, depending on the day—he hadn't told them anything that explained his role in all this.

I still hadn't told anyone except Lena about my visits with

Aunt Prue. But I was beginning to feel like it all fit together, the same way everything in the bowl ends up in the biscuits, as Amma would say.

The Wheel of Fate. The One Who Is Two. Amma and the bokor. John Breed. The Eighteenth Moon. Aunt Prue. The Shadowing Song.

If only I could figure out how, before it was too late.

—— ☙

By the time I got to Ravenwood, Lena was sitting on the front porch. I could see her watching me as I drove through the crooked iron gate.

I remembered what Aunt Prue had said when she gave me the gold rose. *This is for your girl. Ta help me keep an eye on her.*

I didn't want to think about it.

I sat down next to Lena on the top step. She held out her hand and took the charm from me, slipping it onto her necklace without a word.

It's for you. From Aunt Prue.

I know. She told me.

"I fell asleep on the couch, and suddenly she was there," Lena said. "It was exactly the way you described it—a dream, but it didn't feel like a dream." I nodded, and she leaned her head against my shoulder. "I'm sorry, Ethan."

I looked out at the gardens, still green in spite of the heat and the lubbers and everything we had been through. "Did she tell you anything else?"

Lena nodded and reached up to touch my cheek with her

hand. When she turned toward me, I could tell she had been crying.

I don't think she has much time.

Why?

She said she came to say good-bye.

───⌒೨

I never made it home that night. Instead, I found myself sitting alone on Marian's doorstep. Even though she was in there, and I was out, I still felt better at her place than mine.

For now. I didn't know how much longer she'd be there, and I didn't want to think about where I would be without her.

I fell asleep on her carefully swept front porch. And if I dreamed that night, I don't remember.

Crucibles

You know, babies are born without kneecaps." Aunt Grace wedged herself between the sofa cushions before her sister could get there.

"Grace Ann, how could you say such a thing? It's downright disturbin'."

"Mercy, it's the God's honest truth. I read it in *Reader's Digestive*. Those readers are fulla information."

"Why on God's green earth are you talkin' 'bout babies' knees, anyhow?"

"Can't say as I know. Just got me ta thinkin' 'bout the way things change. If babies can just grow them some kneecaps, why can't I learn ta fly? Why don't they build stairs ta the moon? Why can't Thelma get married ta that handsome Jim Clooney boy?"

"You can't learn ta fly 'cause you got no wings. It wouldn't make a lick a sense ta build stairs ta the moon 'cause they don't have any breathin' air up there. And that boy's name is George Clooney, and Thelma can't marry him 'cause he lives all the way over there in Hollywood and he's not even a Methodist."

I listened to them talk in the next room while I ate my cereal. Sometimes I understood what the Sisters were saying, even when it sounded like crazy talk. They were worried about Aunt Prue. They were preparing for the possibility she was going to die. Babies grew kneecaps, I guess. Things changed. It wasn't a good thing or a bad thing, any more than kneecaps were good or bad. At least, that's what I told myself.

Something else had changed.

Amma wasn't in the kitchen this morning. I couldn't remember the last time I'd left for school without seeing her. Even when she was mad and refused to cook breakfast, she would still be banging around in the kitchen, muttering to herself and giving me stinkeye.

The One-Eyed Menace was lying on the spoon rest, bone dry.

It didn't feel right to leave without saying good-bye. I opened the drawer where Amma kept her extra-sharp #2 pencils. I grabbed one and tore a sheet of paper off the message pad. I was going to tell her I left for school. No big deal.

I leaned over the counter and started writing.

"Ethan Lawson Wate!" I hadn't heard Amma come in, and I nearly jumped out of my skin.

"Jeez, Amma. You almost gave me a heart attack." When I turned around, she was the one who looked like she was going to have one. Her face was ashen, and she was shaking her head like a mad woman.

"Amma, what's wrong?" I started to cross the room, but she put her hand out.

"Stop!" Her hand was shaking. "What were you doin'?"

"I was writing you a note." I held up the sheet of paper.

She pointed her bony finger at my other hand, the one still holding her pencil. "You were writin' with the wrong hand."

I looked down at the pencil in my left hand and let it drop, watching it roll across the floor.

I had been writing with my left hand.

But I was right-handed.

Amma backed out of the kitchen, her eyes shining, and tore down the hall.

"Amma!" I called after her, but she slammed her door behind her. I banged on it. "Amma! You have to tell me what's wrong."

What's wrong with me.

"What's all that ruckus out there?" Aunt Grace called from the living room. "I'm tryin' ta watch my stories."

I slid down to the floor, my back against Amma's door, and waited. But she didn't come out. She wasn't going to tell me what was happening. I was going to have to figure it out on my own.

Time to grow a pair of kneecaps.

———— ⌒৯

I didn't feel the same way later that day, when I ran into my dad again with Mrs. English. This time they weren't at the library. They were having lunch at my school. In my classroom. Where anyone could see them, including me. I wasn't that ready for change.

I made the mistake of dropping off the draft of my *Crucible* essay during lunch, because I forgot to give it to her in English class. I pushed through the door without bothering to look through the little glass square, and there they were. Sharing a basket of Amma's leftover fried chicken. At least I knew it would be rubbery.

"Dad?"

My dad smiled before he turned, which is how I knew he'd been waiting for this to happen. He had the smile ready. "Ethan? Sorry to surprise you on your home turf like this. I wanted to go over a few things with Lilian. She has some great ideas about the Eighteenth Moon project."

"I bet she does." I smiled at Mrs. English, holding up the paper. "My draft. I was going to put it in your in-box. Just ignore me." *Like I'm going to ignore you.*

But I didn't get off that easy.

"Are you ready for tomorrow?" Mrs. English looked at me expectantly. I braced myself. The automatic answer to that question was always no, but I had no idea exactly what I wasn't ready for.

"Ma'am?"

"For the reenactment of the Salem witch trials? We're going to try the same cases *The Crucible* is based on. Have you been preparing your case study?"

"Yes, ma'am." That explained the manila envelope marked ENGLISH in my backpack. I hadn't been paying much attention in class lately.

"What an amazing idea, Lilian. I'd love to come watch, if you don't mind," my dad said.

"Not at all. You can videotape the trials for us. We can all watch it as a class afterward."

"Great." My dad beamed.

I felt the cold glass eye rolling over me as I walked out of the classroom.

L, did you know we're reenacting the Salem witch trials in English tomorrow?

Haven't been memorizing your case file? Do you even look in your backpack anymore?

Did you know my dad is videotaping it? I do. Because I walked in on his lunch date with Mrs. English.

Ewww.

What should we do?

There was a long pause.

I guess we should start calling her Ms. English?

Not funny, L.

Maybe you should finish reading The Crucible *before class tomorrow.*

The problem with having actual evil in your life is that regular, everyday evil—administrators giving you detention, the textbook evil that makes up most of high school existence— starts to feel less terrifying. Unless it's your father dating your glass-eyed English teacher.

No matter how you looked at it, Lilian English was evil— the real kind or your everyday variety. Either way, she was eating rubbery chicken with my dad, and I was screwed.

———

Turns out *The Crucible* is more about bitches than witches, as Lena would be the first to say. I was glad I waited until the end of the unit to finish reading the play. It made me hate half of Jackson High, and the whole cheer squad, even more than usual.

By the time class started, I was proud that I actually did the reading and knew a few things about John Proctor, the guy who gets completely shafted. What I hadn't anticipated was costumes—girls in gray dresses and white aprons, and guys in

Sunday school shirts with their pants tucked into their socks. I didn't get the memo, or it was still in my backpack. Lena wasn't wearing a costume either.

Mrs. English doled out our respective one-eyed glares and five-point deductions, and I tried to ignore the fact that my father was sitting in the back of the room with the school's fifteen-year-old video camera.

The classroom was rearranged to look like a courtroom. The afflicted girls were on one side—led by Emily Asher. Apparently, their job was to act like phonies and pretend they were possessed. Emily was a natural. They all were. The magistrates were on one side of them and the witness box on the other.

Mrs. English turned her Good-Eye Side on me. "Mr. Wate. Why don't you start off as John Proctor, and then we'll switch around later on in the period?" I was the guy who was about to have his life destroyed by a bunch of Emily Ashers. "Lena, you can be our Abigail. We'll start with the play and then spend the rest of the week on the actual cases the play was based on."

I went over to my chair in one corner, and Lena went to the other.

Mrs. English waved to my dad. "Let's start rolling, Mitchell."

"I'm ready, Lilian."

Everyone in class turned to look at me.

The reenactment went off without a hitch, which really meant it went on with all the customary hitches. The camera battery died in the first five minutes. The chief magistrate had to use the bathroom. The afflicted girls got caught texting, and the confiscation of their phones was a bigger affliction than the one the Devil was supposed to have brought on them in the first place.

My father didn't say a word, but I knew he was there. His presence kept me from speaking, moving, or breathing when I could help it. Why was he here? What was he doing hanging out with Mrs. English? There was no rational explanation.

Ethan! You're supposed to give your defense.

What?

I looked up at the camera. Everyone in the room was staring at me.

Start talking, or I'm going to have to fake an asthma attack, like Link did during the biology final.

"My name is John Proctor."

I stopped. My name was John.

Just like John at County Care. And John sitting on Ridley's pink shag carpet. Once again, there was me, and there was John. What was the universe trying to tell me now?

"Ethan?" Mrs. English sounded annoyed.

I looked back down at my paper. "My name is John Proctor, and these allegations are false." I didn't know if it was the right line. I looked back at the camera, but I didn't see my father standing behind it.

I saw something else. My reflection in the lens started to shift, like a ripple in the lake. Then it slowly came back into focus. For a second, I was staring at myself again.

I watched my image as the corners of my mouth turned up into a lopsided smile.

I felt like someone had punched me.

I couldn't breathe.

Because I wasn't smiling.

"What the hell?" My voice was shaking. The afflicted girls started laughing.

Ethan, are you okay?

"Do you have anything else to add to that poignant defense, Mr. Proctor?" Mrs. English was more than annoyed. She thought I was screwing around.

I shuffled through my notes, my hands shaking, and found a quote. " 'How may I live without my name? I have given you my soul, leave me my name.' "

I could feel her glass eye on me.

Ethan! Say something!

"Leave me my soul. Leave me my name." It was the wrong line, but something about it felt right.

Something was following me. I didn't know what it was, or what it wanted.

But I knew who I was.

Ethan Wate—son of Lila Jane Evers Wate and Mitchell Wate. Son of a Keeper and a Mortal, disciple of basketball and chocolate milk, of comic books and novels I hid under my bed. Raised by my parents and Amma and Marian, this whole town and everyone in it, good and bad.

And I loved a girl. Her name was Lena.

The question is, who are you? And what do you want from me?

I didn't wait for an answer. I had to get out of that room. I pushed my way through the chairs. I couldn't get to the door fast enough. I slammed against it as hard as I could, and ran down the hall without looking back.

Because I already knew the words. I'd heard them a dozen times, and every time they made less sense.

And every time, they made my stomach turn.

I'M WAITING.

Demon Queen

One of the things about living in a small town is you can't get away with ditching class in the middle of a historical reenactment that your English teacher spent weeks organizing. Not without consequences. In most places, that would mean suspension, or at least detention. In Gatlin, it meant Amma forcing you to show up at your teacher's house with a plateful of peanut butter cookies.

Which is exactly where I was standing.

I knocked on the door, hoping Mrs. English wasn't home. I stared at the red door, shifting my weight uncomfortably. Lena liked red doors. She said red was a happy color, and Casters didn't have red doors. To Casters, doors were dangerous—all thresholds were. Only Mortals had red doors.

My mom had hated red doors. She didn't like people who had red doors either. She said having a red door in Gatlin meant you were the kind of person who wasn't afraid to be different. But if you thought having a red door would do that for you, then you really were just like the rest of them.

I didn't have time to come up with my own theory on red doors, because right then this one swung open. Mrs. English was standing there in a flowered dress and fuzzy slippers. "Ethan? What are you doing here?"

"I came to apologize, ma'am." I held out the plate. "I brought you some cookies."

"Then I suppose you should come in." She stepped back, opening the door wider.

This wasn't the response I was expecting. I figured I'd apologize and give her Amma's famous peanut butter cookies, she would accept, and I would be out of there. Not following her into her tiny house. Red door or not, I definitely wasn't happy.

"Why don't we have a seat in the parlor?"

I followed her into a tiny room that didn't look like any parlor I'd ever seen. It was the smallest house I'd ever been in. The walls were covered with black and white family portraits. They were so old and the faces so small that I would've had to stop and stare to look at any of them, which made them all strangely private. At least, strange for Gatlin, where our families were on display at all times, the dead and the living.

Mrs. English was strange, all right.

"Please, have a seat. I'll bring you a glass of water." It wasn't a question—it seemed to be mandatory. She stepped into the kitchen, which was about the size of two closets. I could hear the running water.

"Thank you, ma'am."

There was a collection of ceramic figurines on the mantel

over the fireplace—a globe, a book, a cat, a dog, a moon, a star. The Lilian English version of the standard junk the Sisters had collected and never let anyone touch, until it was smashed to rubble in their front yard. In the middle of the fireplace was a small television, with rabbit ear antennas that couldn't have worked for about twenty years. Some kind of spidery-looking houseplant sat on top of it, making the whole thing look like a big planter. Except the plant looked like it was dying, which made the planter that wasn't a planter, on top of the TV that wasn't a TV, on top of the fireplace that wasn't a fireplace, all seem pointless.

A tiny bookcase sat next to the fireplace. It actually appeared to be what it was, seeing as it actually had books on it. I bent down to read the titles: *To Kill a Mockingbird. The Invisible Man. Frankenstein. Dr. Jekyll and Mr. Hyde. Great Expectations.*

The front door slammed, and I heard a voice I never would have expected to hear in my English teacher's house.

"*Great Expectations.* One of my personal favorites. It's so... tragic." Sarafine was standing inside the doorway, her yellow eyes watching me. Abraham had ripped into a worn flowered chair in the corner of the room. He looked comfortable, as if he was just another guest. *The Book of Moons* was resting in his lap.

"Ethan? Did you open the front—" It only took a minute for Mrs. English to come back from the kitchen. I don't know if it was the strangers in her parlor, or Sarafine's yellow eyes, but Mrs. English dropped the water, broken glass raining down onto her flowered rug. "Who are you people?"

I looked at Abraham. "They're here for me."

He laughed. "Not this time, boy. We came for something else."

Mrs. English was shaking. "I don't have anything of value. I'm just a teacher."

Sarafine smiled, which made her look even more deranged. "Actually, you have something that is very valuable to us, *Lilian*."

Mrs. English took a step back. "I don't know who you people are, but you should leave. My neighbors have probably already called the police. This is a very quiet street." Her voice was rising. I was pretty sure Mrs. English was only a minute away from a meltdown.

"Leave her alone!" I started to walk toward Sarafine, and she flung open her fingers.

I felt the force, ten times stronger than any hand, slam against my chest. I fell back against the bookcase, sending dusty books falling around me.

"Have a seat, Ethan. I think it's fitting for you to watch the end of the world as you know it."

I couldn't get up. I could still feel the weight of Sarafine's power on my chest.

"You people are crazy," Mrs. English whispered, her eyes wide.

Sarafine fixed her terrifying eyes on Mrs. English. "You don't know the half of it."

Abraham stubbed his cigar out on Mrs. English's side table and rose from the chair. He opened *The Book of Moons* as if he had marked a specific page.

"What are you doing? Calling more Vexes?" I shouted.

This time, they both laughed. "What I'm calling will make a Vex look like a house cat." He started to read in a language I didn't recognize. It had to be a Caster language—Niadic, maybe. The words were almost melodic, until he repeated them in English and I realized what they meant.

"'From blood, ash, and sorrow. For the Demons imprisoned below...'"

"Stop!" I shouted. Abraham didn't even look at me.

Sarafine twisted her wrist slightly, and I felt my chest tighten. "You are witnessing history, Ethan—for both Casters and Mortals. Be a little more respectful."

Abraham was still reading. "'I call their Creator.'"

The moment Abraham spoke the last word, Mrs. English gasped, and her body arched violently. Her eyes rolled back in her head, and she crumpled to the floor like a rag doll. Mrs. English's neck was resting against her chest awkwardly, and all I could think about was how lifeless she looked.

Like she was dead.

Abraham started to read again, but I felt like I was underwater—everything was slow and muffled. How many more people were going to die because of them?

"'...to avenge them. And to serve!'" Abraham's voice echoed through the tiny room, and the walls began to shake. He snapped the Book shut and walked closer to the body of Mrs. English.

The spidery-looking plant fell off the TV, and the pot broke against the stone of the fireplace. The tiny figurines were rocking back and forth, the pieces of Mrs. English's life breaking apart.

"She's coming!" Sarafine called to Abraham, and I realized they were both staring at Mrs. English's body. I tried to get up, but the weight was still bearing down on my chest. Whatever was happening, I couldn't stop it.

It was already too late.

Mrs. English's neck lifted first, her body slowly following, rising from the floor as if an invisible string was pulling it. It was horrible—the way her lifeless body moved like a puppet's. When her body straightened, her eyelids snapped open.

But her eyes were gone. In their place were only dark shadows.

The shaking stopped, and the whole room was still.

"Who calls me?" Mrs. English was speaking, but the voice wasn't hers. It was inhuman. There was no variation in tone, no inflection—it was haunting and ominous.

Abraham smiled. He was proud of whatever he had done. "I do. The Order is broken, and I call you to bring forth the soulless, those who wander the abyss of the Underground, to join us here."

Mrs. English's empty eyes stared past him, but the voice answered. "It cannot be done."

Sarafine looked at Abraham, panicked. "What is she—"

He silenced Sarafine with a look, and turned back to the creature inhabiting the shell of Mrs. English. "I was not clear. We have bodies for them. Bring forth the soulless and offer them the bodies of the Light Casters. This will be the New Order. You will Bind it."

There was a rumbling sound within Mrs. English's body, almost as if the creature was laughing in some sick way. "I am the Lilum. Time. Truth. Destiny. The Endless River. The Wheel of Fate. You do not command me."

Lilum. Lilian English. It was like a sick cosmic joke. Except for the part that wasn't a joke, the part I couldn't stop repeating in my mind.

The Wheel of Fate crushes us all.

Abraham looked stricken, and Sarafine staggered backward. Whatever this Lilum thing was, the two of them had clearly believed they could control it.

Abraham tightened his grip on *The Book of Moons* and changed tactics. "Then I appeal to you as the Demon Queen. Help us forge a New Order. One where the Light will finally be eclipsed by Darkness forever."

I froze. It was all coming together. The Shadowing Song was right. Even if I hadn't heard a word about this Lilum thing, the song had warned me about the Demon Queen and the Wheel of Fate more than once.

I tried not to panic.

The Lilum answered, her voice unnervingly even. "Light and Dark hold no meaning for me. There is only power, born from the Dark Fire, where all power was created."

What was she talking about? She was the Demon Queen. Didn't that make her Dark?

"No." Sarafine's voice was a whisper. "It's not possible. The Demon Queen is true Darkness."

"My truth is the Dark Fire, the origin of power both Light and Dark."

Sarafine looked confused, something I had never seen in her outside of the visions.

That's when I realized she and Abraham didn't understand the Lilum at all. I couldn't pretend that I did, but I knew she wasn't Dark in the way they believed. She was something all her own. Maybe the Lilum was gray, a new shade in the spectrum. Or maybe it was the opposite, and the Lilum possessed neither Dark nor Light—she was the absence of both.

Either way, she wasn't one of them.

"But you can forge a New Order," Sarafine said.

Mrs. English's head jerked toward the sound of Sarafine's voice. "I can. But a price must be paid."

"What's the price?" I called out without thinking.

The head jerked toward me. "A Crucible."

The Demon Queen, the Wheel of Fate—whoever she was, she wasn't talking about my English homework. "I don't understand."

"Shut up, boy!" Abraham snapped.

But the Lilum was still staring blankly in my direction. "This Mortal has the words I require." The Lilum paused. She was talking about Mrs. English. "Crucible. A pot for melting metals. A Mortal allegory." Was she searching Mrs. English's mind for the right words? "A severe test." She stopped. "Yes. A test. On the Eighteenth Moon."

"What's the test?"

"On the Eighteenth Moon," she repeated. "For One who will bring the Order back anew."

It was the message from my Shadowing Song—most of it, anyway.

The One Who Is Two.

"Who?" Abraham demanded. "Tell me now! Who will bring back the Order?"

Mrs. English's neck jerked unnaturally toward Abraham, the black-shadowed eye sockets facing him. A thunderous sound ripped through the house. "You do not command me."

Before he could respond, a blinding light streaked from the dark sockets where Mrs. English's eyes should have been— directly at Abraham and Sarafine. Abraham didn't even have time to rip. The light hit them and exploded around them, filling the room. Sarafine's invisible grip disappeared, and I threw my arm over my eyes to shield them from the light. But I could still sense it, as if I was looking into the sun.

Within seconds, the impossible brightness dimmed and I pulled my arm away from my face. I looked at the place where Abraham and Sarafine had been standing. Black splotches clouded my vision.

Abraham and Sarafine were gone.

"Are they dead?" I found myself hoping. Maybe Abraham had used *The Book of Moons* one time too many. The Book always took something in return.

"Dead." The Lilum paused. "No. It is not their time to be judged."

I disagreed, but I wasn't about to argue with a creature powerful enough to make Abraham and Sarafine disappear. "What happened to them?"

"I willed them away. I do not wish to hear their voices." She didn't really answer the question.

But I had another one, and I had to find the courage to ask it. "The one who has to face the test on the Eighteenth Moon—are you talking about the One Who Is Two?"

The darkened sockets of her eyes turned toward me, and the voice began to speak. "The One Who Is Two, in Whom the Balance is paid. The Dark Fire, from which all power comes, will make the Order anew."

"So we can fix it? The Order, I mean?"

"If the Balance is paid, there will be a New Order." Her voice was completely flat, as if what I had been hoping for meant nothing.

"What do you mean by the Balance?"

"Balance. Payment. Sacrifice."

Sacrifice.

By the One Who Is Two.

"Not Lena," I whispered. I couldn't lose her again. "She can't be the sacrifice. She didn't mean to break the Order."

"Both Dark and Light. Perfect balance. True magic." The Lilum was quiet. Was she thinking, searching for words in the mind of Mrs. English, or just getting tired of hearing my voice, too? "She is not the Crucible. The child of Darkness and Light will Bind the New Order."

It wasn't Lena.

I took a deep breath. "Wait. Then who is it?"

"There is another."

Maybe she didn't understand what I was asking. "Who?"

"You will find the One Who Is Two." The empty black shadows stared at me from the face of Mrs. English.

"Why me?"

"Because you are the Wayward. The one who marks the way between our worlds. The Demon world and the Mortal world."

"Maybe I don't want to be the Wayward." I said it without thinking, but it was true. I didn't know how to find this person. And I didn't want the fate of the Mortal and Caster worlds resting with me.

The walls began to shake again, the ceramic figurines knocking against one another. I watched as the little moon moved dangerously close to the edge of the mantel. "I understand. We cannot choose what we are in the Order. I am the Demon Queen." Did she mean that she didn't want to be what she was either? "The Order of Things exists beyond. The River flows. The Wheel turns. This moment changes the next. You have changed everything." The walls ceased shaking, and the moon stopped just before it fell over the edge.

"This is the way. There is no other."

I understood that.

It was the last thing the Lilum said before the possessed body of Mrs. English dropped to the floor.

⊰ 11.01 ⊱

Bad-Eye Side

With her glasses knocked off, her glass eye closed, and her hair unraveled from its maniacal bun—Lilian English almost looked like a person.

A nice person.

I called 911. Then I sat in the worn flowered chair, staring at Mrs. English's body, waiting for the ambulance. I wondered if she was dead. Another casualty in this war I wasn't sure we could win.

Another thing that was my fault.

The ambulance arrived not long after that. By the time Woody Porter and Bud Sweet found a pulse, I could breathe again. I watched as they loaded the gurney into the back of the "bus," as Woody called it.

"Anyone you can call for her?" Bud asked as he slammed the ambulance doors.

There was one person.

"Yeah. I'll call someone." I went back into Mrs. English's tiny house, through the hall and into the kitchen with the hummingbird wallpaper. I didn't want to call my dad, but I owed Mrs. English that much after everything she'd been through. I lifted the pastel pink receiver off the cradle and stared at the rows of numbers.

My hand started to shake.

I couldn't remember my phone number.

Maybe I was in shock. That's what I kept telling myself, but I knew it was more than that. Something was happening to me. What I didn't know was why.

I closed my eyes, willing my fingers to find the right numbers.

Combinations of numbers marched through my mind. Lena's number and Link's and the Gatlin County Library's. There was only one phone number I couldn't remember.

My own.

Lilian English missed her first day of school in about a hundred and fifty years. The actual diagnosis was severe exhaustion. It made sense, I guess. Abraham and Sarafine could do that to anyone, even without the help of a Demon Queen.

Which left Lena and me hanging out alone in the classroom a few days later. Class was over, and Principal Harper had collected the pile of papers he would never grade, but we were still sitting at our desks.

I think we both wanted to stay a while longer in the place where Mrs. English had never been a puppet, where she'd been a Demon Queen all her own. The real Mrs. English was the hand of justice, even if she wasn't the Wheel of Fate. There was never a curve in her class. Between that and the whole Crucible thing, I could see why the Lilum had thrived in Mrs. English's body.

"I should have known. She was acting creepy all year." I sighed. "And I knew her glass eye was on the wrong side at least once."

"You think the Lilum was teaching our English class? You said the Lilum talked really weird. We would've noticed." Lena was right.

"The Lilum must have been inside Mrs. English some of the time, because Abraham and Sarafine showed up at her house. And, trust me, they knew what they were looking for."

We were sitting in silence at opposite ends of the room. Today, I was on the Bad-Eye Side. It was that kind of day. I had recounted every detail of the other night to Lena three times, except the part about forgetting my phone number. I didn't want her to worry, too. But she was still having trouble wrapping her mind around it all. I couldn't blame her. I had been there, and I wasn't doing much better.

Lena finally said something, from the Good-Eye Side. "Why do you think we have to find this One Who Is Two?" She was more upset than I was, maybe because she had just found out about it. Or maybe because it involved her mother.

"Did you miss the whole Crucible speech?" I'd told her everything I could remember.

"No. I mean, what is this 'One' going to do that we can't? To forge the New Order, or whatever." She left her seat and sat on the edge of Mrs. English's desk, her legs dangling. The New Order. No wonder she was thinking about it. Lena knew the Lilum said that she would be the one to Bind it.

"How do you Bind a New Order, anyway?" I asked her.

She shrugged. "No clue."

There had to be some way to find out. "Maybe there's something in the *Lunae Libri* about it."

Lena looked frustrated. "Sure. Look under N, for *New Order*. Or B, for *Binding*. Or P, for *psycho*, which is how I'm starting to feel."

"Tell me about it."

She sighed, swinging her legs harder. "Even if I knew how to do it, the bigger question is, why me? I broke the last one." She looked tired, her black T-shirt damp with sweat and her charm necklace tangled in her long hair.

"Maybe it needed to be broken. Sometimes things have to break before you can fix them."

"Or maybe it didn't need fixing."

"You want to get out of here? I've had enough Crucible talk for today."

She nodded, grateful. "Me, too."

We walked down the hall, holding hands, and I watched as Lena's hair began to curl. The Casting Breeze. So I wasn't surprised when Miss Hester didn't even look up from painting her long purple nails as we passed by, leaving the Demon and the Mortal worlds behind us.

Lake Moultrie really was as hot and brown as Link said. There wasn't a drop of water in sight. Nobody was around, though there were a few souvenirs from Mrs. Lincoln and her friends, stuck in the cracked mud of the sloping shore.

COMMUNITY WATCH HOTLINE

REPORT ALL APOCALYPTIC BEHAVIOR

She'd even written her home phone number across the bottom.

"What, exactly, constitutes apocalyptic behavior?" Lena tried not to smile.

"I don't know, but I'm sure if we asked Mrs. Lincoln to post a clarification, she'd have it up here tomorrow." I thought about it. "No fishing. No dumping. No calling up the Devil. No plagues of heat and lubbers, or Vexes."

Lena kicked the dry dirt. "No rivers of blood." I'd told her about my dream—that one, anyway. "And no human sacrifice."

"Don't give Abraham any ideas."

Lena put her head on my shoulder.

"Do you remember last time we were here?" I poked her with a dry piece of river grass. "You ran away on the back of John's Harley."

"I don't want to remember that part. I want to remember the good part," she whispered.

"There are a lot of good parts."

She smiled, and I knew I would always remember this day. Like the day I found her crying in the garden at Greenbrier. There were times when I looked at her and everything stopped. When the world fell away and I knew nothing could ever come between us.

I pulled her against me and kissed her harder, in a dead lake where no one could see us and no one cared. With every passing second, the pain was building in my body, the pressure of my pounding heart, but I didn't stop. Nothing else mattered but this. I wanted to feel her hands on my skin, her mouth tugging on my bottom lip. I wanted to feel her body against mine until I couldn't feel anything else.

Because unless we found whoever it was, and convinced the One Who Is Two to do whatever had to be done by the Eighteenth Moon, I had a sinking feeling it didn't matter what happened to either of us.

She closed her eyes, and I closed mine, and even though we weren't holding hands, it felt like we were.

Because what we had, we knew.

The Next Generation

Back off, Boy Scout. I've told you everything I know. Why would I hide anything now?" John smiled and looked over at Liv. "I only wear the pants around here. She's the one wearing the belt."

It was true. His scorpion belt was slung around Liv's waist. Lena had given it to Liv, since she seemed to be John's babysitter when Macon wasn't with him. They never left him alone. At night, Macon even Bound the study with Concealment and Confinement Casts.

But if John was telling the truth about his abilities, he would only have to touch Macon to gain some of his powers. The question was, why didn't he? I was beginning to think he didn't want to leave, but it made no sense.

Lately, nothing did.

Since my conversation with the Lilum—Wheel of Fate,

Demon Queen, Mrs. English Who Was Not Mrs. English—I had more questions than answers. I had no idea how to find the One Who Is Two, and I didn't know how much time we had left.

I needed to figure when the Eighteenth Moon was coming. I couldn't give up on the idea that it had something to do with John Breed, ever since the John in County Care scribbled that message.

This John didn't seem to care. He was lounging around on a cot against the wall, alternating between sleeping and pissing me off.

Lena was frustrated. John's charm didn't get him anywhere with her. "Abraham must have said something to you about the Eighteenth Moon."

He shrugged, looking bored. "Your boyfriend's the one who can't shut up about it."

"Yeah? You want to get off your ass and shut me up?"

Ethan, calm down. Don't let him get to you.

Liv stepped in. "Ethan, I think we can keep things a little more civil down here. For all we know, John is as much a victim of Abraham's reign of terror as the rest of us." She sounded sympathetic—too sympathetic.

"Did he bite any of your *best friends* lately?" I snapped.

Liv looked embarrassed.

"Then I don't want to hear about being civil."

John pushed himself up from the cot. "You don't have to talk to her like that. You're pissed at me. Don't take it out on Olivia. She's busting her ass to help you."

I looked at Liv. She was blushing as she checked the dials on her selenometer. I wondered if John's Incubus magnetism was having an effect on her. "No offense, but shut the hell up."

"Ethan!" Lena gave me her version of the Look. Now I was getting it from all sides.

John was amused. "You want me to talk, you want me to shut up. Let me know when you make up your mind."

I didn't want to talk to him at all. I wanted him to disappear. "Liv, what's the point of keeping him around? He hasn't told us anything. I bet he used his Caster power-sucking abilities to send a message to Abraham and Sarafine, and they're on their way here right now."

Liv crossed her arms, disapprovingly. "John hasn't been sucking anyone's powers. Most of the time, he's alone with me. Or Macon and me." She started to blush. "And yelling at him isn't going to get you anywhere. John is basically a victim of torture. You can't imagine the way Silas and Abraham treated him when he was growing up. Nothing you can say comes close to what he's endured."

I turned to John. "So, this is what you've been doing down here? Telling Liv sob stories so she'll feel sorry for you? Man, you really are a manipulative asshole."

John stood up and walked over to where I was standing. "Funny, I was thinking what a charming asshole you are."

"Really?" I made a fist.

"No." So did he.

"That's enough." Lena stepped between us. "This isn't helping."

"And it isn't scientific, polite, or even remotely entertaining," Liv added.

John wandered back to his cot. "I don't know why everyone is so convinced this has to do with me."

I wasn't about to tell him about the messages from a kid who had suffered a head injury and didn't speak. "This has something to do with the Eighteenth Moon. Lena's isn't until February, unless Sarafine and Abraham are pulling moons out of time again." Lena crossed her arms, watching John.

He shrugged, revealing the black tattoo on his arm. "So you have a few months. Better get cracking."

"I told you, she didn't say it was Lena's Eighteenth Moon. We may not have that much time."

Liv whipped around to look at me. "Who didn't say that?"

Crap. I didn't want to tell her about the Lilum yet, especially not in front of John. Lena wasn't the only girl I knew who was two things. Liv wasn't a Keeper anymore, but she was still acting like one. "No one. It's not important."

Liv was watching me carefully. "You said a guy named John at County Care knew about the Eighteenth Moon—the one in the creepy birthday room. I thought that was the reason you're here hounding John."

"Hounding John? Is that what you think I'm doing?" I couldn't believe how quickly he had gotten to her.

"Actually, I'd call it harassing." John looked smug.

I ignored him. I was too busy trying to cover my tracks with Liv. "It was a guy named John, but he wasn't in the Birthday—"

I stopped.

A guy named John.

Lena looked back at me.

The Birthday Room.

We were thinking the same thing.

What if we've been looking at this all wrong?

"John, when's your birthday?"

He was stretched out, tossing a ball above the spot where his boots were propped against the wall. "Why, you gonna throw me a party, Mortal? I'm not big on cake."

"Just answer the question," Lena said.

The ball hit the wall again. "December 22nd. At least that's what Abraham told me. But it's probably some random day he picked. He found me, remember? It's not like I had a note pinned to my shirt with my birthday written on it."

He couldn't be that stupid. "Does Abraham seem like the kind of guy who would care if you had a birthday or not?"

The ball stopped hitting the wall.

Liv was flipping through an almanac. I heard her breath catch. "Oh my God."

John walked to the table and leaned over Liv's shoulder. "What?"

"December 22nd is the winter solstice, the longest night of the year."

John dropped into the chair next to her. He tried to look bored, his general expression, but I could tell he was curious. "So, it's a long night. Who cares?"

Liv closed the almanac. "Ancient Celts considered winter solstice the most sacred day of the year. They believed the Wheel of the Year stopped turning for a short time at the moment of the solstice. It was a time of cleansing and rebirth—"

Liv was still talking, but I couldn't hear anything but my own thoughts.

The Wheel of the Year.

The Wheel of Fate.

Cleansing and rebirth.

A sacrifice.

It's what the Lilum was trying to tell me at Mrs. English's

house. On the Eighteenth Moon, the night of the winter solstice, the sacrifice would have to be made to bring forth the New Order.

"Ethan?" Lena was staring at me, concerned. "Are you okay?"

"No. None of us are." I looked at John. "If you're telling the truth, and you aren't waiting around for Abraham and Sarafine to come to the rescue, I need you to tell me everything you can about him."

John leaned across the table toward me. "If you think I can't break out of a little study in the Tunnels, you're a bigger idiot than I thought. You have no idea what I can do. I'm here because—" He glanced at Liv. "I have nowhere else to go."

I didn't know if he was lying. But all the signs—the songs, the messages, even Aunt Prue and the Lilum—pointed to him.

John handed Liv a pencil. "Get out that red notebook, and I'll tell you whatever you want to know."

After listening to John talk about his childhood with Silas Ravenwood—who sounded like a military drill sergeant who spent most of his time beating the crap out of John or forcing him to memorize Silas' anti-Caster doctrine—even I was starting to feel a little sorry for him. Not that I would ever admit it.

Liv was writing down every word. "So, basically, Silas hates Casters. Interesting, considering he married two of them." She glanced at John. "And raised one."

John laughed, and there was no way to miss the bitterness in his voice. "I wouldn't want to be around if he heard you call me that. Silas and Abraham never considered me a Caster. According to Abraham, I'm 'the next generation'—stronger, faster, impervious to sunlight, and all that good stuff. Abraham is pretty apocalyptic for a Demon. He believes the end is coming, even if he has to bring it around himself, and the inferior race will finally be wiped out."

I rubbed my hands over my face. I wasn't sure how much more of this I could take. "I guess that's bad news for us Mortals."

John gave me a strange look. "Mortals aren't the inferior race. You're just the bottom of the food chain. He's talking about Casters."

Liv tucked her pencil behind her ear. "I didn't realize how much he hated Light Casters."

John shook his head. "You don't get it. I'm not talking about Light Casters. Abraham wants to get rid of all the Casters."

Lena looked up, surprised.

"But Sarafine—" Liv started to say.

"He doesn't care about her. He only tells her what she wants to hear." John's voice was serious. "Abraham Ravenwood doesn't care about anyone."

———

There were a lot of nights when I couldn't sleep, but tonight I didn't want to. I wanted to forget about Abraham Ravenwood plotting to destroy the world, and the Lilum promising it would destroy itself. Unless, of course, someone wanted to sacrifice themselves. Someone I had to find.

If I fell asleep, those thoughts would twist themselves into rivers of blood as real as the mud in my sheets when I first met Lena. I wanted to find a place to hide from all of it, where the nightmares and the rivers and reality couldn't find me. For me, that place was always inside a book.

And I knew just the one. It wasn't under my bed; it was in one of the shoe boxes stacked against my walls. Those boxes held everything that was important to me, and I knew what was inside all of them.

At least I thought I did.

For a second, I couldn't move. I scanned the brightly colored cardboard boxes, searching for the mental map that would lead me to the right one. But it wasn't there. My hands started shaking. My right hand—the one I used to write with—and my left—the one I used now.

I didn't know where it was.

Something was wrong with me, and it had nothing to do with Casters or Keepers or the Order of Things. I was changing, losing more and more of myself every day. And I had no idea why.

Lucille jumped off my bed when I started tearing through the boxes, tossing the lids, dumping everything from bottle caps and basketball cards to faded pictures of my mom all over my bedroom floor. I didn't stop until I found it in a black Adidas box. I flipped the lid and it was there—my copy of John Steinbeck's *Of Mice and Men*.

It wasn't a happy story, the kind you'd expect a person to reach for when they were trying to chase away whatever was haunting them. But I chose it for a reason. It was about sacrifice; whether it was self-sacrifice or sacrificing someone else to save your own skin—that was a matter of debate.

I figured I could decide tonight, as I turned the pages.

It was too late when I realized someone else must have been searching for answers within the covers of a book.

Lena!

She was turning pages, too—

When Sarafine turned nineteen, she gave birth to a beautiful baby girl. The baby was a surprise, and although Sarafine spent hours staring at her daughter's delicate face, the child was a mixed blessing. Sarafine had never wanted to have a baby. She didn't want a child to live the life of uncertainty that came with being a Duchannes. She didn't want her child to have to fight the Darkness that Sarafine knew was lurking inside her. Until the child would get her real name at sixteen, Sarafine called her daughter Lena, because it meant "the bright one," in the futile hope of staving off the curse. John had laughed. It sounded like something Mortals would do, hanging their hopes on a name.

Sarafine had to hang her hopes on something.

Lena wasn't the only unexpected person to show up in her life.

Sarafine was walking alone when she saw Abraham Ravenwood standing on the same corner where she had first met him, almost a year before. He seemed to be waiting, as if he knew she was coming. As if he could somehow see the war being waged on the battlefield of her mind. A war she never knew if she was winning.

He waved, as though they were old friends. "You look troubled, Miss Duchannes. Is something bothering you? Is there anything I can do to help?"

With his white beard and cane, Abraham reminded Sarafine of her grandfather. She missed her family, even though they refused to see her. "I don't think so."

"Still fighting your nature? Have the voices grown stronger?"

They had, but how could he know? Incubuses didn't go Dark. They were born into the Darkness.

He tried again. "Have you been starting fires by accident? It's called the Wake of Fire."

Sarafine froze. She had inadvertently started several fires. When her emotions intensified, it was as if they actually manifested into flames. Only two thoughts consumed her now: fire and Lena.

"I didn't know it had a name," she whispered.

"There are a number of things you don't know. I would like to invite you to study with me. I can teach you everything you need to know."

Sarafine looked away. He was Dark, a Demon. His black eyes told her everything she needed to know. She couldn't trust Abraham Ravenwood.

"You have a child now, don't you?" It wasn't really a question. "Do you want her to walk the world beholden to a curse that dates back to before you were born? Or do you want her to be able to Claim herself?"

Sarafine didn't tell John she was meeting Abraham Ravenwood in the Tunnels. He wouldn't understand. For John, the world was black or white, Light or Dark. He didn't know they could exist together, within the same person, as they did in her. She hated lying, but she was doing it for Lena.

Abraham showed her something no one in her family had ever spoken of—a prophecy related to the curse. A prophecy that would save Lena.

"*I'm sure the Casters in your family never told you about this. He held the faded paper in his hand as he read the words that promised to change everything: "'The First will be Black / But the Second may choose to turn back.'*"

Sarafine felt her breath catch.

"*Do you understand what it means?*" *Abraham knew the words meant everything to her, and she clung to his as if they were part of the prophecy. "The first Natural born into the Duchannes family would be Dark, a Cataclyst." He was talking about her. "But the second will have a choice. She can Claim herself."*

Sarafine found the courage to ask the question eating away at her. "Why are you helping me?"

Abraham smiled. "I have a boy of my own, not much older than Lena. Your father is raising him. His parents abandoned him because he has some very unusual powers. And he has a destiny as well."

"*But I don't want my daughter to go Dark.*"

"*I don't think you truly understand Darkness. Your mind has been poisoned by Light Casters. Light and Dark are two sides of the same coin.*"

Part of Sarafine wondered if he was right. She prayed he was.

Abraham was also teaching her how to control the urges and the voices. There was only one way to exorcise them. Sarafine set fires, burned down huge cornfields and stretches of forests. It was a relief to allow her powers free reign. And no one got hurt.

But the voices still came for her, whispering the same word again and again.

Burn.

When the voices weren't haunting her, she could hear Abraham in her head, bits and pieces of their conversations looping over and over again: "Light Casters are worse than Mortals. Filled with jealousy because their powers are inferior, they want to dilute our bloodlines with Mortal blood. But the Order of Things will not allow it." Late at night, some of the words made sense. "Light Casters reject the Dark Fire, from which all power comes." Some she tried to force deep into the shadows of her mind. "If they were strong enough, they would kill us all."

I was lying on the floor of my trashed bedroom, staring at my sky blue ceiling. Lucille was sitting on my chest, licking her paws.

Lena's voice found its way into my mind so quietly I almost didn't hear it.

She was doing it for me. She loved me.

I didn't know what to say. It was true, but it wasn't that simple. Sarafine was sinking deeper and deeper into darkness in every vision.

I know she loved you, L. I just don't think she could fight what was happening to her. I couldn't believe I was defending the woman who had killed my mom. But Izabel wasn't Sarafine, at least not right away. Sarafine killed Izabel, just like she killed my mother.

Abraham was what happened to her.

Lena was looking for someone to blame. We all were.

I heard pages turning.

Lena, don't touch it!

Don't worry. It doesn't trigger the visions every time.

I thought about the Arclight, the way it pulled me out of this world and into another randomly. What I didn't want to think about was the last thing Lena said—every time. How many times had she opened Sarafine's book? Lena was Kelting again before I could decide whether or not to ask.

This one's my favorite. She wrote it over and over inside the covers. "Suffering has been stronger than all other teaching, and has taught me to understand what your heart used to be."

I wondered whose heart Sarafine had meant.

Maybe it was her own.

More Wrong Than Right

It was Thanksgiving Day, which meant two things.

A visit from my Aunt Caroline.

And the annual bake-off between Amma's pecan pie, Amma's apple pie, and Amma's pumpkin pie. Amma always won, but the competition was fierce, and the judging the subject of lots of noise around the table.

I was looking forward to it more than usual this year. It was the first time Amma had baked a pie in months, and part of me suspected the only reason she'd done it today was so no one else would notice. But I didn't care. Between my dad dressed in his sport coat instead of pajamas like last year, Aunt Caroline and Marian playing Scrabble with the Sisters, and the smell of pies in the oven, I almost forgot about the lubbers and the heat, and my great-aunt missing from the table. The hard part was that it reminded me of all the other things I'd been forgetting lately —

the things I hadn't meant to forget. I wondered how much longer I would be able to remember.

There was only one person I could think of who might know the answer to that question.

I stood in front of Amma's bedroom door for a good minute before I knocked. Getting answers out of Amma was like pulling teeth, if the teeth belonged to a gator. She had always kept secrets. It was as much a part of her as her Red Hots and crossword puzzles, her tool apron and her superstitions. Maybe it was part of being a Seer, too. But this was different.

I'd never seen her walk away from the stove on Thanksgiving while her pies were still baking, or skip making Uncle Abner's lemon meringue altogether. It was time to grow those kneecaps.

I reached up to knock.

"You gonna come in already or wear a hole in the carpet?" Amma called from inside her room.

I opened the door, prepared to see the rows of shelves lined with mason jars, full of everything from rock salt to graveyard dirt. Bookshelves crammed with cracked volumes that had been handed down, and notebooks with Amma's recipes. It wasn't long ago that I realized those recipes might not have anything to do with cooking. Amma's room had always reminded me of an apothecary, brimming with mystery and the cure for whatever ailed you, like Amma herself.

Not today. Her room was torn apart, the way mine was after I'd dumped the contents of twenty shoe boxes all over my floor. Like she was looking for something she couldn't find.

The bottles that were usually lined up neatly on the shelves, labels facing out, were pushed together on top of her dresser.

Books were stacked on the floor, on her bed, everywhere but on the shelves. Some of them were open—old diaries handwritten in Gullah, the language of her ancestors. There were other things I had never seen in here before—black feathers, branches, and a bucket of rocks.

Amma was sitting in the middle of the mess.

I stepped inside. "What happened in here?"

She held out her hand, and I pulled her up. "Nothin's what happened. I'm cleanin' up. Would do you some good to try it in that mess you call a room." Amma tried to shoo me out, but I didn't move. "Go on, now. Pies are almost done."

She pushed past me. In a second, she'd be out in the hall and on her way to the kitchen.

"What's wrong with me?" I blurted it out, and Amma stopped dead in her tracks. For a second, she didn't say a word.

"You're seventeen. I expect there's more wrong with you than right." She didn't turn around.

"You mean like writing with the wrong hand and hating chocolate milk and your scrambled eggs all of a sudden? Forgetting the names of people I've known my whole life? Is that the kind of stuff you're talking about?"

Amma turned around slowly, her brown eyes shining. Her hands were shaking, and she pushed them into the pockets of her apron so I wouldn't notice.

Whatever was happening to me, Amma knew what it was.

She took a deep breath. Maybe she was finally going to tell me. "I don't know about any a that. But I'm—lookin' into it. Might have something to do with all this heat and these darn bugs, the problems the Casters are havin'."

She was lying. It was the first time Amma had ever given

what sounded like a straight answer in her life. Which made it even more crooked.

"Amma, what aren't you telling me? What do you know?"

" 'I know that my Redeemer lives.' " She looked at me, defiant. It was a line from a hymn I grew up hearing in church, while making spitballs and trying not to fall asleep.

"Amma."

" 'What comfort this sweet sentence gives.' " She clapped her hand on my back.

"Please."

Now she was all-out singing, which sounded kind of crazy. The way you sound when you think something terrible is about to happen, but you're trying to convince yourself that it isn't. The terrible shows up in your voice, even when you think you can hide it.

You can't.

" 'He lives, he lives who once was dead.' " She shoved me out of the room. " 'He lives, my ever-living Head.' "

The door slammed behind me.

"Now." She was already halfway down the hall, still humming the rest of the hymn. "Let's go eat before your aunts get into the kitchen and burn the house down."

I watched her scurry down the hall, shouting before she was halfway to the kitchen. "Everybody get on into the dinin' room, before my food gets cold."

I was starting to think I might have more luck asking my ever-living Head.

When I ducked under the doorframe and walked into the dining room, everyone else was already taking their seats. Lena and

349

Macon must have just arrived; they stood at one end of the dining room while Marian was deep in conversation with my Aunt Caroline at the other. Amma was still shouting orders from the kitchen, where the bird was "resting." Aunt Grace shuffled toward the table, waving her handkerchief. "Don't y'all keep this fine bird waitin' any longer. He died a noble death, and it's downright disrespectable." Thelma and Aunt Mercy were right behind her.

"If you call a noble death a buckshot in the bee-hind, then I reckon you're right." Aunt Mercy pushed past her sister so she could sit in front of the biscuits.

"Don't you start, Mercy Lynne. You know vegetablism is one step closer ta a world without panties an' preachers. That there is a documented fact."

Lena took the seat next to Marian, trying not to laugh. Even Macon was having trouble keeping a straight face. My dad was standing behind Amma's chair, waiting to push it in for her when she finally came in from the kitchen. Listening to Aunt Mercy and Aunt Grace peck away at each other made me miss Aunt Prue even more. But as I slid into my seat, I realized someone else was missing.

"Where's Liv?"

Marian glanced at Macon before she answered. "She decided to stay in tonight."

Aunt Grace caught enough to add her two cents. "Well, that just ain't American. Did you invite her, Ethan?"

"Liv isn't American. And yeah. I mean, yes, ma'am. I invited her."

It was nearly true. I had asked Marian to bring her. That was an invitation, right? Marian unfolded her napkin and placed it on her lap. "I'm not certain she felt comfortable coming."

Lena bit her lip, like she felt bad.

350

It's because of me.

Or me, L. I didn't exactly invite her myself.

I feel like a jerk.

Me, too.

But there was nothing more to say, because right then Amma came in, carrying the green bean casserole. "All right. It's time to thank the Good Lord and eat." She sat down, and my dad pushed in her chair and took his own seat. We all joined hands around the table, and my Aunt Caroline bowed her head to say the Thanksgiving prayer, the way she always did.

I could feel the power of my family. I felt it the same way I did when I joined a Caster Circle. Even though Lena and Macon were the only actual Casters here, I still felt it. The buzz of our own kind of power, instead of lubbers chewing up the town or Incubuses ripping up the sky.

Then I heard it, too. Instead of the prayer, all I could hear was the song, thundering into my mind so loud I thought my head would split.

Eighteen Moons, eighteen dead
Eighteen turned upon their head,
The Earth above, the sky below
The End of Days, the Reaper's Row…

Eighteen dead? Reaper's Row?

By the time Aunt Caroline stopped praying, I was ready to start.

Six pies later, pecan—and, as usual, Amma—had been declared the winners. My dad was falling into his customary post-turkey nap on the couch, wedged in between the Sisters. Dinner was cut short when we were all too full to sit upright in our hard wooden chairs.

I didn't eat as much as usual. I felt too guilty. All I could think about was Liv, sitting alone in the Tunnels on Thanksgiving. Whether it was a holiday to her or not.

I know.

Lena was standing in the kitchen doorway, staring at me.

L. It's not what you think.

Lena walked over to the counter, where the leftovers were piled up. "What I think is that you should pack up some of Amma's pie and take it down to the Tunnels."

"Why would you want me to do that?"

Lena looked embarrassed. "I didn't understand how she felt until the night Ridley Cast the *Furor*. I know what it's like not to have friends. It must be worse to have them and lose them."

"Are you saying you want me to be friends with Liv?" I didn't buy it.

She shook her head. I could see how hard this was for her. "No. What I'm saying is I trust you."

"Is this one of those tests guys don't understand and always fail?"

She smiled, covering the leftover pecan pie with tinfoil. "Not today."

Lena and I hadn't even opened the front door when Amma caught us. "Where do you think you're goin'?"

"We're going to Ravenwood. I'm going to take Liv some of your pecan pie."

Amma tried to give me the Look, but somehow it was just a

look to me. "What you mean is you're goin' down into those Tunnels."

"Only to see Liv, I promise."

Amma rubbed her gold charm. "Straight there and back. I don't want to hear about any Casts or fires, Vexes or any other Demons. Not a one. You hear me?"

I always heard her, even when she wasn't talking.

Lena lifted the Outer Door cut into the floorboards in Ridley's room. I still couldn't believe she was letting me go down alone. But, then again, if you could sense it when your boyfriend was thinking about kissing another girl, it wasn't that big a leap.

Lena handed me the pie. "I'll be in here when you're finished. I've been meaning to look around." I wondered if she had been in here since the night we found John. I knew Lena was worried about Ridley, especially now that she was powerless.

"I won't be long." I kissed her and stepped down onto the stairs I couldn't see.

I heard their voices before I saw their faces.

"I'm not sure this is a proper Southern Thanksgiving, since I've never had Thanksgiving dinner anywhere. But it's quite posh, what with the frozen dinner and all." Liv. She sounded suspiciously happy.

I didn't have to hear the next voice to know who it was.

"You're in luck. I've never had one either. Abraham and Silas weren't big on holidays. Then there's the whole not-needing-to-eat thing. So I have nothing to compare it to."

John.

"What, no Halloween? No Christmas? No Boxing Day?" Liv was laughing, but I could tell it was a real question.

"None of the above."

"That's a bit grim. I'm sorry."

"It's no big deal."

"So this is our first Thanksgiving, then." I heard her laugh.

"Together," he added. The way he said it made me feel sick, like I had eaten too many pieces of pie and then gone back for a turkey and stuffing sandwich.

I stuck my head around the corner. Sure enough, John and Liv were leaning over the table in the study Macon had set up for her. It was set with two candles and one TV dinner in a lopsided aluminum tray. Turkey. I felt terrible, especially after the dinner Amma made.

Liv was holding what had to be John's lighter, trying to light the candles on the table between them.

"Your hand is shaking."

"No, it's not." She looked down at her hand. "Well. It is a bit drafty down here."

"Do I make you nervous?" John smiled. "It's okay. I won't hold it against you."

"Nervous? Please." Liv's cheeks turned a familiar shade of pink. "I'm not afraid of you, if that's what you think." They stared at each other for a second.

"Ouch!" Liv dropped the lighter, shaking her hand. She must have burned her finger.

"Are you okay? Let me see." John grabbed her hand, opening it so he could see her fingers. He put his hand on top of Liv's, his huge palm covering her small one.

354

Liv bit her lip. "I think I need to run it under cold water."

"Hold on."

"What—" Liv stared down at their hands. John moved his, and Liv lifted hers, wiggling her fingers. "It doesn't hurt anymore. It's not even red. How did you do that?"

John looked embarrassed. "Like I said, if I touch a Caster, I get some of their power. I don't steal it or anything. It just happens."

"You're a Thaumaturge. A healer. Like Lena's cousin Ryan. You didn't—"

"Don't worry, it wasn't her. Picked it up from a girl I bumped into." I couldn't tell if he was being sarcastic or not.

Relief flooded Liv's face. "It's remarkable. You do know that, don't you?" She examined her finger again.

"I don't know anything. Except that I'm a freak of nature."

"I'm not so sure nature had much to do with it, since there isn't another person like you in the entire universe, as far as I know. But you are special." She said so it matter-of-factly, I almost would've believed it. If she wasn't talking to John Breed.

"I'm so special, no one wants me around." He laughed, but it sounded bitter. "So special, I do stuff I can't even remember."

"Back home we call that a pub crawl."

"I've lost whole weeks, Olivia." I hated the way he said her name.

O-li-vi-a. Like he wanted to stretch out every syllable and take as long as he could.

"Does it happen all the time?" Now Liv sounded curious, but it seemed like it was more than the wheels in her scientific mind turning. Because she also sounded sad.

He nodded. "Except when I was in the Arclight. Nothing to remember in there."

355

I cleared my throat and stepped into the room. "Yeah? Then maybe we should stick you back in that thing." They were startled. I could tell, because John's face went dark, and the guy who had been talking to Liv disappeared.

"Ethan. What are you doing here?" Liv looked flustered.

"I brought you some of Amma's famous pecan pie. We missed you at dinner. I didn't mean to interrupt." Except I did.

Liv tossed her napkin down on the table. "Don't be ridiculous. You're not interrupting anything. We were just sitting down to a supper of somewhat questionable hen parts."

"Hey. That's our first Thanksgiving you're talking about, sweetheart." John grinned at her—and stared at me.

I ignored him. "Liv, do you think you can help me with something for a minute?"

She pushed her chair away from the table. "Lead on, Wayward."

I could feel John's eyes on me as we left the room.

Sweetheart.

I grabbed Liv by the arm as soon as we were out of Incubus earshot. "What are you doing?"

"Trying to eat my Thanksgiving dinner." Her cheeks went pink, but she didn't slow down.

"I meant, what are you doing *with him*?"

She pulled her arm free. "Are you looking for something in particular? Was there a reason you needed me?" We had made our way to the *Lunae Libri* and disappeared into the stacks, and I watched the torches light along the wall, marking the way we had come. She took one from the wall.

"Last I heard, he doesn't eat anything but Doritos."

"He doesn't. He was keeping me company. Being...a friend."

I stepped in front of her, and she stopped walking. "Liv. He's not your friend."

She was annoyed. "Then what is he? If you're such an expert?"

"I don't know what he is or what he's doing, but I know he's not your friend."

"What do you care?"

"Liv, you could've come over today. You were invited. Macon and Marian were there. They wanted you to come."

"That's quite an invitation. I can't imagine how I missed it."

I knew her feelings were hurt, but I didn't know how to fix it. I should've invited her myself. "I mean, we all wanted you to come."

"I'm sure you did. Just as I'm sure I still have the bruises to show from the last time I saw Lena."

"The *Furor* was a spell. And believe me, you gave as good as you got."

She softened. "I know I could have come to your house today. But I didn't belong there. I don't belong anywhere. And, I suppose, neither does John. Maybe Mortals and Incubuses aren't so different after all."

"You do belong, Liv. And you don't have to stay down here with him. You're not a monster."

Like he is.

Ethan? Is everything okay?

Lena was reaching out to me.

Yeah, L. Be there in a minute.

No rush.

It was Lena's way of saying she didn't mind me talking to Liv,

357

whether or not I would ever get Liv to believe that. I wasn't sure I believed it myself.

Liv was staring at me. "What are you doing here, really? Because I'm fairly certain you aren't concerned about my social life."

"You're wrong." I was still holding the pie tin.

She took it, opening the foil and breaking off a piece of pie. "Delicious. So there is nothing new I should know about?" She broke off another corner. Amma's pie was a good distraction.

"What do you know about the Wheel of Fate?"

She looked surprised. "Funny you should ask." And just like that, the subject of Liv's personal life was closed, and we returned to her favorite subject—anything else.

"Why?"

"I've been thinking about it ever since we found the *Temporis Porta*." Liv pulled out her red notebook and opened it to a page in the middle. There was a sketch of three perfectly formed circles, each divided by spokes set in varying patterns. "This was all I could remember from the door."

"That looks right. You said it was some kind of code?"

She nodded. "I'm not certain, because you opened the door without using them. But I've been researching the symbol in Macon's library."

"And?"

She pointed at the drawing. "The repeated circle. I think it has something to do with what you're calling the Wheel of Fate."

"And the *Temporis Porta*?"

"I think so. But there's one thing I can't understand."

"What is it?" Something Liv didn't understand was a bad sign.

"The door opened by itself. You didn't even touch any of the circles. I wouldn't have believed it if I hadn't seen it with my own eyes."

I remembered the rough feel of the rowan wood beneath my forehead.

"And I couldn't go through it at all."

"But you said you didn't understand why." I wasn't sure where she was going with this.

"Whatever the Wheel of Fate is, I think it has something to do with you, not me."

I let her believe it, but I knew better. I could still hear Amma's voice, echoing in my head.

The Wheel of Fate crushes us all.

Fractured Soul

E than!"

Lena was screaming, and I couldn't find her. I tried to run, but I kept falling because the ground was moving beneath my feet. The pavement on Main was shaking so hard that dirt and rocks were flying up into my eyes. The road rolled on, and it felt like I was standing on the edge of two tectonic plates battling it out.

I stood there, one foot on each plate, while the world shook and the chasm between the plates widened. The crack was so big I knew I was going to fall. And it was getting bigger.

It was only a matter of time.

"Ethan!" I heard Lena's voice, but I couldn't see her.

I looked through the crack and saw her—far below me.

And then I was falling....

My floor hit me harder than usual.

Lena!

I heard her voice, groggy and half asleep.

I'm here. It was just a dream.

I flipped over onto my back, trying to catch my breath. I balled up the sheet and threw it across the room.

Everything's fine.

I knew I didn't sound very convincing.

Seriously, Ethan. Is your head okay?

I nodded, even though she couldn't see me.

My head's fine. It's the Earth's tectonic plates I'm worried about.

She didn't answer for a moment.

And you're worried about me.

Yeah, L. And you.

She knew when I woke up screaming her name that she had suffered another violent, frightening end in one of my dreams we hadn't shared since the Seventeenth Moon. And the dreams were getting worse, not better.

It's because of everything we went through last summer, Ethan. I'm still reliving it, too.

But I didn't tell her it was happening to me every night, or that she wasn't the one in danger this time. I didn't think she wanted to know how much reliving I was doing. I didn't want her to feel like it was getting in the way of living.

There was something else getting in the way of living, at least for me. The answer to the question that Amma wouldn't give me and I couldn't figure out. But I was pretty sure there was someone else who knew, and I finally had enough guts to go see him.

The only question left was whether or not I could get him to tell me.

———⟋℈⟍———

It was pitch-black outside as I pulled the front door closed behind me. When I turned around, Lucille was sitting on the porch, watching me.

"Didn't get enough of the Tunnels last time?" Lucille cocked her head to one side, her standard answer. "Let's get going."

I heard a rip. Actually, it sounded more like a nasty tear.

I spun around. I wasn't ready for another visit from Abraham. But this time it wasn't him—far from it.

Link was lying on his back, caught in the bushes. "Man, this Travelin' thing takes some serious practice." He climbed out of the bushes and brushed himself off. "Where we headed?"

"How did you know I was going somewhere? Were you fishing around in my head?" If he was, he was dead.

"I told you before, I don't wanna mess around in that Temple a Doom." He brushed off his Iron Maiden T-shirt. "I don't sleep, remember? I was wanderin' around outside, and I heard you sneakin' downstairs. It's one of my superpowers. So, where are we goin'?"

I wasn't sure if I should tell him. But the truth was I didn't want to go alone. "New Orleans."

"You don't know anybody in—" Link shook his head. "Dude, why does it always have to be graveyards and crypts with you? Can't we hang out somewhere that isn't full a dead bodies?"

Another question I couldn't answer.

—⟨⟩

The tomb of voodoo queen Marie Laveau was exactly the same. I stared at the Xs carved into the door, and wondered if we should leave our own—in case we never came back out. But there was no time to think about it, because Link had the door open in seconds and we were inside.

The rotted, crooked stairs were still there, leading down into the darkness. So were the smoke and the putrid smell that clung to your skin, even after you took a shower.

Link coughed. "Licorice and gasoline. That's nasty."

"Shh. Be quiet."

We reached the base of the stairs, and I could see the work-shop, or whatever this awful place was called. There was a dim light coming from inside, illuminating the jars and bottles. My skin crawled at the sight of reptiles and tiny mice frantically try-ing to escape.

Lucille hid behind my leg as if she was afraid she might end up in one of those jars.

"How do we know if he's home?" Link whispered.

Before I could answer, a voice rose from behind us. "I am always home, in one form or another."

I recognized the bokor's gravelly voice and heavy accent. He looked even more dangerous up close. His skin was unwrinkled, but scars marred his face. They looked like scratches and puncture wounds, as if he'd been attacked by a creature that wasn't in one of those jars. His long braids were ratty, and I could see tiny objects tied into them. Metal symbols and charms, bits of bone and beads laced so tightly that they'd become part of the hair itself. He was holding his snakeskin staff.

"We're—we're sorry to show up like this," I stammered.

"Was it a dare worth takin'?" His hand tightened on the staff. "Trespassin' is a violation a the law. Yours and mine."

"We didn't come here on a dare." My voice was still shaking. "We came to find you. I have questions, and I think you're the only person who can give me the answers."

The bokor's eyes narrowed, and he rubbed his goatee, intrigued. Or maybe contemplating how to dispose of our bodies after he killed us. "What makes you think I have the answers?"

"Amma. I mean, Amarie Treadeau. She was here. I need to know why." I had his attention now. "I think it was about me."

He studied me carefully. "So, you're the one. Interestin' you would come here, instead a to your Seer."

"She won't tell me anything."

There was something in his expression, beyond recognition. "This way."

We followed him into the room with the smoke and the fumes and the lingering residue of death. Link was next to me, whispering. "You sure this is a good idea?"

"I've got an Incubus with me, right?" It was a bad joke. But I was so scared, I could barely think.

"A quarter." Link took a deep breath. "Hope that's enough."

The bokor stood behind the wooden table as Link and I stood facing him on the other side. "What do you know about my business with the Seer?"

"I know she came to you about a spread she didn't like." I

didn't want to reveal everything I knew. I was afraid he would realize this wasn't our first time here. "I want to know what the cards said. Why she needed your help."

He watched me carefully, as if he could see right through me. It was the way Aunt Del looked at a room when she was sorting through the layers. "That's two questions, and only one a them matters."

"Which one?"

His eyes gleamed in the dark. "Your Seer needs my help to do somethin' she can't. To join the *ti-bon-age*, mend the seams she ripped herself."

I had no idea what he was talking about. What seams had Amma ripped?

Link didn't understand either. "T-bone what? What kinda steak are we talkin' about here?"

The bokor's eyes locked on me. "You really don't know what's waitin' for you? It's watchin' us now."

I couldn't speak.

It's watching us now.

"What—what is it?" I barely choked out the words. "How do I get rid of it?"

The bokor walked over to the terrarium filled with writhing snakes, and lifted the lid. "That's two questions again. I can only answer one."

"What's watching me?" My voice was shaking, and my hands—every part of me.

The bokor lifted a snake, its body ringed in black, red, and white. The snake coiled around his arm, but the bokor held its head as if he knew it might strike.

"I'll show you."

◆ ◆ ◆

He led us to the center of the room, close to the source of the nauseating smoke, a huge pillar that resembled a candle. It looked like it had been made by hand. Lucille crouched under a nearby table, trying to avoid the fumes—or maybe the snake or the crazy guy carrying what looked like eggshells over to a bowl at our feet. He crushed the shells with one hand, careful to keep his other hand on the head of the snake.

"The *ti-bon-age* is meant to be one. Never separated." He closed his eyes. "I will call Kalfu. We need the help of a powerful spirit."

Link elbowed me. "I don't know if I like the sound a that."

The bokor closed his eyes and started to speak. I recognized traces of Twyla's French Creole, but it was mixed with a language I'd never heard before. The words were muffled, as if the bokor was talking to someone close enough to hear him whisper.

I wasn't sure what we were supposed to see, but it couldn't be any weirder than Aunt Prue outside her body or the Lilum inside Mrs. English's.

The smoke started to swirl slowly, growing denser. I watched as it curved and began to take shape.

The bokor was chanting louder now.

The smoke started to change from black to gray, and the snake hissed. Something was forming from the smoke. I'd seen this before, in Bonaventure Cemetery, when Twyla called my mother's Sheer.

I couldn't take my eyes off the smoke. The body formed from the bottom up, just as my mom's had. The feet and the legs.

"What the hell?" Link tried to back up, but he tripped.

The torso and the arms.

The face was the final element to emerge.

It stared back at me.

A face I would have known anywhere.

My own.

I jumped away, scrambling backward.

"Holy crap!" Link shouted, but his voice seemed far away.

Panic gripped me like two hands wrapping themselves around my neck. The figure started to fade.

But before it did, the Sheer spoke. "I'm waiting."

Then it was gone.

The bokor stopped chanting, the sickening candle blew out, and it was over.

"What was that?" I was staring at the bokor. "Why is there a Sheer that looks like me?"

He walked back to the terrarium and dropped the snake inside with the others. "It doesn't look like you. It's your *ti-bon-age*. The other half a your soul."

"What did you say?"

The bokor took a match and relit the candle. "Half your soul is with the livin', and half's with the dead. You left it behind."

"Left it behind where?"

"In the Otherworld. When you died." He sounded almost bored.

When I died.

He was talking about the night Lena and Amma brought me back, on the Sixteenth Moon.

"How?"

The bokor flicked his wrist, and the match went out. "If you come back too fast, the soul can be fractured. Divided. One part

367

a the soul goes back with the livin', and the other half stays with the dead. Caught between this world and the Other, bound to the missin' half until they're brought back together."

Divided.

He couldn't be explaining it right. That would mean I only had half a soul. It didn't even seem possible.

How could a person only have half a soul? What happened to the rest of it? Where did it—

Bound to the missing half.

I knew what had been following me all this time, lurking in the shadows.

Me—the other me.

It was the reason I was changing, losing more and more of myself every day.

The reason I didn't like chocolate milk anymore, or Amma's scrambled eggs. The reason I couldn't remember what was in the shoe boxes in my bedroom, or my phone number. The reason I was suddenly left-handed.

My knees buckled, and I felt myself pitch forward. I could see the floor rising up to meet me. A hand grabbed my arm and hauled me back to my feet. Link.

"So, how do you get the two halves back together? Is there a spell or somethin'?" Link sounded impatient, like he was ready to throw me over his shoulder and run home.

The bokor threw his head back and laughed. When he spoke, it felt like he was looking right through me. "Takes more than a spell. That's why your Seer came to me. But don't you worry, we have an agreement."

I felt like someone had thrown a bucket of cold water on me. "What kind of agreement?"

368

I remembered what he had said to Amma, the night we followed her here. *There is only one price.*

"What's the price?" I was yelling, my voice echoing in my ears.

The bokor lifted his skin-covered staff and pointed it at me. "I've told you more than your share a secrets tonight." He smiled, all the darkness and evil within him twisting itself into a human face.

"How come we don't have to pay you?" Link asked.

"Your Seer will pay enough for you all."

I would have asked him again, but I knew he wouldn't tell us. And if there were deeper secrets than this, I didn't want to know.

Cards of Providence

When I got home, it was way past midnight. Everyone in my house was asleep—except one person. Amma's light was on, her room glowing between the two haint blue shutters. I wondered if she knew I was gone, and where I'd been. I almost hoped she did. It would make what I was about to do a hundred times easier.

Amma wasn't the kind of person you confronted. She was a confrontation all on her own. She lived by her rules, her law— the things she believed, which to her were as sure as the sun rising. She was also the only mother I had left. And, most days, the only parent. The idea of fighting with her made me feel hollow and sick inside.

But not as hollow as it made me feel to know I was only half of myself. Half the person I'd always been. Amma knew, and she had never said a word.

And the words she did say were lies.

I knocked on her bedroom door before I had time to change my mind. She opened it right away, as if she'd been waiting for me. She was wearing her white robe with the pink roses on it, the one I gave her on her birthday last year.

Amma didn't look at me. She looked past me, as if she could see something more than the wall behind me. Maybe she could. Maybe there were pieces of me scattered all over the place, like a broken bottle.

"Been waitin' on you." Her voice sounded small and tired, and she stepped out of the doorway so I could come in.

Amma's room still looked ransacked, but one thing was different. There were cards spread out on the little round table under the window. I walked over to the table and picked one up. The Bleeding Blade. They weren't tarot cards. "Reading cards again? What are they saying tonight, Amma?"

She crossed the room and started pushing the cards into a stack. "Don't have much to say. Think I've seen all there is to see."

Another card caught my eye. I held it up in front of her. "What about this one? The Fractured Soul. What does this one have to say?"

Her hands were shaking so hard that it took her three tries to grab the card from me. "You think you know somethin', but a piece a somethin' is the same as nothin'. Neither one gets you much a anything."

"You mean like a piece of my soul? Is that the same as nothing?" I said it to hurt her, to bust up her soul, so she could see how it felt.

371

"Where did you hear that?" Her voice was shaky. She grabbed the chain around her neck and rubbed the worn gold charm hanging from it.

"From your friend in New Orleans."

Amma's eyes went wide, and she grabbed the back of the chair to steady herself. I knew from her reaction that whatever she'd seen tonight, it wasn't me raising souls with the bokor. "Are you tellin' me the truth, Ethan Wate? Did you go to see that devil?"

"I went because you lied to me. I didn't have a choice."

But Amma wasn't listening to me. She was flipping the cards madly, pushing them around under her tiny palms. "Aunt Ivy, show me somethin'. Tell me what this means."

"Amma!"

She was muttering to herself, rearranging the cards over and over again. "I can't see anything. Has to be a way. There's always a way. Just have to keep lookin'."

I grabbed her shoulders, gently. "Amma. Put the cards down. Talk to me."

She held up a card. On the front was a picture of a sparrow with a broken wing. "The Forgotten Future. Know what these cards are called? Cards a Providence, because they tell more than just your future. They tell your fate. Know the difference?" I shook my head. I was afraid to say anything. She was coming unhinged. "Your future can change."

I looked into her dark eyes, which were filling with tears. "Maybe you can change fate, too."

The tears started falling, and she was shaking her head back and forth hysterically. "The Wheel a Fate crushes us all."

I couldn't stand to hear it again. Amma wasn't just going dark. She was going crazy, and I was watching it happen.

She pulled away, gathered up her robe, and dropped to her knees. Her eyes were shut tight, but her chin was turned up to her blue ceiling. "Uncle Abner, Aunt Ivy, Grandmamma Sulla, I'm in need a your intercession. Forgive me a my trespasses, as the Good Lord forgives us all." I watched as she waited, mumbling the words over and over. It was a good hour before she gave up, exhausted and defeated.

The Greats never came.

When I was little, my mother used to say that everything you needed to know about the South could be found in either Savannah or New Orleans. Apparently, the same was true about my life.

Lena didn't agree. The next morning, we were arguing about it in the back of history class. And I wasn't winning. "A Fractured Soul isn't two things, L. It's one thing split in half."

When I said "two souls," all Lena heard was "two" and assumed I was offering myself up as the One Who Is Two. "It could be any of us. I'm the One Who Is Two, if anyone is. Take a look at my eyes!" I could feel her rising panic.

"I'm not saying I'm the One Who Is Two, L. I'm just a Mortal. If it took a Caster to break the Order, it's going to take more than a Mortal to restore it, don't you think?" She didn't look convinced, but deep down she had to know I was right.

For better or worse, that's all I was—a Mortal. It was the

source of the whole problem between us. The reason we could barely touch, and couldn't really be together. How could I save the Caster world, when I could barely live in it?

Lena lowered her voice. "Link. He's two things, an Incubus and a Mortal."

"Shh." I glanced at Link, but he was oblivious, trying to carve LINKUBUS into his desk with a pen. "I'm pretty sure he barely qualifies as either one."

"John is two things, a Caster and an Incubus."

"L."

"Ridley. There could still be a trace of Siren inside her, even as a Mortal. Two." Now she was reaching. "Amma is a Seer and a Mortal. Two things."

"It's not Amma!" I must have been shouting, because the whole class turned around in their seats. Lena looked hurt.

"It isn't, Mr. Wate? Because the rest of us thought it was." Mr. Evans looked like he was ready to get out the little pink pad of detention slips.

"Sorry, sir."

I ducked down behind my textbook and lowered my voice. "I know it sounds weird, but this is a good thing. Now I know why all that crazy stuff has been happening, like the weird dreams and seeing the other half of myself all over the place. Now everything makes sense."

It wasn't completely true, and Lena wasn't convinced, but she didn't say anything else and neither did I. Between the heat and the bugs, Abraham and the Vexes, John Breed and the Lilum possessing the body of our English teacher, I figured we had enough to worry about.

At least that's what I told myself.

LET IT SNOW! TIME FOR A CHANGE IN THE WEATHER! BUY YOUR TICKETS NOW!

The posters were everywhere, as if the fact needed to be advertised. The winter formal was here, and this year the Dance Committee, made up of Savannah Snow and her fan club, decided to call it the Snow Ball. Savannah insisted it had nothing to do with her and everything to do with the heat wave, which is why everyone was calling it the Slush Ball. And Lena and I were going.

She didn't want to go, especially after what happened at the winter formal last year. When I gave her the tickets, she looked like she wanted to set them on fire. "This is a joke, right?"

"It's not a joke." I was sitting across from her at the lunch table, stabbing at the ice in my soda with my straw. This wasn't going to go well.

"Why would you possibly think I want to go to that dance?"

"To dance with me." I gave her a pathetic look.

"I can dance with you in my bedroom." She held out her hand. "In fact, come here. I'll dance with you right now, in the cafeteria."

"It's not the same."

"I'm not going." Lena was digging in her heels.

"Then I'll go with someone else," I said.

Her eyes narrowed.

"Like Amma."

She shook her head. "Why do you want to go so badly? And don't say to dance with me."

"It could be our last chance." It would be a relief to worry about something as harmless as a disaster at the dance, instead of the destruction of the world. I was almost disappointed Ridley wasn't around to ruin it with style.

So in the end Lena had caved, even though she was still mad about the whole thing. I didn't care. I was making her go. With everything going on, I didn't know if there would ever be another dance at Jackson.

We were sitting on the hot metal bleachers by the field, eating lunch on what should have been a cold December day. Lena and I didn't want to run into Mrs. English, and Link didn't want to run into Savannah, so the bleachers had become our hideout.

"You're still driving tomorrow, right?" I threw the crust of my sandwich at Link. Tomorrow night was the Snow Ball, and between Link and Lena, there was only a fifty-fifty chance we'd get there at all.

"Sure. Just tryin' to decide whether to wear my hair up or down. Can't wait till you see my smokin' new dress." Link threw the crust back at me.

"Wait until you see mine." Lena took a rubber band off her wrist, pulling her hair into a ponytail. "I think I'm wearing a raincoat and boots and bringing an umbrella, in case anyone takes the whole Slush Ball thing literally." She didn't try to hide the sarcasm in her voice.

It had been like this ever since I convinced them to go. "You guys don't have to come with me. But this may be the last dance in Gatlin—maybe anywhere. And I'm going."

"Stop saying that. It won't be the last dance." Lena was frustrated.

"Don't get your panties in a twist." Link punched my shoulder, a little too hard. "It'll be awesome. Lena's gonna fix everything."

"I am?" Lena smiled a little. "Maybe John bit you harder than we thought."

"Sure. Don't you have some kinda Don't-Let-This-Dance-Suck Cast?" Link had been depressed since Ridley took off. "Oh, wait. You don't. 'Cause it's gonna suck no matter what kinda Cast you've got."

"Why don't you try a Stay-Home-and-Shut-Your-Trap Cast? Since you're the one taking Savannah Snow to the dance." I wadded up my sandwich wrapper.

"She asked *me*."

"She asked *you* to her party after the game, and look how well that turned out."

Don't bring it up, Ethan.

Well, it's true.

Lena raised her eyebrow.

You'll only make him feel worse.

Trust me, Savannah's got that down.

Link sighed. "Where do you think she is right now?"

"Who?" I said, though we both knew exactly who he was talking about.

He ignored me. "Probably makin' trouble somewhere."

Lena folded her lunch bag into tinier and tinier squares. "Definitely making trouble somewhere."

The bell rang.

"It's probably better this way." Link stood up.

"It's definitely better this way," I agreed.

377

"Coulda been worse, I guess. It wasn't like I was that hung up on her. Like I was in love with her or somethin'." I wasn't sure who he was trying to convince, but he jammed his hands into his pockets and took off across the field before I could say anything.

"Yeah. That really would have sucked." I squeezed Lena's hand, letting it drop before I got light-headed.

"I feel so bad for him." She stopped walking and slipped her hands around my waist. I pulled her close, and she rested her head against my chest. "You know I'd do anything for you, right?"

I smiled. "I know you'd go to a stupid dance for me."

"I would. And I am."

I kissed her forehead, letting my lips stay on her skin as long as I could.

She looked up at me. "Maybe we can make tomorrow really fun. Help Link forget about my cousin for a little while."

"That's what I'm talking about."

"I have an idea. Something to fix a broken Linkubus heart."

The tip of her ponytail began to curl, and I walked across the field wishing there was a Cast for that.

⤙ 12.12 ⤚

Slush Ball

When Link pulled up in front of my house, Savannah was already in the front seat of the Beater. He got out and met me at the curb, like he had something to tell me. He was wearing a tacky ruffled tux shirt that made him look like he was in a mari-achi band, and tux pants with his high-top Vans.

"Nice threads."

"Thought Savannah would hate it. Thought she wouldn't get in the car. I swear, I tried everything." Normally, he would've been gloating. Tonight, he sounded miserable.

Rid's really gotten to him, L.

Just get him up here to the house. I have a plan.

"I thought you were meeting Savannah at the dance. Isn't she supposed to be there with Emily and the rest of the Dance Com-mittee?" I lowered my voice, but I didn't have to. I could hear a

Holy Rollers demo track blasting from the stereo, as if Link had been trying to drown Savannah out.

"I tried that. She wanted to take pictures." He shuddered. "Her mom and my mom. It was a nightmare." He broke into his standard impression of his mother. "Smile! Wesley, your hair is stickin' up. Stand up straight. Take the picture!"

I could only imagine. Mrs. Lincoln was fierce with a camera, and there was no way she was going to watch her son take Savannah Snow to the winter formal without documenting it for future generations. Mrs. Lincoln and Mrs. Snow were too much to take when you put them together in the same room. Especially when the room was Link's living room, where there wasn't a place to sit or look or even lean your hand against that wasn't shrink-wrapped in plastic.

"Bet you five bucks Savannah doesn't set foot in Ravenwood."

Link finally cracked a smile. "That's what I'm hopin'."

From the backseat of the Beater, Savannah looked like she was sitting in a big puddle of pink whipped cream. She tried to talk to me a few times, but it was impossible to hear anything over the music. When we turned at the fork in the road that led to Ravenwood, she started to squirm.

Link turned off the radio. "You sure you're okay with this, Savannah? You know folks say Ravenwood's been haunted ever since the War." He said it like he was telling a ghost story.

Savannah lifted her chin. "I'm not afraid. People say lots a things. Doesn't mean they're true."

"Yeah?"

"You should hear what they say about you and your friends." She turned back to look at me. "No offense."

Link blasted the radio, trying to drown her out, as Ravenwood's gates creaked open. *"This church picnic ain't no picnic. / You're my fried chicken. / Holy finger-lickin'..."*

Savannah yelled at him over the music. "Are you callin' me a piece a fried chicken?"

"Nah. Not you, Slush Queen. Never." He closed his eyes and pounded out the drums on the dashboard of the Beater. As I got out of the car, I felt sorrier for Link than ever.

Link started to open his door, but Savannah didn't move. The idea of setting foot inside Ravenwood must not have sounded so good after all.

The door opened before I knocked. I saw a swirl of fabric — green, with a gold shine to it, so it looked like both colors at the same time. Lena pulled the door wide, and the fabric floated off her shoulders, hanging down toward her waist almost like bits of wing.

Do you remember?

I remember. You look beautiful.

I did remember. Lena was the butterfly tonight, like the moon on the night of her Seventeenth Moon. What had looked like magic then still looked like magic now.

Her eyes sparkled.

One green, one gold. One Who Was Two.

A chill swept over me, out of place on the warm December night. Lena didn't notice, and I forced myself to ignore it. "You look — wow."

She twirled around, smiling. "You like it? I wanted to do something different. Come out of my cocoon a little."

You were never in a cocoon, L.

Her smile widened, and I said it again out loud. "You look...
like you. Perfect."

She pushed a curl back to show me her earlobe—a tiny gold
butterfly, with one gold wing and one green. "Uncle Macon had
them made. And this." She pointed to a tiny butterfly that rested
in the hollow of her neck, attached to a delicate gold chain.

I wished she was wearing her charm necklace, too. The only
times I'd ever seen her without it didn't end well. And I never
wanted anything about Lena to change.

She smiled.

I know. I'll put it on my charm necklace after tonight.

I leaned in and kissed her. Then I held up the small white box
I was holding. Amma had made her a corsage by hand, like she
did last year.

Lena opened the box. "It's perfect. I can't believe there's a
flower still blooming anywhere near here." But there it was, a
single golden blossom, nestled between looping green leaves. If
you looked at them right, they were their own version of wings,
almost as if Amma had known.

Maybe there were still some things she could see coming.

I slid the corsage onto Lena's wrist, but it snagged. As I
tugged on it, I noticed she was wearing the thin silver bracelet
from Sarafine's box. But I didn't say anything. I didn't want to
ruin the night before it even started.

Link honked the horn and cranked up the music even louder.

"We'd better go. Link's crashing and burning out there. At
least, he wishes he was crashing and burning."

Lena took a deep breath. "Wait." She put her hand on my
arm. "There's one more thing."

"What?"

"Don't be mad." There was no guy in the world who didn't know what those words meant. She was about to give me a reason to be mad.

"I won't." My stomach curled into a ball.

"You have to promise." Even worse.

"I promise." My stomach tightened, and the ball became a knot.

"I told them they could come." She said it quickly, as if I would be less likely to hear her.

"You told who what?" I wasn't sure I wanted to know. There were so many wrong answers to that question.

Lena pushed open the doors to Macon's old study. Through the crack, I could see John and Liv standing together in front of the fireplace. "They're together all the time now." Her voice dropped to a whisper. "I was pretty sure something was going on. Then Reece saw them repairing Macon's broken grandfather clock, and she saw their faces."

A clock. Like a selenometer, or a motorcycle. Things that worked the way Liv's mind did. I shook it off. Not John Breed, not with Liv.

"Fixing a clock?" I looked at Lena. "That's the big giveaway?"

"I told you, Reece saw them. And look at them. You don't have to be a Sybil to figure it out."

Liv was wearing an old-looking dress, like something she probably found in Marian's attic. It was low across her shoulders and hung in some complicated lacy way that only the worn leather scorpion belt interrupted. She looked like someone out of a movie you would watch in your English class after you'd read the book. Her blond hair was loose, instead of in braids.

She looked different. She looked...happy. I didn't want to think about it.

L? What's going on?

Watch.

John was standing behind her, wearing what was probably one of Macon's suits. He looked like Macon used to—dark and dangerous. He was pinning a corsage to a lacy strap on Liv's shoulder. She was teasing him, and I recognized the tone.

And Lena was right. Anyone who saw them together could tell something was going on.

Liv caught his hand as he fumbled. "I'd appreciate it if you didn't actually draw blood."

He tried again. "Then hold still."

"I am. It's the pin that's not." His hand was shaking.

I cleared my throat, and they looked up. Liv turned even pinker when she saw me. John stood taller.

"Hello there." Liv was still blushing.

"Hi." I couldn't think of what else to say.

"This is awkward." John smiled as if we were friends. I turned to Lena without answering, because we weren't.

"Even if this wasn't the weirdest idea you've ever come up with—and I'm not saying it isn't—how do you think we're going to pull this off? Neither one of them goes to Jackson."

Lena held up two more tickets to the Slush Ball. "You bought two, I bought two." She gestured to John. "Meet my date."

Excuse me?

She looked at Liv. "And yours."

Why are you doing this?

"We can bring whoever we want as our dates. It's just until we get inside."

Are you crazy, L?

No. It's a favor for a friend.

I looked at John and Liv.

Which one is suddenly your friend?

She reached up to put her hands on my shoulders, and kissed my cheek. "You."

"I don't understand."

We're moving forward. Let things be as they are.

I looked at John and Liv.

This is your idea of moving forward?

Lena nodded.

"Hello? If you two want to actually talk out loud, we can wait in the other room." John was watching us impatiently.

"Sorry. We're good now." Lena gave me a meaningful look. "Right?"

Maybe we were, but I knew someone who wouldn't be. "Do you have any idea what Link is gonna say about this? He's waiting in the car with Savannah right now."

Lena nodded at John, and I heard the ripping noise again, coming from outside. The music blasting from the Beater suddenly stopped. "Link's already at the dance. So I guess we go, right?" John grabbed Liv's hand.

"You *ripped* Link?" I felt my shoulders stiffen. "You weren't even touching him."

John shrugged. "I told you, I'm not really a rules kinda guy. I can do a lot of things. Most of the time, I don't even know how."

"That makes me feel a lot better."

"Relax. It was your girlfriend's idea."

"What's Savannah gonna think?" I could imagine her telling this story to her mom.

"She won't remember a thing." Lena grabbed my hand. "Come on. We can take the hearse." Lena picked up her keys.

I shook my head. "Going to the dance alone with Savannah is the last thing Link wanted."

"Trust me." Two more words no guy wants to hear from his girlfriend.

What are you up to? Help me out here.

"The band had to be there early." She dragged me after her.

"The band? You mean the Holy Rollers?" Now I was really confused. Principal Harper wouldn't let the Holy Rollers play at a dance any more than—actually, there was no comparison. It would never happen.

Lena's hair curled in the nonexistent breeze, and she tossed me the keys.

⊰ 12.12 ⊱

A Light in the Dark

I could see lights flashing through the upper windows of the gym all the way from the parking lot. The party was already in high gear.

Lena pulled me by the arm. "Come on! We can't miss this!"

I heard the unmistakable howl of Link's vocals and froze. The Holy Rollers were in there performing, just like Lena said they would be.

I felt a moment of panic. The Eighteenth Moon was almost here, and we were about to walk into a dance at Jackson. It seemed stupid, but then so did staying home and worrying about the end of the world when there was nothing we could do to stop it. Maybe the stupidest part was thinking I could keep it from happening.

So I did the only logical thing, which was keep my mouth

shut and tighten my arm around the prettiest girl in the parking lot. "All right, L. Come clean. What did you do?"

"I wanted him to have one good night without Ridley." Lena slid her arm through mine. "And I wanted it for you." She looked over her shoulder to where John's low voice and Liv's laughter floated up behind us. "For everyone, I guess."

The weirdest part was that I understood why she did it. We had all been stuck since the summer, as if it never really ended. Amma couldn't read cards or talk to the Greats. Marian wasn't allowed to do her job. Liv wasn't training to be a Keeper. Macon barely came up from the Tunnels. Link was still trying to figure out how to be an Incubus and get over Ridley. And John had been stuck for real, in the Arclight. Even the heat stuck around, like the endless summer from hell.

Everything in Gatlin was stuck.

What Lena did tonight wasn't going to change any of that, but maybe we could leave the summer behind us. Maybe it would end one of these days, taking the heat and the bugs and the bad memories with it.

Maybe we could feel normal again. Our version of normal, at least. Even if the clock was still ticking and the Eighteenth Moon was getting closer.

We can do more than feel normal, Ethan. We can be normal.

Lena smiled at me, and I pulled her even closer as we walked into the gym.

The inside of the gym had been transformed, and the theme seemed to be—Link. The Holy Rollers were onstage, lit by spotlights the Dance Committee could never afford to rent. And Link was in the center of it all, his ruffled shirt unbuttoned and drenched with sweat. He was alternating between playing the drums and singing, sliding along the stage with the mic stand in his hand. Every time he moved near the edge, a group of freshmen girls screamed.

And for the second time in my life, the Holy Rollers sounded like a real band—without a cherry lollipop in sight.

"What did you do?" I shouted to Lena over the music.

"Consider it a Don't-Let-the-Dance-Suck Cast."

"So, I guess the whole thing was Link's idea in the first place." I smiled, and she nodded at me.

"Exactly."

On the way to the dance floor, we walked past a cardboard backdrop. There was a stool, but the photographer was nowhere in sight. The whole thing looked a little suspicious. "Where's the photographer, L?"

"His wife went into labor." Lena wouldn't look at me.

"Lena."

"Really. You can ask anyone. Well, don't ask her. She's a little busy right now."

We passed Liv and John, who were sitting at a table near the dance floor. "I've only seen this on TV," Liv said, taking it all in.

"An American high school dance?" John smiled. "It's my first, too." John reached out to tug on a length of her blond hair. "Let's dance, Olivia."

An hour later, I had to admit Lena was right. We were all having a good time, and it didn't feel like summer anymore. It felt like a regular high school dance, where you wait for the slow songs to get close to your girlfriend. Savannah was holding court in her puffy cotton candy dress, and she even danced with Earl Petty—once. The only exception was the return of Link as a rock god. But tonight even that didn't seem so impossible.

Fatty was busting the rest of the Holy Rollers for smoking in front of the gym while the Dance Committee's pre-approved playlist blasted through the speakers. But there wasn't much Fatty could do, since they were all around twenty-five and confirmed dirtbags. That was obvious when the lead guitarist whispered something in Emily Asher's ear that actually left her speechless for the first time in her life.

I went to find Link, who was hanging out in the hallway by the lockers. The hallway was dark, except for one blinking fluorescent panel on the ceiling, which made it a good place to hide from Savannah. I figured I'd tell him how great he was onstage, because there was nothing you could say to Link that would make him happier than that. But I didn't get to tell him.

He was wiping the sweat off his face when I saw her turn the corner.

Ridley.

So much for Link being happy.

I ducked into the doorway of the bio lab before they saw me. Maybe Ridley was going to tell him where she'd been all this time. She would definitely lie to Lena and me when we asked her.

"Hey there, Hot Rod." She was sucking on a cherry lollipop, wearing lots of black and showing lots of skin. Something was off, but I couldn't put my finger on it.

"Where the hell have you been?" Link threw his sweaty shirt onto the floor.

"Around."

"Everyone's been worried about you. Even after the stunt you pulled." *Everyone* meaning *him*.

Ridley laughed. "Yeah, I bet."

"So, where—" For a second, he didn't say anything. "Why are you wearin' sunglasses, Rid?"

I pushed myself flatter against the wall and looked around the corner. Ridley was wearing black sunglasses, the kind she used to wear all the time.

"Take them off." He was almost shouting. If the music wasn't so loud, someone would've heard him.

Ridley leaned up against the locker next to Link. "Don't be mad, Shrinky Dink. I was never cut out to be a Mortal. We both knew that."

Link pulled her sunglasses off, and I could see her yellow eyes from where I was standing. The eyes of a Dark Caster.

"What did you do?" Link sounded defeated.

She shrugged. "You know, I begged forgiveness and all that. I think everyone knew I'd been punished enough. Being a Mortal was *torture.*"

Link was staring at the linoleum. I knew that look. It was the same one he had whenever his mom started on one of her tirades, threatening moral damnation if he didn't bring his grades up or stop reading books she was trying to ban. It was the look that said: *Nothing I do is going to make any difference.*

"Who's 'everyone,' Rid? Sarafine? Abraham?" He was shaking his head. "Did you go to them after everything they did to you? After they tried to kill us? The way you let John Breed outta the Arclight after what he did to me?"

She stepped in front of him, resting her hands on his chest. "I had to let him out. He gave me power." Her voice was rising, the sarcastic tone gone. "Don't you understand? It was the only way I could feel like myself again."

Link grabbed her wrists and pushed her away. "I'm glad you feel like yourself. Guess I never really knew who you were. I'm the idiot." He started walking back toward the double doors that led into the gym.

"I did it for us!" Ridley actually looked hurt. "If you can't see that, then you really are an idiot."

Link turned around. "For us? Why would you do this to yourself for us?"

"Don't you get it? We can be together now. We're the same. I'm not some stupid Mortal girl you'll get sick of in six months."

"You think I cared about that?"

She laughed. "You would've, trust me. I was nothing."

"You were something to me." He looked up at the ceiling, as if the answer to this mess was written on the worn squares.

Ridley closed the distance between them. "Come with me. Tonight. I can't stay here, but I came back for you."

As I watched her, I saw Sarafine—the one from the visions. The one who was trying to fight her nature, the Darkness taking hold within her. Maybe Lena's family was wrong.

Maybe there was still Light in the Dark.

Link leaned his head against hers, their foreheads touching for a second. "I can't. Not after what they did to my friends, and to you. I can't be one of them, Rid. I'm not like you—and I don't want to be."

She was stunned. You could see it in her eyes, even if they were yellow.

"Rid?"

"Take a good look, Hot Rod. This is the last time you're ever gonna see me." She was walking backward, still looking at him. Then she turned and ran.

A cherry lollipop rolled across the floor.

Link's voice was so quiet I barely heard him as his hand closed around it.

"Bad or not, you'll always be my girl."

After seeing Ridley, Link didn't care about being a rock god. He was in bad shape, and he wasn't the only one. Lena had barely said a word since I told her about Ridley. The dance was over for us.

The parking lot was deserted. No one left a Jackson dance this early. The hearse was parked at the far end of the lot, under the broken streetlight. Link was behind us, and Liv and John were walking in front, holding hands. I listened to our shoes against the asphalt as we walked. That's how I knew John had stopped walking.

"No. Not now," he whispered.

I followed his eyes, but it was pitch-black and I couldn't see anything. "What is it?"

"What's up, man?" Link stepped up next to me, his eyes focused on the hearse. I knew he could see in the dark, like John. "Please tell me that isn't who I think it is."

John didn't move. "It's Hunting and his Blood Pack."

Liv tried to find them in the darkness, but it was impossible until Hunting stepped into the pale glow of another streetlight.

She pushed John. "Go! Get back in the Tunnels." Liv wanted him to rip, dematerialize before Hunting had the chance to do the same.

He shook his head. "I can't leave you. I won't."

"You can rip us out of here." Liv reached for his hand.

"I can't take all of you at once."

"Then go!"

It didn't matter what Liv said. There was no time.

Hunting leaned against the streetlight, a cigarette burning between his fingers. Two more Incubuses stepped into view. "So, this is where you've been hiding out. High school. I never would've guessed. You never were that smart."

John pushed Liv behind him. "How did you find me?"

Hunting laughed. "We can always find you, kid. You've got your own personal LoJack. Which makes me wonder how you managed to hide out this long. Wherever you were, you should've stayed there."

Hunting started walking toward us, his lackeys right behind him.

Lena squeezed my hand.

Oh my God. He was safe in the Tunnels. This is all my fault. It's Abraham's fault.

John stood his ground. "I'm not going anywhere with you, Hunting."

Hunting flicked his cigarette into the darkness. "It's almost a shame I have to take you back. You've got a lot more fight in you when Abraham isn't messing with your head. Does it feel any different to think for yourself?"

I flashed on John wandering like a zombie through the cave at the Great Barrier. He swore he didn't remember what happened that night. Was it possible Abraham was controlling him then?

John froze. "What are you talking about?"

"Guess you haven't been doing much thinking after all. Oh, well. You won't miss it, then." Hunting lowered his voice. "You know what I won't miss? Watching you twitch all the time, like someone's poking you with a cattle prod."

John's hands started to shake. "Shut up!"

I remembered the way John's body used to jerk all the time. The way his muscles had seemed to seize involuntarily—the way it had gotten worse when he was with Abraham the night of Lena's Seventeenth Moon. I hadn't seen it happen once since we found him in Ridley's room.

Hunting laughed. "Come over here and make me. Or we can skip the part where I beat some sense into you before I take you back."

Link stepped up next to John. "So, tell me how it works. Is this like a regular fight, or do I need to use some kinda Jedi mind tricks I don't know about?"

I was stunned. Link was clearly trying to even the odds. John looked as surprised as the rest of us. "I got this one. But thanks."

"What are you—" Link never had a chance to finish.

John threw his hands out in front of him, the way Lena did when she was using her powers to tear up the ground or bring on torrential rain.

Or hurricane-force winds.

John was using Lena's powers—the ones he absorbed the last time he touched her.

The wind picked up so fast that it knocked Hunting off his feet. The other two Incubuses were thrown backward, skidding across the parking lot at a speed that would result in serious asphalt burn. But Hunting ripped before the full force of the wind caught him.

He started to materialize a few feet away, but the wind pulled him back again.

"He's still coming!" Liv screamed. She was right.

Lena pushed past me.

I have to help John. He can't do it alone.

She threw her own hands forward, her palms facing Hunting. Lena's powers were stronger than ever. And as unpredictable.

Rain poured from the sky as the clouds broke open.

No! Not now!

The rain hammered down on us—and the wind, which was dying down fast.

Hunting was dry, the rain running off his jacket in rivulets. "Nice trick, kid. It's a shame Sarafine's daughter destroyed the Order. If her powers weren't so screwed up, you might've been able to save your ass."

I heard a dog barking and caught a glimpse of Boo Radley running around the side of one of the cars.

Macon was behind him, rain running down his face. "As luck would have it, mine seem to be developing in quite an *interesting* manner."

Hunting was as shocked to see Macon as the rest of us, but he did a good job hiding it. He lit another cigarette, despite the rain. "You mean after I killed you? It'll be a pleasure to do it again."

The members of Hunting's pack had picked themselves up and crossed the parking lot the old-fashioned way. Now they were standing behind Hunting.

Macon closed his eyes.

Everything went quiet and still. Too still. The way it feels right before something horrible is going to happen. I wasn't the only one who sensed it.

Hunting vanished, ripping through the shiny black sky—

As he materialized, inches from Macon, a pulsating green light enveloped us. The light hummed with power.

It was coming from Macon.

Hunting froze in the eerie green glow, his hand outstretched, canines bared.

"What is that?" Link was shielding his eyes.

"It's light," Liv said, transfixed.

"How can he create light?" I asked.

Liv shook her head. "I have no idea."

The light grew brighter, and Hunting dropped to the ground, thrashing on the glowing concrete. An agonizing sound tore through him, like his vocal cords were shredding. The other two Incubuses were writhing on the ground, too, but I couldn't take my eyes off Hunting.

The color started to leach out of him, beginning at the top of his head and moving down over his face. It was like watching a sheet being pulled off someone, slowly. But this sheet was a black mist, and as it moved down, his neck—and his hair, his skin, his empty black eyes—became almost translucent. It was happening to other members of his Blood Pack, too.

"What's happening to them?" I don't know if I was expecting an answer, but it was John who had one.

"They're losing their power. Their Darkness." I could tell from the panicked look on John's face that he'd never seen this firsthand. "That's what happens to Incubuses when they're exposed to daylight." I looked at John. It wasn't affecting him.

"He's really creating light," Liv whispered.

John said something else, but I wasn't listening anymore. I was staring at the other two Incubuses, who were translucent now. The Darkness had seeped out of them much faster. I watched as their bodies stiffened, like statues, their eyes fixed and lifeless. But that wasn't the most disturbing part.

The black mist—the Dark power that had drained out of their bodies—was seeping into the ground.

"Where is it going?" Lena asked.

"The Underground." John took a step back, as if he didn't want to get too close to what he could've been. "Energy can't be destroyed. It just changes form."

I froze. The words replayed themselves in my mind.

It just changes form.

I thought about Twyla and the Greats and Aunt Prue. My mom and Macon.

I remembered the green glow of the Arclight.

The same light that was washing over us now. Had something happened to Macon within its walls? Had my mother changed him somehow? Remade the man she had loved and lost?

"What will it become?" Liv sounded frightened. John was actually telling her something she didn't know.

The color had drained from Hunting's body, all the way down to his hands. Macon hadn't moved, his eyes squeezed tightly shut, like he was in the middle of a terrible nightmare.

John didn't answer for a second. When finally he did, I wished he hadn't. "Vexes."

"Macon would never want to do that." Liv was as shocked as I was.

John took her hand. "I know. But he doesn't get to decide the way the universe operates, Liv. None of us do."

"Oh my God." Lena was pointing at the two Incubuses, now completely void of color. The air around them seemed to shift, but then I realized what was really happening. They were disintegrating. But they didn't turn to ash, the way zombies and vampires in the movies do. The tiny pieces of them vanished, as if they had never been at all.

I heard Macon inhale sharply. This was draining him, too. I watched him fight to hold on long enough to finish off Hunting, but the light began to dim, until the black night swallowed up the parking lot again.

Hunting's body dropped to the ground. He was moaning, dragging himself across the asphalt. His face and torso were still rigid and completely translucent.

Macon dropped to his knees, and Lena knelt down next to him. "How did you do that?"

Macon didn't reply right away. When his breath sounded regular again, he answered. "I'm not entirely sure myself. But it seems I can channel my Light energy. Create light, for lack of a better explanation."

John wandered over, shaking his head. "And I thought I was different. You give new meaning to Light Caster, Mr. Ravenwood."

Macon looked at John, the hybrid who could stand in the sunlight. "In Light there is Darkness, and in Darkness there is Light."

I heard the rip as Hunting disappeared, his body marked by the Light.

⇥ 12.13 ⇤

Tears and Rain

After what happened in the parking lot, Macon and Liv took John back down into the Tunnels, where he would be safe under the veil of Concealment Casts and Bindings. We hoped. There was no doubt Hunting would tell Abraham everything, but Liv wasn't sure if he was strong enough. I didn't ask if she meant strong enough to make it back to Abraham, or to survive at all.

Later that night, Lena and I sat together on the steps of her uneven porch, my body pressed into hers. I tried to memorize the way it fit perfectly with mine. I buried my face in her hair. It still smelled like lemons and rosemary. One thing hadn't changed.

I tilted her chin up and pressed my mouth against hers. I wasn't kissing her as much as I was feeling her lips against mine. I could have lost her tonight.

She leaned her head against my chest.

But you didn't.

I know.

I let my mind drift, but all I could think about was what it had felt like without her last summer, when I thought I'd lost her. The dull ache that never went away. The emptiness. It was the same way Link must have felt when Ridley walked away. I'd never forget the look on his face. He was so broken. And Ridley, with those haunting yellow eyes.

I felt Lena's mind churning even harder than mine.

Stop it, L.

Stop what.

Thinking about Ridley.

I can't. She reminds me of Sara—of my mom. And look how she turned out.

Ridley's not Sarafine.

Not yet.

I slid the corsage off her thin wrist. There it was. Her mother's bracelet. My hand brushed against the metal, and the second it did, I knew everything that belonged to Sarafine was tainted. The porch started to spin—

It was getting harder and harder to keep track of the days. Sarafine felt as though she was in a constant fog, confused and detached from her everyday life. Emotions seemed beyond her grasp, floating on the periphery of her mind as if they belonged to someone else. The only place she felt grounded was in the Tunnels. There was a connection to the Caster world and the elements that had created the power running through her veins. It gave her comfort, allowed her to breathe.

Sometimes she spent hours down there, sitting in the small study Abraham had created for her. It was usually peaceful, until Hunting arrived. Her half brother believed Abraham was wasting his time with her, and he didn't attempt to hide it.

"Here again?" Sarafine could hear the contempt in Hunting's voice.

"I'm just reading." She tried to avoid confrontations with Hunting. He was vicious and cruel, yet there was always a thread of truth in his words. Truth she tried desperately to ignore.

Hunting leaned against the door, a cigarette hanging between his lips. "I'll never understand why Grandfather Abraham wastes his time with you. Do you have any idea how many Casters would kill to have him as a teacher?" Hunting shook his head.

She was tired of being bullied. "Why am I a waste?"

"You're a Dark Caster pretending to be Light. A Cataclyst. If that isn't a waste, I don't know what is."

The words stung, but Sarafine tried to hide it. "I'm not pretending."

Hunting laughed, baring his canines. "Really? Have you told your Light Caster husband about your secret meetings down here? I wonder how long it would take him to turn on you."

"That's none of your business."

Hunting dropped his cigarette into an empty soda can on the desk. "I'll take that as a no."

Sarafine felt her chest tighten, and for a second everything went black.

The desk caught fire just as Hunting pulled his hand away.

There was no warning. One minute she was angry at Hunting; the next, the desk was going up in smoke.

Hunting coughed. "Now, that's more like it."

Sarafine scrambled to put out the fire with an old blanket. Predictably, Hunting didn't help. He disappeared into Abraham's private study down the hall. Sarafine stared at her hands, covered in black ash. Her face was probably filthy, too. She couldn't go home to John like this.

She wandered down the hall toward the small bathroom. But as soon as she came within a few feet of Abraham's door, she heard voices.

"I don't know why you're so obsessed with that kid." Hunting's voice was bitter. "Who cares if he can go out in the daylight? He's barely old enough to walk, and Silas will probably kill him before he can be useful." He was talking about the boy Abraham told her about when they first met. The one who was a little older than Lena.

"Silas will control his temper and do what I tell him," Abraham snapped. "Have some vision, boy. That child will be the next generation. An Incubus with all of our strengths and none of our weaknesses."

"How can you be sure?"

"You think I picked his parents by accident?" Abraham didn't like being questioned. "I knew exactly what I was doing."

For a moment there was silence. Then Abraham spoke again. "It won't be long before the Casters are

*out of the way. I'll see it in my lifetime. I promise you
that."*

Sarafine shivered. A part of her wanted to run for the
door and never look back. But she couldn't. She had to
stay for Lena.

She had to stop the voices.

When Sarafine got home, John was in the living room.

"Shh. The baby's asleep." He kissed her on the cheek
as she sat down next to him on the couch. "Where have
you been?"

For a second she considered lying, telling him she
was at the library or walking in the park. But Hunting's
words mocked her. "I wonder how long it would take
him to turn on you." *He was wrong about John.*

"I was in the Tunnels."

"What?" John sounded as if he thought he had mis-
understood her.

"I met one of my relatives, and he told me things
about the curse. Things I didn't know. The second Natural born into the Duchannes family can Claim herself.
Lena can choose." It all came tumbling out, so many
things she had longed to share with him.

John was shaking his head. "Wait a minute. What
relative?"

There was no stopping now. "Abraham Ravenwood."

John stood up, towering above her. "Abraham Ravenwood, the Blood Incubus? He's dead."

Sarafine jumped up. "No. He's alive, and he can help
us save Lena."

John was studying her face as if he didn't recognize it. "Help us? Have you lost your mind? He's a blood-drinking Demon! How do you even know if anything he told you is true?"

"Why would he lie? He has nothing to gain from telling me that Lena has a choice."

John grabbed her by the shoulders. "Why would he lie? How about because he's a Blood Incubus? He's worse than a Dark Caster." *Sarafine cringed beneath his fingers. It didn't matter if John called her Izabel; her eyes were still golden yellow, and her skin ice-cold. She was one of them.*

"He can help Lena." *He's helping me, too. That's what she wished she could tell him.*

John was so angry he didn't notice how her face had crumbled. "You don't know that. He could be lying. We don't even know if Lena's a Natural."

Sarafine felt something rising inside her, like the crest of a wave. She didn't recognize it for what it was. Rage. But the voices did. He doesn't trust you. He thinks you're one of them.

She tried to push the thoughts away and focus on John. "When she cries, it rains. That isn't proof enough for you?"

John let go of her shoulders and ran his hands through his hair. "Izabel, this guy is a monster. I don't know what he wants with you, but he's playing on your fears. You can't speak to him again."

Panic welled up inside her. She knew Abraham was telling the truth about Lena. John hadn't seen the

405

prophecy. But there was something else. If she couldn't see Abraham, she couldn't control the voices.

John was staring at her. "Izabel! Promise me."

She had to make him understand. "But, John—"

He cut her off. "I don't know if you are losing your judgment or losing control, but if you go anywhere near Abraham Ravenwood, I'll leave. And I'll take Lena with me."

"What did you say?" He couldn't mean it.

"If what he says is true, and Lena has a choice, she will choose Light. I will never allow any Darkness into her life. I know you've been struggling. You disappear all day, and when you're here, you look distracted and confused."

Was it true? Could he see it on her face?

John was still talking. "But it's my job to protect Lena. Even if it's from you."

He loved Lena more than he loved her.

He was ready to walk away and take her daughter.

And one day, Lena would Claim herself. John would be sure she turned her back on Sarafine.

Something clicked within her, two chambers locking into place. The rage wasn't cresting anymore. It was crashing down on her, drowning her beneath it. And she could hear the voice.

Burn.

The drapes ignited, sending fire racing up the walls behind John. Smoke started to fill the room, black and dark, a living, breathing shadow. The sound was so loud as the flames ate away at the wall and spread to the floor. The fire created a perfect circle around John, following an invisible path only she could see.

"Izabel! Stop!" John screamed, his voice twisted by the roaring of the fire.

What had she done?

"How could you do this to me? I stood by you, even after you Turned!"

After you Turned.

He believed she was Dark.

He always had.

She looked at him through the cloud of smoke quickly filling the room. Sarafine watched the flames with remove. She wasn't standing in her house, about to watch her husband burn to death. He didn't look like the man she loved. Or even a man she could love.

He's a traitor. *The voice was perfectly clear now, and there was only one. Sarafine recognized it right away.*

Because it was her own.

Before she walked away from the house and the smoke, her life and memories that were already fading, she remembered something John used to say to her. She looked into his green eyes with her gold ones.

"I'll love you until the day after forever."

———&⁊

Lena fell to her knees on the step beneath me, sobbing.

I wrapped my arms around her, but I didn't say a word. She had just watched her mother kill her father and leave her for dead.

There was nothing left to say.

⊰ 12.13 ⊱

The Verdict

A few hours later, Lena was shaking me.

Wake up. You have to wake up, Ethan—

I sat up with a start. "I'm awake!" Only I looked around, confused, because it wasn't Lena shaking me, it was Liv. Even though I could still hear the echo of Lena's voice lingering in my head.

"Ethan. It's me. Please—you've got to wake up."

I looked at her through half-open eyes. "Am I dreaming?"

Liv frowned. "I'm afraid not. This is real."

I rubbed my hand through my hair, confused. It was still pitch-dark outside, and I couldn't even remember dreaming. I only remembered Lena's voice and the urgent feeling something was wrong. "What's going on?"

"It's Marian. She's gone. Come on."

Things were starting to fall into place. I was in my room. Liv was in my room. I wasn't dreaming. Which meant—

"Wait. How did you get in here?"

Liv looked embarrassed. "I hitched a ride." She pointed to the scorpion belt around her waist and glanced behind her.

An Incubus was sitting in the corner of my bedroom.

Great.

John picked up my jeans from the floor and tossed them at me. "Hurry up, Boy Scout." For a guy who didn't have to sleep, he was as grouchy in the middle of the night as I was.

Liv blushed, turning around, and a few seconds later I heard the familiar ripping sound. Only for the first time, it was for me.

"Where are we?"

Nobody answered. Then I heard John's voice in the darkness. "No clue."

"Don't you have to know where you're going to rip? Isn't that the way it works?" I asked.

"Is that some kind of Mortal word for Traveling? Real clever." He sounded annoyed, which I was used to by now. "Sort of. Usually."

The shadows were shifting, and I rubbed my eyes, trying to see in the dark. I stretched out my hands, but I couldn't feel anything.

"Usually?"

"I was following the signal."

"What signal?"

My eyes adjusted from the darkness of Traveling to the darkness of wherever we had Traveled to. As the blurry shadows lightened from black to gray, I realized we were crammed into a tiny space.

Liv looked at John. "An *Ad Auxilium Concitatio*. It's an ancient Homing Cast, like a Caster SOS. But only a Cypher can detect one."

John shrugged. "I hung out with one at Exile with Rid and—" He didn't finish, but we all knew who he was talking about. "I picked up some Cypher skills."

I shook my head. Cyphers? There was so much about Lena's world I would never understand, no matter how hard I tried.

"You're a handy guy," I said, annoyed.

"Who sent it?" Liv asked.

"I did." Lena was standing behind us in the darkness. I could barely see her face, but her green and gold eyes were shining. She looked over at John. "I was hoping you would pick it up."

"Glad I'm good for something."

"The Far Keep is trying Marian for treason. It's going on right now." Lena sounded grim. "Uncle Macon went after Marian, but he wouldn't let me come. He said it was too dangerous."

Marian was on trial. It was really happening, the way I was afraid it would, ever since the day Liv and I found the *Temporis Porta*.

Everything I'd been feeling—the doubt, the panic, the wrongness—caught up with me in a crashing wave that nearly knocked my feet out from under me. Like I was drowning. Or falling.

"Don't worry." Liv tried to sound reassuring. "I'm sure she's fine. This whole thing is my fault, not hers. The Council will have to admit that, sooner or later."

John held up his hand. *"Ignis."* A warm yellow flame flickered from the center of his palm.

"New party trick?" I asked.

He shrugged. "Fire was never really my thing. Guess I picked it up from hanging out with Lena." Normally I would have punched him. At least, I would have wanted to.

Lena grabbed my hand. "These days I can't even light a candle without torching the place."

Light flooded the room, and I didn't have time to hit him, because now I knew exactly where we were. Again.

I was on the other side of the pantry door. Ten feet under my kitchen, in my own house.

I grabbed the old lantern and took off down the crumbling tunnel, toward the door in the ceiling no one ever opened, to the place where the ancient doors would be waiting for me.

"Wait up! You don't know where this tunnel ends," John called after me.

"It's all right," I heard Liv say. "He knows where he's going."

I heard their footsteps behind me, but I only ran faster.

———⟨ℨ———

I started banging on the *Temporis Porta* as soon as I reached it. This time it didn't open. Splinters dug into my skin, but I didn't stop pounding on the thick wood.

Nothing I did mattered.

I rested my face against the wood. "Aunt Marian, I'm here! I'm coming."

Lena came up behind me.

Ethan, she can't hear you.

I know.

John shoved me aside and touched the surface of the doors with his hand. Then he yanked it away as if the wood burned. "That's some serious mojo."

Liv grabbed his hand, but there wasn't a mark on it. "I don't think there's anything we can do to open those doors, unless they want to be opened." She was talking about the last time they opened—for me. But they weren't opening this time.

Liv examined the side of the doors, where the carvings were clearest.

"There has to be a way." I threw myself back against the thick, carved planks. Nothing. "We have to think of something. Who knows what they might do to Marian."

Liv looked away. "I can imagine. But we can't help her if we can't get inside. Give me a minute." She pulled her red notebook out of her worn leather backpack. "I've been trying to figure out these symbols since the first time we saw them."

Lena shot me a look. "The first time?"

Liv didn't look up. "Didn't Ethan tell you? He found these doors weeks ago. They let him pass, but they left me behind. And he wouldn't tell me much about what he saw on the other side. But I've been studying the doors ever since."

"Weeks ago?"

"I haven't the exact date," Liv answered.

Ethan?

I can explain. I was going to tell you the night at the Cine-plex, but you were already mad because I had invited Liv to the party.

412

Secret doors? With your secret friend? And something secret you found behind them? Why would that make me mad?

I should've told you. It's not like you're worried about Liv.

I wasn't getting off that easy. I tried not to look at Lena, focusing on a page of sketches in Liv's red notebook. "That's it." I recognized the symbols in her notebook.

Liv held the paper up against the symbols carved into the doors, moving it from one wooden panel to the next, as she compared them. "See the recurring pattern in these three circles?"

"The Wheel," I said automatically. "You said they were the Wheel of Fate."

"Yes, but perhaps not *only* the Wheel of Fate. I think each circle might represent one of the Three Keepers. The Council of the Far Keep."

"The ones who showed up in the archive?" Lena asked.

She nodded. "I've read everything I could find about them, which isn't much. From what I can determine, the Three Keepers must have been the ones who visited us."

I thought about it. "It makes sense. The first time I went through those doors, I ended up at the Far Keep."

"So you think these signs stand for the three of them?" John looked over at me. "Those freaks that wanted to take Liv?"

I nodded. "And Marian." He seemed more concerned about Liv than Marian, which didn't surprise me, but it still made me angry. Like just about everything that came out of his mouth.

Liv ignored us both, pointing to the first circle, the one with the fewest spokes. "I think this one represents what's happening now, the present. And this" — she pointed to the second circle, the one crossed with more spokes—"symbolizes what has been. The past."

"Then what's that one?" John pointed to the last circle, the one with no spokes.

"What will never be, or what will always be." Liv traced the drawing with her finger. "In other words, the future."

"If each of these symbols represents one of the Keepers, then which is which?" I asked.

Lena studied the circle with the most spokes. "I think that huge guy is the past. He was carrying that empty hourglass when we saw him in the archive."

Liv nodded. "I agree."

I reached out and touched the circles. They were hard and cool, different from the texture of the rest of the wooden door. I moved my hand to the empty circle, with no spokes. "The woman from the Council, the one who looked albino. She's what hasn't happened yet, right? The future? Because she's nothing. I mean, she was practically invisible."

Liv reached up to the circle with the fewest spokes. "Which would make the tall one the present."

The light in the room flickered, and John looked frustrated. "This sounds like a whole lot of crap. What will be? What won't be? What are you talking about?"

"What will be and what will not be are equally possible and impossible," Liv explained. "I guess you could say they are the absence of history, the place *The Caster Chronicles* cannot touch. You can't tell a story or Keep a record of what hasn't happened yet. That's Keeper 101." Liv sounded dreamy, and I wondered what she knew about *The Caster Chronicles*.

"The Caster what?" John shifted the light from one hand to the other.

"It's a book," Lena said, without taking her eyes off the

doors. "The Keepers had it with them when they came to see Marian."

"Whatever." John looked bored. "If you're talking about the future, how about we call it that?"

Liv nodded. "But you have to remember, we're not just talking about the Mortal future. We're talking about everything unknown, for Casters and Mortals. Including the unknown realm, the place where the Demon world touches our own."

"Demon world?" I felt the prickling of recognition. I had to tell Liv. "I know the place where the Demon world touches ours. I mean, I don't know it, but I know her. The Lilum. The Demon Queen."

Liv went pale, but it was John who was the most freaked out. "What are you talking about?"

"The Lilum thing—"

"There's no Lilum here." Liv was shaking her head. "The very presence of the Lilum in our world would mean the total destruction of existence itself."

"What does that have to do with her?" I asked.

"Her? Is that who you were talking about? The *she* who told you about the Eighteenth Moon was the Lilum? The Demon Queen?" Liv knew from the look on my face that she was right.

"Great," John muttered.

Liv froze. "Where is the place, Ethan?" She closed her eyes, which made me think she knew what I was going to say.

"I don't know for sure. But I can find it. I'm the Wayward. The Lilum said it herself." I touched the circles again with my hands, over and over, feeling the rough wood beneath my fingers.

The past. The present. The future that will be, and the future that will not.

415

The way.

The wood began to hum beneath my hands. I touched the carved circles again.

The color drained from Liv's face. "The Lilum said that to you?"

I opened my eyes, and everything was clear. "When you look at the door, you see a door, right?"

Liv nodded.

I looked at her. "I see a path."

It was true. Because the *Temporis Porta* was opening for me.

The wood turned to mist, and I slid my hand right through. Beyond it, I could see a path leading into the distance. "Come on."

"Where are you going?" Liv grabbed my arm.

"To find Marian and Macon." This time, I made sure to grab Liv and Lena before I stepped inside the door. Liv grabbed John's hand.

"Hold on." I took a breath and ducked into the mist—

Perfidia

We found ourselves nearly crushed in the center of a mob. I recognized the robes. Only I was tall enough to see over them, but it didn't matter. I knew where we were.

It seemed like the middle of a trial, or something like one. Liv's pencil was moving inside the red notebook as quickly as it could, trying to keep up with the words that were flying all around us.

"*Perfidia*. It's Latin for 'treason.' They're saying she's going to be tried for treason." Liv was pale, and I could barely hear her voice over the clamor of the crowd surrounding us.

"I know this place." I recognized the tall windows with the heavy gold drapes, and the wood benches. Everything was the same—the thick noise of the crowd, the stone walls, the beamed ceiling that was so high that it seemed to go on forever. I held on to Lena's hand, pushing my way to the front of the hall, directly under the empty wooden balcony. Liv and John threaded their way through the robed crowd behind me.

"Where's Marian?" Lena was panicking. "And Uncle Macon? I can't see anything over all these people."

"I don't like this," Liv said quietly. "Something doesn't feel right."

I felt it, too.

We were standing in the center of the same crowded hall where I stood the first time I crossed through the *Temporis Porta*. But last time, it seemed like I was somewhere in medieval Europe, in a place from an illustration in the World History textbook we never seemed to crack at Jackson. The room was so big I'd thought it might be a ship or a cathedral. A place that transported you somewhere, whether it was across the sea or to the paradise the Sisters were always talking about.

Now it seemed different. I didn't know where this place was, but even in their dark robes, the people—the Casters, Mortals, Keepers, or whatever they were—seemed like regular old people. The kind of people I knew something about. Because even though they were crowded on the glossy wooden bench that surrounded the perimeter of the room, they could've been sitting in the gym at Jackson, waiting for the Disciplinary Committee meeting to start. On the benches or the bleachers, these people were looking for the same thing. Drama.

Even worse, they were looking for blood. Someone to blame, and to punish.

It felt like the trial of the century, or a bunch of reporters waiting outside South Carolina's Broad River Correctional Institution when someone from death row was about to get a lethal injection. The executions were covered by every TV station and newspaper. A few people showed up to protest, but they looked like they had been bused in for the day. Everyone else was hanging out, waiting to watch the spectacle. It wasn't much different from the burning of the witches in *The Crucible*.

The crowd rushed forward, murmuring, just as I knew they would, and I heard the banging of a gavel. *"Silentium."*

Something's happening.

Lena grabbed my arm.

Liv pointed across the room. "I saw Macon. He's over there."

John looked around. "I don't see Marian."

Maybe she's not here, Ethan.

She's here.

She had to be, because I knew what was about to happen. I forced myself to look up to the balcony.

Look—

I pointed up at Marian, once again hooded and robed, once again tied at the wrists with a golden rope. She was standing on the balcony, high above the room, just as she had been the last time. The tall Keeper who had come to the archive was next to her.

The people around us were still whispering. I looked at Liv, who interpreted. "He's the Council Keeper. He's going to—"

Liv's eyes welled up. "It's not a trial, Ethan. It's a sentencing."

I heard the Latin, but this time I didn't try to understand. I knew what it meant before the Council Keeper repeated the words in English.

Marian would be found guilty of treason.

I listened without listening, my eyes locked on Marian's face. "The Council of the Far Keep, which answers only to the Order of Things, to no man, creature, or power, Dark or Light, finds Marian of the Western Keep guilty of Treason."

I remembered the first time I heard those words.

"These are the Consequences of her inaction. The Consequences shall be paid. The Keeper, though Mortal, will return to the Dark Fire from which all power comes."

I might as well have been the one sentenced to death. Pain gutted my whole body. I watched as Marian's hood was pulled from her shaved head. I stared into her eyes, surrounded by dark rings as if she had been hurt. I couldn't tell if it was physical pain or mental or even Mortal. I imagined it was something worse.

I was the only one prepared for it. Liv broke down sobbing. Lena stumbled against me, and I held her up by the arm. Only John stood there, unfazed, his hands jammed into his pockets.

The Council Keeper's voice echoed through the room again. "The Order is broken. Until the New Order comes forth, the Old Law must be upheld, and the Consequences paid."

"All this courtroom drama. If I didn't know you better, Angelus, I would think you were vying for a spot on cable television." Macon's voice carried over the crowd, but I couldn't see him.

"Your Mortal levity defiles this sacred space, Macon Ravenwood."

"My Mortal levity, Angelus, is something you cannot understand. And I warned you, Angelus, that I would not stand for this."

The Council Keeper shouted over the crowd. "You have no power here."

"You have no business finding a Mortal guilty of treason against the Order."

"The Keeper is of both worlds. The Keeper knew the price.

The Keeper chose to allow the destruction of the Order," he answered.

"The Keeper is a Mortal. Her name is Marian Ashcroft. She has already been sentenced to death, like every Mortal. In forty or fifty years, she will face that sentence. It is the Mortal way."

"This is not your matter to speak of." The Council Keeper's voice was rising, and the spectators were getting restless.

"Angelus, she is weak. She has no powers, no way to protect herself. You cannot punish a wet child for the rain."

"I do not understand."

" 'The one thing that doesn't abide by majority rule is a person's conscience.' " Macon was quoting Harper Lee. I never knew any of Marian's quotes, but I remembered that one from reading *To Kill a Mockingbird* in English class last year. And from my mom.

John's head was bent toward Liv's, and they were whispering about something. When he noticed me watching them, he stopped. "This is crap," he said.

For once I agreed with him. "But we can't stop it."

"Why not?"

There was no way he would understand. "I know how it ends. They've found her guilty of treason. She's going to be sent back to the Dark Fire, or whatever happens after that. There's nothing we can do," I said miserably. "I was here before."

"Yeah? I wasn't." John stepped forward, clapping dramatically. The whole room went dead silent. He squeezed Lena's shoulder as he passed. "Well, doesn't this suck?" John shoved his way to the front of the hall, where Macon was standing. I could finally see him. John held up his hand, like he was waiting for Macon to give him a high-five. "Nice try, old man."

Macon was surprised but held up his hand. His cuff was pulled down a little too far, as though his shirt was too long.

What's going on, L?

I have no idea.

Lena's hair started to curl. I smelled a faint trace of smoke in the air.

L, what are you doing?

I think you mean what is he doing?

John wove slowly toward the Council Keeper, who was holding Marian on the balcony. "I'm starting to think you're not really listening to this fine former Incubus brother of mine." He jumped up onto the pew, shoving a robed man out of his way.

"You're out of line, spawn of Abraham. And do not think *The Caster Chronicles* have been kind to you, Breedling."

"Oh, I don't think they've been kind. Since when are people kind to me? I'm a jerk. On the other hand, you're kind of a jerk, too." John jumped up above the pew, barely catching the bottom of the wooden balcony. His black boots swung back and forth in the air.

The massive gold drapes behind us exploded into flames.

John kicked a bald, tattooed man in the head. I recognized the tattoo. It was the mark of a Dark Caster.

Now John had climbed up onto the wooden balcony, above us all. He put one arm around Marian, the other around the Council Keeper. "Angelus, that's your name, right? Man, who came up with that one? Here's the thing. My friend Lena over there, she's a Natural." There was a murmuring around us, and I saw the crowd part around Lena as they backed a few feet away.

"Why don't you show them?" Lena smiled at him, and the

drapes closest to the altar caught fire. The whole room was beginning to fill with smoke.

"And Macon Ravenwood, he's—messed up. Okay, I don't really know what he is. It's a long story. There's this ball, and this fire, and some bad, bad Casters.... But you've probably read all about that, haven't you?" John snapped. "In your little Caster spy book."

Between Marian and Angelus, I didn't know who looked more surprised.

"Anyway, back to Macon. Powerful guy. He likes to do this trick—come on, don't be shy." Macon closed his eyes, and a green glow flared above him. The crowd tried to rush back toward the walls, but there was too much smoke.

"Which leaves me. I'm not a Natural." John nodded in Macon's direction. "I'm not whatever he is either." John grinned. "But the thing about me is, I've touched both of them. So now I can do whatever they can do. It's kinda my thing. Bet you don't have a Caster like that in your little book, do you?" As the Keeper tried to pull away, John yanked him even closer. "So, Angelus. Let's go for a spin and see what a strange guy like you can do."

The Keeper was furious and backed away, holding up his hand, fingers pointed at John. John imitated him, exactly.

There was a flash of light, like lightning—

We were all standing back on the other side of the *Temporis Porta*.

Even Marian.

The Day After Forever

Was that real?" Lena whispered. I pointed to the doors, where smoke was snaking out from under the bottom of the wood.

I grabbed Marian and hugged her, at the same time Liv did. I backed away, awkwardly, and Lena took my place.

"Thank you," Marian whispered.

Macon clapped his hand on John's arm. "I can't decide if that was a brilliant act of pure selflessness back there, or if it was simply an attempt to collect all our powers for yourself."

John shrugged. "I noticed you didn't give me any skin." I remembered the cuff of Macon's shirt pulled down over his hand.

"You aren't quite ready to share my power. Either way, I owe you greatly. You showed real courage back there. I won't soon forget it."

"Oh, come on. Those guys were jerks. It was nothing." He

walked away from Macon, but I could see the pride on his face. I could see it on Liv's face even more clearly.

Marian took Macon's arm, and he started helping her back through the tunnel. At the rate they were going, even the short span of the dirt tunnel was going to be a long hike.

"This is ridiculous," said John, and in a rip we were all gone.

In seconds, we were in Macon's study.

"What are Angelus' powers, exactly?" I was still trying to figure out what we had witnessed.

"I don't know, but he certainly didn't seem to want us to find out." Macon was deep in thought.

"Yeah. He got us out of there pretty fast. I didn't get to touch him," John said.

"I feel horrible. Do you think I torched that beautiful old room?" Lena was lost in a different thought entirely.

John laughed. "No, I did."

"It's an evil room," Macon said. "We can only hope you did."

"Why would that guy Angelus involve himself so closely with this case? What could this be, like one page in *The Caster Chronicles*?" John asked.

Macon helped Marian into a chair. "He loathes Mortals."

She was still shaking. Macon pulled a blanket from the foot of his bed and wrapped it around her. I remembered Marian doing the same for the Sisters the night of the Vex attack. The worlds—they weren't two separate universes anymore, Caster and Mortal. It was all crashing together now.

Things couldn't stay like this, not for long.

Liv pulled her chair next to Marian's and put her arms around her. Lena twitched a finger in the direction of Macon's

425

fireplace grating. Flames lurched up from the logs, shooting ten feet up to the ceiling. At least it wasn't rain.

"Maybe it's not just him. Maybe it's Abraham." John sighed. "He doesn't give up easily."

Macon's brow furrowed. "That's interesting. Angelus and Abraham. A common goal, perhaps?"

Liv spoke up. "Are you suggesting that the Keepers are in collusion with Abraham? Because that is so wrong, on so many levels. It can't possibly be true."

John warmed his hands in front of the fire. "Did anyone notice how many Dark Casters were in that room?"

"I noticed the one you kicked in the head." I smiled.

"That was an accident." John shrugged.

Macon shook his head. "Either way, the sentencing occurred. We have a week to figure something out before..." We all looked at Marian. She was in shock, it was pretty clear. Her eyes were closed, and she pulled the blanket closer around her shoulders, rocking herself. I think she was reliving the whole night.

Macon shook his head. "Hypocrites."

"Why?" I asked.

"I have my own suspicions about what the Far Keep is up to, and I can't say it has anything to do with keeping the peace. Power changes people. I'm afraid they are no longer the principled leaders they once were." Macon had trouble hiding the disappointment in his face.

And the exhaustion. He was making a good show of it, but he looked like he hadn't slept in days. And now that he did sleep, I was always surprised to find he needed it as much as the rest of us. "But Marian is back home with us, safe and sound." He placed a hand on her shoulder. She didn't look up.

"For now." I wanted to go back, bash down the *Temporis Porta*, and beat the crap out of everyone in that room. I couldn't stand to see Marian like this.

Macon sank into the chair next to her. "For now. Which is all I can say for any of us, these days. We have a week until the sentence—since she was found guilty of treason. It should take that long for a *Perfidia* Proclamation to take effect. I won't let anything else happen to her, Ethan. That is more than a promise."

Liv slumped at the study table, an inconsolable mess. "If someone is going to make sure nothing else happens to Marian, it's me. If I hadn't gone with you—if I had stayed in the library, like I was supposed to..."

"Now who's the emo Caster girl?" Lena poked Liv in the arm. "That's my thing. You're supposed to be the chipper blond brainiac, remember?"

"How rude of me. I do apologize." Liv smiled and Lena smiled back, drawing her arm around Liv, as if they were friends. I guess, in a way, they were. These days, we were bound by the common threat of our fate. Because the Eighteenth Moon was almost here, and none of us had any answers.

John sat down next to Liv, protectively. "It's not your fault." He shot me a dirty look. "It's his." So much for friendship.

I stood up. "We've got to get Aunt Marian home."

For the first time, she looked up at me. "I...can't."

I understood. She wouldn't be sleeping alone, not anytime soon. That was the first night Liv and Marian were under one roof again, only this time it was in Liv's room, and their roof was the ceiling of the Tunnels. I wondered if Concealment Casts worked against Keepers, too. Mostly, I just hoped they worked.

There was one place we could go, no matter how badly our worlds were spiraling out of control. The place where it had all started for Lena and me. The place that was ours.

The morning after Marian's trial, we went to find it again.

The crumbling garden at Greenbrier was still black and charred, but you could see where the grass had started to grow. The tiny stems weren't green, though. They were brown, like everything else in Gatlin County. The invisible walls that protected Ravenwood from being ravaged didn't extend here.

Still, it was our place. I led Lena through the garden to the hearthstone where we first discovered Genevieve's locket. It seemed like it had all happened years ago, instead of the year before.

Lena sat on the stone, pulling me down after her. "Do you remember how beautiful it was here?"

I looked at her, the most beautiful girl I'd ever seen. "It still is."

"Do you think about what it would be like if this was all gone? If we can't fix this, and there's no New Order?"

I barely thought about anything else, beyond heat and bugs and dried-up lakes. What would be next? A flood? "I don't know if it would matter. Maybe we'd be gone, too, and we wouldn't even know the difference."

"I think we've both seen enough of the Otherworld to know that's not true." She knew I was trying to make her feel better. "How many times have you seen your mom? She knows what's happening, maybe better than anyone."

There was nothing I could say. Lena was right, but I couldn't let her shoulder the burden of all this alone. "You didn't do this intentionally, L."

"I don't know if that makes me feel any better about destroying the world."

I pulled her against my chest, feeling the gentle rhythm of her heartbeat. "The world isn't destroyed. Not yet."

She picked at the dry grass. "But someone's life will be. The One Who Is Two has to be sacrificed to create the New Order." Neither one of us could forget it, though we hadn't gotten any closer to figuring it out.

And if the Eighteenth Moon really was on John's birthday, then we had only five days left to find the One. Marian's life — all our lives — hung in the balance.

Him.

Her.

It could be anyone.

Whoever it was, I wondered what they were doing now — if they had any idea. Maybe they weren't worried at all. Maybe they would never even see it coming.

"Don't worry. John bought us some time. We'll think of something." She smiled. "It was cool to see him doing something for us, instead of against us."

"Yeah. If he was." I don't know why, but I still couldn't give that guy a break. Even if Lena was willing to give Liv a chance.

"What's that supposed to mean?" Lena sounded annoyed.

"You heard Macon. What if he was using the opportunity to siphon off all of your powers?"

"I don't know. Maybe we have to take it on faith."

I didn't want to do that. "Why should we?"

"Because people change. Things change. Everything and everyone we know has changed."

"What if I don't want to?" I didn't.

"It doesn't matter. We change whether we want to or not."

"Some things don't," I said. "We don't get to decide how the world works. Rain falls down, not up. The sun rises in the east and sets in the west. That's the way it is. Why is that concept so hard for you Casters to understand?"

"I guess we're sort of control freaks."

"You think?"

Lena's hair curled. "It's hard not to do things when you can do them. And in my family, there's not much we can't do."

"Really?" I kissed her.

She smiled underneath my lips. "Shut up."

"Is it hard not to do this?" I kissed her neck. Her ear. Her lips.

"How about this?" She opened her mouth to complain, but no words came out.

We kissed until my heart was faltering. Even then, I'm not sure we would have stopped, but we did.

Because I heard a rip.

Time and space opened up. I saw the tip of his cane as Abraham Ravenwood slipped through a hole in the sky, the air slamming shut behind him.

He was wearing a dark suit and his stovepipe hat, which made him look like Abraham Lincoln's father. "Did I hear something about the New Order?" He took off his hat and tapped the brim, shaking off nonexistent dust. "Turns out, broken suits me just fine. And I'm sure my boy John will feel the same way, once he's back where he belongs."

Before I had a chance to respond, I heard the sound of footsteps in the dirt. A second later, I saw her black motorcycle boots.

"I would have to agree." Sarafine was standing outside the stone arch, her black hair as curly and wild as Lena's. Even though it was a hundred degrees, she was wearing a long black dress with strips of fabric crisscrossing her body. It reminded me of a straitjacket.

Lena—

She didn't answer, but I could sense her heart pounding.

Sarafine's gold eyes fixed on me. "The Mortal world is in a state of beautiful chaos and destruction, which will ultimately lead to an exquisite end. We couldn't have planned this better ourselves." That was easy for her to say, since their original plan failed.

There was something chilling about seeing Sarafine here, after watching her set Lena's childhood home on fire with Lena and her father still inside. But it was also impossible to shake the images of the girl, not much older than Lena, battling the Darkness within her—and losing.

I pulled Lena to her feet, her hand burning mine the moment our skin touched.

Lena. I'm right here with you.

I know.

Her voice sounded empty.

Sarafine smiled at Lena. "My damaged, half-shadowed daughter. I would love to say how nice it is to see you again, but that would be a lie. And I am nothing if not honest."

The color had drained from Lena's face, and she was standing so still I almost wasn't sure she was breathing. "Then I guess you're nothing, Mother. Because we both know you're a liar."

Sarafine flexed her fingers. "You know what they say about glass houses and stones. I wouldn't throw any if I were you, darling. You *are* looking at me through one gold eye."

Lena flinched, and the wind started to blow.

"It's not the same." I said. "Lena has Light *and* Dark in her."

Sarafine waved her hand as if I was an annoying insect, a lubber trying to crawl my way out of the sunshine. "There is Light and Darkness within us all, Ethan. Haven't you learned that by now?"

A chill crawled up my spine.

Abraham leaned forward on his cane. "Speak for yourself, my dear. The heart of this old Incubus is as black as the tar in hell."

Lena wasn't interested in Abraham's heart, or Sarafine's lack of one. "I don't know what you want, and I don't care. You should leave before Uncle Macon senses you're here."

"I'm afraid we can't do that." Abraham's empty black eyes were fixed on Lena. "We have business to attend to."

Every time I heard his voice, the rage welled up inside me. I hated him for what he'd done to Aunt Prue. "What kind of business? Destroying the whole town?"

"Don't worry, I'll get to that." Abraham pulled a polished gold pocket watch from his jacket and checked it. "But first, we have to kill the One Who Is Two."

How does he know who it is, L?

Don't Kelt. She can hear you.

I held Lena's hand tighter, feeling my skin blister beneath hers. "We don't know what you're talking about."

"Don't lie to me, boy!" He lifted his cane in one hand, pointing it at me. "Did you think we wouldn't figure it out?"

Sarafine was staring at Lena's eyes. She hadn't seen them the night she called the Seventeenth Moon. She had been locked in some kind of Dark Caster dream state. "We do have *The Book of Moons*, after all."

Thunder rumbled through the air, but even as angry as she was, Lena couldn't bring the rain. "You can have the Book. We don't need it to forge the New Order."

Abraham didn't appreciate being challenged, especially not by a Caster who was half Light. "No. You're right, little girl. You need the One Who Is Two. But we aren't going to let you sacrifice yourself. We're going to kill you first."

I forced my thoughts into the part of my mind I could lock away from Lena, because if she knew what I was thinking, Sarafine would, too. Even in that private part of my mind, the same thought kept fighting its way out.

They thought the One Who Is Two was Lena.

And they were going to kill her.

I tried to push Lena behind me. But the second I moved, Abraham extended his hand and lifted it into the air. My feet rose off the ground, and I was thrown back, an iron grip locked around my throat. Abraham began to close his hand, and I could feel an invisible glove closing around my neck. "You have caused me enough trouble for two lifetimes. That ends here."

"Ethan!" Lena screamed. "Leave him alone!"

But the hand only tightened. I could feel it beginning to crush my windpipe. My body was jerking and shaking, and I remembered John when he was in the Tunnels with Lena. The weird jerking and twitching he seemed unable to control.

Was this what it felt like to be in the grip of Abraham Ravenwood?

Lena started to run toward me, but Sarafine flicked out her

433

fingers, and a perfect circle of fire flew up around Lena. It reminded me of Lena's father, standing in the midst of the flames as Sarafine watched him burn to death.

Lena threw her own palm forward, and Sarafine flew back. She hit the ground hard, skidding across the dirt faster than was humanly possible.

She stood up, brushing off her dirty dress with her bloody hands. "Someone's been practicing." Sarafine smiled. "Me, too."

She turned her hand in a circle in front of her, and a second ring of fire surrounded the first.

Lena! Get out of there!

I couldn't choke out the words. I didn't have enough air.

Sarafine advanced. "There will be no New Order. The universe has already brought Darkness upon the Mortal world. But things will get worse." Lightning sliced across the Carolina blue sky, touching down on the old stone arch, reducing it to rubble.

Sarafine's golden yellow eyes were glowing, and Lena's gold and green ones started to glow, too. The flames of the outer circle around Lena were spreading, touching the perimeter of the inner one.

"Sarafine!" Abraham shouted. "Enough of these games. Kill her, or I will."

Sarafine stalked toward Lena, her dress blowing around her ankles. The Four Horsemen had nothing on her. She was rage and vengeance, wrath and malice, in beautifully twisted human form. "You have shamed me for the last time."

The sky began to darken above us, forming a dense black cloud.

I tried to pull away from the supernatural grip, but every time I moved, Abraham closed his hand more and the vise around my neck tightened. It was hard to force my eyes to stay open. I kept blinking, trying not to pass out.

Lena thrust her open hands into the fire, and the circle pushed away from her. The flames didn't die down, but they were expanded outward at Lena's command.

The black cloud followed Sarafine, swirling above her. I blinked harder, trying to concentrate. I realized it wasn't a storm cloud trailing Sarafine.

It was a swarm of Vexes.

Sarafine called out above the hissing fire. "On the first day, there was Dark Matter. On the second, an Abyss from which, on the third day, the Dark Fire rose. On the fourth day, from the smoke and flame, all Power was born." She stopped just outside the blazing circle. "On the fifth, the Lilum, the Demon Queen, was spun from the ash. And on the sixth came the Order, to balance an energy that knew no bounds."

Sarafine's hair began to singe from the heat. "On the seventh, there was a book."

The Book of Moons appeared on the ground in front of her, the pages flipping themselves. They stopped abruptly, and the Book lay open at Sarafine's feet, impervious to the flames.

Sarafine began to recite from memory.

> "FROM THE VOICES IN THE DARKNESS, I COME.
> FROM THE WOUNDS OF THE FALLEN, I AM BORN.
> FROM THE DESPAIR I BRING FORTH, I AM
>   CLAIMED.
> FROM THE HEART OF THE BOOK, I HEAR
>   THE CALL.

The moment she spoke the last word, the fire parted, creating a path through the center of the blaze.

I saw Sarafine raise her hands in front of her and close her eyes. She flicked her fingers open on both hands, and fire sparked on the tips. But her face twisted in confusion. Something wasn't right.

Her powers weren't working.

The flames never left her fingers, and the sparks rained down, igniting her dress.

I struggled with the last bit of strength I had left in me. I was going to lose consciousness. I heard a voice in a remote corner of my mind. It wasn't Lena or the Lilum, or even Sarafine. It was whispering something over and over, so softly I couldn't hear it.

The death grip around my neck loosened, but when I glanced at Abraham, the position of his hand hadn't changed. I gasped, inhaling so fast the air choked me. The words in my head were getting louder.

Two words.

I'M WAITING.

I saw his face—my face—for a split second. It was my other half, my Fractured Soul. He was trying to help me.

The invisible hand was ripped from my neck, and air tore through my lungs. Abraham's expression was a mixture of shock, confusion, and fury.

I stumbled as I ran toward Lena, still trying to catch my breath. By the time I reached the edge of the burning circle,

Sarafine was trapped inside another, clutching the bottom of her burnt dress.

I stopped a few feet away. The heat was so intense I couldn't get any closer. Lena was standing in front of Sarafine, on the other side of the blazing ring. Her hair was singed from the heat, her face black from the smoke.

The cloud of Vexes was moving away from her and toward Abraham. He was watching, but he wasn't helping Sarafine.

"Lena! Help me!" Sarafine called, dropping to her knees. She looked so much like Izabel the night she was Claimed, lying at her mother's feet. "I never wanted to hurt you. I never wanted any of this."

Lena's blackened face was filled with rage. "No. You wanted me dead."

Sarafine's eyes were watering from the smoke, which almost made it look like she was crying. "My life has never been about what I wanted. My choices were made for me. I tried so hard to fight the Darkness, but I wasn't strong enough." She coughed, trying to rub the smoke away. With her face streaked and her eyes swollen and red, the gold in them was hard to see. "You have always been the strong one, even as a baby. That's how you survived."

I recognized the confusion in Lena's eyes. Sarafine was a victim of the curse Lena had feared her whole life—the curse that had spared Lena. Was this who her mother could have been? "What do you mean, how I survived?"

Sarafine coughed, black smoke swirling around her. "There was a terrible storm, and the rain put out the fire. You saved yourself." She sounded relieved, as if she hadn't left Lena for dead.

Lena stared at her mother. "And today you were going to finish what you started."

An ember fell onto Sarafine's dress, and it caught fire again. She slapped at the charred fabric with her bare hand until it went out. She lifted her eyes to meet Lena's. "Please." Her voice was so hoarse, it was hard to hear. She reached out her hand toward Lena. "I wasn't going to hurt you. I just had to make him believe I was."

She was talking about Abraham, the one who had lured Lena's mother into the Dark, the one who was standing there watching her burn.

Lena was shaking her head, tears streaming down her face. "How can I trust you?" But even as she said it, the flames began to die down in the space between them.

Lena started to reach out her hand.

Their fingertips were inches apart.

I could see the burns on Sarafine's arm as she reached for Lena. "I've always loved you, Lena. You're my little girl."

Lena closed her eyes. It was hard to look at Sarafine, with her hair singed and her skin blistering. It had to be even harder if she was your mother. "I wish I could believe you...."

"Lena, look at me." Sarafine seemed to be breaking. "I'll love you until the day after forever."

I remembered the words from the vision. The last thing Sarafine said to Lena's father before she left him to die. *"I'll love you until the day after forever."*

Lena remembered, too.

I saw her face twist in agony as she yanked her hand back. "You don't love me. You aren't capable of love."

The fire surged up where it had died down only a minute

before, trapping Sarafine. She was being consumed by the flames she once controlled, her powers as unpredictable as any Caster's.

"No!" Sarafine screamed.

"I'm sorry, Izabel," Lena whispered.

Sarafine lunged forward, catching the sleeve of her dress on fire. "You little bitch! I wish you had burned to death like your miserable father! I will find you in the next life—"

But screams reached a crescendo as the flames swept over Sarafine's body in seconds. It was worse than the bloodcurdling shrieking of the Vexes. It was the sound of pain and death and misery.

Her body fell, and the flames moved over it like a swarm of locusts, leaving nothing but the raging fire. At the same moment, Lena dropped to her knees, staring at the place where her mother's hand had hung in the air a minute before.

Lena!

I closed the distance between us, dragging her away from the fire. She was coughing, trying to catch her breath.

Abraham came closer, the black cloud of demonic spirits above him. I pulled Lena to me as we watched Greenbrier burn for the second time.

He was standing over us, the tip of his cane practically touching the melted toe of my sneaker. "Well, you know what they say. If you want something done right, do it yourself."

"You didn't help her." I don't know why I said it. I didn't care that Sarafine was dead. But why hadn't he?

Abraham laughed. "Saved me the trouble of killing her myself. She wasn't worth her weight in salt anymore."

I wondered if Sarafine had realized how expendable she was.

How worthless she was in the eyes of the master she served? "But she was one of you."

"Dark Casters are nothing like me and my kind, boy. They're like rats. Plenty more where Sarafine came from." He looked at Lena, his face darkening to match his empty eyes. "Once your little girlfriend's dead, getting rid of them will be my next order of business."

Don't listen to him, L.

But she wasn't listening to Abraham. She wasn't listening to anyone. I knew, because I could hear her stumbling over the same words in her mind, again and again.

I let my mother die.

I let my mother die.

I let my mother die.

I pushed Lena behind me, even though she had a better chance of fighting Abraham than I did. "My aunt was right. You are the Devil."

"She's too kind. But I wish I was." He pulled out his gold pocket watch, checking the time. "But I do know a few Demons. And they've been waiting a long time to pay this world a visit." Abraham slid the watch back into his jacket. "Looks like you kids are out of time."

⊰ 12.14 ⊱

Demon Door

Abraham lifted *The Book of Moons*, and the pages began to turn again, flipping so fast I was sure they would tear. When they stopped, he ran his fingers over the pages reverently. This was his bible. Framed by the black smoke behind him, Abraham began to read.

> "ON DARKEST DAYS, WHEN BLOOD IS SPILLED,
> A LEGION OF DEMONS TO AVENGE THOSE KILLED.
> IF A MARKED DOOR CANNOT BE FOUND,
> THE EARTH WILL OPEN, TO OFFER ONE FROM
> THE GROUND.

> "SANGUINE EFFUSO, ATRIS DIEBUS,
> ORIETUR DAEMONUM LEGIO UT INTERFECTOS
> ULCISCATUR.

SI IANUA NOTATA INVENIRI NON POTUERIT,
TELLUS HISCAT UT DE TERRA IPSA IANUAM
OFFERAT."

I didn't want to hang around to see the legion of Demons that Abraham was calling to finish us off. The Vexes were enough for me. I grabbed Lena's hand and pulled her up, running from the fire and Lena's dead mother, from Abraham and *The Book of Moons* and whatever evil he was summoning.

"Ethan! We're going the wrong way."

Lena was right. We should have been running toward Ravenwood, instead of through the tangled cotton fields that used to be part of Blackwell, the plantation that once stood on the other side of Greenbrier. But there was nowhere else to go. Abraham was standing between Ravenwood and us, his sadistic smile revealing the truth. This was a game, and he was enjoying it.

"We don't have a choice. We have to—"

Lena cut me off before I could finish. "Something's wrong. I can feel it."

The sky darkened above us, and I heard a low rumbling sound. But it wasn't thunder or the unmistakable screams of Vexes.

"What is that?" I was dragging Lena up the hill that used to lead from the road to Blackwell Plantation.

Before she could answer, the ground started moving beneath us. It felt like it was rolling under my feet, and I struggled to keep my balance. The rumbling sound was getting louder, and there were other noises—trees splitting and falling, the strangled symphony of thousands of lubbers, and a faint cracking coming from behind us.

Or below us.

442

Lena saw it first. "Oh my God!"

The earth was cracking down the middle of the dirt road, the split heading right for us. As the crack spread, the ground opened up, and dirt poured into the fissure like quicksand being sucked into a hole.

It was an earthquake.

It seemed impossible because quakes didn't happen in the South. They happened in places out west, like California. But I'd seen enough movies to recognize one.

The sound was as terrifying as the sight of the ground consuming itself. The black streak of Vexes above us reared back, heading straight for us.

The ground behind us was splitting faster, tearing like a seam.

"We can't outrun it! Or them!" Lena's voice was ragged. "We're trapped!"

"Maybe not." I looked over the side of the hill and saw the Beater skidding across the road below us. Link was driving like his mom had just caught him drinking in church. There was something in front of the Beater, moving even faster than the car.

It was Boo. Not the lazy black dog that slept at the foot of Lena's bed. This was a Caster dog that looked like a wolf, and ran faster than one.

Lena looked back. "We'll never make it!"

Abraham was still standing in the distance, untouched by the winds swirling around him. He turned to look over the side of the hill, where the Beater was racing along the road below.

I looked down, too. Link was hanging out the window shouting at me. I couldn't hear him, but whatever he was urging us to do—jump, run, I didn't even know—there was no time.

I shook my head silently, glancing back at Abraham one last time. Link's eyes followed mine.

Then he was gone.

The Beater was still moving, but the driver's seat was empty. Boo jumped out of the way as the car sped past him, ignoring the curve in the road. The Beater flipped, crashing down onto the road over and over.

I saw the roof cave in at the same time I heard the rip—

A hand fumbled for my arm. I was pitched into the black void that transported Incubuses from one place to another, but I didn't need to see to know it was Link's hand digging into my skin.

I was still spiraling through the void when I felt his fingers slipping. Then I was falling, and the world came back into view. Slices of the dark sky and flashes of brown—

My back hit something hard, more than once.

I watched the sky pull farther and farther away as I got closer to the ground. But my body slammed against something solid, and suddenly I wasn't falling anymore.

Ethan!

My arm was caught, and the pain tore up my shoulder. I blinked. I was trapped in a sea of long, brown...branches?

"Dude, are you okay?" I turned slowly toward the sound of his voice. Link was standing at the base of the tree, staring up at me. Lena was beside him, completely panicked.

"I'm trapped in a tree. What do you think?"

Relief spread across Lena's face.

"I think I just saved your ass with my superpowers." Link was grinning.

"Ethan, can you get down?" Lena asked.

"Yeah. I don't think anything's broken." I untangled my legs from the branches carefully.

"I can rip you down," Link offered.

"No, thanks. I got it." I was afraid of where I might end up if he gave it another shot.

It hurt every time I moved, so it took me a few minutes to climb down. As soon as I hit the ground, Lena threw her arms around me. "You're okay!"

I didn't want to mention that if she squeezed me any tighter, I wouldn't be. I could already feel what little energy I had left draining out of me. "I think so."

"Hey, you two are heavier than you look. And it was my first time. Cut me some slack." Link was still grinning. "I did save your lives."

I held out my fist. "You did, man. We'd be dead if it wasn't for you."

He tapped his knuckles against mine. "I guess that makes me a hero."

"Great. Now your head's gonna be even bigger, if that's possible." He knew what I was really saying — *thanks for saving my ass and the girl I love.*

Lena hugged him. "Well, you're my hero."

"I did sacrifice the Beater." Link looked over at me. "How bad was it?"

"Bad."

He shrugged. "Nothin' a little duct tape can't fix."

"Hope you've got a lot of it. How did you find us, anyway?"

"You know how they say animals can sense tornados and earthquakes and stuff like that? Guess it's the same for Incubuses."

"The earthquake," Lena whispered. "Do you think it made it to town?"

"It's already hit," Link said. "Main Street split open right down the middle."

"Is everyone okay?" I meant Amma, my dad, and my hundred-year-old aunts.

"I dunno. My mom took a mess a people down to the church, and they're holed up in there. She said somethin' about the foundation and the steel in the beams and some show she saw on the nature channel." Leave it to Mrs. Lincoln to rescue everyone on her street with educational programming and a talent for ordering people around. "When I left, she was screamin' about the apocalypse and the seven signs."

"We have to get to my house." We didn't live as close to church as Link did, and I was pretty sure Wate's Landing wasn't built to withstand earthquakes.

"There's no way. The road split right behind me as soon as I turned off a Route 9. We're gonna have to go through Perpetual Peace." It was hard to believe Link was volunteering to go into the cemetery at night, in the middle of a supernatural earthquake.

Lena put her head on my shoulder. "I have a bad feeling about this."

"Yeah? Well, I've had a bad feelin' since I got back from Neverland and turned into a Demon."

⁓☙

When we walked through the gates of His Garden of Perpetual Peace, it was anything but peaceful. Even with the glowing

446

crosses, it was so dark I could barely see. The lubbers were going nuts, buzzing so loud that it sounded like we were in the center of a wasps' nest. Lightning cut through the darkness, cracking the sky the way the earthquake had cracked the earth.

Link was leading the way, since he was the only one who could see much of anything. "You know, my mom's right about one thing. In the Bible, it says there'll be earthquakes at the end."

I looked at him like he was nuts. "When was the last time you read the Bible? In Sunday school, when we were nine?"

He shrugged. "Just sayin'."

Lena bit her bottom lip. "Link could be right. What if Abraham didn't cause this, and it's a result of the Order being broken? Like the heat and the bugs and the lake drying up?"

I knew she felt responsible, but this wasn't caused by a Mortal End of Days. This was a supernatural apocalypse. "And Abraham just happened to be reading about cracking open the earth to let all the Demons out?"

Link looked over at me. "What do you mean, lettin' the Demons out? Lettin' them outta where?"

The ground started to tremble again. Link stopped, listening. It seemed like he was trying to determine where the quake was coming from, or where it would hit next. The rumbling changed to a creaking sound, as if we were standing on a porch that was about to collapse. It sounded like a thunderstorm underground.

"Is another one going to hit?" I couldn't decide if it was better to run or stand still.

Link looked around. "I think we should—"

The ground underneath us seized, and I heard the asphalt splitting. There was nowhere to go, and not enough time to get there, anyway. The asphalt was crumbling around me, but I wasn't falling down. Pieces of the road were jutting up toward the sky.

They scraped against each other, forming a crooked concrete triangle, until they stopped. The glowing crosses started flickering out.

"Tell me that isn't what I think it is." Link was backing away from the dead grass, dotted with plastic flowers and headstones. It looked like the headstones were shifting. Maybe another aftershock was coming, or worse.

"What are you talking about?" The first gravestone came out of the dirt before he had time to answer. It was another earthquake—at least, that's what I thought.

But I was wrong.

The gravestones weren't falling over.

They were being pushed up from underneath.

Stones and dirt were flying into the air and coming back down like bombs being dropped from the sky. Rotted caskets forced their way out of the ground. Hundred-year-old pine boxes and black lacquered coffins were rolling down the hill, breaking open and leaving decaying corpses in their wake. The smell was so disgusting, Link was gagging.

"Ethan!" Lena screamed.

I grabbed her hand. "Run!"

Link didn't need to be told twice. Bones and boards were flying through the air like shrapnel, but Link was taking the hits for us like a linebacker.

"Lena, what's happening?" I didn't let go of her hand.

"I think Abraham opened some kind of door into the Underground." She stumbled, and I pulled her back to her feet.

We reached the hill that led to the oldest part of the cemetery, the one I had pushed Aunt Mercy's wheelchair up more times than I could count. The hill was dark, and I tried to avoid the huge holes I could barely see.

"This way!" Link was already at the top. He stopped, and I thought he was waiting for us. But when we made it up the hill, I realized he was staring out into the graveyard.

The mausoleums and tombs had exploded, littering the ground with hunks of carved stone, bones, and body parts. There was a plastic fawn lying in the dust. It looked like someone had dug up every grave on the hill.

There was a corpse standing at the far end of what used to be the good side of the hill. You could tell it had been buried for a while by the state of decay. The corpse was staring at us, but it had no eyes. The sockets were completely empty. Something was inside it, animating what was left of the body—the way the Lilum had been inside Mrs. English.

Link put up his arm to keep us behind him.

The corpse cocked its head to one side, as if it was listening. Then a dark mist poured out of its eyes, nose, and mouth. The body went slack and dropped to the ground. The mist spiraled like a Vex, then shot across the sky and out of the graveyard.

"Was that a Sheer?" I asked.

Link answered before Lena. "No. It was some kinda Demon."

"How do you know?" Lena whispered, as if she was afraid she might wake more of the dead.

Link looked away. "The same way a dog knows when it sees another dog."

"It didn't look like a dog to me." I was trying to make him feel better, but we were way past that.

Link stared at the body lying on the ground where the Demon

stood only moments ago. "Maybe my mom's right and this is the End a Days. Maybe she's gonna get a chance to use her wheat grinder and her gas masks and that inflatable raft after all."

"A raft? Is that what's strapped to the roof of your garage?"

Link nodded. "Yeah. For when the waters rise and the Lowcountry floods and God takes his vengeance on all us sinners."

I shook my head. "Not God. Abraham Ravenwood."

The ground had finally stopped shaking, but we didn't notice.

The three of us were shaking so hard, it was impossible to tell.

⊰ 12.17 ⊱

Passing Strange

Sixteen bodies were lying in the county mortuary. According to the Shadowing Song from my mom, there should have been eighteen. I didn't know why the earthquakes had stopped and Abraham's army of Vexes had disappeared. Maybe destroying the town had lost its appeal once we were gone and the town was, well, destroyed. But if I knew anything about Abraham, there was a reason. All I knew was that this kind of broken math, the place where the rational met the supernatural, was what my life was like now.

And I knew without a doubt that two more bodies would join the sixteen. That's how much I believed in the songs. Number seventeen and number eighteen. Those were the numbers I had in the back of my mind as I drove out to County Care. The power was out there, too.

And I had a terrible feeling I knew who number seventeen would be.

The backup generator was flickering on and off. I could tell by the way the safety lights were flashing. Bobby Murphy wasn't at the front desk; in fact, nobody was. Today's catastrophic events at His Garden of Perpetual Peace weren't going to raise too many eyebrows at County Care, a place most people didn't know about until tragedy struck. Sixteen. I wondered if there were even sixteen autopsy tables at the mortuary. I was pretty sure there weren't.

But a trip to the mortuary was probably a regular event around here. There was more than one revolving door between the dead and the living as you made your way down these hallways. When you walked through the doors of County Care, your universe shrunk, smaller and smaller, until your whole world was your hallway, your nurse, and your eight-by-ten antiseptic peach of a room.

Once you walked in here, you didn't care much about what happened out there. This place was a kind of in-between world. Especially since every time I took Aunt Prue's hand, it felt like I ended up in another one.

Nothing seemed real anymore, which was ironic because outside these walls, things were more real than they'd ever been. And if I didn't figure out what to do about a few of them—like a powerful Lilum from the Demon world, an unpaid blood debt that was destroying Gatlin, and a few larger worlds beyond—there weren't going to be any antiseptic peaches left to call home.

I walked down the dark hallway toward Aunt Prue's room.

The safety lights flashed on, and I saw a figure in a hospital gown standing at the end of the hallway, holding an IV. Then the safety lights flashed off, and I couldn't see anything. The lights came on again, and the figure was gone.

The thing is, I could have sworn it was my aunt.

"Aunt Prue?"

The lights went out again. I felt really alone—and not the peaceful kind of alone. I thought I saw something moving in the darkness, and then the safety lights flashed back on.

"What the—" I jumped back, spooked.

Aunt Prue was standing right in front of me, her face inches from mine. I could see every wrinkle, every mark from every tear, and every road, like a map of the Caster Tunnels. She beckoned me with one finger, like she wanted me to follow. Then she held her finger to her lips.

"Shh."

The lights went out, and she was gone.

I ran, fumbling my way through the darkness until I found my aunt's room. I pushed on the door, but it didn't open. "Leah, it's me!"

The door swung open, and I saw Leah holding a finger to her lips. It was almost exactly like the gesture Aunt Prue had made in the hallway. I was confused.

"Shh." Leah locked the door behind me. "It's time."

Amma and Macon's mother, Arelia, were sitting next to the bed. She must have come to town for Aunt Prue. Their eyes were closed, and they held hands over Aunt Prue's body. At the foot of the bed, I could barely make out a shimmering presence, the flutter of a thousand tiny braids and beads.

"Aunt Twyla? Is that you?" I saw a flash of smile.

Amma shushed me.

I felt Aunt Prue's gnarled hand clutching mine, patting me reassuringly.

Shh.

I smelled something burning, and realized a handful of herbs was smoking in a painted ceramic bowl on the windowsill. Aunt Prue's bed was covered with her familiar bedspread, the one with the little balls stitched all over it, instead of her hospital sheets. Her flowered pillows were behind her head. Harlon James IV was curled by her feet. There was something different about Aunt Prue. There wasn't a tube or a monitor or even a piece of tape attached to her body. She was dressed in her crocheted slippers and her best pink flowered housecoat, the one with the mother-of-pearl buttons. As if she were going out for one of her drives, to inspect every front yard on the street and complain about who needed a new coat of paint on their house.

I was right. She was number seventeen.

I pushed between Amma and Arelia and took Aunt Prue's hand. Amma opened one eye and shot me a look. "Hands to yourself, Ethan Wate. You don't need to go where she's goin'."

I stood taller. "She's my aunt, Amma. I want to say good-bye."

Arelia shook her head, without opening her eyes. "No time for that now." Her voice sounded like it was drifting into the room from far away.

"Aunt Prue came to find me. I think she has something to tell me."

Amma opened her eyes, raising an eyebrow. "There's the world a the livin', and there's the world a the done-livin'. She's had a good life, and she's ready. And right now, I've got enough trouble keepin' the folks I care about here with the livin'. So if you don't mind..." She sniffed, as if she was trying to get dinner on the table and I was getting in the way.

I gave her a look I'd never given Amma before. One that said: *I mind.*

She sighed and took my hand in one of hers, my aunt's hand in the other. I closed my eyes and waited. "Aunt Prue?"

Nothing happened.

Aunt Prue.

I opened one eye. "What's wrong?" I whispered.

"Can't say as I know. All that fussin', and those Demons makin' all that racket, probably scared her off."

"All those bodies," Arelia whispered.

Amma nodded. "Too many folks movin' to the Otherworld tonight."

"But it's not finished yet. There'll be eighteen. That's what the song said."

Amma looked at me, her expression broken. "Maybe the song's wrong. Even the cards and the Greats are wrong sometime or another. Maybe not everything rolls down the hill as quick as you think."

"Those are my mom's songs, and she said eighteen. She's never wrong, and you know it."

I know, Ethan Wate. She didn't have to say it. I could see it in her eyes, in the way her jaw was set and her face was lined.

I held out my hand again. "Please."

Amma looked over her shoulder. "Leah, Arelia, Twyla, come give us a hand here."

We joined hands, creating a circle — Mortal and Caster. Me, the lost Wayward. Leah, the Light Succubus. Amma, the Seer who was lost in the darkness. Arelia, the Diviner who knew more than she wanted to. And Twyla, who had once called the spirits of the dead, a Sheer in the Otherworld. The light to show Aunt Prue the way home.

They were all part of my family now.

Here we were, holding hands in a hospital room, saying good-bye to someone who was in so many ways already long gone.

Amma nodded to Twyla. "You mind doin' the honors?"

Within seconds, the room disappeared into shadow instead of light. I felt the wind blowing, even though we were inside.

Or so I thought.

The darkness solidified, until we were standing in an enormous room, facing a vault door. I recognized it immediately— the vault in the back of Exile, the club from the Tunnels. This time, the room was empty. I was alone.

I put both hands on the door, touching the silver wheel that opened it. I pulled as hard as I could, but I couldn't make the wheel turn.

"You're gonna have ta put a little more muscle inta it, Ethan." I turned around, and Aunt Prue was standing behind me, in her crocheted slippers and her housecoat, leaning heavily on her IV pole. It wasn't even attached to her body.

"Aunt Prue!" I hugged her, feeling the bones behind her papery skin. "Don't go."

"That's enough a your fussin'. You're as bad as Amma. She's been here 'most every night this week, tryin' ta get me ta stay. Keeps putting somethin' that smells like Harlon James' old diapers under my pillow." She wrinkled her nose. "I've had my fill a this place. They don't even have my stories on the TV here."

"Can't you stay? There are so many parts of the Tunnels left to map. And I don't know what Aunt Mercy and Aunt Grace are going to do without you."

"That's why I wanted ta talk ta you. It's important, so you pay attention, ya hear?"

"I'm listening." I knew there was something she needed to tell me, something none of the others could know.

Aunt Prue leaned in on her IV and whispered. "You gotta stop 'em."

"Stop who?" The hair on the back of my neck was standing up.

Another whisper. "I know exactly what they're fixin' ta do, which is invite half a the town ta my party."

Her "party." She'd mentioned it before. "You mean your funeral?"

She nodded. "Been plannin' it since I was fifty-two, and I want it ta go just the way I want. Good china and linens, the good punch bowl, and Sissy Honeycutt singin' 'Amazin' Grace.' I left a list a the D-tails underneath a my dresser, if it made it over ta Wate's Landin'."

I couldn't believe this was the reason she'd brought me here. But then again, it was Aunt Prue. "Yes, ma'am."

"It's all about the guest list, Ethan."

"I get it. You want to make sure all the right people are there."

She looked at me like I was an idiot. "No. I want ta make sure the wrong ones aren't. I want ta make sure *certain people* stay out. This isn't a pig pick at the firehouse."

She was serious, although I saw a sparkle in her eye that made it seem like she was about to break out into one of her

457

infamously unharmonic fake-opera versions of "Leaning on the Everlasting Arms."

"I want you ta slam the door before Eunice Honeycutt sets foot in the buildin'. I don't care if Sissy's singin', or *that woman* brings the Lord Almighty on her arm. She's not havin' any a my punch."

I grabbed her in a hug so big that I lifted her tiny crocheted feet right off the ground. "I'm going to miss you, Aunt Prue."

" 'Course ya are. But it's my time, and I got things ta do and husbands ta see. Not ta mention a few Harlon Jameses. Now, would you mind gettin' the door for an old woman? I'm not feelin' like myself today."

"That door?" I touched the metal vault in front of us.

"The very one." She let go of the IV stand and nodded at me.

"Where does it go?"

She shrugged. "Can't tell you. Just know it's where I'm meant to go."

"What if I'm not supposed to open it or something?"

"Ethan, are you tellin' me you're afraid ta open a silly little door? Turn the durned wheel already."

I put my hands on the wheel and yanked on it as hard as I could. It didn't move.

"You gonna make an old woman do the heavy liftin'?" Aunt Prue pushed me aside with one feeble hand and reached out to touch the door.

It sprang open beneath her hand, blasting light and wind and spraying water into the room. I could see a glimpse of blue water beyond. I offered her my arm, and she took it. As I helped her over the threshold, we stood there for a second on opposite sides of the door.

458

She looked over her shoulder, into the blue behind her. "Looks like this here's my path. You want ta walk me a ways, like you promised you would?"

I froze. "I promised I'd walk you out there?"

She nodded. "Sure did. You're the one who told me 'bout the Last Door. How else would I know 'bout it?"

"I don't know anything about a Last Door, Aunt Prue. I've never been past this door."

"Sure ya have. You're standin' past it this very minute."

I looked out, and there I was—the other me. Hazy and gray, flickering like a shadow.

It was the me from the lens of the old video camera.

The me from the dream.

My Fractured Soul.

He started walking toward the vault door. Aunt Prue waved in his direction. "You goin' ta walk me up ta the lighthouse?"

The moment she said it, I could see the pathway of neat stone steps leading up a grassy slope to a white stone lighthouse. Square and old, one simple stone box on top of another, then a white tower that reached high into the unbroken blue of the sky. The water beyond was even bluer. The grass that moved with the wind was green and alive, and it made me long for something I had never seen.

But I guess I had seen it, because there I was coming down the stone pathway.

A sick feeling turned in my stomach, and suddenly someone twisted my arm behind me, like Link was practicing wrestling moves on me.

A voice—the loudest voice in the universe, from the strongest person I knew, thundered in my ear. "You go on ahead,

Prudence. You don't need Ethan's help. You've got Twyla now, and you'll be fine once you get up there to the lighthouse."

Amma nodded with a smile, and suddenly Twyla was standing next to Aunt Prue—not a made-of-light-Twyla but the real one, looking the same as she did the night she died.

Aunt Prue caught my eye and blew me a kiss, taking Twyla's arm and turning back toward the lighthouse.

I tried to see if the other half of my soul was still out there, but the vault door slammed so hard it echoed through the club behind me.

Leah spun the wheel with both hands, as hard as she could. I tried to help, but she pushed me away. Arelia was there, too, muttering something I couldn't understand.

Amma still had me in a hold so tight that she could've won the state championship if we really were at a wrestling match.

Arelia opened her eyes. "Now. It has to be now."

Everything went black.

_____ ᘓ

I opened my eyes, and we were standing around Aunt Prue's lifeless body. She was gone, but we already knew that. Before I could say or do anything, Amma had me out of the room and halfway down the hall.

"You." She could barely speak, a bony finger pointing at me. Five minutes later, we were in my car, and she only let go of my arm so I could drive us home. It took forever to figure out a way to get back to the house. Half of the roads in town had been closed off because of the earthquake that wasn't an earthquake.

I stared at the steering wheel and thought about the wheel on the vault door. "What was that? The Last Door?"

Amma turned and slapped me in the face. She'd never laid a hand on me, not in her entire life or mine.

"Don't you ever scare me like that again!"

Cream of Grief

The cream-colored paper was thick and folded eight times, with a purple satin ribbon tied around it. I found it in the bottom drawer of the dresser, just like Aunt Prue said I would. I read it to the Sisters, who argued about it with Thelma until Amma stepped in.

"If Prudence Jane wanted the good china, we're usin' the good china. No sense arguin' with the dead." Amma folded her arms. Aunt Prue had only been gone two days. It seemed wrong to be calling her dead so soon.

"Next you'll be tellin' me she didn't want fun'ral potatoes." Aunt Mercy wadded up another handkerchief.

I checked the paper. "She does. But she doesn't want you to let Jeanine Mayberry make them. She doesn't want stale potato chips crumbled on the top."

Aunt Mercy nodded as if I was reading from the Declaration

of Independence. "It's the truth. Jeanine Mayberry says they bake up better that way, but Prudence Jane always said it was on account a her bein' so cheap." Her chin quivered.

Aunt Mercy was a mess. She hadn't done much of anything but wad up handkerchiefs ever since she heard that Aunt Prue had passed. Aunt Grace, on the other hand, had busied herself with writing condolence cards, letting everyone know how sorry she was that Aunt Prue was gone, even though Thelma explained that it was the other folks who were supposed to send them to her. Aunt Grace had looked at Thelma like she was crazy. "Why would they send them ta me? They're my cards. An' it's my news."

Thelma shook her head, but she didn't say anything after that.

Whenever there was a disagreement about something, they made me read the letter again. And Aunt Prue's letter was about as eccentric and specific as my Aunt Prue herself.

"*Dear Girls,*" the letter began. To each other, the Sisters were never the Sisters. They were always the Girls. "*If you're reading this, I've been called to my Great Reward. Even though I'll be busy meeting my Maker, I'll still be watching to be sure my party goes according to my specifications. And don't think I won't march right outta my grave and up the center aisle a the church if Eunice Honeycutt sets one foot into the building.*"

Only Aunt Prue would need a bouncer for her funeral.

It went on and on from there. Aside from stipulating that all four Harlon Jameses be in attendance along with Lucille Ball, and selecting a somewhat scandalous arrangement of "Amazing Grace" and the wrong version of "Abide With Me," the biggest surprise was the eulogy.

She wanted Amma to deliver it.

"That's nonsense." Amma sniffed.

"It's what Aunt Prue wanted. Look." I held out the paper.

Amma wouldn't look at it. "Then she's as big a fool as the rest a you."

I patted her on the back. "No sense arguing with the dead, Amma." She glared at me, and I shrugged. "At least you don't have to rent a tuxedo."

My dad stood up from his seat on the bottom stair, defeated. "Well, I'd better go start rounding up the bagpipes."

In the end, the bagpipes were a gift from Macon. Once he heard about Aunt Prue's request, he insisted on bringing them in all the way from the Highlands Elks Club in Columbia, the state capital. At least, that's what he said. Knowing him, and the Tunnels, I was convinced they came from Scotland that same morning. They played "Amazing Grace" so beautifully when folks first arrived that nobody would walk into the church. A huge crowd formed around the front walkway and the sidewalk, until the reverend insisted they all come inside.

I stood in the doorway, watching the crowd. A hearse—a real hearse, not Lena and Macon's—sat parked out in front of the building. Aunt Prue was being buried in the Summerville Cemetery until His Garden of Perpetual Peace reopened for business. The Sisters called it the New Cemetery, since it had only been open about seventy years.

The sight of the hearse brought back a memory, the first time

I saw Lena drive through Gatlin on my way to school last year. I remembered thinking it was an omen, maybe even a bad one.

Had it been?

Looking back on everything that had happened, everything that had brought me from that hearse to this one, I still couldn't say.

Not because of Lena. She would always be the best thing that had ever happened to me. But because things had changed.

We both had. I understood that.

But Gatlin had changed, too, and that was harder to understand.

So I stood in the doorway of the chapel, watching it happen. Letting it happen, because I didn't have a choice. The Eighteenth Moon was two days away. If Lena and I didn't figure out what the Lilum wanted—who the One Who Is Two actually was—there was no way to predict how much more things would change. Maybe this hearse was another omen of things to come.

We had spent hours in the archive, with nothing to show for it. Still, I knew that was where Lena and I would be again, as soon as the funeral was over. There was nothing left to do but try. Even if it seemed hopeless.

You can't fight fate.

Was that what my mom had said?

"I don't see my horse-drawn carriage. White horses, that's what my letter said." I would've known that voice anywhere.

Aunt Prue was standing next to me. No glimmer, no shine. Just plain as day Aunt Prue. If she wasn't still wearing the clothes she died in, I would've mistaken her for one of the guests at her own funeral.

"Yeah, well. We had a little trouble finding one. Since you're not Abraham Lincoln."

She ignored me. "I thought I made it clear, I wanted Sissy Honeycutt ta be the one singin' 'Amazin' Grace,' just like she did at Charlene Watkins' service. And I don't see her. But these fellas really put some lung inta it, which I 'preciate."

"Sissy Honeycutt said we'd have to invite Eunice if we wanted her to sing." That was explanation enough for Aunt Prue. We turned back to the pipers. "I think it's the only hymn they know. I'm not sure they're actually Southern."

She smiled. " 'Course they ain't."

The music spun out over the crowd, drawing everyone a few feet closer. I could tell Aunt Prue was pleased, no matter what she said.

"Still, it's a fine crowd. Biggest one I seen in years. Bigger than all my husbands' put together." She looked at me. "Don't you think so, Ethan?"

I smiled. "Yes, ma'am. It's a fine crowd." I pulled on the collar of my tux shirt. In the hundred-degree winter heat, I was about to pass out. But I didn't tell her that.

"Now, put your jacket on an' show a little respect for the D-ceased."

⁓

Amma and my dad reached a compromise on the eulogy. Amma wouldn't deliver it, but she would read a poem. When she finally told us what she was reading, nobody gave it much thought. Except that it meant we got to cross off two items on Aunt Prue's list at the same time.

"Abide with me; fast falls the eventide,
The darkness deepens, Lord, with me abide.
When other helpers fail and comforts flee,
Help of the helpless, O abide with me.
Swift to its close ebbs out life's little day;
Earth's joys grow dim; its glories pass away;
Change and decay in all around I see;
O Thou who changest not, abide with me."

The words hit me like bullets. The darkness was deepening, and though I didn't know what the eventide was, it felt like it was falling fast. It wasn't just comforts that were fleeing, and it was more than Earth's joys and glories that were passing away.

Amma was right. So was the guy who wrote the hymn. Change and decay was all I could see.

I didn't know if there was anyone or anything who changest not, but if there was, I would do more than ask them to abide with me.

I wanted them to rescue me.

By the time Amma folded the paper back up, you could've heard a pin drop. She stood at the podium, every bit Sulla the Prophet as the original. That's when I realized what she had done.

It wasn't a poem, not the way she had read it. It wasn't even a hymn anymore.

It was a prophecy.

⊰ 12.20 ⊱

Hybrid

I was standing on the top of the white water tower, with my back to the sun. My headless shadow fell across the warm, painted metal, disappearing off the edge and into the sky.

I'M WAITING.

There he was. My other half. The dream staggered on like a movie I'd seen so many times that I started to cut and recut it myself, as it erupted into flashes—

Hard hitting.

Chucks kicking.

Deadweight.

Falling...

"Ethan!"

I rolled out of my bed and landed on my bedroom floor.

"No wonder Incubuses keep showing up in your room. You sleep like the dead." John Breed was standing over me. From where I was lying, he looked twenty feet tall. He also looked like he could kick my ass better than I had been kicking my own in my dream.

It was a weird thought. But what came next was weirder.

"I need your help."

———⁓

John was sitting in the chair at my desk, which I had started to think of as the Incubus chair.

"I wish you guys could figure out some way to sleep." I pulled my faded Harley Davidson shirt over my head. Ironic, considering I was sitting across from John.

"Yeah. That's not really an option." He stared up at my blue ceiling.

"Then I wish you could figure out that the rest of us need to—"

John cut me off. "It's me."

"What?"

"Liv told me everything. The One Who Is Two guy—it's me."

"Are you sure?" I wasn't even sure I believed him.

"Yeah. I figured it out today at your aunt's funeral."

I glanced at the clock. He should have said yesterday, and I should've been asleep. "How?"

He got up and paced across the room. "I always knew it was

469

me. I was born to be two things. But at the funeral, I knew this was something I had to do. I felt it, when the Seer was talking."

"Amma?" I knew Aunt Prue's funeral had been emotional for my family, the whole town really, but I hadn't expected it to affect John. He wasn't part of either of those things. "What do you mean, you always knew?"

"It's my birthday tomorrow, right? My Eighteenth Moon." He didn't sound too happy about it, and I couldn't blame him. Considering it was bringing on the end of the world and everything.

"Do you know what you're saying?" I still didn't trust him.

He nodded. "I'm supposed to make the trade, like the Demon Queen said. My pathetic screwed-up experiment of a life for a New Order. I almost feel bad for the universe. I'm getting a bargain. Except for the fact that I won't be around to see it."

"But Liv will," I said.

"Liv will." He dropped back down in the chair, holding his head in his hands.

"Damn."

He looked up. "Damn? That's the best you can come up with? I'm ready to lay down my life here."

I almost couldn't imagine what was going through his mind — what would make a guy like him willing to die. Almost.

I knew what it felt like to be willing to sacrifice yourself for the girl you loved. I was going to do the same thing at the Great Barrier, when we faced Abraham and Hunting. At Honey Hill, when we faced the fires and Sarafine. I would have died for Lena a thousand times over.

"Liv's not going to be happy."

"No. She's not," he agreed. "But she'll understand."

"I think things like this are pretty hard to understand. And I've been trying for a while now."

"You know what your problem is, Mortal?"

"The end of the world?"

John shook his head. "You think too much."

"Yeah?" I almost laughed.

"Trust me. Sometimes, you gotta trust your gut instincts."

"So, what does your gut want me to do?" I said it slowly, without looking at him.

"I didn't know until I got here." He walked over to me and grabbed my arm. "The place you were dreaming about. The big white tower. That's where I need to go."

Before I could tell him what I thought about him digging through my dreams, Incubus-style, I heard the rip and we were gone. . . .

I couldn't see John. I couldn't see anything but darkness and a silver streak of widening light. When I stepped through, I heard the ripping sound again, and saw her face.

Liv was waiting for us on the top of the water tower.

She stormed toward us, furious. But she wasn't looking at me. "Are you completely insane? Did you think I wouldn't know what you were up to? Where you'd come?" She started to cry.

John stepped in front of me. "How did you know where I was?"

She waved a piece of paper in the air. "You left a note."

"You left her a note?" I asked.

"It just said good-bye . . . and some other stuff. It didn't say where I was going."

I shook my head. "She's Liv. You didn't know she'd figure it out?"

471

She held up her wrist. The dials were practically exploding off her selenometer. "The One Who Is Two? You didn't think I would instantly know it was you? If you hadn't walked in on me writing about it, I would never have even told you."

"Liv."

"I've been trying to find a way around this for months now." She closed her eyes.

He reached out for her. "I've been trying to find a way around you."

"You don't have to do this." Liv shook her head, and John pulled her close against his chest, kissing her forehead.

"Yeah. I do. For once in my life, I want to be the guy who does the right thing."

Liv's blue eyes were red from crying. "I don't want you to go. We only just—I never had a chance. We never had a chance."

He put his thumb on her lip. "Shh. We did. I did." He looked out into the night, but he was still talking to her. "I love you, Olivia. This is my chance."

She didn't respond, except for the tears running down her face.

He took a step toward me, pulling me up by the arm. "Take care of her for me, will you?"

I nodded.

He leaned closer. "If you hurt her. If you touch her. If you let anyone break her heart, I will find you and kill you. And then I'll keep hurting you from the other side. Understand?"

I understood better than he knew.

He let go of me and took his jacket off. He handed it to Liv. "Keep it. To remember me by. And there's something else." He reached into one of the pockets. "I don't remember my mother, but Abraham said this belonged to her. I want you to have it." It was a gold bracelet with an inscription in Niadic, or some other Caster language only Liv would know how to read.

Liv's knees buckled, and she started sobbing.

John held her so tight that the tips of her toes were barely touching the ground. "I'm glad I finally met someone I wanted to give it to."

"Me, too." She could barely speak.

He kissed her gently and stepped away from her.

He nodded at me.

And threw himself over the edge of the railing.

I heard her voice, echoing through the darkness. The Lilum.

The Balance is not paid.

Only the Crucible can make the sacrifice.

The Wrong One

When I opened my eyes, I was back in my bedroom. I stared up at my blue ceiling, trying to figure out how I got here. We had ripped, but it couldn't have been because of John. I knew that much, because he was lying on my bedroom floor, unconscious.

It must have been someone else. Someone who was more powerful than an Incubus. Someone who knew about the Eighteenth Moon.

Someone who had known everything, all along—including the one thing I was just starting to figure out for myself, right now.

Liv was shaking John, still sobbing. "Wake up, John. Please, wake up."

He opened his eyes for a second, confused. "What the hell?"

She threw her arms around him. "Not hell. Not even heaven."

"Where am I?" He was disoriented.

"My room." I sat up and leaned against the wall.

"How did I get here?"

"Don't ask." I wasn't about to try to explain that the Lilum had somehow transported us here.

I was more worried about what it meant.

It wasn't John Breed.

And there was someone I had to talk to.

⇥ 12.21 ⇤

Plain English

I knocked on the door and stood waiting in a pale yellow circle of porch light. I stared at the door, shifting my weight uncomfortably, my hands jammed in my pockets. Wishing I wasn't there. Wishing my heart would stop pounding.

She was going to think I was crazy.

Why wouldn't she? I was beginning to think so myself.

I saw the bathrobe first, then the fuzzy slippers and the glass eye.

"Ethan? What are you doing out there? Are you with Mitchell?" Mrs. English peeked outside, patting her plastic curlers as if there was a way to make them look more attractive.

"No, ma'am."

She looked disappointed and switched to her classroom voice. "Do you have any idea how late it is?"

It was nine.

"Can I come in for a minute? I really need to talk to you."

Well, not you. Not you exactly.

"Now?"

"It'll only take a minute. It's about *The Crucible*."

Just not the one you taught us about.

That finally got her, like I knew it would.

I followed her into the parlor for the second time, but she didn't remember. The collection of ceramic figurines on the mantel over the fireplace was lined up perfectly again, as if nothing had ever happened there. The only giveaway was the spidery plant. It was gone. I guess some things were too broken to fix.

"Please have a seat, Ethan."

I automatically sat in the flowered chair, and then stood right up, because there was nowhere else to sit in the tiny room. No son of Gatlin would sit while a lady stood. "I'm fine standing. You go ahead, ma'am."

Mrs. English adjusted her glasses as she sat down. "Well, I have to say, this is a first."

Anytime now. Wade on in.

"Ethan? Did you want to tell me something in particular about *The Crucible*?"

I cleared my throat. "This might sound sort of weird, but I need to talk to you."

"I'm listening."

Don't think about it. Say the words. She'll hear you somehow.

"Yeah, well. That's sort of the thing. I don't need to talk to you. I need to talk to—you know. Only you don't know. The other you."

"Pardon me?"

477

"The Lilum. Ma'am."

"First of all, it's pronounced Lilian, but I hardly think it's appropriate for you to call me by my first name." She faltered. "It must be confusing, my friendship with your father—"

I didn't have time for this. "The Demon Queen? Is she there?"

"I beg your pardon!"

Don't stop.

"The Wheel of Fate? The Endless River? Can you hear me?"

Mrs. English stood up. Her face was red, and she was the angriest I'd ever seen her. "Are you on drugs? Is this some kind of a prank?"

I looked around the room, desperate. My eye stopped on the figurines on the mantel, and I walked over to them. The moon was a stone, pale and round, a full circle with a crescent shape carved on top of it. "We need to talk about the moon."

"I'm calling your father."

Keep trying.

"The Eighteenth Moon. Does that mean anything to you?"

Out of the corner of my eye, I saw her reach for the phone.

I reached for the moon.

The room filled with light. Mrs. English froze in her chair, holding the phone, the room fading around her—

I was at the *Temporis Porta*, but the doors were wide open. There was a tunnel on the other side, the walls crudely covered in mortar. I stepped through the doors.

The tunnel was small, the ceiling so low I had to crouch down as I walked. There were marks on the wall, thin lines that looked as if someone was using them to count. I followed the tunnel a half a mile or so, when I saw the rotted wooden stairs.

Eight steps.

There was a wooden hatch at the top, with an iron ring hanging down toward the stairs. I climbed them carefully, hoping they held my weight. When I reached the top, I had to slam my shoulder against the wooden hatch to get it open.

Sunlight flooded into the tunnel as I pulled myself out.

I was in the middle of a field, a path just beyond where I was standing. Not a path so much as two snaking, parallel lines where the tall, waving grass was worn down to dirt. The fields on either side looked gold, like corn and sunshine—not brown, like lubbers and drought. The sky was blue, what I had come to think of as Gatlin blue. Thin and cloudless.

Hello? Are you there?

She wasn't here, and I couldn't believe where I was.

I would've recognized it anywhere; I had seen enough pictures of this place—my great-great-great-great-granddaddy Ellis Wate's plantation. He was the one who had fought and died on the other side of Route 9 during the Civil War. Right here.

I could see my house—and his—Wate's Landing in the distance. It was hard to tell if it looked the same, except for the haint blue shutters staring back at me. I looked down at the hatch, hidden by the dirt and grass, and understood instantly. It was the tunnel that led to the pantry, in the cellar at my house. I had come out on the other side—the safe side, where slaves using the Underground Railroad could lose themselves in the thick fields.

Why did the *Temporis Porta* bring me here? What was the Lilum doing at my family's farm, more than a hundred fifty years in the past?

Lilum? Where are you?

479

Half of a rusty bicycle lay in a heap by the side of the road. At least, it looked like part of a bicycle. I could see where the metal had been sawed off in the middle and a hose threaded through the frame. It had been rigged to water the field. A pair of muddy rubber boots stood in the dirt next to the bike wheel. In the distance, the fields stretched as far as I could see.

What do I have to do?

I looked back down at the rusted half of a bike, and I knew.

A tide of helplessness washed over me. There was no way I could water the field. It was too big, and I was just one person. The sun was growing hotter, and the leaves were turning browner, and soon the field wouldn't be gold at all, but burnt and dead, like everything else. I heard the familiar hum of a swarm. The lubbers were coming.

Why are you showing me this?

I sat down in the dirt and stared up at the blue sky. I saw a fat bee, drunkenly buzzing in and out of the wildflowers. I felt the soil beneath me, soft and warm even though it was dry. I pressed my fingers deeper into the dirt, dry as coarse sand.

I knew why I was here. Whether or not I could finish it, I had to try.

That's it, isn't it?

I yanked on the hot, muddy boots and picked up the rusting metal wheel. I held the handlebars, pushing the wheel in front of me. I started watering the field, one row at a time. The wheel groaned as it turned, and the heat prickled my neck as I bent into the job, pushing as hard as I could through the bumps and ruts of the field.

I heard a sound like a massive stone door opening for the first time in a century, or an enormous stone being pushed out of the mouth of a cave.

It was water.

Slowly coming up, returning to the field from whatever old pump or well the hose was attached to.

I pushed harder. Water started to run through the dirt in rivulets. As it ran down the dry trenches in the field, it created tiny rivers that formed small rivers, which formed decent-sized rivers that I knew would eventually flood the path entirely, to form even bigger ones as far as I could see.

An endless river.

I ran fast as I could. I watched the spokes of the wheel turn faster, pumping the water harder, until the wheel was moving so fast that it looked like a blur. The force of the water was so strong that the irrigation hose split open like the back of a gutted snake. There was water everywhere. The dirt was turning to mud beneath my feet, and I was soaking wet. It was like I was riding a bike for the first time, like I was flying—doing something only I could do.

I stopped, out of breath.

The Wheel of Fate.

I was staring at it, rusty and bent and older than dirt. My Wheel of Fate, here in my hands. In my family's old field.

I understood.

It was a test. My test. It was mine all along.

I thought about John, lying on my bedroom floor. The Lilum's voice when she said he wasn't the Crucible.

It's me, right?

I'm the Crucible.

I'm the One Who Is Two.

It was always me.

I watched the field as it started to turn green and gold again. The heat subsided. The fat bee flew off into the sky, because the sky was real, not just a painted bedroom ceiling.

I heard the rumble of thunder, then the crack of lightning, and I stood in the middle of the field, holding the rusty wheel, as the rain began to fall.

The air hummed with magic, like the feeling I had the first time I stepped onto the beach at the Great Barrier—only a hundred times stronger. The sound was so loud my ears were ringing.

"Lilum?" I shouted with my Mortal voice, sounding small in the middle of the massive field. "I know you're here. I can feel it."

"I am." The voice echoed down from above, from the blinding blue sky. I couldn't see her, but she was there—not the Mrs. English Lilum, but the real Lilum. In her nameless, formless state, all around me.

I took a deep breath. "I'm ready."

"And?" It was a question.

I knew the answer now. "I know who I am. And what I have to do."

"Who are you?" The question hung in the air.

I looked up toward the sky, letting the sun fall on my face. I said the words I had been dreading, since the moment they first whispered themselves in the deepest, darkest reach of my mind.

"I am the One Who Is Two." I shouted it as loud as I could. "I have one soul in the Mortal world and one soul in the Otherworld." My voice sounded different. Sure. "The One Who Is Two."

I waited in the silence. It was a relief to finally say it, like a crushing weight had been lifted off my back. Like I had been holding up the burning blue sky.

"You are. There is no other." There wasn't a trace of emotion in her voice. "The price must be paid to forge the New Order."

"I know."

"It is a crucible. A severe test. You must be sure. By the solstice."

I stood there for a long time. I felt the cool air and the stillness. I felt all the things I hadn't felt since the Order had changed.

"If I do this, then everything goes back to the way it was. Lena will be okay without me. The Council of the Far Keep will leave Marian and Liv alone. Gatlin will stop drying up and cracking open." I wasn't asking. I was bargaining.

"Nothing is certain. But—" I stood there and waited for the Lilum to answer. "There will be order again. A New Order."

If I was going to die, there was one more thing I wanted. "And Amma won't have to pay whatever price she owes the bokor."

"That bargain was made willingly. I cannot alter it."

"I don't care! Do it anyway!" But I knew she wouldn't, even as I said it.

"There are always consequences."

Like me. The Crucible.

I closed my eyes and thought about Lena and Amma and Link. Marian and my dad. My mom. All the people I loved.

All the people I'd lost.

The people I couldn't risk losing.

There wasn't a lot to decide. Not as much I thought there would be. I guess some decisions are made before you make them. I took a step and found my way back into the light. "Promise me."

"It is binding. An oath. A promise, as you call it."

That wasn't good enough. "Say it."

"Yes. I promise." Then she said a word that wasn't in any language or even any kind of sound I could understand. But the word itself sounded like thunder and lightning, and I understood the truth in it.

It was a promise.

"Then I'm sure."

A second later, I was standing in Lilian English's parlor again, while she lay collapsed in the flowered chair. I could hear my father's voice coming from the other end of the phone in her hand.

"Hello? Hello—"

My brain shifted to autopilot. I picked up the phone, hung up on my dad, and called 911 for the very Mortal Lilian English. I had to put the phone down without saying a word, because Sissy Honeycutt worked dispatch down at the station house, and she'd recognize my voice for sure. I couldn't get caught at my unconscious English teacher's house twice. But it didn't matter. Now they had the address. They would send out the ambulance, like they did before.

And Mortal Mrs. English wouldn't remember I had been there at all.

I drove straight to Ravenwood without stopping, without thinking, without turning on the radio or rolling down the window. I didn't remember how I got there. One minute I was driving through town, and the next I was pounding on Lena's front door. I couldn't breathe. I felt like I was trapped in the wrong atmosphere, in some kind of terrible nightmare.

I remember slamming my fist on the Caster moon as many times as I could, but it didn't respond to my touch. Maybe there was no way to hide how different I was. How incomplete.

I remember calling and crying and Kelting her name, until Lena finally opened the door in her purple Chinese pajamas. I remembered them from the night she told me her secret, that she was a Caster. Sitting on my front steps in the middle of the night.

Now, sitting on hers, I told her mine.

What happened after that was too painful to remember at all.

We lay in Lena's old iron bed, tangled together like we could never be taken apart. We couldn't touch, but we couldn't *not* touch. We couldn't stop staring at each other, but every time our eyes met, it only hurt more. We were exhausted, but there was no way we could sleep.

There wasn't enough time to whisper all the things we needed to say. But the words themselves didn't matter. We were only thinking one thing.

I love you.

We counted the hours, the minutes, the seconds.

We were running out of all of them.

⊰ 12.21 ⊱

The Last Game

It was the last day. There was nothing left to decide. Tomorrow was the solstice, and my mind was made up. I lay in my bed and stared up at my blue plaster ceiling, painted the color of the sky to keep the carpenter bees from nesting. One more morning. One more painted blue sky.

I got home from Lena's and went back to sleep. I left my window open, in case anyone wanted to see me, haunt me, or hurt me. No one came.

I could smell the coffee and hear my dad walking around downstairs. Amma was at the stove. Waffles. Definitely waffles. She must have been waiting for me to wake up.

I decided not to tell my dad. After everything he'd gone through with my mom, I didn't think he would be able to understand. I couldn't stand to think what this might do to him. The way he went crazy when my mom died, I understood now. I had been too scared to let myself feel those things before. And now, when it didn't matter how I felt, I was feeling every one of them. Sometimes life was weird that way.

Link and I tried to have lunch at the Dar-ee Keen, but we finally gave up. He couldn't eat, and I couldn't either. You know how prisoners get to choose their last meal, and it's such a big deal? It didn't work that way for me. I didn't want shrimp 'n' grits or brown sugar pound cake. I couldn't keep anything down.

And they can't give you the one thing you really want, anyway.

Time.

Finally, we went to the basketball court at the elementary school playground and shot some hoops. Link let me win, which was weird because I used to be the one who let him win. Things had changed a lot in the last six months.

We didn't talk much. Once, he caught the ball and held it after I passed it to him. He was looking at me the same way he had when he sat down next to me at my mom's funeral, even though the section was all roped off and only the family was supposed to sit there. "I'm not good at this stuff, you know?"

"Yeah. Me neither."

I pulled out an old comic I had rolled up in my back pocket. "Something to remember me by."

He unrolled it and laughed. "Aquaman? I gotta remember you and your lame powers with this sucky comic?"

I shrugged. "We can't all be Magneto."

487

"Hey, man." He dribbled the ball from one hand to the other. "Are you sure you want to do this?"

"No. I mean, I'm sure I don't want to. But I don't have a choice." Link understood about not having choices. His whole life was about not having them.

He bounced the ball harder. "And there's no other way?"

"Not unless you want to hang out with your mom and watch the End of Days." I was trying to make a joke. But my timing was always off now. Maybe my Fractured Soul was holding on to it.

Link stopped dribbling and held the ball under his arm. "Hey, Ethan."

"Yeah?"

"Remember the Twinkie on the bus? The one I gave you in second grade, the day we met?"

"The one you found on the floor and gave me without telling me? Nice."

He grinned and shot the ball. "It never really fell on the floor. I made that part up."

The basketball hit the rim and bounced into the street.

We let it go.

I found Marian and Liv in the archive, back together where they belonged.

"Aunt Marian!" I was so relieved to see her that I almost knocked her out cold as I hugged her. When I finally let go, I could tell she was waiting for me to say it. Something, anything—about the reason they let her go.

So I waded in, slowly. Giving them bits and pieces of the story that didn't quite fit together. At first, they were both relieved to hear some good news. Gatlin, and the Mortal world, wasn't going to be destroyed in a supernatural apocalypse. Casters weren't going to lose their powers or accidently set themselves on fire, although in Sarafine's case it had saved our lives. They heard what I wanted them to hear: Everything was going to be okay.

It had to be.

I was trading my life for it—that's the part I left out.

But they were both too smart to let the story end there. And the more pieces I gave them, the quicker their minds fit the pieces together to create the twisted truth of it all. I knew exactly when the last piece slid into place.

There was the terrible moment when I saw their faces change and the smiles fade. Liv wouldn't look at me. She was winding her selenometer compulsively and twisting the strings she always wore around her wrist. "We'll figure something out. We always do. There has to be another way."

"There isn't." I didn't need to say it; she already knew.

Without a word, Liv untied one of the frayed strings and tied it onto my wrist. Tears were running down her cheeks, but she didn't look at me. I tried to imagine myself in her place, but I couldn't. It was too hard.

I remembered losing my mom, staring at my suit laid out on the chair in the corner of my room, waiting for me to put it on and admit she was dead. I remembered Lena kneeling in the mud, sobbing, the day of Macon's funeral. The Sisters staring glassy-eyed at Aunt Prue's casket, handkerchiefs wadded in their hands. Who would boss them around and take care of them now?

That's what no one tells you. It's harder to be the one left behind.

I thought about Aunt Prue stepping through the Last Door so calmly. She was at peace. Where was the peace for the rest of us?

Marian didn't say a word. She stared at me like she was trying to memorize my face and freeze this moment so she could never forget it. Marian knew the truth. I think she knew something like this was coming the moment the Council of the Keep let her come back.

Nothing came without a price.

And if it had been her, she would have done the same thing to protect the people she loved.

I was sure Liv would've, too. In her own way, that's exactly what she did for Macon. What John tried to do for her on the water tower. Maybe she felt guilty that it was me instead of him.

I hoped she knew the truth—that it wasn't her fault, or my fault, or even his fault. No matter how many times I wanted to believe it was.

This was my life, and this was how it was ending.

I was the Wayward. And this was my great and terrible purpose.

It was always in the cards, the ones Amma was so desperate to change.

It was always me.

But they didn't make me say any of that. Marian gathered me up in her arms, and Liv wrapped her arms around us both. It reminded me of the way my mom always hugged me, like she would never let go if she had a choice. Finally, Marian whispered something softly. It was Winston Churchill. And I hoped I would remember it, wherever I was going.

" 'This is not the end. It is not even the beginning of the end. But it is, perhaps, the end of the beginning.' "

490

12.21

Remainders

Lena wasn't in her bedroom at Ravenwood. I sat down on her bed to wait, staring up at the ceiling. I thought of something and picked up her pillow, rubbing it against my face. I remembered smelling my mom's pillowcases after she was gone. It was magic to me, a piece of her that still existed in my world. I wanted Lena to at least have that.

I thought about Lena's bed, the time we broke it, the time the roof caved in on it, the time we broke up and the plaster had rained down on everything. I looked at the walls, thinking about the words that wrote themselves there the first time Lena told me how she felt.

You're not the only one falling.

Lena's walls weren't glass anymore. Her room was the same as it was the day we first met. Maybe that was how she was trying to keep things. The way it was at the beginning, when things were still full of possibility.

I couldn't think about it.

There were bits of words everywhere, I guess because that's how Lena felt things.

WHO CAN JUDGE THE JUDGE?

It didn't work like that. You couldn't reset the clock. Not for anyone. Not even for us.

NOT WITH A BANG BUT A WHIMPER

What was done was done.

I think she must have known, because she left a message for me, written across the walls of her room in black Sharpie. Like the old days.

> DEMON MATH
> what is *JUST* in a world
> you've ripped in two
> as if there could be
> a half for me
> a half for you
> what is *FAIR* when
> there is nothing
> left to share
> what is *YOURS* when
> your pain is mine to bear
> this sad math is mine

this mad path is mine
subtract they say
don't cry
back to the desk
try
forget addition
multiply
and i reply
this is why
remainders
hate
division

I rested my head against the wall next to the words.

Lena.

She didn't respond.

L. You're not a remainder. You're a survivor.

Her thoughts came slowly, in a jagged rhythm.

I won't be able to survive this. You can't ask me to.

I knew she was crying. I imagined her lying in the dry grass at Greenbrier. I would look for her there next.

You shouldn't be alone. Wait for me. I'm coming.

There was so much to say that I stopped trying to say it. Instead, I wiped my eyes with my sleeve, and opened my backpack. I pulled out the spare Sharpie Lena kept there, the way people have a spare tire in the back of their car.

For the first time, I uncapped it and stood on the girly chair in front of her old white dresser. It groaned under my weight, but it held. And I didn't have long, anyway. My eyes were stinging, and it was hard to see.

I wrote on her ceiling, where the plaster had cracked, where so many times other words, better words, more hopeful words had appeared above our heads.

I wasn't much of a poet, but I had the truth, and that was enough.

I will always love you.
Ethan

———৪৩

I found Lena lying in the charred grass at Greenbrier, the same place I had found her the day she shattered the windows in our English class. Her arms were flung over her head, the same way they were that day, too. She stared up at the thin stretch of blue.

I lay down next to her.

She didn't try to stop the tears. "It's different, you know that? The sky looks different now." She was talking, not Kelting. Suddenly talking was special. All the regular things were.

"It does?"

She took an uneven breath. "When I first met you, that's what I remember. I looked up at the sky and thought, *I'm going to love this person because even the sky looks different.*" I couldn't say anything. My breath was caught in my throat.

But she wasn't finished. "I remember the exact moment I saw you. I was in my car. You were playing basketball outside with your friends. And the ball rolled off the court and you went to get it. You looked at me."

"I remember that. I didn't know you saw me."

She smiled. "See you? I almost crashed the hearse."

I looked back up at the sky. "Do you believe in love before first sight, L?"

Do you believe in love after last sight, Ethan?

After death — that's what she meant.

It wasn't fair. We should have been complaining about our curfews. Trying to find a place besides the Dar-ee Keen where we could get summer jobs together. Worrying about whether or not we would get into the same college. Not this.

She rolled away from me, sobbing and pulling at the grass with her hands. I wrapped my arms around her, holding her close. I brushed her hair aside carefully and whispered in her ear. "Yes."

What?

I believe in love after death.

She took a ragged breath.

Maybe that's how I'll remember, L. Maybe remembering you is life after death for me.

She turned to look at me. "You mean, the way your mom remembers you?"

I nodded. "I don't know exactly what I believe in. But because of you and my mom, I know I believe."

I believe, too. But I want you here. I don't care if it's a hundred degrees and every blade of grass dies. Without you, none of that matters to me.

I knew how hard this was for her, because all I could think about was how much I didn't want to leave her. But I couldn't say that. It would only make it worse.

We're not talking about dead grass. You know that. The world will destroy itself, and the people we love.

Lena was shaking her head. "I don't care. I can't imagine a world without you in it."

"Maybe you can imagine the world I always wanted to see." I reached into my back pocket and pulled out the folded, beat-up map, the one that had been on my wall for so many years now. "Maybe you can see it for me. I marked the routes in green. You don't have to use it. But I wish someone would. It's kind of something I was planning for a while—my whole life, actually. They're places from my favorite books."

"I remember." Her voice was muffled. "Jack Kerouac."

"Or you can make your own." I felt her breath catch. "Funny thing is, until I met you all I wanted to do was to get as far away from here as I could. Kind of ironic, isn't it? Can't get much farther away than where I'm going, and now I'd give anything to stay."

Lena put her hands on my chest, pushing herself away from me. The map dropped on the ground between us. "Don't say that! You aren't doing it!"

I bent down and picked up the map that marked all the places I'd dreamed of going, before I finally figured out where I belonged. "Just hold on to it for me, then."

Lena stared at the folded paper like it was the most dangerous thing in the world. Then she reached up and unhooked her charm necklace from around her neck. "If you hold this for me."

"L, no." But it was hanging in the air between us, and her eyes were begging me to take it. I opened my hand, and she dropped the necklace—the silver button, the red string, the Christmas tree star, all of her memories—into my hand.

I reached out and lifted her chin so she was looking at me. "I know this is hard, but we can't pretend it isn't happening. I need you to promise me something."

"What?" Her eyes were red and swollen as she stared back at me.

"You have to stay here and Bind the New Order, or whatever your part is in all this. Otherwise, everything I'm about to do will be for nothing."

"You can't ask me to do that. I went through this when I thought Uncle Macon was dead, and you saw how well I handled that." Her voice cracked. "I won't make it without you."

Promise you'll try.

"No!" Lena was shaking her head, her eyes wild. "You can't give up. There has to be another way. There's still time." She was hysterical. "Please, Ethan."

I grabbed her and wrapped my arms around her, ignoring the way her skin burned mine. I would miss these burns. I would miss everything about her. "Shh. It's okay, L."

It wasn't.

I swore to myself that I'd find a way back to her somehow, like my mom found her way back to me. That was the promise I made, even if I couldn't keep it.

I closed my eyes and buried my face in her hair. I wanted to remember this. The feeling of her heart beating against mine as I held her. The smell of lemons and rosemary, which had led me to her before I even met her. When it was time, I wanted this to be the last thing I remembered. My last thought.

Lemons and rosemary. Black hair and green and gold eyes.

She didn't say a word, and I gave up trying, because you couldn't hear either one of us over the shattering noise of hearts breaking and the looming shadow of the last word, the one we refused to say.

The one that would come anyway, whether or not we said it.

Good-bye.

⊰ 12.21 ⊱

Broken Bottles

Amma was sitting at the kitchen table when I got home. The cards and the crosswords and the Red Hots and the Sisters were nowhere in sight. Only an old, cracked Coke bottle sat on the table. It was from our bottle tree, the one that never caught the spirit Amma was looking for. Mine.

I'd been rehearsing this conversation in my mind from the moment I realized the Crucible was me, not John. Thinking of a hundred different ways to tell the person who loved me as much as my mom had that I was going to die.

What do you say?

I still hadn't figured it out, and now that I was standing in Amma's kitchen, looking her in the eye, it seemed impossible. But I had a feeling she already knew.

I slid into the seat across from her. "Amma, I need to talk to you."

She nodded, rolling the bottle between her fingers. "Did everything wrong this time, I reckon. Thought you were the one pickin' a hole in the universe. Turns out it was me."

"This isn't your fault."

"When a hurricane hits, it's not the weatherman's fault any more than God's—no matter what Wesley's mamma says. Either way, doesn't matter to those folks left without a roof over their heads, now, does it?" She looked up at me, defeated. "But I think we both know this was all my doin'. And this hole is too big for me to stitch up."

I put my big hands over her small ones. "That's what I needed to tell you. I can fix it."

Amma jerked back in her chair, the worry lines in her forehead deepening. "What are you talkin' about, Ethan Wate?"

"I can stop it. The heat and the drought, the earthquakes, and the Casters losing control of their powers—all of it. But you already knew that, didn't you? That's why you went to the bokor."

The color drained from her face. "Don't you talk about that devil in this house! You don't know—"

"I know you went to see him, Amma. I followed you." There was no time left to play games. I couldn't walk away without saying good-bye to her. Even if she didn't want to hear it. "I'm guessing this is what you saw in the cards, wasn't it? I know you were trying to change things, but the Wheel of Fate crushes us all, doesn't it?"

The room was so still that it felt like someone had sucked the air right out of it.

"That's what you said, isn't it?"

Neither one of us moved, or breathed. For a second, Amma

looked so spooked that I was sure she was going to bolt or douse the whole house in salt.

But her face crumpled and she rushed at me, clutching my arms like she wanted to shake me. "Not you! You're my boy. The Wheel doesn't have any business with you. This is my fault. I'm goin' to set it right."

I put my hands on her thin shoulders, watching as the tears ran down her cheeks. "You can't, Amma. I'm the only one who can. It has to be me. I'm going before the sun comes up tomorrow—"

"Don't you say it! Not another word!" she shrieked, digging her fingers into my arms like she was trying to keep from drowning.

"Amma, listen to me—"

"No! You listen to me!" she pleaded, her expression frantic. "I've got it all worked out. There's a way to change the cards, you'll see. Made a deal a my own. You just have to wait." She was muttering to herself like a madwoman. "I've got it all worked out. You'll see."

Amma was wrong. I wasn't sure if she knew it, but I did. "This is something I have to do. If I don't—you and dad, this whole town, will be gone."

"I don't care about this town!" She hissed. "It can burn to the ground! Nothin's gonna happen to my boy! You hear me?" Amma whipped her head around the room, from one side to the other, like she was looking for someone hiding in the shadows.

When she looked back at me, her knees buckled, and her body swayed dangerously to one side. She was going to pass out. I grabbed Amma's arms and pulled her up, as her eyes locked on mine. "Already lost your mamma. Can't lose you, too."

I lowered her into one of the chairs and knelt next to it, watching as she slowly came back to herself. "Take deep breaths." I remembered hearing Thelma say that to Aunt Mercy when she had one of her fainting spells. But we were way past deep breaths.

Amma tried to wave me off. "I'm all right. Long as you promise me you won't do anything stupid. I'm gonna stitch this mess back together. I'm just waitin' on the right thread." One dipped in the bokor's brand of black magic, I was willing to bet.

I didn't want the last thing I said to Amma to be a lie. But she was beyond reason. There was no way I'd be able to convince her that I was doing the right thing. She was sure there was some kind of loophole, like Lena. "All right, Amma. Let's get you to your room."

She held on to my arm as she stood up. "You have to promise me, Ethan Wate."

I looked her right in the eye. "I won't do anything stupid. I promise." It was only half a lie. Because saving the people you love isn't stupid. It isn't even a choice.

But I still wanted the last thing I said to Amma to be as true as the sun rising. So after I helped her into her favorite chair, I hugged her tight and whispered one last thing. "I love you, Amma."

There was nothing truer.

The front door slammed as I pulled Amma's bedroom door shut.

"Hey everybody. I'm home," my dad's voice called from the hall. I was about to answer, when I heard the familiar sound of another door opening. "I'll be in the study. I have lots of reading to do." It was ironic. My dad spent all his time researching the Eighteenth Moon, and I knew more about it than I wanted to.

As I walked back through the kitchen, I saw the old Coke bottle sitting on the table, exactly where Amma left it. It was too late to catch anything in that bottle, but I picked it up anyway.

I wondered if there were bottle trees where I was going.

On my way to my room I passed the study, where my dad was working. He was sitting at my mom's old desk, the light filling up the room, his work, and the caffeinated coffee he'd smuggled into the house. I opened my mouth to say something. I didn't know what—just as he rummaged in the drawer for his earplugs, twisting them into his ears.

Good-bye, Dad.

I rested my forehead on the doorway in silence. I let things be what they were. He would know the rest, soon enough.

It was after midnight when Lena finally cried herself to sleep. I was sitting on my bed reading *Of Mice and Men* one last time. Over the last few months, my memories had faded so much that I couldn't remember a lot of it, anyway. I still remembered one part, though. The end. It bothered me every time I read it—the way George shot Lennie while he was telling Lennie about the farm they were going to buy one day. The one Lennie would never see.

When we read the novel in English class, everyone agreed that George was making this big sacrifice by killing his best friend. It was ultimately a mercy kill, because George knew Lennie was going to be hanged for accidentally killing the girl at the ranch. But I never bought it. Shooting your best friend in the head, instead of making a run for it, doesn't seem like a sacrifice to me. Lennie made the sacrifice, whether he knew it or not. Which was the worst part—I think Lennie would've knowingly sacrificed himself for George in a minute. He wanted George to get that farm, to be happy.

I knew my sacrifice wasn't going to make anyone happy, but it was going to save their lives. That was enough. I also knew none of the people who loved me would let me make that kind of sacrifice for them, which is why I was pulling on my jeans at one in the morning.

I took one last look around my room—the shoe boxes stacked along the walls that held everything important to me, the chair in the corner where my mother sat when she visited me two months ago, the piles of my favorite books hidden under my bed, and the swivel chair that hadn't swiveled the time Macon Ravenwood sat in it. I wanted to remember it all. As I swung my leg over the windowsill, I wondered if I would.

The Summerville water tower loomed above me in the moonlight. Most people probably wouldn't have picked this place, but this is where it happened in the dreams, so I knew it was right. I was taking a lot of things on faith lately. Knowing you don't have much time left changes things. You get kind of philosophical. And you figure things out—more like, they figure themselves out—and everything gets real clear.

Your first kiss isn't as important as your last.
The math test really didn't matter.
The pie really did.

The stuff you're good at and the stuff you're bad at are just different parts of the same thing.

Same goes for the people you love and the people you don't—and the people who love you and the people who don't.

The only thing that mattered was that you cared about a few people.

Life is really, really short.

I took Lena's charm necklace out of my back pocket and looked at it one last time. Then I reached through the open window of the Volvo and dropped it on the seat. I didn't want anything to happen to it when this was all over. I was glad she gave it to me. I felt like part of her was here with me.

But I was alone. I wanted it this way. No friends, no family. No talking, no Kelting. Not even Lena.

I wanted to let things feel the way they really were.

The way things felt was terrible. The way things were was worse.

I could feel it now. My fate was coming for me—my fate, and something else.

The sky ripped open a few feet from where I was standing. I expected Link to step out of the darkness with a pack of Twinkies or something, but it was John Breed.

"What's going on? Are Macon and Liv okay?" I asked.

"Yeah. Everyone's fine, all things considered."

"Then what are you doing here?"

He shrugged, flipping the top of his lighter open and closed. "I thought you might need a wingman."

"Why? To push me over the edge?" I was only half kidding.

He snapped the lighter shut. "Let's just say it's harder

than you think when you're up there. Besides, you were there with me, right?" It was twisted logic, but things were pretty twisted.

I didn't know what to say. It was hard to believe he was the same dirtbag who'd kicked my ass at the fair and tried to steal my girlfriend. He was a halfway decent guy now. Falling in love can do that to you. "Thanks, man. What's it like? I mean, on the way down."

John shook his head. "Trust me, you don't wanna know."

We walked toward the water tower. An enormous white moon blocked the light of the real one. The white metal ladder was only a few feet away.

I knew she was behind me before John sensed her and spun around.

Amma.

Nobody else smelled like pencil lead and Red Hots. "Ethan Wate! I was there the day you were born, and I'll be there the day you die, from this side or the other."

I kept walking.

Her voice grew louder. "Either way, it won't be today."

John sounded amused. "Damn, Wate. You sure have a creepy family, for a Mortal."

I braced myself for the sight of Amma armed with her beads and her dolls and maybe the Bible, too. But when I turned around, my eyes fell on the tangled braids and snakeskin-wrapped staff of the bokor.

The bokor smiled back at me. "I see you haven't found your *ti-bon-age*. Or have you? It's easier to find than to capture, isn't it now?"

"Don't you talk to him," Amma snapped. Whatever the bokor was here for, it obviously wasn't to talk me down off the ledge.

"Amma!" I called her name, and she turned back to face me. For the first time, I could see how lost she was. Her sharp brown eyes were confused and nervous, her proud posture bent and broken. "I don't know why you brought that guy here, but you shouldn't be mixed up with someone like him."

The bokor threw his head back and laughed. "We have a deal, the Seer and me. And I intend to fulfill my end a the bargain."

"What deal?" I asked.

But Amma shot the bokor a look that said *Keep your mouth shut.* Then she waved me over, the way she used to when I was a kid. "That's nobody's business except mine and my Maker's. You come on home, and he'll go back to where he belongs."

"I don't think she's asking," John said. He looked over at Amma. "What if Ethan doesn't want to go?"

Amma's eyes narrowed. "I knew you'd be here, the devil on my boy's shoulder. I can still see a thing or two. And you're Dark as a piece a coal in the snow—no matter what color your eyes are. That's why I brought some Darkness a my own."

The bokor wasn't here for me or my Fractured Soul. He was here to make sure John didn't get in Amma's way.

John put his hands up in mock surrender. "I'm not trying to make Ethan do anything. I came as a friend."

I heard the sound of bottles clinking. That's when I noticed the string of bottles tied to the bokor's belt, like the kind you found on bottle trees.

The bokor held one in front of him, his hand on the corked

stopper. "I brought some friends, too." He uncorked the bottle, and a thin trail of dark mist escaped. It swirled slowly, almost hypnotically, until it formed the body of a man.

But this Sheer didn't look like the others I'd seen. His limbs were mangled and awkwardly bent in unnatural positions. His facial features were grotesque, and whole pieces were missing where they seemed to have rotted away. He looked like a zombie from a horror movie—torn and broken. His eyes were unfocused and vacant.

John took a step back. "You Mortals are even more screwed up than Supernaturals."

"What the hell is that?" I couldn't stop staring at it.

The bokor threw some kind of powder on the ground around him. "One a the souls a the Unclaimed. When families don't tend to their dead, I come for them." Smiling, he shook the bottle in front of him.

I felt sick. I thought trapping evil spirits in bottles was one of Amma's crazy superstitions. I didn't know there were evil voodoo practitioners trolling graveyards with old Coke bottles.

The tortured spirit moved toward John, its expression frozen in a terrifying and silent scream. John opened his hands in front of him, the way Lena always did. "Back up, Ethan. I don't know what this thing's gonna do."

I stumbled back as flames surged from John's hands. He didn't pack as much power as Lena or Sarafine did, but there was still plenty of fire. The flames hit the spirit, enveloping it. I could see the outline of its limbs and body in the center of the blaze, its face frozen in an eternal scream. Then the mist dissipated, and the form vanished. Within seconds, the dark mist was spiraling in front of the fire, until the spirit was hovering a few feet away.

"Guess that didn't work." John rubbed his hands on his jeans. "I haven't—"

The Unclaimed flew at John, but it didn't stop when it reached him. The dark mist flew inside him, almost disappearing completely when John ripped. The spirit was forced out violently, like it was being sucked backward into a vacuum.

John materialized a few feet away, shocked. He ran his hands over his body, like he was trying to see if anything was missing. The spirit was spiraling up through the mist, unfazed.

"What did that thing do to you?"

John was still trying to shake it off. "It was trying to get inside me. Dark spirits need a body to possess if they're gonna do any real damage."

I heard the sound of clinking glass again. The bokor was opening the bottles, and a shadowy mist rose slowly from each one. "Look. He's got more of them."

"We're screwed," John said.

"Amma, stop it!" I yelled. But it didn't matter. Amma's arms were crossed, and she looked more determined and crazy than I'd ever seen her. "You come on home with me, and he'll fill those bottles back up faster than you can spill a glass a milk." This time, Amma had gone so dark that I didn't know how to find her—or bring her back.

I looked at John. "Can't you make them disappear, or turn them into something?"

John shook his head. "I don't have any powers that work on angry Unclaimed spirits."

Circles of smoke floated into the air as someone stepped out from the shadows. "Fortunately, I happen to have a few." Macon

Ravenwood took a couple of puffs on the cigar he was holding. "Amarie, I am disappointed. This is not your finest hour."

Amma pushed past the bokor, the bottles still tied to his belt rattling dangerously. She pointed a bony finger at Macon. "You would do the same thing for your niece, quicker than a sinner would steal money outta the collection plate, Melchizedek! Don't you stand there with your high and mighty because I won't let my boy be your sacrificial lamb!"

The bokor released another Unclaimed spirit behind Amma. Macon watched it rise into the air. "Excuse me, sir. I'm going to have to ask you to collect your belongings and be on your way. My friend was not thinking straight when she procured your services. Grief addles the brain, you know."

The bokor laughed, pointing his staff at one of the spirits and guiding it in Macon's direction. "I'm not a hired hand, Caster. The bargain she made with me can't be undone."

The spirit circled once and shot down toward Macon, its mouth torn and slack.

Macon closed his eyes and I shielded mine, anticipating the blinding green light that had almost destroyed Hunting. But there was no light. It was the opposite—a complete absence of light. Darkness.

A wide circle of absolute blackness formed in the sky above the Unclaimed spirit. It looked like one of those satellite pictures of a hurricane, except there were no churning winds. This was a real hole in the sky.

The Unclaimed turned as the black hole pulled it across the sky like a magnet. When the spirit hit the outer edge of the hole, it disappeared, little by little, as it was sucked inside. It reminded me of the way my hand disappeared into the grate outside the *Lunae Libri,* except this didn't look like an illusion. When the spirit's hazy fingers were finally swallowed by the void, the hole closed and vanished.

"Did you know he could do that?" John whispered.

"I don't even know what he did."

The bokor's eyes widened, but he wasn't deterred. He pointed his staff at the remaining spirits one by one, and their broken forms jerked toward Macon. Ink-black holes opened up behind each of them, dragging the Unclaimed inside. Then the holes disappeared like the pop of fireworks.

One of the empty bottles slipped out of the bokor's hand and dropped to the ground. I heard it crack against the dry earth. Macon opened his eyes and met the bokor's, calmly. "As I said before, your services are no longer required. I suggest you return to your hole in the ground before I create one for you."

The bokor opened a crude pouch and scooped a handful of the chalky white powder he had sprinkled on the ground around him. Amma backed away, raising the bottom of her dress so it didn't drag across the powder. The bokor lifted his hand and blew the particles at Macon.

They blew through the air like ash. But before they reached Macon, another black hole opened and sucked them in. Macon rolled his cigar between his fingers. "Sir, and I use the term loosely, unless you have something more, I suggest you take your walking stick home."

"Or what, Caster?"

"Or the next one will be for you."

The bokor's eyes glittered in the darkness. "This was a mistake, Ravenwood. The old woman owes me a debt, and she will

pay it—in this life or the next. You should not have interfered."
He threw something to the ground, and smoke rose from the
place where it hit. When the smoke cleared, he was gone.

"He can Travel?" That was impossible.

Macon walked toward us. "Parlor tricks, from a third-rate
magician."

John stared at Macon in awe. "How did you do whatever
you just did? I knew you could create light, but what was that?"

"Patches of darkness. Holes in the universe, I suppose." He
answered. "It's not a particularly pleasant business."

"But you're a Light Caster now. How can you create darkness?"

"I'm a Light Caster now, but I was an Incubus long before
that. In some of us, both Light and Darkness exist. You should
know that better than anyone, John."

John was about to say something else, when Amma called
out across the thin stretch of dirt between us. "Melchizedek
Ravenwood! This is the last time I'm askin' you to stay outta my
affairs. You take care a your family, and I'll see to mine! Ethan
Wate, we're leavin' this minute!"

I shook my head. "I can't."

Amma pointed at Macon with a venomous look in her eye.
"This is your doin'! I will never forgive you for this, you hear
me? Not today or tomorrow, or when I see you in hell for the
sins we've both committed. For the one I'm about to commit."
Amma sprinkled something around her feet, creating a circle.
The white crystals glittered like snowflakes. Salt.

"Amarie!" Macon called out to her, but his voice was gentle.
He knew she was coming unhinged.

"Aunt Delilah, Uncle Abner, Aunt Ivy, Grandmamma Sulla.

I'm in need a your intercession." Amma stared up into the black sky. "You're the blood a my blood, and I call you to help me fight the one whose threatenin' what I love most."

She was calling the Greats, trying to turn them on Macon. I felt the weight of it—her desperation, her madness, her love. But it was too tangled with the wrong things to be right. Only she couldn't see it.

"They won't come," I whispered to Macon. "She tried to call them before, and they didn't show."

"Well, perhaps they lacked the proper motivation." I followed Macon's eyes up beyond the water tower, and I could see the figures looming above us in the moonlight. The Greats— Amma's ancestors from the Otherworld. They had finally answered her.

Amma pointed at Macon. "He's the one tryin' to hurt my boy and take him outta this world. You stop him! Do what's right!"

The Greats stared down at Macon, and for a second I held my breath. Sulla had strands of beads wrapped around her wrist, like a rosary from a religion all her own. Delilah and Ivy were at her sides, watching Macon.

But Uncle Abner was looking right at me, his eyes searching mine. They were huge and brown and full of questions. I wanted to answer them, but I wasn't sure what he was asking.

He found the answers somehow, because he turned to Sulla and spoke to her in Gullah.

"Do what's right!" Amma called out into the darkness.

The Greats looked at Amma and joined hands. Then they slowly turned their backs to her. They were doing what was right.

Amma let out a strangled scream and dropped to her knees. "No!"

The Greats were still holding hands, facing the moon, when they disappeared.

Macon put his hand on my shoulder. "I'll take care of Amarie, Ethan. Whether she wants me to or not."

I started walking toward the rusty metal ladder.

"Do you want me to come with you?" John called after me.

I shook my head. This was something I had to do alone. As alone as you can be, when half of your soul is trailing you everywhere you go.

"Ethan—" It was Macon. I held the side of the ladder. I couldn't turn around.

"So long, Mr. Wate." That was it, a handful of meaningless words. All there was left to say.

"You'll take care of her for me." It wasn't a question.

"I will, son."

I tightened my hands on the ladder in front of me.

"No! My boy!" I heard Amma screaming, and the sound of her feet kicking as Macon held her back.

I started climbing.

"Ethan Lawson Wate—" With every ragged scream, I pulled myself higher. The same thought playing over and over again, in my mind.

The right thing and the easy thing are never the same.

Finally

I was standing on the top of the white water tower, facing the moon. I had no shadow, and if there were any stars, I couldn't see them. Summerville was stretched out before me, a scattering of tiny lights, all the way to the blackness of the lake.

This had been our happy place, mine and Lena's. One of them, at least. But I was alone now. I wasn't feeling happy. I wasn't feeling anything but fear—and like I wanted to throw up.

I could still hear Amma screaming.

I knelt for a second, resting my hands on the painted metal. I looked down and saw a heart, drawn in black Sharpie. I smiled, remembering, and stood up.

It is time. There is no turning back now.

I stared out at the tiny lights, waiting to get up the courage to do the unthinkable. The dread churned in my stomach, heavy and wrong.

But this was right.

As I closed my eyes, I felt the arms slam into my waist, knocking the air out of me, dragging me down to the metal ladder. I caught a glimpse of him—of me—when my jaw hit the side of the railing, and I stumbled.

He was trying to stop me.

I tried to throw him off. I leaned forward and saw my Chucks kicking. Then I saw his Chucks kicking. They were so old and thrashed they could have been mine. This was how I remembered it from the dream. This was how it was supposed to be.

What are you doing?

This time, he was asking me.

I threw him against the floor, and he landed on his back. I grabbed the collar of his shirt, and he grabbed mine.

We looked into each other's eyes, and he saw the truth.

We were both going to die. It seemed like we should be together when it happened.

I pulled out the old Coke bottle Amma had left sitting on the kitchen table earlier. If a whole bottle tree could catch a whole lot of lost souls, maybe one Coke bottle could hold on to mine.

I've been waiting.

I saw his face change.

His eyes widen.

He lunged at me.

I wouldn't let go.

We stared into each other's eyes and clawed at

each other's throats.

As we rolled over the edge of the water tower

and fell

515

the
whole
way
down,
I
was
only
thinking
one
thing
.
.
.
L
E
N
A

Nineteen Moons —

Acknowledgments

Three Moons and more than 1,600 pages from the day we sat down to prove to a few smack-talking teenagers that we could write a book, our extended Caster family couldn't even fit on one or two pages, if we tried to name you all.

We are grateful to all of our incredibly talented publishers in the thirty-eight countries that have welcomed the Beautiful Creatures novels into their world. You have shown our readers, ourselves, and the Casters of Gatlin County many kindnesses. We are grateful to our writer and reader friends, our agent and editor friends, our online and marketing/PR friends, our teacher and librarian friends, and our bookstore friends. We owe a huge debt to our translator friends, particularly Dr. Sara Lindheim, our Classicist and Keeper. More than anything, we are grateful to the teens (and the teens at heart) who read our books, and particularly our Caster Girl & Boy beta readers, who are infamously brutal editors and who, we hope, will one day make other writers weep more loudly than they have us. Good Lord willin' and the creek don't rise.

Finally, we are grateful to our families, our tribes, our inner circles—all of you who already know this means you because you're probably sitting here while we're writing this. Our books are about holding on to your family and finding your tribe, more than anything else. To us, that is magic. It took us a long time to find you, and we love you all.

Emma, May, Kate & Lewis; Nick, Stella & Alex—
We love you first, best, and last.

Some loves are cursed.
Others are
dangerous....

Turn the page for a look at the new series
from the authors of the *New York Times*
bestselling Beautiful Creatures series.

Ridley

There are only two kinds of Mortals in the backwater town of Gatlin, South Carolina—the stupid and the stuck. At least, that's what they say.

As if there are other kinds of Mortals anywhere else.

Please.

Luckily, there's only one kind of Siren, no matter where you go in this world or the Otherworld.

Stuck, no.

Stuck-*up*? Maybe.

Stupid?

It's all a matter of perspective. Here's mine: I've been called a lot of things, but what I really am is a survivor—and while there are more than a few stupid Sirens, there are zero stupid survivors.

Consider my record. I outlasted some of the Darkest Casters

and creatures alive. I withstood whole *months* of Stonewall Jackson High School. Beyond that, I survived a thousand terrible love songs written by one Wesley Lincoln, a clueless Mortal boy who became an equally clueless quarter Incubus. And who, by the way, is not the most gifted musician.

For a while, I survived wanting to write him a love song of my own.

That was harder.

This Siren gig is meant to be a one-way street. Ask Odysseus and two thousand years' worth of dead sailors if you don't believe me.

We didn't choose for it to be that way. It's the hand we were dealt, and you won't hear me whining about it. I'm not my cousin Lena.

Let's get something straight: I'm *supposed* to be the bad guy. I will always disappoint you. Your parents will hate me. You should not root for me. I am not your role model.

I don't know why everyone seems to forget that. I never do.

No matter what she says, Lena was meant to be Light. I was meant to be Dark. Respect the teams, people. At least learn the rules.

My own parents disowned me after the Dark Claimed me as a Siren on my Sixteenth Moon. Since then, nothing rattles me—nothing and no one.

I always knew my incarceration in the sanitarium that my Uncle Macon called Ravenwood Manor was a temporary pit stop on the way to *bigger* and *better*, my two favorite words. Actually, that's a lie.

My two favorite words are my name, *Ridley Duchannes*.

Why wouldn't they be?

Sure, Lena gets the credit for being the most powerful Caster of all time.

Whatever. It doesn't make *me* any less excellent. Neither does her too-good-to-be-true Mortal boyfriend, Ethan "the Wayward" Wate, who defeats Darkness in the name of true love every day of the week.

So what?

I was never going for perfect. I think that should be clear by now.

I've done my part, played my hand, even thrown in my cards when I had to. I've bet what I didn't have and bluffed until I had it. Link once said: *Ridley Duchannes is always playing a game.* I never told him, but he was right.

What's so bad about that? I always knew I'd rather play than watch from the sidelines.

Except once.

There was one game I regretted. At least, one that I regretted losing. And one Dark Caster I regretted losing to.

Lennox Gates.

Two markers. That's all I owed him, and it was enough to change everything. But I'm getting ahead of myself.

It all started long before that. There were blood debts to be paid—though this time it wasn't up to my cousin and her boy-friend to pay them.

Ethan and Lena? Liv and John? Macon and Marian? This wasn't about them anymore.

This was about Link and me.

I should've known we wouldn't get off easy. No Caster goes.

down without a fight, even when you think the fight is over. No Caster lets you ride off into the sunset on some lame white unicorn or in your boyfriend's beat-up excuse for a car.

What's a Caster fairy-tale ending?

I don't know, because Casters don't get to have fairy tales—especially not Dark Casters. Forget the sunset—the whole castle burns to the ground, taking Prince Charming down with it. Then the seven dwarves go all ninja and drop-kick your butt straight out of the kingdom.

That's what a Dark Caster fairy tale looks like.

What can I say? Payback's a bitch.

But here's the thing:

So am I.

Four survivors.
One unstoppable enemy.

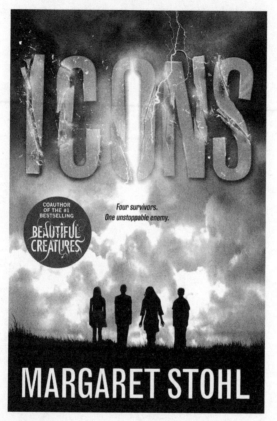

Keep reading for a look at the first book in Margaret Stohl's thrilling series set in a haunting new world where four teens must piece together the mysteries of their past in order to save their future.

THE PIETÀ OF LA PURÍSIMA

Feelings are memories.

That's what I'm thinking as I stand there in the Mission chapel, the morning of my birthday. It's what the Padre says. He also says that chapels turn regular people into philosophers.

I'm not a regular person, but I'm still no philosopher. And either way, what I remember and how I feel are the only two things I can't escape, no matter how much I want to.

No matter how hard I try.

For the moment, I tell myself not to think. I focus on trying to see. The chapel is dark but the doorway to outside is blindingly bright. That's what morning always looks like in the chapel. The little light there prickles and stings my eyes.

Like in the Mission itself, in the chapel you can pretend

that nothing has changed for hundreds of years, that nothing has happened. Not like in the Hole, where they say the buildings have fallen into ruins, and Sympa soldiers control the streets with fear, and you think about nothing but The Day, every day.

Los Angeles, that's what the Hole used to be called. First Los Angeles, then the City of Angels, then the Holy City, then the Hole. When I was little, that's how I used to think of the House of Lords, as angels. Nobody calls them *alien* anymore, because they aren't. They're familiar. We never see them, but we've never known a world without them, not Ro and me. I grew up thinking they were angels because back on The Day they sent my parents to heaven. At least, that's what the Grass missionaries told me, when I was old enough to ask.

Heaven, not their graves.

Angels, not aliens.

But just because something comes from the sky doesn't make it an angel. The Lords didn't come here from the heavens to save us. They came from some faraway solar system to colonize our planet, on The Day. We don't know what they look like inside their ships, but they're not angels. They destroyed my family the year I was born. What kind of angel would do that?

Now we call them the House of Lords—and Ambassador Amare, she tells us not to fear them—but we do.

Just as we fear her.

On The Day, the dead dropped silently in their homes, never seeing what hit them. Never knowing anything about our new Lords, about the way they could use their Icons to control the energy that flowed through our own bodies, our machines, our cities.

About how they could stop it.

Either way, my family is gone. There was no reason for me to have survived. Nobody understood why I did.

The Padre suspected, of course. That's why he took me.

First me, and then Ro.

I hear a sound from the far end of the chapel.

I squint, turning my back to the door.

The Padre has sent for me, but he's late. I catch the eye of the Lady from the painting on the wall. Her face is so sad, I think she knows what has happened. I think she knows everything. She's part of what General Ambassador to the Planet Hiro Miyazawa, the head of the United Embassies, calls the old ways of humanity. How we believed in ourselves—how we survived our-selves. What we looked up to, back when we thought there was someone up above.

Not something.

I look back to the Lady a moment longer, until the sadness surges and the pain radiates through me. It pulses from my temples and I feel my mind stumble, folding at the edge of unconsciousness. Something is wrong. It must be, for the familiar ache to come on so suddenly. I press my hand to my temple, willing it to stop. I breathe deep, until I can see clearly.

"Padre?"

My voice echoes against the wood and stone. It sounds as small as I am. An animal has lurched into my leg, one of many more entering the chapel, and my nostrils fill with smells—hair and hides and hooves, paint and mold and manure. My birthday falls on the Blessing of the Animals, which will begin just hours from now. Local Grass farmers and ranchers will come to have the Padre bless their livestock, as they have for three hundred years. It is Grass tradition, and we are a Grass Mission.

Appearing in the door, the Padre smiles at me, moving to light the ceremonial candles. Then his smile fades. "Where's Furo? Bigger and Biggest haven't seen him at all this morning."

I shrug. I can't account for every second of Ro's day. Ro could be lifting all the dried cereal cakes out of Bigger's emergency supplies. Chasing Biggest's donkeys. Sneaking down the Tracks toward the Hole, to buy more parts for the Padre's busted-up old *pistola*, shot only on New Year's Eve. Meeting people he doesn't want me to meet, learning things he doesn't want me to know. Preparing for a war he'll never fight with an enemy that can't be defeated.

He's on his own.

The Padre, preoccupied as always, is no longer paying attention to himself or to me. "Careful..." I catch his elbow, pulling him out of the way of a pile of pig waste. A near miss.

He clicks his tongue and leans down to chuck Ramona Jamona on the chin. "Ramona. Not in the chapel." It's an act—really, he doesn't mind. The big pink pig sleeps in his chamber on cold nights, we all know she does. He loves Ro and me just as he does Ramona—in spite of everything we do and beyond anything he says. He's the only father we have ever known, and though I call him the Padre, I think of him as my Padre.

"She's a pig, Padre. She's going to go wherever she wants. She can't understand you."

"Ah, well. It's only once a year, the Blessing of the Animals. We can clean the floors tomorrow. All Earth's creatures need our prayers."

"I know. I don't mind." I look to the animals, wondering. The Padre sinks onto a low pew, patting the wood next to him. "We can take a few minutes to ourselves, however. Come. Sit."

I oblige.

He smiles, touching my chin. "Happy birthday, Dolly." He holds out a parcel wrapped in brown paper and tied with string. It materializes from his robes, a priestly sleight of hand.

Birthday secrets. My book, finally.

I recognize it from his thoughts, from yesterday. He holds it out to me, but his face is not full of joy.

Only sadness.

"Be careful with it. Don't let it out of your sight. It's very rare. And it's about you."

I drop my hand.

"Doloria." He says my real name and I stiffen, bracing myself for the words I fear are coming. "I know you don't like to talk about it, but it's time we speak of such things. There are people who would harm you, Doloria. I haven't really told you how I found you, not all of it. Why you survived the attack and your family didn't. I think you're ready to hear it now." He leans closer. "Why I've hidden you. Why you're special. Who you are."

I've been dreading this talk since my tenth birthday. The day he first told me what little I know about who I am and how I am different. That day, over sugar cakes and thick, homemade butter and sun tea, he talked to me slowly about the creeping sadness that came over me, so heavy that my chest fluttered like a startled animal's and I couldn't breathe. About the pain that pulsed in my head or came between my shoulder blades. About the nightmares that were so real I was afraid Ro would walk in and find me cold and still in my bed one morning.

As if you really could die from a broken heart.

But the Padre never told me where the feelings came from. That's one thing even he didn't know.

I wish someone did.

"Doloria."

He says my name again to remind me that he knows my secret. He's the only one, Ro and him. When we're alone, I let Ro call me Doloria—but even he mostly calls me Dol, or even Dodo. I'm just plain Dolly to everyone else.

Not Doloria Maria de la Cruz. Not a Weeper. Not marked by the lone gray dot on my wrist.

One small circle the color of the sea in the rain.

The one thing that is really me.

My destiny.

Dolor means "sorrow," in Latin or Greek or some other language from way, way before The Day. BTD. Before everything changed.

"Open it."

I look at him, uncertain. The candles flicker, and a breeze shudders slowly through the room. Ramona noses closer to the altar, her snout looking for traces of honey on my hand.

I slip my finger through the paper, pulling it loose from the string. Beneath the wrapping is hardly a book, almost more of a journal: the cover is thick, rough burlap, home-made. This is a Grass book, unauthorized, illegal. Most likely preserved by the Rebellion, in spite of and because of the Embassy regulations. Such books are usually on subjects the Ambassadors won't acknowledge within the world of the Occupation. They are very hard to come by, and extremely valuable.

My eyes well with tears as I read the cover. *The*

Humanity Project: The Icon Children. It looks like it was written by hand.

"No," I whisper.

"Read it." He nods. "I was supposed to keep it safe for you and make sure you read it when you were old enough."

"Who said that? Why?"

"I'm not sure. I discovered the book with a note on the altar, not long after I brought you here. Just read it. It's time. And nobody knows as much about the subject as this particular author. It's written by a doctor, it seems, in his own hand."

"I know enough not to read more." I look around for Ro. I wish, desperately, he would walk through the chapel door. But the Padre is the Padre, so I open the book to a page he's marked, and begin to read about myself.

Icon doloris.

Dolorus. Doloria. Me.

My purpose is pain and my name is sorrow.

One gray dot says so.

No.

"Not yet." I look up at the Padre and shake my head, shoving the book into my belt. The conversation is over. The story of me can wait until I'm ready. My heart hurts again, stronger this time.

I hear strange noises, feel a change in the air. I look to

Ramona Jamona, hoping for some moral support, but she is lying at my feet, fast asleep.

No, not asleep.

Dark liquid pools beneath her.

The cold animal in my chest startles awake, fluttering once again.

An old feeling returns. Something really is wrong. Soft pops fill the air.

"Padre," I say.

Only I look at him and he is not my Padre at all. Not anymore.

"Padre!" I scream. He's not moving. He's nothing. Still sitting next to me, still smiling, but not breathing.

He's gone.

My mind moves slowly. I can't make sense of it. His eyes are empty and his mouth has fallen open. Gone.

It's all gone. His jokes. His secret recipes—the butter he made from shaking cream together with smooth, round rocks—the rows of sun tea in jars—gone. Other secrets, too. My secrets.

But I can't think about it now, because behind the Padre—what was the Padre—stands a line of masked soldiers. Sympas.

Occupation Sympathizers, traitors to humanity. Embassy soldiers, taking orders from the Lords, hiding behind plexi-masks and black armor, standing in pig mess and casting long shadows over the deathly peace of the chapel. One wears golden wings on his jacket. It's the only detail I see, aside from the weapons. The guns make no noise, but the animals panic all the same. They are screaming—which is something I did not know, that animals could scream.

I open my mouth, but I do not scream. I vomit.

I spit green juices and gray dust and memories of Ramona and the Padre.

All I can see are the guns. All I can feel is hate and fear. The black-gloved hands close around my wrist, overwhelming me, and I know that soon I will no longer have to worry about my nightmares.

I will be dead.

As my knees buckle, all I can think about is Ro and how angry he will be at me for leaving him.

I never believed in ghosts.
Until one tried to kill me.

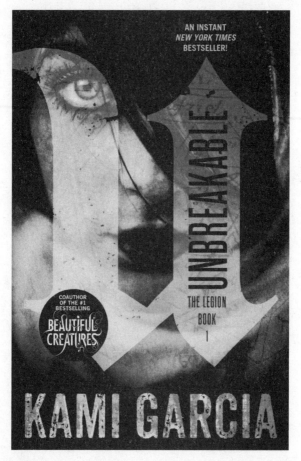

AN INSTANT
NEW YORK TIMES
BESTSELLER!

UNBREAKABLE

THE LEGION
BOOK
1

COAUTHOR
OF THE #1
BESTSELLING
BEAUTIFUL
CREATURES

KAMI GARCIA

Take a look at the first book in Kami Garcia's
action-packed paranormal thriller... if you dare.

1. SLEEPWALKER

As my bare feet sank into the wet earth, I tried not to think about the dead bodies buried beneath me. I had passed this tiny graveyard a handful of times but never at night, and always outside the boundaries of its peeling iron gates.

I would've given anything to be standing outside them now.

In the moonlight, rows of weathered headstones exposed the neat stretch of lawn for what it truly was—the grassy lid of an enormous coffin.

A branch snapped, and I spun around.

"Elvis?" I searched for a trace of my cat's gray and white ringed tail.

Elvis never ran away, usually content to thread his way

between my ankles whenever I opened the door—until tonight. He had taken off so fast that I didn't even have time to grab my shoes, and I had chased him eight blocks until I ended up here.

Muffled voices drifted through the trees, and I froze.

On the other side of the gates, a girl wearing blue and gray Georgetown University sweats passed underneath the pale glow of the lamppost. Her friends caught up with her, laughing and stumbling down the sidewalk. They reached one of the academic buildings and disappeared inside.

It was easy to forget that the cemetery was in the middle of a college campus. As I walked deeper into the uneven rows, the lampposts vanished behind the trees, and the clouds plunged the graveyard in and out of shadow. I ignored the whispers in the back of my mind urging me to go home.

Something moved in my peripheral vision—a flash of white.

I scanned the stones, now completely bathed in black.

Come on, Elvis. Where are you?

Nothing scared me more than the dark. I liked to see what was coming, and darkness was a place where things could hide.

Think about something else.

The memory closed in before I could stop it....

My mother's face hovering above mine as I blinked

myself awake. The panic in her eyes as she pressed a finger over her lips, signaling me to be quiet. The cold floor against my feet as we made our way to her closet, where she pushed aside the dresses.

"Someone's in the house," she whispered, pulling a board away from the wall to reveal a small opening. "Stay here until I come back. Don't make a sound."

I squeezed inside as she worked the board back into place. I had never experienced absolute darkness before. I stared at a spot inches in front of me, where my palm rested on the board. But I couldn't see it.

I closed my eyes against the blackness. There were sounds—the stairs creaking, furniture scraping against the floor, muffled voices—and one thought replaying over and over in my mind.

What if she didn't come back?

Too terrified to see if I could get out from the inside, I kept my hand on the wood. I listened to my ragged breathing, convinced that whoever was in the house could hear it, too.

Eventually, the wood gave beneath my palm and a thin stream of light flooded the space. My mom reached for me, promising the intruders had fled. As she carried me out of her closet, I couldn't hear anything beyond the pounding of my heart, and I couldn't think about anything except the crushing weight of the dark.

I was only five when it happened, but I still remembered

every minute in the crawl space. It made the air around me now feel suffocating. Part of me wanted to go home, with or without my cat.

"Elvis, get out here!"

Something shifted between the chipped headstones in front of me.

"Elvis?"

A silhouette emerged from behind a stone cross.

I jumped, a tiny gasp escaping my lips. "Sorry." My voice wavered. "I'm looking for my cat."

The stranger didn't say a word.

Sounds intensified at a dizzying rate—branches breaking, leaves rustling, my pulse throbbing. I thought about the hundreds of unsolved crime shows I'd watched with my mom that began exactly like this—a girl standing alone somewhere she shouldn't be, staring at the guy who was about to attack her.

I stepped back, thick mud pushing up around my ankles like a hand rooting me to the spot.

Please don't hurt me.

The wind cut through the graveyard, lifting tangles of long hair off the stranger's shoulders and the thin fabric of a white dress from her legs.

Her legs.

Relief washed over me. "Have you seen a gray and white Siamese cat? I'm going to kill him when I find him."

Silence.

Her dress caught the moonlight, and I realized it wasn't a dress at all. She was wearing a nightgown. Who wandered around a cemetery in their nightgown?

Someone crazy.

Or someone sleepwalking.

You aren't supposed to wake a sleepwalker, but I couldn't leave her out here alone at night either.

"Hey? Can you hear me?"

The girl didn't move, gazing at me as if she could see my features in the darkness. An empty feeling unfolded in the pit of my stomach. I wanted to look at something else—anything but her unnerving stare.

My eyes drifted down to the base of the cross.

The girl's feet were as bare as mine, and it looked like they weren't touching the ground.

I blinked hard, unwilling to consider the other possibility. It had to be an effect of the moonlight and the shadows. I glanced at my own feet, caked in mud, and back to hers.

They were pale and spotless.

A flash of white fur darted in front of her and rushed toward me.

Elvis.

I grabbed him before he could get away. He hissed at me, clawing and twisting violently until I dropped him. My heart hammered in my chest as he darted across the grass and squeezed under the gate.

I looked back at the stone cross.

The girl was gone, the ground nothing but a smooth, untouched layer of mud.

Blood from the scratches trailed down my arm as I crossed the graveyard, trying to reason away the girl in the white nightgown.

Silently reminding myself that I didn't believe in ghosts.

When I stumbled back onto the well-lit sidewalk, there was no sign of Elvis. A guy with a backpack slung over his shoulder walked by and gave me a strange look when he noticed I was barefoot, and covered in mud up to my ankles. He probably thought I was a pledge.

My hands didn't stop shaking until I hit O Street, where the shadows of the campus ended and the lights of the DC traffic began. Tonight, even the tourists posing for pictures at the top of *The Exorcist* stairs were somehow reassuring.

The cemetery suddenly felt miles away, and I started second-guessing myself.

The girl in the graveyard hadn't been hazy or transparent like the ghosts in movies. She had looked like a regular girl.

Except she was floating.

Wasn't she?

Maybe the moonlight had only made it appear that way. And maybe the girl's feet weren't muddy because the ground where she'd been standing was dry. By the time I reached my block, lined with row houses crushed together like sardines, I convinced myself there were dozens of explanations.

Elvis lounged on our front steps, looking docile and bored. I considered leaving him outside to teach him a lesson, but I loved that stupid cat.

I still remembered the day my mom bought him for me. I came home from school crying because we'd made Father's Day gifts in class, and I was the only kid without a father. Mine had walked away when I was five and never looked back. My mom had wiped my tears and said, "I bet you're also the only kid in your class getting a kitten today."

Elvis had turned one of my worst days into one of my best.

I opened the door, and he darted inside. "You're lucky I let you in."

The house smelled like tomatoes and garlic, and my mom's voice drifted into the hallway. "I've got plans this weekend. Next weekend, too. I'm sorry, but I have to run. I think my daughter just came home. Kennedy?"

"Yeah, Mom."

"Were you at Elle's? I was about to call you."

I stepped into the doorway as she hung up the phone. "Not exactly."

She threw me a quick glance, and the wooden spoon slipped out of her hand and hit the floor, sending a spray of red sauce across the white tile. "What happened?"

"I'm fine. Elvis ran off, and it took forever to catch him."

Mom rushed over and examined the angry claw marks. "Elvis did this? He's never scratched anyone before."

"I guess he freaked out when I grabbed him."

Her gaze dropped to my mud-caked feet. "Where were you?"

I prepared for the standard lecture Mom issued whenever I went out at night: always carry your cell phone, don't walk alone, stay in well-lit areas, and her personal favorite—scream first and ask questions later. Tonight, I had violated them all.

"The old Jesuit cemetery?" My answer sounded more like a question—as in, exactly how upset was she going to be?

Mom stiffened and she drew in a sharp breath. "I'd never go into a graveyard at night," she responded automatically, as though it was something she'd said a thousand times before. Except it wasn't.

"Suddenly you're superstitious?"

She shook her head and looked away. "Of course not.

You don't have to be superstitious to know that secluded places are dangerous at night."

I waited for the lecture.

Instead, she handed me a wet towel. "Wipe off your feet and throw that away. I don't want dirt from a cemetery in my washing machine."

Mom rummaged through the junk drawer until she found a giant Band-Aid that looked like a leftover from my Big Wheel days.

"Who were you talking to on the phone?" I asked, hoping to change the subject.

"Just someone from work."

"Did that *someone* ask you out?"

She frowned, concentrating on my arm. "I'm not interested in dating. One broken heart is enough for me." She bit her lip. "I didn't mean—"

"I know what you meant." My mom had cried herself to sleep for what felt like months after my dad left. I still heard her sometimes.

After she bandaged my arm, I sat on the counter while she finished the marinara sauce. Watching her cook was comforting. It made the cemetery feel even farther away.

She dipped her finger in the pot and tasted the sauce before taking the pan off the stove.

"Mom, you forgot the red pepper flakes."

"Right." She shook her head and forced a laugh.

My mom could've held her own with Julia Child, and

marinara was her signature dish. She was more likely to forget her own name than the secret ingredient. I almost called her on it, but I felt guilty. Maybe she was imagining me in one of those unsolved crime shows.

I hopped down from the counter. "I'm going upstairs to draw."

She stared out the kitchen window, preoccupied. "Mmm...that's a good idea. It will probably make you feel better."

Actually, it wouldn't make me feel anything.

That was the point.

As long as my hand kept moving over the page, my problems disappeared, and I was somewhere or *someone* else for a little while. My drawings were fueled by a world only I could see—a boy carrying his nightmares in a sack as bits and pieces spilled out behind him, or a mouthless man banging away at the keys of a broken typewriter in the dark.

Like the piece I was working on now.

I stood in front of my easel and studied the girl perched on a rooftop, with one foot hanging tentatively over the edge. She stared at the ground below, her face twisted in fear. Delicate blue-black swallow wings stretched out from her dress. The fabric was torn where the wings had ripped through it, growing from her back like the branches of a tree.

I read somewhere that if a swallow builds a nest on your roof, it will bring you good luck. But if it abandons the nest, you'll have nothing but misfortune. Like so many things, the bird could be a blessing or a curse, a fact the girl bearing its wings knew too well.

I fell asleep thinking about her. Wondering what it would be like to have wings if you were too scared to fly.